Saving Shallmar

"But Saving Shallmar's Christmas story is a tale of compassion and charity, and the will to help fellow human beings not only survive, but also be ready to spring into action when a new opportunity presents itself. Bittersweet yet heartwarming, Saving Shallmar is a wonderful Christmas season story for readers of all ages and backgrounds, highly recommended."

- *Small Press Bookwatch*

Battlefield Angels

"Rada describes women religious who selflessly performed life-saving work in often miserable conditions and thereby gained the admiration and respect of countless contemporaries. In so doing, Rada offers an appealing narrative and an entry point into the wealth of sources kept by the sisters."

- *Catholic News Service*

Canawlers

"A powerful, thoughtful and fascinating historical novel, Canawlers documents author James Rada, Jr. as a writer of considerable and deftly expressed storytelling talent."

- *Midwest Book Review*

Between Rail and River

"The book is an enjoyable, clean family read, with characters young and old for a broad-based appeal to both teens and adults. Between Rail and River also provides a unique, regional appeal, as it teaches about a particular group of people, ordinary working 'canawlers' in a story that goes beyond the usual coverage of life during the Civil War."

- *Historical Fiction Review*

OTHER BOOKS BY JAMES RADA, JR.

Fiction

Between Rail and River

Canawlers

Lock Ready

October Mourning

The Rain Man

Non-Fiction

Battlefield Angels: The Daughters of Charity Work as Civil War Nurses

Beyond the Battlefield: Stories from Gettysburg's Rich History

Echoes of War Drums: The Civil War in Mountain Maryland

Looking Back: True Stories of Mountain Maryland

Looking Back II: More True Stories of Mountain Maryland

No North, No South…: The Grand Reunion at the 50th Anniversary of the Battle of Gettysburg

Saving Shallmar: Christmas Spirit in a Coal Town

BETWEEN RAIL AND RIVER

by
James Rada, Jr.

LEGACY
PUBLISHING

A division of AIM Publishing Group

BETWEEN RAIL AND RIVER

This is a work of fiction. All the characters and events portrayed in this book are either fictitious or used fictitiously.

Published by Legacy Publishing, a division of AIM Publishing Group.
Gettysburg, Pennsylvania.
Printed in the United States of America.
Second printing: July 2014.

Cover photo courtesy of the National Park Service.

315 Oak Lane • Gettysburg, Pennsylvania 17325

For Sam,
my son who has yet to experience
the wonders of his new country

BETWEEN RAIL AND RIVER

by
James Rada, Jr.

1

END OF SEASON

JANUARY 1863

David Windover woke up shaking with his teeth chattering. He had curled himself into a tight ball and pulled the patchwork quilt tightly around him during the night. The quilt was colorful, but it was too thin. He was still cold. His teeth continued to bang together so hard that David thought that he might chip a tooth. However, the itch he felt on his shoulder was gone. His shaking fingers had unconsciously scratched the troublesome spot.

All the warmth from his body escaped right through the thin quilt. A cold breeze sneaked through the cracks around the shutters and shot straight across the hay house. It tore right through David as if he and the quilt were full of holes.

He opened his eyes. The hay house was dark except for where the morning sun peeked through the cracks in the shutters. It was Sunday; otherwise, the canal boat would already be underway. Any other day of the week, the *Freeman* began moving so early in the morning that it was dark outside. Now in the faint light coming from under the shutters, David could see his breath evaporating in a misty cloud as he exhaled.

"It's the middle of winter, David, what do you expect?" he muttered to himself. He almost bit his tongue because his teeth wouldn't stop chattering while he spoke.

As he lay there shaking, David knew that it wasn't going to get any warmer. He didn't have a stove in the room because the danger of starting a fire was too high with all the hay that was stored in the room. The hay was for the mules in the mule shed at the fore end of

1

the canal boat. When the hay house was full, David had no floor space in the room. He would have to stand on his bed of hay to dress. Now, the room was half-empty, which only allowed the empty space to be filled with cold January air.

The winter had started out mild enough through the end of last year that David had had foolish hopes of avoiding the cold altogether. He'd been proven wrong with a vengeance as the temperatures had plummeted to single digits during the nights. Now the canal was kept open only through the use of icebreakers to carve a navigable channel through the canal.

David straightened his body quickly. He threw off the blanket and pulled on his pants and shirt, all the while muttering to himself about the cold. He stomped his feet into his boots, wincing as he wondered if there were ice cubes in the toes of the boots that made his toes go numb. He tugged on his overcoat and buttoned it all the way to the neck. Other than the boots and his long underwear, the clothes were Hugh Fitzgerald's, the former owner of the *Freeman*. Hugh was dead, though, and David had needed clothes other than his Confederate army uniform for his work on the canal.

Once clothed, he wrapped himself in the quilt and lay back down.

Outside the hay house, Thomas Fitzgerald screamed. It was a high-pitched wail that sounded as if the young boy was in trouble.

The sound of Thomas's fear moved David to action.

Cold forgotten, David jumped up and grabbed his pistol from where it hung in its holster on the wall. The gun was a Colt Navy .36, a remnant from his days serving as a lieutenant in the army.

Had Confederate raiders boarded the boat again intent on sinking it so that it would block other boats on the Chesapeake and Ohio Canal? They had tried once before and nearly succeeded.

David threw open the shutters and quickly hopped up onto the race plank, the foot-wide walkway that went around the edge of the boat. He dropped into a crouch and spun around searching for a gray or butternut uniform, but he didn't see any.

"Mama, stop it! That water's cold enough to be ice!" Thomas yelled.

David looked around the side of the hay house. Thomas stood on the opposite side of the boat on the race plank. He was bare to the waist and dripping wet. He hugged himself as he bounced up and down in front of his mother.

"It serves you right for running off and getting so dirty," Alice Fitzgerald replied as she scrubbed at the nine-year old's face with a wet cloth. "You would think that the ground is too frozen for any of it to get onto you."

"I was trying to dig into a beaver's burrow. I wanted to see what it looked like inside. I might have... Ahhggh! That's cold! I'm turning blue!" Thomas screamed as Alice poured another bucket of water on him. He jumped from foot to foot, hugging himself and shivering.

David sighed and uncocked his pistol. There was no danger here, just a mischievous boy. David tucked the gun into the waistband of his pants behind his back and smiled at Thomas's predicament. It shouldn't be any surprise that Thomas was dirty. Thomas could find dirt in the cleanest home.

David took a moment to stretch with his hands over his head. He looked over the Chesapeake and Ohio Canal. The canal boat *Freeman* was tied up on the side of the canal opposite the towpath so that any boats that might have passed during the night could do so unimpeded.

The canal was about sixty feet wide at this point. The oak, maple and sycamore trees that had held beautiful yellow, red and orange leaves a couple months ago were now bare. David could look through the crisscrossing branches and see the Potomac River rushing by just a few dozen yards away.

When David looked into the water of the canal, he saw a thin crust of ice at the edges of the boat and the sides of the canal. Thomas hadn't just been complaining because he didn't want a bath. The water was cold enough to ice up.

The Canal Company had been running ice breakers — heavy boats with wedges attached to the fore to crack the ice — up and down the canal to keep the water flowing and the canal open for as long as possible. Last year had been so bad financially for the Canal Company that the board of directors wanted to keep it open as long as possible to try and recoup some of their losses.

The talk on the canal, besides war, was that the tonnage transported on the canal was noticeably down. That meant that toll revenues to the Canal Company were down as well.

The additional time the canal was open also helped the Fitzgeralds earn more money to get through the winter.

"David, help me," Thomas called when he noticed David standing next to the hay house.

"I'm going to get a pail of water and wash up myself, Thomas," David called as he straightened up. Of course, he was going to heat it up over the stove in the family cabin first. No use in turning his skin blue if he didn't have to.

"Mama's not using water. She's using ice," Thomas complained through chattering teeth.

Alice rolled her eyes as she dipped the bucket into the canal to fill it. "Hush, Thomas. Maybe this time you'll learn to stay clean. No, that would be too much to hope for."

David walked over the hatch covers that hid the full holds of coal and onto the race plank on the other side of the boat. A cleated board was laid out between the race plank and the canal bank. David walked across the board to the bank where the three canal mules were tied.

Each one had a blanket on its back because they had stood outside all night. The three of them would have fit in the mule shed, but they wouldn't have had much room to move around. Besides, they were used to being outside in just about all types of weather.

Until November, the Fitzgeralds had owned four mules. When Confederate soldiers had ambushed a Union patrol on the canal at the river lock near Dam 4, King Edward had been shot and killed in the crossfire. That left Jigger, Ocean, and Seamus to pull the canal boat. Since King Edward had been killed, the other mules, which usually pulled the boat in pairs, had been working shorter tricks. At the end of each trick, one of the mules was given a rest, and the fresh mule was hooked up in the harness. Using this method, each mule pulled the boat for eight hours and rested for four. It wasn't the best way to run the mules, but with winter coming on, Alice Fitzgerald wanted to get as many trips in before the canal was drained for the winter as she could. She also wanted to take her time and choose a mule that had the strength to pull a loaded canal boat and the endurance to do it for years.

David patted each of the mules and spoke softly to them. He inspected each of the twelve legs, looking for sores, loose shoes, worn shoes, and cracked hooves. He ran his hands across their shoulders to check for sores caused by the rubbing of the harness as the mules pulled the boat. Alice insisted that the mules be well cared for. David could understand why. If the mules didn't pull well, the *Freeman* wouldn't move. A sick mule or a thin mule couldn't do the work demanded of him.

Tony climbed out of the mule shed, holding the thick, padded harnesses over his small shoulders. He waved to David and the harness chains jangled loudly.

"Are they ready?" Tony asked.

"Let me water them first," David replied.

He picked up the empty bucket and walked to the bank where he dipped it into the water. The thin crust of ice broke easily. David filled the bucket and carried it back to the mules so they could drink their fill while he brushed the knots out of their coats.

Tony walked across the fall board and laid the harnesses on the ground. The eleven-year-old boy stood in front of the trio of mules and pointed to each one.

"Which one of you will get to rest for a little while longer? Any volunteers?" He paused for a moment. "No? Then I guess I'll have to draft two of you. We are at war you know."

David smiled and shook his head. Sometimes Tony seemed about thirty years old, but other times he seemed like the eleven-year-old boy that he was. David pulled the portable feed bin out of the ground and carried it onto the *Freeman*. He would store it in the mule shed until they stopped for dinner.

When David finished stowing the feed bin in the mule shed, he walked to the other end of the boat. The smells of breakfast cooking got stronger every step of the way. Since Alice was busy with Thomas, it would have to be Elizabeth who was cooking up breakfast.

David walked down the three steps to the door of the family cabin. He knocked lightly on the wooden door.

"Come in," Elizabeth said.

David opened the door and stepped inside. It was comfortable and warm inside the small cabin. The fire in the small, pot-belly stove on his right emanated heat that spread throughout the room. Elizabeth stood close by the stove frying eggs in an iron skillet. David inhaled deeply enjoying the smells of eggs, sausage, and coffee.

"Good morning, Elizabeth," he said.

"Good morning. Breakfast will be ready in a moment. Sit down," Elizabeth said.

The family cabin seemed nearly as small as the table. The room was ten feet by ten feet square, and a six-foot by five-foot portion of that was taken up by the stateroom where Alice and Elizabeth slept.

The pot-belly stove stood against the wall between the stateroom and the door to the family cabin. On the other side of the entry door was the pantry. Then came the table that tended to dominate the room. Against the wall opposite the pantry were the two bunks where Tony and Thomas slept.

David sat down at the small table next to the two windows. It was only big enough for two people to sit comfortably, though they had been known to squeeze four people around it at meal times. When all five of them tried to eat at once, though, someone usually wound up sitting on the lower bunk with his plate on his lap.

The door to the cabin opened again. Thomas ran inside with his teeth chattering and jumped onto the lower bunk. He pulled his wool blanket over himself and curled into a ball. David could still see the boy shaking, but not a speck of skin showed from under the blanket.

David smiled but managed to keep from laughing. Just barely.

Alice stepped into the cabin and shut the door behind her. She saw the shivering lump on the bunk and rolled her eyes.

"Thomas, it wasn't that bad," Alice said.

"Was too," came a muffled reply.

David finally laughed out loud. Still chuckling, he took his cup off the table and filled it from the coffee pot on the stove.

Elizabeth tossed the last few chunks of coal into the stove from the pail next to the small pot-belly stove. Then she shut the grate.

"I need more coal," she said, holding out the pail.

"Thomas, that's your job," Alice said.

From under the blanket, Thomas groaned. He folded back the blanket to expose his head and glared at his mother.

"Aren't you afraid that I might get dirty? After all, coal is pretty dirty, and you went to a lot of trouble to clean me up," Thomas said.

"I guess you'll have to be careful then. Otherwise, I might have to give you another bath," Alice warned him.

Thomas frowned, but he didn't say anything else. He sat up and walked over to the pantry. He opened the two doors to show three shelves filled with cans and jars. He shifted the cans and jars from the lower shelves up to the highest shelves. When the shelves were completely empty, he pulled them off their brackets and set them on the floor. Behind the shelves was a thin board that served as a backing to the shelves. Thomas squatted down, pushed back the wall and stepped behind it.

The pantry was actually a small low-ceilinged room beneath the

Freeman's quarterdeck. David had seen a few other canal boats and knew that, in many of them, the shelves lined the side walls. The way Alice had her pantry set up created a hidden area behind the shelves. Though Alice said the hidden room was merely used to store coal the Fitzgeralds kept for personal use, David had hidden in the room when Union soldiers had searched the boat for him. They hadn't been able to find him, either.

Thomas crawled back into the family cabin holding a full pail of coal. He walked across the room and set the pail next to the stove. While he was still generally clean, his arms were black up to his elbows.

"Go wash your arms, Thomas, and do it right or we will repeat what we went through this morning," Alice told her son.

Thomas sighed and headed outside. When he had left the room, David asked, "Is a coal bin all that room is ever used for?"

Alice stared across the table at him. Her green eyes revealed nothing. "Why do you ask?" she replied.

"I was just thinking that even with the coal behind there, there's still a lot of space back there that you're not using. It seems a waste when space is such a premium here."

Alice glanced at the opening in the pantry and at Elizabeth who was flipping sausage links onto a plate. David thought she wasn't going to answer him, but then she turned to face him.

"Coal's all that's back there," Alice said.

David realized that she hadn't really answered his question, but he wasn't going to push for a different answer. Alice said what she did very carefully so that while she might never lie, she certainly wasn't always saying what someone might think she was saying.

"How much longer do you think the canal will stay open?" David asked, changing the subject. "There was ice on the canal again this morning."

Alice shrugged. "It depends on how good a job the ice-breakers do. If they can keep things moving fairly steadily, I would guess that the Canal Company will keep things running year-round. Last year, the canal was only completely closed at the beginning of the year for the winter. Even though it was closed beyond Hancock, they ran boats up to Hancock for a good portion of the winter."

"That makes it hard to earn a living, doesn't it?"

"No harder than a farmer. You should realize that." David was the son of a plantation owner. "Too much rain. Too little rain. Fire. In-

7

sects. Early winter. Late spring. All those things affect the growing season and quality of your harvest. The same thing applies here. Flooding will close the canal and so will drought. An early winter will close us, and a late spring will keep us closed."

"Well, if the canal is going to stay open for a while yet, I'm going to need some blankets. It's hard to get up in the morning when the hay is frozen to me," David said, smiling.

Alice didn't smile. She pressed her lips in a tight line and got a faraway look in her eyes.

"We haven't had any hands on board in many seasons. It's been the family doing all of the work for the most part," she said finally.

David wasn't sure if he should say something so, he remained quiet and sipped his coffee. He was almost sure that she was thinking about her dead husband, Hugh, and David had no place in those memories.

"Even Thomas never sleeps out in the hay house when it gets cold." She looked around the cabin. "Tony's going to have to share the lower bunk with Thomas. You can have the top bunk."

"Won't that be too cramped for them?"

Alice shook her head. "It shouldn't be. They are both still pretty small. If it does get to that point, Thomas can sleep on a pallet on the floor."

That settled, Alice turned to the plate of food that Elizabeth had set in front of her. Elizabeth looked out the window and called, "Tony, breakfast's ready."

Just as she finished, the door opened. "I was already on my way in," Tony said.

Tony sat down at the table and took a bite from a hot buttered biscuit. A soft moan escaped his mouth but no crumbs. He loved Elizabeth's biscuits.

"Tony, winter's coming on so we've got to make some adjustments so nobody freezes to death during the night. David is going to take your bunk, and you'll sleep with Thomas on the lower bunk," Alice said.

Tony stopped chewing and looked at the bunks. He took a deep breath and swallowed the mouthful of biscuit.

"Is there anything wrong?" Alice asked.

Tony's head snapped around to stare at her. "No, ma'am. I've got a few things under my mattress. I'll move them down before tonight, though," Tony said.

After breakfast, David took the first trick of the day at the rudder. He stood on the quarterdeck that was two steps above the race planks but still two steps below the roof of the family cabin. He leaned back against the railing with one hand on the rudder. It was the only control on the canal boat, and the boat was still slow to respond to the rudder commands.

David pulled his gray sack suit tightly around him and looked over the edge into the clear water. Most of the ice had either melted or was floating around in small chunks. There was still a chill in the air that sent him to wrap his hands around the hot mug of coffee sitting on the roof of the family cabin every few minutes.

Thomas stood on the shore with Ocean and Jigger. He shared pieces of an apple with the two Kentucky mules.

"Let's go, Thomas. Georgetown's waiting," David said.

Thomas waved to him. Then he grabbed hold of the harness chain between the two mules and gave it a tug. The two mules began walking east on the towpath. Thomas let the mules walk ahead, and he fell into step beside them.

They walked about twenty feet before they had taken up the slack to the tow line. The thick rope rose from the water, dripping wet and taut. As the slack disappeared, the mules' steps froze. Now they were pulling against the dead weight of a canal boat loaded with 121 tons of coal.

The pair of mules leaned against the harnesses, letting their weight and the buoyancy the water gave the boat nudge it forward. It took minutes as the mules took their first slow-motion step and then another. The steps became quicker but still only a plodding walk. Quicker still until finally, they were walking at the normal four-mile-per-hour pace that controlled the pace of life on the canal.

A faster pace wasn't allowed on the canal. Speedier boats could cause damage to the canal beds through erosion. Faster boats were harder to maneuver. Faster-moving mules would also tear up the towpath as they dug in more to pull loaded boats.

David didn't mind the slow pace. It gave him plenty of time to think. Now that he was used to working on the canal, he valued that thinking time. He still had decisions to make about his future. He wasn't sure if he had been counted as missing in action among his regiment yet, but sooner or later, David was going to have to let his father know what had happened to him and why. When that occurred, he wanted to be able to tell his father what his plans for the future were.

What were his plans for the future?

That was the big question, and the one David still wasn't able to answer.

The *Freeman* had been moving for about an hour when Alice came out of the family cabin. She walked up to the quarterdeck and sat down on the roof of the family cabin. Even covered by her coat and bonnet, he still found her very attractive. She was thirty-six years old. Life on the canal hadn't worn her down or weathered her skin as it did some women. Alice would still turn men's heads in any town.

David glanced at her from time to time but kept most of his attention on the canal. Though he didn't have to worry too much about running into the side of the canal, he did need to watch for deadfalls in the water or even damage caused by guerrillas trying to disrupt the flow of coal into Washington City.

"They'll close the canal soon. Have you thought about what you'll do then?" Alice asked.

She brushed a loose strand of her auburn hair out of her face and tucked it under her bonnet.

David shrugged. "I sort of burned some of my bridges behind me when I decided to stay with you and your family."

David had been a Confederate spy on the canal, but now he was technically a deserter from the army. He still didn't know if anyone had reported him as such, though.

"Do you regret it?" Alice asked.

David thought for a moment. "No."

"Have you thought about going back to Charlottesville?" Alice asked.

"All the time. I love Grand Vista, but I don't think I have a life there any longer. It would never have been mine anyway."

He dreamed of Grand Vista, his family's plantation, every evening with its three-floor brick mansion and rolling hills, but he also dreamed of being on Grand Vista with Alice, Elizabeth, Tony, and Thomas. He even dreamed of Seamus, Jigger, and Ocean pulling a carriage rather than a canal boat.

"I'm sorry."

David shook his head. "Don't be. I made my own choices. I am sure there are other places just as lovely as Grand Vista. I'll just have to find one and make it my own."

"You can stay with us, though life on the canal is a little different in the winter than you've seen so far." David had only been with the Fitzgeralds for three months.

David smiled. "Thank you for that generous offer. I certainly feel comfortable here with you and your family. I will definitely consider it."

That seemed to be enough for Alice. She stood up and walked back down to the family cabin. David watched her go and shook his head.

What did she want from him? At times, she treated him like a friend and at other times like one of her children. He didn't understand women.

The *Freeman* stopped that night about thirty-five miles west of Georgetown and the end of the journey. They were near Balls Bluff and Harrison Island. Near the end of October 1861, a battle had been fought on the Virginia side of the river within sight of where they are now.

The C&O Canal ran along the Maryland side of the Potomac River for the most of its 184.5-mile length. Because of that, it was essentially the border between the United States of America and the Confederate States of America.

As David climbed into his new bunk that night, he found himself rolling around trying to get comfortable. He couldn't. Of all things, it was because he was too warm. Finally, David climbed off his bunk as quietly as possible and sat down at the table. The room was dark. David lit a lantern and opened up a book he had bought from another boatman two weeks ago. It was a book of poetry by Edgar Allan Poe, who had spent some of his short life in Charlottesville and Richmond.

David read one poem called "The Sleeper," which actually began to make him feel drowsy. Another poem called "Lenore" filled him with such longing that he had to close the book and set it aside.

He had other works by Poe in his room at Grand Vista. He had collected the man's writings not only because they were uncommonly good but also because Poe had attended the University of Virginia in Charlottesville for a short time. David felt a kinship to Edgar Allan Poe, who never seemed to feel at home anywhere. He even identified with characters in some of Poe's works. The stories reminded David

11

of the nightmares he used to have while he was still fighting in the war. Those had been troubling times for him when every time he closed he eyes, he saw macabre visions filled with walking dead men and death. For most soldiers, sleep was an escape from the horrors of wars. For David, it had been something worse.

He walked across the room and tossed a few chunks of coal into the stove. He might be warm now, but if the stove wasn't tended, it could get cold very fast.

When David turned back, he saw Tony, now sleeping in the lower bunk with Thomas, roll over. His arm drooped over the edge to fall to the floor. Even in his sleep, Tony jerked his hand back so quickly that it surprised David. After that explosive motion, Tony went back to sleeping in a stiff pose that seemed almost unnatural.

David stared at him. It wasn't natural. David had seen Tony sleeping before, and he didn't look anything like the statue of a child that David was watching now. Something was wrong with Tony. Something about the sleeping arrangements bothered the boy.

David walked over to the lower bunk and scooped Tony up in his arms. He lifted the boy from the lower bunk and set him on the upper bunk. Tony immediately relaxed as if he realized in his sleep that he was back where he liked to sleep. David pulled the blanket up over Tony and stepped back.

On the lower bunk, Thomas had spread out, flinging his arms and legs wide.

David grinned and shook his head. He sat down in one of the straight-back chairs around the table and tipped it back on its legs so that he was leaning against the wall at a forty-five-degree angle. He crossed his arms over his chest, closed his eyes and fell asleep.

The *Freeman* reached Georgetown the next day and waited at the wharf to offload its cargo. The talk was that the canal was going to be drained at the end of the month. Needed repairs would be made while the canal bed was empty. Some of the repairs made last year had merely been patches until time and conditions allowed for more permanent repairs to be made.

"If we're not stuck here for too long, we should be able to make it back to Cumberland by the time they let the water out," Alice explained to David after she told him when the canal would be drained.

"I thought you usually wintered in Sharpsburg?" David asked.

Alice frowned, and she sighed. "That was when we had a home there. It burned down during the Battle of Antietam. If we winter in Cumberland, we can probably find temporary work to help us through the winter. We had such a poor season this year that we'll need help."

David had fought and been wounded during the Battle of Antietam, though the Confederates had called it the Battle of Sharpsburg. He had seen Sharpsburg and the damage the nearby battle had caused to the homes. He had also seen the dead. Too many men had died there. The sight had been like one of his nightmares come true.

"Why not just stay here then? Washington City is larger than Cumberland. It would be easier to find winter work here."

"Because when the canal is flooded again, if we are in Cumberland, we'll be one of the first boats to be loaded. It will give us a quick start next season, and we'll need the money."

It made sense, but all David could think of was that once the water was drained from the canal, he would be stuck wherever they were. Now he was on the move, but what would happen when he was stuck in one place?

2

ROCK COLLECTING

JANUARY 1863

David stood at the rudder as the *Freeman*, lightened by the removal of 121 tons of coal in Georgetown, headed back toward Cumberland. David wore his overcoat and gloves and still felt the cold. His lack of movement allowed the cold to affect him to a greater degree than if he had been moving around. His breath turned to mist each time he exhaled so that someone looking at him from a distance would have thought he was smoking.

He could see the *Harvest Moon* moving west about a half mile ahead of the *Freeman*. The gap between the two boats remained relatively steady except when they stopped at the locks.

Elizabeth walked with Ocean and Seamus, taking her turn as a mule driver. She had taken over for Thomas at Lock 30 at Weverton. Instead of resting, Thomas still played on the towpath. He walked along with his sister, ran ahead and dashed into the woods to explore something only he noticed. The boy never seemed to tire or stop playing.

The canal boat passed under the B&O Railroad bridge that led into Harpers Ferry, Virginia, at the intersection of the Potomac and Shenandoah Rivers. Currently, most of this area of Northern Virginia was under control of the Union, so the trains were running again. One of the problems that the B&O Railroad kept running into during this war is that their tracks crossed into Virginia at Harpers Ferry and stayed south of the Potomac River until they neared Cumberland. When the Confederacy controlled Northern Virginia, it made sure that once the trains crossed the river into the South, they didn't cross back.

David enjoyed the quiet of not having the trains rumble by and blow their whistles to try and frighten canal mules. At the bridge, he could hear the Potomac as its waters crashed and mixed with the Shenandoah River. The river of the North met the river of the South and mixed.

Or did they?

The waters might mix at this point, but the river remained the Potomac River, the river of the Union. David pondered that message from nature as the *Freeman* approached Lock 33. Elizabeth stopped the mules while the *Harvest Moon* locked through and the lock doors were reset for the *Freeman.*

Once the lock doors were open, Elizabeth started Ocean and Jigger forward with a sharp "Gee haw!" David made sure that the *Freeman* was straight as he eased the large boat into the lock. Near Harpers Ferry, there were three locks within a mile and a half of each other. Lock 33 was the middle lock. It was also the one that had a small community growing up around it.

The lockhouse occupied a strategic position along the canal. Fort Duncan was only a few miles to the west and Harpers Ferry was just across the railroad bridge and within easy walking distance. In fact, there was also an outlet lock at this point so that boats could be taken across the river to Virginia at this point. Right now, that lock wasn't used because of the war.

Four years ago, William Walsh had opened a feed store on a vacant piece of ground above the lock's bypass flume. Then on the berm side of the canal, the Salty Dog Tavern was opened. Now it serviced only the soldiers from Fort Duncan, but since there were more soldiers than usual because of the war, it made up the trade lost from Harpers Ferry. Other buildings in the tiny community included a small bakery and more homes.

Tony walked out of the family cabin and tossed one of the coiled snubbing lines to Daniel Bretzl, the lockkeeper. Bretzl looped the thick, sturdy rope around the snubbing post, a stump-like piece of wood set into the ground next to the canal. Tony tossed the other line onto the other side of the canal. He then jumped from the boat as it neared the lock and ran up to the snubbing post and looped his line around it.

"How are things here?" David asked the lockkeeper.

"Been quiet 'cept at night, but that's normal around here," Bretzl answered.

The soldiers enjoyed their free time in the Salty Dog Tavern, and more than a few of them had been known to wander across the railroad bridge when they were drunk to cause trouble in Harpers Ferry.

"No war trouble?" David asked.

"War? That's for armies and generals. Truth be told, things is so scarce over there with all the fightin' and shelling that was done last year that we get Virginians comin' over wanting to buy from us."

"Do you sell to them?"

Bretzl spit a wad of brown tobacco into the canal. "Of course we do."

"The soldiers don't stop them?"

David remembered how the squad of Union soldiers had searched the *Freeman* for him after he had escaped from them last year.

"Those soldiers aren't fighting to starve women and children. Those folks are our friends and family. You don't turn your back on friends just because some men further east can't agree on things," Bretzl said.

"That's good to know."

Bretzl grinned. "I thought you might like it. I'm not going to harm a man who's done me no wrong no matter what colors he's wearing or *wore*."

David smiled. He didn't fool too many people. Many of the canallers at least realized that David had been a former Confederate soldier, but for the most part, they kept the information to themselves. Canallers were a tight-knit community who dealt with their problems among themselves without involving outsiders.

As the *Freeman* entered the lock, Elizabeth halted the mules so that the boat floated into the lock. Tony and Bretzl tightened up on their snubbing lines so that the boat wouldn't crash into the closed west-end lock doors. When the *Freeman* was entirely inside the lock and stopped, David turned the rudder all the way to the side so that it lay against the side of the boat and wouldn't interfere with the east-end lock doors.

Tony and Bretzl pulled on the swing arms for the lock doors on their respective sides of the lock to shut the east-end doors on the lock. Bretzl then walked onto the west-end doors and used his lock key to open the sluice gates at the bottom of the lock doors.

Water flooded in under the *Freeman* and began to raise the boat. It bounced around, but Tony and Bretzl kept the snubbing lines tight so that the boat didn't crash into either the lock walls or doors. It took about ten minutes for the *Freeman* to rise about eight feet.

Once the water level inside the lock was the same height as the water on the west side of the lock, Bretzl used the huge iron lock key to shut the sluice gates. Then he and Tony leaned on the swing arms of the west-end lock doors and opened them.

Tony and Bretzl tossed their snubbing lines onto the cargo hatches. Tony jumped onto the boat and began coiling the ropes so they would be ready for the next lock, which was only about a mile further west. Elizabeth started the mules moving again, and the *Freeman* moved out of the lock.

David waved to Bretzl. "I guess I'll be seeing you next season."

Bretzl waved back. "Have a good winter."

Lock 34 was about a mile away to the west. It was the closest lock to Fort Duncan, which had been built last year to defend Harpers Ferry. The lock was also part of a canal that had originally been built by George Washington to skirt the rapids in the area. Washington's Potowmack Company, founded in 1785, had been the C&O Canal's predecessor. David saw it as another example of a Southern man's dreams being consumed by the North's avarice.

Thomas picked up a flat stone off the towpath and skipped it across the canal. It traveled on a diagonal path across the canal in four jumps and then hopped out of the water and into the dirt on the far side of the canal.

David watched the stone disappear into the brush. It gave him an idea. "Thomas!" David called.

The boy stopped running and turned to look at David. "What?"

Thomas wore a navy peacoat that Alice had purchased for him in Georgetown. It was unbuttoned, though, and Thomas was still barefoot. The winter weather just didn't seem to affect him.

"Can you do me a favor? Find me some stones. I'm looking for nice round stones somewhat smaller than my fist. The rounder they are, the better." David put his hands together in a circle to show the size and shape of the stones he wanted.

"How many do you want?" Thomas asked.

"Let's start with ten."

Thomas grinned and ran off the side of the towpath to look for the stones. David looked at his hand and closed it slowly into a fist. Then he quickly flung his arm out and opened his hand. His idea just might work and be fun at that.

Tony finished coiling the snubbing lines and walked up on the quarterdeck with David. He leaned back against the railing on the other side of the rudder from David.

Tony was beginning to fill out some from his time as a canal boat hand. His bony frame was losing its sharp edges as the hollows were filling in. David wondered if it was because the former thief and scavenger was eating well for the first time in his life or developing muscles from his labors.

Tony looked around uncomfortably and then asked, "Why did you put me in your bunk the other night?"

David watched him look at his feet and not make eye contact, which was quite unusual for Tony. The boy was usually very straightforward with what he thought.

"You seemed more comfortable there," David said. He had been letting Tony sleep in the bunk since that first night while he slept on a pallet on the floor.

"How could you tell?"

David explained what he had seen while he watched Tony sleep. Tony sighed.

"I guess you think I'm crazy," he said.

David shook his head. "Actually, I figured you were afraid that Thomas had wet the bed."

Tony laughed and looked at David.

"I wish it was something like that. The problem's not Thomas. It's me."

"Do you want to tell me about it?"

Tony hesitated. "How much did Mrs. Fitzgerald tell you about me?"

David shrugged. "Not much. It's not her story to tell."

Tony nodded. "I used to live with my mother in Cumberland. She had a lot of what she called 'men friends.' You understand?" David nodded. "Well, when she was with her men friends, I was under her bed. I took extra money from their pockets while they were busy on the bed, but their pants were on the floor."

Tony's face flushed red, and he stared at his feet again.

"So now you don't want to sleep under a bed even if you're on your own bed," David guessed.

Tony shrugged. "Probably."

"Well then, you're welcome to the top bunk."

"Why'd you send Thomas looking for stones for you?" Tony asked, changing subjects. He had made his confession, and now he wanted to forget the embarrassment.

Tony was just as curious as Thomas about things, but where Thomas had to find the answers on his own from first-hand experience, Tony settled for asking questions and evaluating the answers.

"I'm just trying to keep Thomas occupied and out of trouble," David said innocently.

Tony snorted. "Maybe you're going to eat those rocks when he gives them to you, too."

David shook his head. His relationship with Tony was far different than Alice's relationship with the eleven-year-old. Tony treated the two adults on the boat quite differently. He respected and obeyed Alice as if she was his mother. He treated David like a good friend or brother and sometimes a younger brother at that.

"I was just remembering when I was your age. My brother and I would skip stones across the ponds on Grand Vista. It was a great competition," David recalled.

"You didn't ask for flat stones," Tony said quickly.

David nodded. "I know that. You see, I always beat Peter at skipping stones. I could get more jumps out of them, and they would go farther. He hated that because he's three years older than me. So we started throwing stones at targets. He thought he could beat me at that because he was stronger than me, and at first, Peter did win. Then I began to get better. Not more powerful but more accurate. We moved to smaller targets and farther away, and I still kept beating him. He hated it."

"You still remember something like that?" Tony asked, surprised.

"Of course, it was one of the few times that the number two son was number one, and even my father couldn't dispute it."

Tony cocked an eyebrow. "So, you're looking for something to throw rocks at?"

David shook his head. "No, I have an idea what I'd like to throw stones at."

"What?"

"Ver-r-r-rmints," David said, imitating the canaller accent.

"You had better not let Thomas catch you at it then. He'll be mad, especially when he realizes he gave you the stones," Tony said.

"I don't think he'll be mad at me hitting these varmints."

"Why's that?"

David grinned, but he didn't say anything else.

3

SOLDIER BOY

JANUARY 1863

George Fitzgerald knelt behind the earthen rampart somewhere in eastern Virginia. He had marched around in so many directions lately that he had lost all sense of where he was. He simply marched along with the rest of the Union army. George believed that he was northeast of Richmond.

His body shook, and it wasn't all from the cold. He was about to take part in his first battle. He rubbed his hands together to warm them. Then he cupped his hands and blew into them. He had taken his gloves off a few minutes ago so that he could fire his rifle, which was propped up beside him.

George inched his head up until he could see over the rampart. In the distance, he could see the Confederate Army line. In the open space between the two lines, hundreds of men would die soon. He wasn't even sure what the significance of fighting this battle would be. This wasn't a strategic battle. Two groups of soldiers had simply met up with each other on their way to join up with larger armies.

Would history call this "The Accidental Battle"?

George's left hand began to shake. He dropped down and shoved his hand under his thigh. He didn't want anyone to see that he was scared.

"You can't shoot if you're sitting on your hand," Brian Langdon said.

Brian was a blond-haired young man of George's age. Brian was a merchant's son in Washington City. He had a slight paunch around his middle from comfortable living and a pleasant sense of humor that made him popular among the men. Brian and George had joined up at the same time at the Georgetown recruiting station. They had become friends as they went through the scant training together and shared a tent in the field.

"I don't know that I can shoot if I wasn't sitting on my hand," George said.

He held out his hand, and Brian watched it quiver.

"If that's as bad as it gets, you're lucky. I don't even think I can look over the rampart. I don't want to see what's coming at me," Brian said.

George was glad that he had at least managed that much.

"There's nothing to be seen yet. The Rebels are just sitting over there doing the same thing we are," George said.

"You mean afraid to look over at us and sitting on shaking hands?"

"I only wish. If that were the truth, then maybe we wouldn't see each other and would keep on marching past each other."

"Or if we do see each other, we won't be able to shoot." Brian laughed. "Wouldn't that be a hoot?" Brian suddenly stopped laughing. "George, do you think you can kill a man?"

George shrugged. "I don't know. I've shot animals."

"Rabbit and deer don't look like you, though. They aren't related to you. They can't ask you not to shoot them," Brian said.

George agreed, but he just wasn't sure what would happen when he actually came face to face with a person he was trying to shoot.

The cannons began to fire, and George covered his ears to drown out the frightening booms. He felt the ground shake as the enemy returned fire. None of the shells fell close, but the Rebels would soon have the troop lines in range if the Union army stayed where it was.

"It won't be long now," Brian said.

George nodded and picked up his rifle.

The bugler blew charge. George took a deep breath and stood up along with the other men on the line. They began to run forward, firing as they moved. Ahead of them, a gray line rose up, and the Confederates screamed and charged at the Union soldiers.

From the corners of his eyes, George saw Union soldiers fall. He concentrated on staring forward at the enemy coming toward him. Men collapsed. Other soldiers filled in the gaps the fallen men left in the line and the line continued to edge forward.

George raised his rifle to his shoulder and fired into the mass of men charging at him. He wasn't sure if he hit anyone, but he was more worried about being shot himself. He paused only to reload and then he advanced again. He felt safe being on the move. Each puff of smoke meant a bullet aimed in his direction, and there was a large cloud of smoke forming around the Rebel army. It was cutting down visibility on both sides of the fighting.

George fired and paused to reload. A soldier walked around him and then suddenly fell. Blood spread on the ground around the soldier's neck.

That could have been him. If he hadn't paused, he would have been lying there on the ground.

George closed his eyes and took a deep breath.

"We've got to keep going," Brian said beside him.

His friend was also reloading his rifle. They both managed to finish and started walking toward the enemy again and fired into the Rebel line.

A shell exploded on George's left. The sound was deafening, and so was Brian's scream. The shrapnel tore through his friend's body, turning it red. Brian standing on George's left shielded George from most of the shrapnel.

George screamed as the shrapnel hit his left arm, his shoulder, and his head. Then Brian fell on top of him, and they tumbled to the ground.

His breath went out of him as he hit so that he couldn't even scream. He gasped to try and catch his breath. He sucked in foul air filled with the scent of blood and gunpowder.

George felt the weight of his friend on him and tried to rouse him. George figured that he would have to help Brian to the rear of the fighting so that the doctors could help him.

"Brian, how bad are you hit? I can help you, but you've got to get off me," George asked.

Brian didn't respond, and George tried to raise himself up to look at Brian. His left arm wouldn't move when he tried to push up. Instead, he rolled to the side to look at Brian.

Brian wasn't there.

Or rather, a lump of bloody flesh lay across George, but it no longer looked like Brian Langdon.

George screamed, but he couldn't be heard among the gunfire and

22

other yells. Even if the soldiers could have heard him, they were too busy fighting to pay George much attention. Soldiers moved around him, back and forth. Blue. Gray. Blue. Blue. Gray. Blue. Gray. Gray.

George realized that he must be right on the front line. He only hoped that when the fighting ended, all the soldiers around him would be wearing blue uniforms.

He tried to crawl away on his backside, but Brian's body kept him pinned down. He tried to wiggle out from under the body.

Before he managed to free himself, George saw a Rebel soldier charge at him. The man raised his rifle with his bayonet attached, intending to spear George. George clenched his eyes shut and turned his head away, but the pain of being skewered didn't come.

He opened his eyes and saw the soldier was on his knees. The man stared blankly ahead, and the rifle hung unfired at his side. A small round hole in the man's head was the only indication that he had been shot. Then the man fell over, adding more weight to pin George to the ground.

George tried to push the bodies off of him, and this time he was able to raise his arms to push at the bodies on his thighs and stomach.

George stopped and stared at his left hand. It wasn't there. His left arm was shredded, and his hand was missing entirely. Blood pumped out of the wound, and George realized that he was bleeding to death.

He tucked his arm against his side, hoping that would slow the blood that he was losing. He felt lightheaded and weak, which was probably why he wasn't able to push the bodies off him. He could feel the warmth of his blood pumping out of his arm in contrast to the snow he felt on his back.

George yelled for help until everything went black.

23

4

DECISIONS TO MOVE ON

JANUARY 1863

As the *Freeman* floated out of Lock 39, Alice Fitzgerald walked out of the family cabin and stood on the race plank. She looked around to get her bearings and waved to Jackson Myers, the lockkeeper. He tipped his straw hat to her and turned to walk back to the warmth of the lockhouse.

"We're close to where we used to stop at the end of every season. Sharpsburg's not far from here," Alice said to David, who stood at the rudder.

David nodded as he eased the *Freeman* into the curve the canal made as it paralleled the Potomac River.

"I want to stop here, David," Alice said.

"Did you change your mind about spending the winter in Cumberland?" he asked.

Alice shook her head and walked up on the quarterdeck with him. "No, but I've got some business in town that I would like to get started now. The next lock is more than four miles away."

She had been thinking about this for some time. Her life had changed irreversibly with everything that had happened to her last year, and she needed to move on and rebuild her life. This was one of the steps she had decided that she needed to take to do that. She needed to act now before she changed her mind. Otherwise, she would be delayed a couple months from doing anything.

"Elizabeth, we're stopping," David called.

"The mules aren't that tired," Elizabeth Fitzgerald replied.

"Your mother wants to go into Sharpsburg."

24

Elizabeth stopped the mules, and David turned the rudder to the side so that the *Freeman* came to rest against the berm side of the canal. The tow rope slackened and slipped into the water.

"Should I bring the mules over there?" Elizabeth asked.

David looked over at Alice.

"Just unhitch them and let them rest over there," Alice called. "I'll take Seamus into town. I don't expect that I'll be gone more than a couple of hours. We'll still have some daylight to make a few miles more." Once they stopped, Alice asked David, "Can you help me lay out the fall board?"

David Windover nodded and followed Alice toward the mule shed. They picked up the fall board off the cargo hatches. They lifted the cleated board up on one end and lowered the other end to the ground so that they could walk from the boat to the shore. Alice could have done it herself, but the board was long, and it was awkward for one person to handle alone.

Alice climbed into the mule shed and put a harness and blanket on Seamus. She led the gray mule out of the shed and across the fall board.

"Can you help me up, David?" Alice asked. She could ride into town from the road that ran near the lockhouse.

David put his hands around Alice's waist and lifted her up so that she could sit sidesaddle on the mule's back. She thought he hesitated a bit too long before he began lifting her and before he let her go, but Alice didn't want to get into what that discussion would lead to right now.

"Do you want me to go in with you?" David asked.

Alice shook her head. "No. Someone needs to watch the boat. There may still be guerillas on the canal."

Thomas came running up on the north side of the canal. He had crossed over from the towpath on the closed canal doors.

"Can I come, too, Mama?" he asked.

Alice didn't really want to have to watch Thomas while she was in town. If he saw any of his friends, she would have to tie him to her to keep him from running off. There was too much trouble the nine-year-old boy could get into there, but it might be the last chance he had to see the town for a long time.

"Fine," Alice conceded, nodding.

"Yea!" Thomas shouted.

25

"Mama, can I go?" Elizabeth called from across the canal.

Having said "yes" to Thomas, she couldn't very well say "no" to Elizabeth. Besides, Elizabeth could help Alice watch Thomas.

"Yes," Alice said.

Elizabeth smiled. She led Ocean and Jigger across the canal at Lock 39 and brought them up next to her mother and Seamus. Thomas climbed up on Seamus's back, and David lifted Elizabeth onto Jigger.

"We'll be back as soon as we can," Alice said. "Do you need anything while I'm in town?"

David shook his head.

Alice, Thomas, and Elizabeth rode away. Tony came out of the family cabin to watch them leave. He waved to them one last time as they passed out of sight.

"Why are we going into Sharpsburg, Mama?" Elizabeth asked.

"I have some business to take care of that I don't want to leave until next season," Alice replied.

Sharpsburg was not Alice's hometown. It had been where Hugh had grown up. Still, Alice had liked the town and the people, though she had never made any strong relationships because she was only in town a few months out of the year.

Five roads came together in Sharpsburg, which made it a popular stopover point with travelers. The town had its own fire company and newspaper. Farmers in the area grew wheat, rye, and hay. They raised sheep, geese, beef, and the farm lanes were well-rutted from travel to and from the town. Alice wondered how much that had changed since the battle.

Alice hadn't been here since she and Hugh had walked through the town after the Battle of Antietam. That had been four months ago. Sharpsburg had still been burning at the time, and people had been wandering the streets in a daze.

"Where's our house?" Thomas asked as they rode into town.

Alice tried to keep from crying at the sight of the empty lot. "I told you, Thomas, it burned down during the battle."

Thomas's brow wrinkled in confusion. "But there's nothing left. I thought there would be something left of the outside like when the Taylors' house burned down a while back. You could still tell it had been a house, but there's nothing left of our house," Thomas said.

"He's right, Mama. It doesn't look right. You expect to see our house there when you look in that direction, but there's nothing there," Elizabeth said.

Alice nodded, but she didn't trust herself to say anything.

She dismounted in front of the empty lot. All that remained of their house was the stone foundation. Thomas was right. The fire had done its work, and then some, on their house. This had been Alice's home for fifteen of the twenty years she had been married to Hugh.

Now they were both gone, and her life was very different.

She paced the edge of the foundation making a large T. The stones were still tight fitting and level. Another house could be placed on the foundation with no problem.

The problem was that Alice didn't have a new home to put here or the money to have one built.

She looked into the empty basement. Though the food items were gone, some of the storage shelves remained. She could see the spot where she and Hugh had hidden slaves as they helped them along the Underground Railroad to freedom.

Alice looked at her children. She pulled her coat tighter around her.

"Do you miss it?" she asked.

Thomas shrugged and wandered away. He quickly lowered himself into the basement to rummage around in the rubble.

Elizabeth said, "I'm sad because it was our house, but I don't think I'll miss it as much as I should. Is that wrong?"

"What do you mean?" Alice asked.

"We didn't live here that much, just a couple months a year. The *Freeman* is our home. If we lost that, I would miss it much more than I do the house." She paused. "It was a nice house, though. I liked having my own room."

Alice nodded slowly. Elizabeth understood how Alice was feeling and Elizabeth had been able to put it in words, too. Alice had had a house in Sharpsburg fifteen years, but she might only have actually lived here for three of those fifteen years. The rest of the time she was on the canal and lived on the *Freeman*.

That was her real home. "I'm going to sell the property and the mule barn," Alice said suddenly.

"Do we need money that bad?"

Alice nodded. "We do, but that's not the primary reason. We may not see the money from selling this lot for a while. The property is of no use to us. We wouldn't be able to live here again for years anyway. It takes time to save money to buy a house. Why should we go through all of that saving and sacrifice to rebuild a house that we don't miss? It's time for us to move on."

Elizabeth slowly nodded her agreement, though unshed tears filled her eyes.

Alice turned away from the foundation and took hold of Seamus's bridle.

"Come along, Thomas," Elizabeth called.

They walked the mules down Main Street and past the town center. The United States flag flew proudly at the top of the flagpole right now. Early in the war, when loyal Unionists had raised the flag in town square, someone stole the rope. When another flag was raised, it was set afire. It seems like most people felt the Union had a chance at winning the war now and were rallying behind their country.

Alice found the Arnold house and knocked on the door. It was a brick two-story home with a small front porch that barely held all of the Fitzgeralds.

John Arnold answered the door. He was a wiry thin man whose hair was as white as snow, though he was only forty years old. He was a friend of Hugh's and Hugh had allowed him to rent the mule barn and house when they were canalling. Now Alice hoped the man might do her a bigger favor.

"Alice!" John smiled broadly. "Come in! Come in! Does this mean that they've drained the canal for the winter?" He stepped back and waved them into the house.

"Not yet, John, but soon," Alice told him.

Alice walked inside the parlor with Elizabeth and Thomas. John closed the door and hurried forward to show them to the sofa. Alice, Thomas and Elizabeth sat down and relaxed. John sat down in a rocking chair across the room from them.

"So what can I do for you? I suppose you've come to collect the rental on the barn?" he said.

Alice shook her head. "I've got a favor to ask of you, John."

"If it's in my power to give, you've certainly got it. I heard about what happened to Hugh. I'm so sorry, but I'll do what I can to help you."

Alice smiled. "Thank you, John. I know you were a good friend to both Hugh and me. I am going to winter in Cumberland this year. I can find work there to keep me busy until the canal reopens. I would like you to sell the mule barn and house lot."

"Sell?"

Alice nodded.

"Does this mean you're not coming back to Sharpsburg?"

"Not to live. I'll still be back now and then to visit. Without the house to hold us here, there's really no reason for us to stay. We're canawlers. Our home is on our boat moving up and down the canal," Alice explained.

John rubbed his chin. "I'm not sure how much I can get for the land, especially right now. Given what happened here last fall, people aren't exactly flocking to buy up all of the property hereabouts. They're afraid that it might happen again."

"I understand, John. Get whatever you can. There's no rush. I know that it may take a while to get a decent price, and you keep five percent of what you get for all of your work on my behalf," Alice said.

John sighed. "I appreciate the offer, but are you sure this is the right decision?"

Alice shrugged. "No, not totally, but it feels right. I'm not sure what my future will hold, but I don't feel like it will be in Sharpsburg any longer."

"Sharpsburg's a good place to live," John said quickly.

"I'll take your word for it. I haven't actually lived here that long when you think about it."

John grinned. "I understand." He clapped his hands against his thighs. "Well, it's not my property to tell you what to do or not to do with it. It's just my responsibility to see that you get a good price. I will do that for you."

He held out his hand and Alice shook it.

"Thank you."

The Fitzgeralds stood up to leave.

"Can't you stay for dinner? I'll take you all to Grant's Tavern," John offered.

Alice shook her head. "We have to get heading to Cumberland. I want to make sure I'm there when the company drains the canal. That's where we will winter."

"Good luck to you then. Hopefully, I'll have sold the properties by the time you're back to see me again," John said.

As the three of them rode the mules back to the *Freeman*, Alice felt as if she should be feeling melancholy about what she had just done. She had just cut all of her ties to Sharpsburg. She didn't feel sad, though. She felt free and light. It was as if she had opened up a multitude of possibilities for her and her family by deciding to sell the property.

Her future was ahead of her once again.

5

DANGEROUS GAMES

JANUARY 1863

The *Freeman* passed the mid-point of the canal the next day. They were only a few miles from Martinsburg, Virginia. David looked across the river into Virginia and felt his chest swell a bit. He found himself looking toward Virginia a lot. There was something about the land that he loved. It was his homeland. It was in his blood, but he didn't feel that the land itself would welcome him right now, let alone the people.

As he watched, David saw a black man run from a stand of trees toward the river. The man was barefoot and dressed in lightweight clothing that couldn't keep him warm. The man ran hard, occasionally looking over his shoulder.

David watched silently, knowing the man was running for his life. He was a slave hoping to make it to the Potomac River and freedom.

Behind the man, two mounted riders appeared from the woods. They rode their horses hard toward the escaping slave. One of the men lifted a long bullwhip from his saddle. He shook it free and snapped it out. The lash hit the slave on the back and sent the man sprawling headfirst on the ground.

The riders galloped past the fallen slave and circled around him. The slave pushed himself to his feet and ran again, still heading for the river as if the water would stop the men from chasing him. The slave had spirit; David gave him that, though he didn't give him a chance at reaching freedom.

The whip snaked out again. This time, the end wrapped around the slave's neck. The rider jerked the whip back hard and the slave flipped backward and fell.

31

The second rider dismounted and walked up to the fallen slave. He kicked the black man in the side three times. Then he rolled the slave onto his stomach and bound his hands behind his back. The man tied a rope around the slave's neck and remounted. He turned his horse and led the slave away toward the south.

The rider with the whip recoiled his whip and tied it to his saddle. Then he actually waved to David as he turned and rode away.

David watched the display in silence. He was surprised to find himself clenching the rudder so tight that his knuckles turned white.

He knew runaway slaves had to be captured. Plantation owners like his father paid too much money for them to let them go without attempting to chase them down. Grand Vista had its share of slaves who had tried to escape and David had seen them brought back hungry, thin and beaten.

He had never seen the process of capturing a slave, though. He had seen the overseer by himself and returning with the escaped slaves. David knew the punishment was whipping, but he had never seen it happen or even heard the smack of the whip against bare flesh.

The whole thing reminded him of hunting. It was hunting. It was a hunt for a man.

The *Freeman* neared Cumberland and David saw more and more boats as they tried to jockey for a good position in the basin before the end of the season. Others were racing to see if they could make a short run to Williamsport before the canal closed.

David came out of the family cabin and walked up to the quarter-deck where Alice piloted the boat. She smiled at him.

"We're almost there," she said.

"What happens when we get to Cumberland?" David asked.

"We find the best place to tie up that we can. Hopefully, we'll be close to town and in the basin."

"Do we wait then until the canal reopens?"

"Usually, but everyone did so poorly this year because of the war and the problems with keeping water in the canal that I think they'll be a lot of canawlers looking for work to get by until the canal reopens," Alice explained.

A large black locomotive picked up speed as it approached the *Freeman*, heading toward Baltimore and other points north. David watched it come. The B&O tracks and the canal paralleled each other on the approach into Cumberland. As the locomotive neared the mules, it blew its whistle, hoping to startle the mules into bolting. David expected it. In fact, he had grown used to it, but it didn't mean he would accept it.

Thomas did a good job maintaining control of Seamus and Jigger. They hesitated, but they didn't rear or bolt. David nodded his approval. Thomas was an excellent mule driver. He had a way with animals.

As the locomotive approached the boat, David grabbed one of the round stones that Thomas had collected for him. He kept them lined up along one edge of the family cabin. The stone felt comfortable in his fist. He hurled it at the train. The rock soared into the open window of the engine and David was rewarded with a yell from the man inside.

He laughed. He felt like he was ten years old again and had just beaten his brother at a rock-throwing competition.

"Why did you do that?" Alice asked, frowning. "It will only make things worse."

"I don't think so."

"It will. Tensions between the railroaders are bad enough, but things like that will just make it worse," she told David.

He had learned a lot about the canal in his short time with the Fitzgeralds. One thing was that the canal had one foot in the grave. Another thing was that the B&O Railroad was trying to kick the other foot out from under the canal.

"It might if the railroad wanted peace with the canal, but it doesn't. Nor do the people who work for it. There's been a war going on along the Potomac River a lot longer than the war between the Union and the Confederacy. The railroad declared war on the canal, and you all sit around and still act like pacifists. When you don't respond to their stupid stunts like trying to spook mules or stealing the grain trade that the canal lost to the railroad, they see that as your weakness and their victory," David said.

"And you think throwing a rock at a man changes all that?"

David nodded. "It does. Now that man knows that when he tries that again, he might get hit with another rock, and if he wasn't paying attention, he won't even be sure which boat to watch out for. If enough canallers did it, then maybe the railroaders would stop blowing their whistles."

"Or they might just think of something worse to do," Alice shot back.

"Then it's up to the canallers to be ready. We didn't start this fight with the railroad, but we shouldn't let that stop us from being the victor."

6

WOMEN'S WORK

FEBRUARY 1863

Harlan Armentrout sat behind his large desk in his study. His elbows rested on the cherry surface and his fingers formed a steeple in front of his face. He was a tall man with wide shoulders. He was completely bald, but he had a very thick mustache as if to distract people from noticing the lack of hair on his head.

He wore a matching brown suit, waistcoat and pants. It surprised Alice a bit that he wore the coat inside the house. It gave her the impression that her potential employer was a very formal man.

Armentrout looked across the room at Alice and Elizabeth. They stood in their Sunday dresses, waiting nervously. Alice was surprised that Armentrout hadn't offered them a place to sit.

"Mrs. Fitzgerald, you do understand that I am looking for a housekeeper and cook who can serve long term," Armentrout said.

Alice nodded and looked Armentrout in the eye. "I do, sir, but I'm afraid I can't offer that type of commitment. We're canawlers."

"So why do you want to do domestic work?"

"The canal was drained yesterday because the ice got too thick for the icebreakers. Usually, we make enough during the season to get by for the winter season. Last year was very bad, though."

Armentrout nodded. He laid his hands down to rest on the desk. "Yes, the war was quite nasty. It has taken many of our finest young men and given us nothing but broken souls and corpses in return. I've had to amputate more limbs in the past two years than I did in my eighteen years of practicing medicine up until that point."

"The war was part of it, sir. We also lost our home during the Battle of Antietam. We lived in Sharpsburg."

Alice thought it wouldn't hurt to generate a little sympathy from Armentrout if she could.

Alice wasn't willing to go into the other part of her concern. Sympathy or not. She had some pride, but she was a widow with two children of her own to support and one whom she had adopted. In addition, there was David to worry about. She wanted to get a job quickly before other canawlers filled the vacancies.

"So how long will you be able to work for me if I should choose to hire you?" Armentrout asked.

Alice thought for a moment and shrugged. "It's hard to say. When the canal fills, we'll have to be ready to load up and head for Georgetown. That could be a month or it may be three. The Canal Company managed to keep the canal open relatively late in the season because January was somewhat mild, but if spring comes early, they'll be putting water back in as soon as they can."

"You put me in a bit of a predicament then."

Alice was getting tired of standing. She wondered what kind of gentleman Harlan Armentrout was not to offer her and Elizabeth a seat. Alice wondered if he also made his patients stand.

"I understand, sir, but those who can afford them have slaves do this type of household work. Not many people have a need for labor they have to pay for."

Armentrout straightened his back. "I can afford slaves, but I would never purchase another human being. I do not believe in it. I only wish President Lincoln had extended his Emancipation Proclamation last year to include all of the United States, not simply those states in rebellion," Armentrout told her.

"I don't disagree with you," Alice said.

"That is easy for you to say, madam. You have never been in a position to own slaves so you can't miss what you have never experienced," Armentrout corrected.

Alice glanced at her daughter. She didn't want to say the wrong thing in front of Elizabeth. "I have proven my devotion to the cause of freedom for all, Dr. Armentrout." That was all she was going to say about that. He didn't need to know that she and Hugh used to transport slaves along the Underground Railroad. Even the children, except for Tony, didn't know about that.

Her covert help had ended when she had taken David aboard the

Freeman. Alice didn't know how he would react to the situation since his father owned slaves.

Armentrout decided not to press the point, much to Alice's relief.

"You can handle the duties that are required of the position?" he said instead.

"Yes, sir. I've been working on a canal boat for most of my life. I've driven mules, cooked, sewed, hauled hay, and on occasion, shoveled coal."

Armentrout raised his eyebrows. "That's quite a variety of jobs, I must say. However, we'll not need you to drive mules or haul hay. The other skills may come in handy."

"It's all part of one job...being a canawler."

"And Elizabeth? Are you as well versed as your mother?"

Elizabeth looked a bit startled that she had been spoken to. She recovered quickly and said, "Yes, sir. I've done all those things, but I may not be as good as my mother in some."

Armentrout stood up and began to pace the hardwood floor. "I find myself in a bit of a quandary. My wife needs the assistance in running the house now." He paused and shook his head. "I will accept the conditions you set as far as your limited time. It will give me time to search out help of a more-permanent nature while not feeling rushed. You are qualified...both of you. It's a pity you are not seeking employment on a more-permanent basis."

Armentrout walked around the desk and shook both Elizabeth's and Alice's hands. Alice noticed that his hands were strong but soft. He could never pass for a canawler.

"When can you start?" Armentrout asked.

Alice smiled. She and Elizabeth had work. They should be able to get through the winter without too much worry now.

"As soon as we can walk back to our boat and change into clothes more suited for doing housework," Alice replied.

Armentrout nodded. "Good. I'll let my wife know that she can expect you in about an hour. She will give you a list of work you can begin doing. You and Elizabeth can work out your own schedule as to who will be here at what times."

"Yes, sir."

Alice and Elizabeth returned within an hour wearing the wool work dresses they usually wore when they were on the canal in the fall. A woman about Alice's age answered their knock on the door to the Armentrout home. She wore a blue dress with a skirt widened so much by crinolines that Alice thought the woman would have trouble fitting through the door. Did everyone dress so formally in this house?

The woman's chignon formed her black hair into looped braids at the back of her head. It was interwoven with blue silk netting. Her make-up hid the wrinkles in her face and she would have been attractive if she didn't look so angry.

"I'm Minerva Armentrout," the woman said.

"We are the Fitzgeralds. I'm Alice and this is my daughter Elizabeth. Your husband hired us to do the housework here."

Minerva nodded sharply. "Please come inside."

She walked away from the door and Alice and Elizabeth followed her inside. They walked back into the kitchen. Elizabeth thought it was nearly as large as their home in Sharpsburg had been. The fireplace was large enough to hold more than one large cook pot and there was also a large cook stove for smaller pots. Two doors led from the kitchen; one to the pantry and one to the back porch. The counter in the middle of the room had more space on it than the bed Elizabeth shared with her mother. The house had two iceboxes to keep food cold.

"My husband said that he had hired you and your daughter to be our temporary household staff. If you ask me, it is all a waste. I'll go to the trouble of getting you both trained and you'll leave. I wish he would simply purchase a pair of slaves. Then I would know that they would stay around and behave in an acceptable way," Minerva said.

Elizabeth stiffened. She was not sure whether she should be surprised or offended by the woman's comments. She did not like being compared to a slave.

"Aren't you an abolitionist like your husband?" Alice asked.

Minerva looked aghast. "An abolitionist? Me? My maiden name is Ferol. I am one of the Richmond Ferols."

"Oh, I didn't know."

Elizabeth had no clue who the Ferols were, but judging by the way Minerva said it and where she said they were from, Elizabeth figured she was safe in assuming that Mrs. Armentrout did not share her husband's distaste of slavery.

"We eat breakfast at seven in the morning, dinner at noon and supper at five. I will give you the menus for each day and will expect you to prepare them. Laundry is to be done daily, as is house cleaning. Particularly the house cleaning. With all of the coal trains going through town, there always seems to be a coating of coal dust on everything. It is your job to keep it clean. Do you understand?"

"Yes, ma'am," Alice said.

Minerva glanced at the clock on the wall. "Good. It's ten o'clock now. You had better get to work preparing dinner. I will expect it on the table in two hours."

"Where is the menu?" Alice asked.

"It is on the nail by the pantry. That will be where I post the menus each day."

Minerva then turned and walked out of the kitchen without so much as a goodbye. Elizabeth watched her go and turned to her mother.

"I don't like her," Elizabeth said. "She's too strict. She reminds me of Miss Duckworth."

Constance Duckworth was the teacher at the school in Sharpsburg that Elizabeth used to attend. Miss Duckworth was rumored to have come from Boston. She was an excellent teacher, but the children had all thought that she was too strict and quick to anger.

"She's just setting the rules of her house, Elizabeth. I'm sure she can't be too bad. Mr. Armentrout is very nice, though a bit formal," Alice told her daughter.

"They seem very different."

Her mother nodded. She walked over to the pantry and picked up the menu. She read the list to Elizabeth. It was fairly extensive, but luckily it could all be completed in two hours. Barely.

"Can you get some wood for the fire, Elizabeth?" Alice stirred the ashes in the fireplace with the poker. "There are still some embers glowing that we can use to get the fire going."

Elizabeth was happy about that. A fire would take the chill off the kitchen. The kitchen was the size of four family cabins on the *Freeman*. There was only kindling and small logs next to the fireplace, though. Elizabeth stoked the fire with what she had. It would allow her mother to get started with the meal.

"I'll have to get some logs from outside," Elizabeth said.

She put on her coat and walked out the back door. There was no pile of firewood on the back porch as she would have expected. The Armentrouts must not have bothered to chop and stack any firewood since they lost their house help.

Elizabeth went back inside and sought out Mrs. Armentrout. She found her in the sitting room reading *The Alleghenian*. It was a weekly newspaper with a southern slant.

"Excuse me, ma'am. There's no firewood," Elizabeth said.

Mrs. Armentrout rolled her eyes. "Well, what do you expect me to do about that? I know Dr. Armentrout had some men deliver some wood within the past few days. Use that."

"Where is it?"

"Out in the backyard somewhere."

Elizabeth nodded and left.

The wood pile was just that. A pile of wood that still needed to be chopped into usable pieces of firewood and stacked near the back door of the house. Seeing no other alternative, Elizabeth fetched an axe from the tool shed and began chopping the large pieces of wood into smaller pieces.

It took her a while to get into the rhythm of swinging the axe, but eventually, she got used to the weight. Then there was the problem with the power of her swing. When she had seen her brother and father chop wood, they had always managed to split the larger pieces in half in a single swing. It took Elizabeth two or three swings to do the same thing, and she always managed to get the axe stuck in the log. She took three times as long freeing the blade from the log as she did swinging the axe.

She carried the first dozen pieces of wood she had split into the kitchen so that her mother would have enough firewood to get a good-sized fire going to cook dinner. Then she went back outside to continue chopping because wood would be needed for more than just this meal.

She had been chopping wood for about fifteen minutes when she realized someone was watching her. She turned around, still holding the axe over her shoulder. A young man was standing by the railing of the back porch. He was tall and had wide shoulders. He had blond hair and dark eyes.

"Don't worry, I won't hurt you," the young man said.

Elizabeth realized how she was holding the axe and lowered it.

"I'm sorry. Hello," she said.

He smiled at her. "I'm Michael Armentrout," the young man said.

"I'm Elizabeth Fitzgerald."

"Should I ask why you are chopping wood?"

"Because it's needed. Your father just hired my mother and me to be the household servants. My mother's in the kitchen."

Michael came down the stairs and walked over next to her. He took the axe from her hands and held it up. "But this is not a household chore."

"I didn't see any stacked wood by the door, and your mother told me the woodpile was out here."

"Ah, leave it to Mother to expect you to chop wood."

"I can do it. I've been doing it."

"But it takes you four times longer than it would me. Besides, who do you think has been doing it since Mr. and Mrs. Barnaby left?"

He quickly raised the axe over his head and swung it in a smooth arc. It cleaved the log Elizabeth had upended in half. One swing and no catching. She had to admit that he did do it faster.

"Look here, why don't you set the logs in position for me? I'll split them. Then when we're done, we'll both stack them. With both of us working, we should have this finished in no time at all," Michael offered.

"I think that's a good idea."

She set a log in front of Michael and then moved away. He quickly split it, and the two halves flew off to the side. Elizabeth set another log in front of him, and he duplicated his action. They moved quickly because Michael could chop better than Elizabeth could, and he didn't have to stop between each swing to set up a log.

They said very little as they worked and Michael began to work up a sweat. They were nearly finished chopping the wood into manageable pieces when Elizabeth heard a shrill voice shout, "Michael!"

He stopped in mid-swing and turned to face the house. His mother was standing on the porch where he had been standing earlier. Her brown eyes were wide and angry.

"What are you doing?" Minerva asked.

"I'm helping Elizabeth do what I should have done yesterday. I forgot to do it then so I'm doing it now," he said.

"Chopping the wood is her job." Minerva pointed to Elizabeth.

"It was my job yesterday," Michael said.

"Yesterday, we did not have servants. Today, we do." Minerva faced Elizabeth. "And, you, young lady, should know better than to slack off and beguile my son into doing your work."

"I didn't. I…" Elizabeth started to say.

Minerva held up her hand. "Don't back talk me."

Michael said, "Mother, Elizabeth didn't do anything. I…"

"Michael," Minerva interrupted. "We will not discuss this in front of the help. Come up here this instant."

Michael looked at Elizabeth and rolled his eyes. He passed her the axe and walked up the stairs to the back porch. Then he and his mother went inside.

Elizabeth laid the axe down and began to pick up the logs to stack them on the porch. She was not going to like working here. She only hoped that the canal would reopen very quickly.

7

REPUTATIONS

FEBRUARY 1863

Tony hopped down to the floor from his bunk and stretched out. The fire in the pot-belly stove was going strong, and the room was toasty.

Life had changed two days ago. Nothing dramatic. It just used to be that there was always plenty of work to be done to keep the canal boat moving. Now with the *Freeman* stopped and sitting in the empty basin, things to do on the boat had nearly stopped, too.

During his free time, Tony was trying to learn to read. He thought that reading would be a mighty useful skill if he could learn it. And if Thomas could learn to read, Tony was sure that he could also.

"I'm glad you're awake Tony. I was going to leave a note for you before I left," Alice said.

"About what, ma'am?"

"We need some things from town. Would you get them for me today?"

Tony nodded. "Sure."

"I've already made up the list. Take Thomas with you. He can read the list and help you carry everything." Alice handed Tony a five-dollar bill. "And this should cover the costs. You and Thomas can treat yourselves to a penny's worth of candy each, but only a penny's worth. Depending on how long the canal stays closed, we may need all the money we can save."

Tony took the money and shoved it into his front pocket. He expected that he and Thomas would be carrying quite a few items home if Mrs. Fitzgerald needed to give them five dollars to pay for it all.

42

She leaned over and kissed him on the top of his head. "Elizabeth and I have to go to work now. Your breakfast is on the table."

Impulsively, Tony reached out and hugged her. "Have a good day."

Alice smiled and said, "With a start like that, how could it be bad?"

She left the cabin, and Tony sat down to eat. He was halfway through the ham and eggs when Thomas bounded into the room holding a piece of paper.

"Mama gave me this list of things she wants us to buy today," Thomas said.

"What does she want us to buy?"

Thomas glanced at the list. "Food things."

"Any particular place she said to go?"

Thomas shook his head.

"Well then, read me the list so I can figure out where the best place to get the stuff will be."

Tony had been born and raised in Cumberland, well, Shanty Town actually. It was still considered a part of Cumberland, though that is not where they would be going to buy the items they needed. No, they would be going downtown. That, too, was a place that Tony was intimately familiar with. He had spent many hours there, stealing whatever was available and either using it for his own survival or selling it for a few cents to add to his cash can.

It had been more than six months since Tony had wandered the streets of Cumberland, trying to steal enough food to supplement the meager meals his mother had given him. After Mr. Fitzgerald had hired him as a hand, Tony hadn't planned on going into Cumberland ever again. He had been introduced to small towns like Hancock and Williamsport and the large cities like Georgetown and Washington City. They were all new and exciting to him.

Cumberland had become just a place he had lived. He didn't have good memories of the city. He had been there as a thief and many times he had been caught and had to serve time in the city jail. He did know the stores with the best quality merchandise from the time he had spent in town. He could put that experience to good use now and help the Fitzgeralds.

As Thomas read down the list of items, Tony began to recall the different stores in downtown Cumberland. He imagined their stock and compared one store to another in his head. The produce would be best from Ben Hansom's Groceries. The canned items would be cheapest at Luke Twigg's Groceries on South Liberty. The meat should come from Centre Street Meats.

As the number of stops they would have to make added up, Tony realized that he and Thomas might not be able to carry everything in one trip. They might be making multiple trips from town to the *Freeman*, which would make running the errands take longer.

Tony didn't mind that, but Thomas might. He liked to play. Tony knew that if he wanted to be treated as a member of the family, he would need to do what was asked of him whether it was fetch groceries or walk mules. He wasn't asked to do anything that anyone else on the boat wasn't asked to do.

He had learned since coming to live with the Fitzgeralds that a good family worked together, willing to take on greater burdens to make someone else's lighter. The more they were willing to do, the stronger the family would be. Tony thought it was interesting that for a family to be strong they had to serve each other and help everyone else grow stronger.

"I know where we can get the penny candy Mama said we could get," Thomas offered.

"First, we have to get everything else on the list," Tony cautioned him.

Thomas frowned. "If we get the candy first, then we can eat it while we're doing all that other shopping."

"Knowing you, we also probably wouldn't get the shopping done."

After Tony finished his breakfast, he and Thomas walked into town. It was cold, but Thomas didn't seem to mind. He dawdled after any little distraction.

Luke Twigg's Groceries was the closest place where they needed to shop, so Tony and Thomas headed in that direction from the canal basin. One wall of the store was filled with cans of vegetables and meat from floor to ceiling. Luke drew a lot of business from canawlers. They tended to use a lot of canned goods because sometimes fresh food was hard to come by.

Tony felt odd coming into the store. He felt he should be looking around for the sheriff or one of his deputies. He patted the five-dollar bill in his pocket. He wasn't coming to steal something. He was here as a paying customer this time. Luke Twigg would even have to wait on him like he did the adults who stood in his store.

While they were waiting to be served, Thomas pointed to a can sitting on the counter. Tony looked at the words on it and the picture.

"What's this word?" Thomas asked Tony.

Tony looked at the can. He recognized the letters, but he wasn't quite sure how they all fit together. Then he realized that the picture on the can was the same as the word just like in the primers that Thomas was always showing him.

"Corn," Tony said.

"Wrong," Thomas said, grinning. "You're only looking at the picture and not making the letter sounds."

"How do you know what I'm doing?"

"Because this word is 'cut'." Thomas pointed at the word below the picture. "This word is 'corn.' We're going to have to work a lot harder on your lessons if you want to learn to read."

Tony sighed. Sometimes he wondered if he was ever going to be able to read. Learning twenty-six letters had been easy, but learning all the different sound and word combinations that those twenty-six letters could make was nearly impossible.

But everyone else seemed to be able to learn how to read. It wasn't impossible. He just had to keep trying until he could read like everyone else. He knew he could do it.

All of the Fitzgeralds were able to read and David, too. Even George Fitzgerald could read, and Tony didn't consider him all that smart. George had run away from a family who loved him. And where had he run? To join the war. Now, how smart was that?

Luke Twigg noticed the boys, and he eyed them suspiciously. He was a heavyset man who could have passed for a blacksmith with the size of his forearms. Luke Twigg was a tough man, but he operated near the edge of Shanty Town, so he had to be tough.

"What are you two doing in here?" he asked.

"We came to buy some things," Thomas said.

Twigg looked at Tony. "I know you. You're that no-good thief I've caught stealing in here before."

"I am not a thief," Tony said defensively. At least not anymore he wasn't.

"Then how come every time you leave, something from my store disappears? Now get out of here before I send for the sheriff." He

45

leaned over the counter toward them and, for a moment, Tony thought the man would growl.

Thomas tugged on Tony's arm. "Let's go somewhere else, Tony. We don't have to get the canned vegetables here."

Tony shook his head. He wasn't going to leave this time. He had no reason to run, and he wasn't going to act like he was a thief. He was going to buy what Mrs. Fitzgerald had asked him to buy.

Tony pulled the five-dollar bill from his pocket and held it up so that Luke Twigg could see it. The man's eyebrows went up.

"You still want us to leave and take our money with us?" Tony asked.

Luke leaned against the counter on his forearms. He tried to stare down Tony, but Tony didn't back down.

"What can I get you?" Luke asked.

Tony smiled and turned to Thomas. "Give him the list, Thomas."

Thomas passed the list to the grocer. Luke read it over.

"I don't have all of this," Luke said.

Tony nodded. "We know that. We just want you to get us the canned foods. You've got the best prices in town for them."

Luke smiled at the compliment. "I do at that. It will take a few minutes for me to gather up all of this. Some of the stock is in the back."

Tony shrugged. "We'll look around then and wait."

Thomas tugged on Tony's arm. "Tony, look over there."

Tony turned and looked where Thomas was pointing. A smoky gray cat was creeping around the edge of the door, trying to sneak into the store. It molded its body to the doorframe as it tried to slink into the back where the smoked meats were kept. It was a creature after Tony's heart and Thomas's, too.

Luke saw the cat. "Get out of here, you beast!"

He ran around the side of the counter, stomping hard, and the cat quickly ran back outside. Luke stopped at the door and waved his fist after the cat.

"I'd close the door, but I need to watch my outside displays for thieves." Luke glanced at Tony suspiciously as he said this, but Tony didn't react.

Thomas came up behind Luke. "What are you so mad at the cat for?"

"Because anytime I happen to get some fish in here to sell that beast tries to sneak in and steal some," Luke told him.

"You don't have any fish right now."

Luke turned and went back behind the counter. "Not right now, but I don't want that cat getting into the habit of looking for food in here, unless, of course, it walks in with a five-dollar bill in its mouth."

"Tony, I'm going to go and try to catch that cat."

"Why?" Tony replied.

Thomas shrugged. "I don't know. A cat might be handy to have around on a canal boat."

"To do what?"

"I don't know. I just haven't had a cat lately."

Thomas was notorious for catching animals and trying to make pets of them. He collected turtles, rabbits, birds, fish or anything else that he could catch. Of course, that also included things like spiders, snakes and last year, a bear cub. Tony thought that Thomas's collecting days had ended after a copperhead's bite had nearly killed the boy last year. It didn't seem to be the case, though.

Tony also knew he wouldn't be able to curb Thomas's curiosity.

"Just don't let it claw you," Tony said.

"I won't." Then Thomas headed out the door after the cat.

Luke was steadily stacking the cans on the counter. Tony hoped that he had a box that could hold all of these things.

"I've got some more canned tomatoes in the back that I haven't had a chance to put out yet. I'll go get them because your list says three cans and there are only two out here."

Luke walked into the back room, and Tony was left alone in the store. He grabbed one of the cans from the pile and began trying to figure out the words.

"P...E...A...S," he read. "Pee...as. Well, this has to be 'peas,' it sounds too much like the picture to be something else. Where is the 'a' sound in all of that? Peas. Peeeeasss."

Tony just couldn't hear it. He set the can back down and reached out for another one. Footsteps sounded on the floor behind him, and he turned to see who had come into the store.

"You just stay where you are, boy."

Tony turned and saw Sheriff Whittaker standing there. The sheriff was a tall, wide man who looked like he could lift a cow. A Cumberland sheriff had to be powerful. He was expected to deal with railroaders and canallers when they got into their squabbles. Not that

47

Sheriff Whittaker, or any sheriff for that matter, spent much time in Shanty Town where most of the rough types spent their free time. Tony guessed that if Sheriff Whittaker could keep the trouble in that part of town, most of the respectable folks would just stay away from Shanty Town and consider the sheriff successful.

"I've been wondering where you've been hiding, Tony. This is about as long as you've gone without getting yourself caught. Either you're getting better at thieving, or I'm slipping," Sheriff Whittaker said.

"I'm not doing anything wrong," Tony said.

"When you were born, you probably stole the doctor's eyeglasses." The sheriff grinned at his own humor.

"I'm not stealing nothing. I'm a paying customer."

Luke walked out from the back room. He set the box of cans he was carrying on the counter.

"I caught Tony here trying to lift a couple cans from your counter, Luke," the sheriff said.

"Tell him I came to pay, Mr. Twigg," Tony said.

Sheriff Whittaker hesitated. "Is that true, Luke?"

Luke glanced at Tony. The grocer licked his lips and said, "Of course not, Sheriff. You know this boy. He's a liar and a thief. I was in the back getting some more cans to restock my shelves. I didn't even know he was in here."

"That's a lie!" Tony shouted.

The sheriff grabbed Tony's arm and cuffed him in the back of the head with his free hand. Tony grunted in pain, but he couldn't pull away from the sheriff. The man's hands could reach all the way around Tony's arm.

"Looks like your luck ran out, Tony. Of course, if I had caught you yesterday, you could have shared a cell with your mother. I just let her go this morning."

Tony was thankful for that. He certainly had no wish to see his mother. She had sent him out to fend for himself last spring after she thought that he had spoiled an outing with one of her "man friends."

Luke walked over to his cash register and opened it. "Hey, Sheriff, before you go, could you look and see if the boy has a five-dollar bill on him? I'm missing one from my register."

Then Tony realized what Luke Twigg's game was. He was going to take all of Tony's money and not have to sell a thing to get it. Everyone had his or her own scam to run.

Tony tried to twist away from the sheriff. "He's lying! He's trying to rob me!"

The sheriff laughed. "That's pretty funny coming from you, Tony."

The sheriff's hand went into Tony's shirt pocket and came out with the five-dollar bill. He stared at it a moment and then passed it to Luke.

"Let's go, Tony."

The sheriff pulled Tony out onto Liberty Street. Tony was still kicking and struggling to get away from the larger man. If he could just get free, he could outrun the sheriff and hide on the canal boat, but the sheriff's grip was too tight.

Then Tony saw Thomas walking up the street cuddling the gray cat in his arms.

"Thomas! Get your Mama! Come to the city jail," Tony called.

Thomas looked up and realized that Tony was in trouble. He turned quickly and ran toward the river.

"Who was that?" the sheriff asked.

"A good friend."

"A brat like you don't have friends."

"I've got more than friends. I've got family," Tony said proudly.

The jail was a small, brick building in the center of town, which Tony was all too familiar with. The sheriff shoved Tony into the building. The two cells at the back of the first floor were empty; otherwise one of the deputies would have been on guard duty.

The sheriff pushed Tony into one of the two cells and locked the door behind him. Tony stumbled and fell against the cot in the cell.

"Get comfortable. You'll be there a while," the sheriff told him.

"I don't think so."

Tony laid down on the bunk anyway. He was sure Thomas would get Mrs. Fitzgerald, but he wasn't sure how long it would take her to get away from where she worked to come and help him.

It only turned out to take about fifteen minutes. Mrs. Fitzgerald opened the door to the jail and stepped inside with Thomas behind her.

"See, there he is, Mama," Thomas said, pointing to Tony.

Tony stood up and walked to the bars of his cell. Mrs. Fitzgerald stared at him, and Tony wondered if he might not be better off in jail. What was she angry with him for? He hadn't done anything wrong.

"Are you the sheriff?" Alice asked Sheriff Whittaker.

The sheriff nodded sharply and stood up. "That's what the badge says."

He must have been blind to not see that Mrs. Fitzgerald was not in a joking mood. Tony just hoped it was the sheriff and not him, whom she was angry with.

"What did you arrest that boy for?" Alice said, pointing at Tony.

"What business is it of yours?"

"He's living with my family. I have to decide whether he needs a good switching or whether you need one," Alice said.

It might have sounded like a joke, but Tony could tell that she was serious. He could even picture Mrs. Fitzgerald swatting the sheriff's backside with a switch. It brought a smile to his face.

The sheriff drew back at that comment. "Now listen here, missy…"

"My name is Alice Fitzgerald, but you can call me Mrs. Fitzgerald."

The sheriff took a deep breath and said, "Mrs. Fitzgerald, that boy is in jail for thievery, and he'll stay there until I say he can go."

"I didn't do anything, Mrs. Fitzgerald. Luke Twigg robbed me, and the sheriff was too dumb to figure out what was going on. It happened right in front of him, and he even helped Luke do it," Tony called.

Sheriff Whittaker grabbed a stick and rapped it against the bars of the cell. Tony jumped back. "You had better watch your mouth, boy," the sheriff said.

Alice asked, "Who is Luke Twigg?"

"He's a grocer on South Liberty Street. Tony took a five-dollar bill from his register and was about to steal some cans of food when I grabbed him."

Alice cocked her head to one side. She turned to Thomas and waved him to stand in front of her.

"Thomas, tell the sheriff the errand I sent you and Tony on this morning," Alice said.

Thomas gulped and said, "You gave us a list of stuff you wanted Tony and me to buy. Tony divided the list up to different places where we could get the best deal. Luke Twigg's Grocery was the first place we went. Tony said they had the cheapest canned goods."

"How much money did I give you?"

"Five dollars," Thomas said, and then he added, "and you said

Tony and I could each use a penny for candy when we were done."

"Well, sheriff?" Alice asked.

Sheriff Whittaker shrugged. "Well, what? That boy wasn't even in the store when I caught Tony. We didn't see him until we were on the street. He's probably just a brat like Tony. You and he probably made up that story just to try and get Tony out of jail. For all I know, you're just a Shanty Town whore like..."

The sound of Alice slapping the sheriff sounded like a gunshot. Thomas wrapped his arms around his mother's waist, and Tony's mouth fell open. The sheriff stepped back and grabbed his cheek. It was red where Alice's hand had hit him.

Alice's voice was as hard as the sheriff's head when she spoke. "If you ever call me something like that again, I will make sure you are the one who is in that jail cell. I am a widow, a mother, and a canawler. Nothing else. Now let that boy out of that cell before I go find a lawyer."

Sheriff Whittaker looked like he was going to say something, but instead, he took the key ring off the wall and opened Tony's cell.

"Get out of here," he said to Tony.

Tony rushed over and hugged Mrs. Fitzgerald. "Thank you, ma'am. I really didn't do anything wrong." He wanted her to know that he was innocent. He had given up his past when he had come to live with the Fitzgeralds last year.

"I believe you, Tony," she said.

They turned and walked outside the jail and walked back toward the canal basin.

Tony said, "Ma'am, Luke Twigg still has your money."

Alice nodded. "He won't for long. Show me where his store is."

They crossed Bedford Street and headed down Liberty. Tony pointed out the store as they came nearer. Cans were stacked in towers in front of the store, and smoked hams hung from the edge of the roof.

"It looks like it would fit in Shanty Town. Why would you ever come here?" Alice asked Tony.

"I know most of the stores in town and what they have that's good and what's not. I know what they charge for it, too. Luke Twigg has the lowest prices on canned goods in the city, but his meats are expensive. Maybe now I can see why his prices are so low."

Alice ruffled Tony's hair. "That was good thinking. I appreciate

51

you being thrifty, but I don't think Mr. Twigg will be getting any more business from us."

"No, ma'am."

They walked into the store. Luke Twigg froze when he saw the three of them. When he regained his composure, he climbed down off the ladder he was standing on. He had been stacking cans on the high shelves.

"What are you doing here?" Luke asked Tony.

"We came for my five dollars back," Alice answered before Tony could say anything.

"You mean this boy stole from you, too?"

Alice's eyes narrowed as she glared at Luke. "No, you stole from him, and in doing so, you stole from me. The money was mine."

"I don't know what you're talking about, ma'am." Luke did a poor job of looking innocent. He was too big. He looked like a bear trying to impersonate a lamb.

"Don't lie to me, Mr. Twigg. I've obviously been to see the sheriff since Tony is with me. I know you accused him of stealing money, but it was my money. He didn't steal it. Not from me. Not from you. Now, do I have to get the sheriff over here to charge you with theft?"

Luke Twigg sighed and took a five-dollar bill out of his pocket. He passed it to Alice. She gave it to Tony who put it back in his own pocket.

"The boy's a thief, ma'am. I know. He's stolen from me before. I was just getting payment for all those things he stole from me all those times before," Luke said.

Alice wasn't buying his excuses. She stepped up close to him, and Luke dwarfed her, but he was the one who backed away. "So that makes it all right for you to become a thief? Two wrongs do not make a right, sir, and in trying to make it so, you robbed me not Tony."

She turned and headed for the door with Tony and Thomas. Then Tony stopped and turned back. He walked up to Luke and stared him in the eye.

"The sheriff was awfully mad when he found out I hadn't robbed you and that he had helped you rob me. He came out of the whole thing looking pretty foolish, and Sheriff Whittaker doesn't like people laughing at him," Tony said.

"So?" Luke said.

"So, I don't think you want to draw any attention to yourself for a while at least until he calms down," Tony advised. "Otherwise, he might want to investigate, and that might mean he'll look at your books."

Luke was acting like he didn't care, but Tony knew he did. Tony had realized why Luke was able to charge so little for his canned goods. He wasn't paying for them. He was probably buying stolen merchandise for a portion of what it was worth and selling it.

"I've got nothing to hide," Luke said defensively.

Tony nodded. "That's good. That's real good. The other problem is that we still need our order for canned goods."

"You didn't pay for them."

"I think I did more than pay for them. I went to jail for them. I had Mrs. Fitzgerald's money taken from me. I had my time wasted when I have other errands to do. All because you were greedy and you thought that I was an easy mark."

"Go away, Tony."

"Bring me my order first," Tony said.

"I will not!" Luke snapped.

"Are you sure about that?"

"Get out of here before I throw you out!" Luke shouted.

Tony held up his hands and backed away. "Fine, fine. I'm leaving." He turned to Alice. "Mrs. Fitzgerald, we need to stop back at the sheriff's office."

"Whatever for?" Alice asked.

"I want to press charges against Mr. Twigg for theft and making a false accusation," Tony told her.

"You can't do that!" Luke shouted.

Tony turned back. "Why can't I? You caused us a lot of trouble. Besides, now is the best time to do it. The sheriff is still mad, and he'll want to take it out on somebody."

Tony started to walk away. He thought that Luke might call his bluff, but just as he reached the door, Luke called, "Wait."

Tony didn't have to ask, "For what?" When he turned around, Luke had set a box on the counter and was filling it with a variety of cans. Tony doubted that it was exactly what Mrs. Fitzgerald had asked for, but he wasn't going to push his luck that far.

Luke passed him the box.

"Now will you go home and not to the sheriff?" Luke asked.

Tony took the heavy box in his arms. "Gladly."

When they were well down the street, Alice said, "It appears you have a reputation in town."

"With some people."

"Is it true?"

"It used to be," Tony admitted. "I told you about that, but I haven't done anything like that in a while. I don't need to."

"You stole those groceries from Mr. Twigg," Alice said.

"I did not. He gave them to me."

"But after you threatened him."

"If he hadn't been in the wrong, ma'am, what I said wouldn't have mattered, and he would have let us walk away with our hands empty," Tony explained.

Alice looked in the box at the variety of canned goods. "Well, you sure got us a bargain."

8

COMMUNICATION

FEBRUARY 1863

Alice and Elizabeth trudged back to the *Freeman* after a long day working for the Armentrouts. Alice hoped that things would get easier the longer they were there. Right now, the house was in disarray because the Armentrouts hadn't had house servants for a couple of months. The Barnabys had moved to Philadelphia to be farther away from the war and closer to their only son, who practiced law there. Once things were put into order, the house should be relatively easy to maintain. Of course, that would be about the time she and Elizabeth would have to leave to work again on the canal.

"You're quiet," Alice said to Elizabeth.

Elizabeth sighed and nodded.

"I'm tired. That house is a lot larger than the *Freeman* or even our old house, and it's harder to keep clean. If the least little thing is dirty or out of place, it shows. You wouldn't think that would be the case when there are so many things in the house."

The problem wasn't the number of things. The problem was whose things they were. Minerva Armentrout noticed those things. She even noticed things that weren't dirty or out of place and insisted that they be cleaned or straightened.

Alice nodded. "You get one room clean, and there always seems to be another room that needs dusting."

The *Freeman* sat in the empty canal basin along with two dozen other canal boats. These would be the first boats out of Cumberland with their holds full of coal when the canal was reopened. Alice hoped she would be able to make the first run to Georgetown quickly

55

and have the coal off-loaded before Georgetown began to back up with canal traffic.

They walked down the steep Washington Street hill as it sloped toward Wills Creek. They passed Emmanuel Church on the right. Alice glanced over the edge of the bridge as they crossed Wills Creek. The Potomac River was running, but there was ice on the creek.

She quickened her step when she saw the *Freeman*, anticipating the warmth of the snug family cabin. As she entered the cabin, the smells of cooked beef hit her. She smiled.

"I wouldn't smile until you try it," David warned.

He was standing over the small stove, cooking steaks. They sizzled in the frying pan as he stabbed one with a fork and lifted it onto a plate.

"Go ahead and sit down. I've been holding supper for you," David said.

"That was kind of you," Alice said.

David never ceased to amaze her. He was full of small kindnesses and was generous with sharing them.

"It was only fair. You and Elizabeth have been working all day. I figured you would be hungry and tired when you came home, so I thought I should help out."

Alice and Elizabeth sat at the table. David laid the steaks on their plates and then added fried potatoes and boiled carrots. Elizabeth took a deep breath and sighed.

"I didn't know you could cook, David," Elizabeth said.

"I wouldn't call it cooking until you've tasted it," David told her.

"It smells all right."

Alice said, "I thought you said you were raised on a plantation."

"I was," David answered.

"Then where did you learn to cook?"

"I was in the army for two years and for a good part of that time, I was spying along the canal with McLaughlin and Thelen. We didn't have cooks, so I had to take my turn cooking along with them. I either had to learn quickly, or we went hungry."

Jonas Thelen was dead now; shot by a Union patrol he had tried to ambush. Where Tim McLaughlin was David had no idea. Nor did he care. The man was a rapist and killer, and the last David had seen of him, he had been lying unconscious on the towpath.

Alice and Elizabeth began eating their dinner.

56

"This is good, David," Elizabeth said after she swallowed the first bite of steak.

David smiled and nodded his head toward her in appreciation. Then he took a bow.

"Where are Tony and Thomas?" Alice asked.

"They are in the hay house working through one of the lessons in Elizabeth's school books. Thomas is teaching Tony, or so he says," David said.

"That's good. I worry about them not having enough education. Both of those boys are smart, but they need to have a way to use their brains, so they don't spend most of their time trying to figure out how to cheat adults," Alice said, referring to her incident yesterday with Luke Twigg.

Because canawlers moved back and forth along the canal during their working days, there was little opportunity for canawler children to attend school. Most just got a month or two of schooling during the winter when the canal was closed. Unless they continued their lessons during the season on their own, they tended to fall further and further behind in their education.

"Enough education for what, Mama? All of us can run the boat and do sums and read a way bill. What else do you need to be a canawler?" Elizabeth said.

Alice was surprised at Elizabeth's attitude. George had always been the one who Alice and Hugh had to struggle with to get to do his lessons.

"Life is not just the canal, Elizabeth. Do you think Michael Armentrout knows just a little reading or math?" Alice asked.

Elizabeth blushed but said quickly, "He's a rich boy."

"He's a boy who is prepared to take advantage of whatever opportunities life offers him. I want you to be prepared like that. I want you to be able to live away from the canal and prosper."

Elizabeth nodded absently, not giving Alice any argument.

Tony and Thomas ran into the family cabin and sat down on the bottom bunk. Thomas slid the book they had been studying underneath the bunk.

"Hi, Mama," Thomas said.

"Hello, you two. I'm glad to see you were studying," Alice said.

"I'm trying to teach Tony how to read."

"You don't know how to read, Tony?"

The young boy shook his head. "No, ma'am. My mother never sent me to school, but I'd really like to be able to read. If Thomas can do it, I'm sure I can, too."

That comment earned Tony a punch on the arm from Thomas. In moments, the two boys were wrestling on the bunk.

"I didn't know you couldn't read either, Tony," David said.

"I don't go telling people I'm stupid," Tony said.

"You're not stupid. I know plenty of people who can read whom I would say you are smarter than. You just haven't been taught to read. I'm sure you'll pick it up quite easily. I'll help you, too, if you want," David offered.

Tony nodded. "Thank you. I would. Thomas is not the best teacher. He keeps wanting to play before we even finish one lesson."

Alice finished her meal, enjoying the conversation going on around her. With David and Tony on the boat, it felt as if her family was complete once more. The absence left by George and Hugh was at least somewhat filled by David's and Tony's presence.

Then she felt a pang of guilt at her acceptance of things as they were. But why shouldn't she accept things? She couldn't bring Hugh back to life. She couldn't find George wherever he had run off to fight in this horrible war. This was what life had given her right now, and it wasn't that bad.

Should she be feeling this way so soon after Hugh had been killed, though?

What way did she feel?

That stopped her. She didn't know how she felt. All she knew was that things felt right. They felt good. She was content.

She forced a smile at something Elizabeth said and then concentrated on finishing her meal. She would have a long day of work tomorrow, cleaning up the Armentrout home.

David sat on one of the fourteen curved hatch covers that hid the coal holds on the *Freeman*. He leaned back against the hay house and stretched out his legs. He put his pipe to his mouth and puffed on the shank. Blowing out a thin trail of smoke, he watched it roll toward the south.

He looked across the river into Virginia. Cumberland sat right on the Potomac River so he could sit here and look across the water to his homeland. It was so close now and yet, it felt farther away than ever. He was now a deserter from the Confederate Army. Would he ever be able to return to Virginia?

"What are you thinking about?"

David turned his head and saw Alice standing near him. She stood on the race plank and leaned against the hay house. Her shawl was pulled around her shoulders, but David doubted that it did much to keep her warm. She didn't act as if she was cold.

"I was thinking that my father probably thinks I'm dead. After not hearing from me for so long, Colonel Collins has probably assumed I'm dead or captured and reported it as such," David said. He scooted to the side and patted the hatch cover. "Please sit down."

Alice pulled her shawl tighter around her and sat down beside David. "How can you stand to be out here? It's freezing."

"I'll go in soon, but I didn't want my pipe smoke filling up the family cabin. Besides, a little cold air keeps me alert and awake. It helps the sky stay clear so that the stars sparkle brightly."

"And so do the lights of Ridgeley."

David nodded. "I'm a Virginian. I like those lights. They call to me."

"Why don't you write him a letter and tell him what has happened?"

David knew Alice was speaking of his father just as she knew that David was thinking about his father.

David chuckled. "And how would I get it to him? There is not a lot of correspondence across the river right now."

"There's more than you think."

"What would it accomplish?"

"It would let your father know you're alive. I wish George would send me a letter so that I would know what happened to him."

The comparison to George startled David. He didn't like being compared to the teenage boy. When George had joined the army, he had done so to prove he was a man and that Alice should have been treating him like one. David had joined to fight for Virginia.

"There's a difference between George and me," David said.

Alice shook her head. "Not really. You both have parents who don't know what happened to you. You are both causing your parents pain."

Alice had no idea what his father was feeling. She had never even met the man. She had never seen how proud he had been of Peter, David's older brother, and how offended he had been when the North had attacked the Confederacy. David had always been the spare son. Peter had been groomed to inherit Grand Vista. David had been left to find his own future.

"George left by his own free will. I was basically sent away to serve in the army by my father," said David.

"Then why are you worried about letting him know how you are? If he sent you to fight, do you think he will be pleased to hear that you are not fighting?"

David sighed. "He might not care, but I do. Even if he doesn't love me as much as my brother, I still love him."

"All parents love their children."

David snorted. "Does Tony's mother love him?"

Alice had no response to that or rather she didn't want to respond because the answer was "no." Tony's mother was a whore who had used him to help her fleece her customers for more money than they had bargained for. When things had gone sour for his mother, she had thrown her son out to fend for himself.

David told her, "George left because he was a boy trying to prove to everyone that he was a man. I'm not a child."

"Then stop acting like one."

David glared at her. Without saying a word, he stood up and walked away from her. He crossed the fall board and headed into Cumberland. Alice watched him go.

Alice walked back into the family cabin. It was quiet inside, which was unusual. Elizabeth, Thomas and Tony all stared at her.

"What's wrong?" she asked.

"Is David...is David going to leave?" Tony asked.

Then Alice realized that the children had heard her and David's argument. Privacy was almost unheard of on a canal boat, but she hadn't thought that she and David had been talking that loudly. Besides, the windows were closed.

"I don't know what David is going to do. He is an adult. He almost left us once. If he does leave, we'll get by," Alice said.

Tony's lower lip quivered. He nodded and then lay down on his bunk facing the wall. He and David had formed a strong bond because David had rescued him from a saloon in Shanty Town and Tony had rescued David from Union soldiers taking him to a prison camp.

"We don't want him to go, Mama," Elizabeth said.

"Why?" Alice said sharply.

Elizabeth shrugged.

"I like him. He helped us when he didn't have to," Thomas said.

"He just feels like he's part of our family," Elizabeth added.

"He's not, though," Alice said a bit too quickly.

Tony rolled over and said, "I'm not a member of your family either. Does that mean you don't care for me as much as Elizabeth, Thomas or George?"

Alice rushed over and laid a hand on Tony's shoulder. "Of course not, Tony. You are just like one of my own children. I love you."

"Then why can't you treat David like one of your family?"

"It's different with David. I can't treat him like one of my children. He's a grown man," Alice explained, but her words didn't sound true even to her.

"Then treat him like a grown man."

Alice shook her head. "I can't, Tony. It just wouldn't be right."

"Why not? I can treat him like a grown man. I can treat him like family. I treat you all like family. It's not hard at all. You just have to care," Tony insisted.

"It's not that easy."

Tony looked her directly in the eye. "It is if you're not afraid to care."

Alice backed off a step and nodded. She knew Tony was right.

9

ESCAPE TO SHANTY TOWN

FEBRUARY 1863

David walked south from the *Freeman* along the edge of the canal basin. He wasn't sure where he was going. He just knew that he had to get away from the canal boat, and the lights from Shanty Town attracted him.

He cursed himself silently for stalking off like an angry child. And after he argued with Alice that he wasn't a child! He had proven her right!

Alice just didn't know what she was talking about where he was concerned. Yes, he enjoyed being on the *Freeman* and working with Alice and the children. It felt right. He felt like he belonged here with the Fitzgeralds. Still, he couldn't forget that he had a family near Charlottesville. Was that so wrong? He didn't miss his brother too much, but he did miss his father. Louis Windover was a hard man, but David had learned a lot from him. Striving for his father's approval had been hard, but it hadn't been impossible. Now David was a deserter from the Confederate army and living in enemy territory. What would his father think about that?

David looked up. He was on Wineow Street in Shanty Town. Though Shanty Town might have once had the shanties that gave it its name, now it was filled with saloons that catered to canawlers and railroaders, which wasn't always a good mix. As the rough area of Cumberland, a lot was tolerated in Shanty Town that wasn't accepted in other places in town. It began at the loading basin and stretched south, encompassing Wineow Street and a few side streets. Some stores sold food and dry goods during the day, but the more-popular businesses were the saloons. It was a place known for its rowdiness because so many canawlers spent their free time getting drunk in the saloons since the sale of alcohol was forbidden along the canal. Fights were a form of greeting in Shanty Town, at least among the men. The women had another way to greet the canawlers and railroaders.

David walked down the middle of the dirt street. He listened to the loud piano music coming through the closed doors of saloons like Aunt Maud's Inn, The Rail and the River, The Waterman's Tavern and The Queen's Crown.

David saw McKenney's Tavern and stopped walking. He was tempted to step inside, but he was afraid that he might be recognized. His last time inside — his only time inside — hadn't been a pleasant experience. Tony had been in trouble because some of the men had recognized him as his mother's son. They had been threatening Tony because Tony had helped his mother take the men for more money than they had bargained for her company. David had gone inside the tavern looking for Tony. He had bluffed his and Tony's way out of the saloon, eventually pulling his pistol to ensure that they would be able to leave. It had been the beginning of the friendship between David and Tony.

David shook his head. Things had seemed so cut and dried then. There had been no doubt, no hesitation in his actions. He had known what was right and had done it.

Why weren't things like that now? Why couldn't he see what the right thing to do was?

He started walking again, not sure where he was going. A few moments later, he paused in front of The Queen's Crown and stared at the building. It stood out from the other taverns because it had a fresh coat of paint where the other buildings on the street looked worn and old. The Queen's Crown wasn't a new business, but the building was only four months old, having been built to replace another The Queen's Crown that had burned to the ground five months ago and killed four railroaders when it had burned. Because of that, most railroaders assumed a canawler had burned the building down.

As far as David knew, he was the only one who knew that Tony had burned the original The Queen's Crown as revenge against the railroaders inside. Tony had acted in anger because the railroaders had killed Hugh Fitzgerald, a man Tony had respected, earlier in the evening. Tony had soaked the front wall of the old building in oil and had set it afire. The wooden structure had burned quickly.

David smiled and walked inside. Clouds of smoke from pipes and cigarettes filled the air. David wondered if the smoke made anyone nervous, knowing what had happened when smoke had filled the building last year. There were a half a dozen tables on the main floor. Four were filled with people playing poker. One had two people sitting at it talking, and one table was empty.

David walked past the tables to the new bar. It was about twenty feet long, and the wooden surface was already well stained with spilled drinks and marred with scratches.

The bartender walked over when he saw David. The man didn't smile.

"Whiskey," David said.

"Cash," the bartender said with no attempt to sound friendly.

David laid a coin on the bar. The man picked it up, and it disappeared into his pocket. A few moments later, he set a glass down in front of David.

David picked up the glass and stared into it. He sniffed it and then tasted it. He wondered if it was supposed to be his drink. It was so watered down that it was probably more water than whiskey. At least he hoped that water was what was in it.

David downed it in a gulp and was surprised by how much it burned. It was definitely more than water, but it certainly wasn't whiskey. Who cared as long as it got him drunk? He waved the bartender over with a coin and ordered another drink. David wasn't in the mood for fine liqueurs tonight. He wanted to get drunk and forget about things for a while.

Someone bumped into him from the side. He ignored the slight as he downed the second whiskey and ordered a third. His stomach and throat burned and David hoped that there wasn't too much poison in the whiskey. With another couple of drinks, he wouldn't even care about that.

"There are better ways to forget your troubles."

David turned at the smoky sound of the female voice to look at the woman standing next to him. She had auburn hair that looked like Alice's. David had never seen Alice wear a tight red dress like this woman wore, however. It hugged her figure and accented every delightful curve of her body.

"I'm sure there are," David said.

He realized that he was grinning stupidly.

"Buy me a drink?" the woman asked.

David liked the sound of her voice. It massaged his ears and seemed to go well with the harsh-tasting drinks.

David considered how much money he had in his pocket and how much drinking he wanted to do. He nodded and waved for the bartender to bring two more drinks. The woman smiled and leaned closer to him, revealing her cleavage.

"What's your name?" David asked.

"Sarah. What's your name?"

"David."

"Are you a canaller or a railroader?" Sarah asked.

David grinned. "You mean that you can't tell?"

Sarah stepped back from the bar and looked him over. "You're too clean to be a railroader, but you don't have the hands of a canaller. You look like a soldier."

David stiffened. He wasn't so drunk that he couldn't realize that he needed to head that thought off quickly. It could get him in a lot of trouble if people realized just how right that Sarah was.

"I'm a canaller," he said quickly.

"Fairly new then," Sarah said, moving closer to him.

David accepted that without comment.

"What are you doing on this side of the river?" Sarah asked.

"What do you mean?"

"You sound like a Virginian. You're a bit north of home."

This woman could read men too well. It worried David. He didn't want to walk away from her, though. He liked to look at her hair. It reminded him of Alice.

"I was born in Virginia, but I live here, or rather, on the canal, now."

The woman nodded and didn't pursue the comment. She moved closer to David so that she was rubbing her body against him. David wasn't so drunk that his body didn't respond to her.

"Are you interested in heading upstairs?" Sarah asked.

"Upstairs?" David's head was ringing a bit from the bad liquor, and his stomach twisted itself in knots.

"My room is up there."

David looked at the woman and blinked. The bar was dark and smoky, and it was hard to see the woman's face clearly. What he could see of the rest of her was inviting, though. Her red dress was so tight that David thought if the woman took a deep breath, the seams on her dress would split. Still, she had the beautiful auburn hair just like Alice did.

Because David was taking so long to answer, the woman took the initiative. She took David by the arm and led him across the floor toward the back door of the tavern.

David just stared at the woman's head. She was about the same height as Alice, too. He wondered what Alice would look like in a dress like Sarah wore. Not that she would wear one, of course. No, Alice was a lady, a mother, and a canaller.

They went through the back door and the cold air cleared David's head a bit in the cold air. How many drinks had he downed? He could remember two, but when he felt the change in his pocket, it was nearly gone.

Sarah felt David shiver. She turned to him and said, "Worried?"

"Cold."

She raised up on her toes and kissed him. David leaned backward, slightly startled. He wasn't sure if he was trying to get away from the woman, but the wall was behind him. It kept him from getting too far away. He felt her lips on his and then her leaning against him.

How long had it been since he had kissed a woman?

It had been Eliza Bennett. She had kissed him as he had prepared to go off to war. That had been nearly two years ago.

David ran his hand through Sarah's auburn hair and pulled her closer to him. Sarah moaned slightly and rubbed her hands between his legs.

Is this how Alice would kiss?

He tried to picture her leaning against him. His arms tightened around her waist.

Sarah pulled back so quickly that David let out a small gasp. "That's all until we get upstairs. You do have more money, don't you?"

David nodded numbly.

Sarah turned away from him and walked toward a crooked staircase that led up to the floor above the saloon. David started to follow her. A lantern hung over the staircase to light it for the people who had rooms above. As Sarah passed beneath it, David stopped.

He saw her face clearly. Yes, she had auburn hair like Alice, but that is where the similarity ended. Sarah might have been young or old. It was hard to tell under all of her make-up. Her nose was straight except for a small, upward hook at the end. Her lips were full and red, perhaps more of each because of her make-up. Her cheeks were drawn. Her dark eyes were narrow and without emotion.

Not like Alice at all.

It didn't matter to his body, though. He had responded to Sarah.

She wasn't offering much; just what
comfort and release two dollars could buy.

She waved for him to come up the stairs. "Come on, David. My
room is up here."

David took a step forward and then stopped. He shook his head
and took a deep breath.

"I can't. This is wrong," David said.

Sarah frowned and put her hands on her hips. "What are you? A
preacher or something?"

David rubbed his forehead. "I'm sorry. I just wasn't thinking
straight because of the whiskey."

Sarah smiled again. She reached down and lifted the edge of her
dress, exposing a shapely leg. "That's okay. I'll help you clear your
head," she said.

David shook his head. "No, Sarah, you don't understand. I'm not
changing my mind. I'm just offering you an explanation."

Sarah dropped her dress and frowned.

David turned and walked around the side of the saloon to Wineow
Street. He was surprised that he was staggering slightly. How much
had he drunk? If the wrong person saw him weaving, it would be an
invitation to an attack by the thieves that wandered Shanty Town.
David needed to get back to the loading basin and onto the *Freeman*.

David didn't see any lights on in the family cabin as he walked
across the fall board. He figured that was probably a good thing. If
Alice saw him in this condition, she would give him a good dressing
down since she considered him a child. It also wouldn't do for the
children to see him drunk. It set a bad example for them.

He opened the shutters to the hay house and climbed inside. He
thought that he had seen the last of this place for a while. It was a
small room about six-feet long and ten-feet wide. It sat right in the
middle of the canal boat and usually housed the hay for the mules,
though it would also be used as a spare room during the season.

He closed the shutters behind him and stood for a moment in the
complete darkness. He held his hands out and found the hay bales that
used to be his bed and fell into them gratefully. There was no blanket
on the hay, so it poked at him through his clothes. He was too tired to
care.

Though he was exhausted, he shivered throughout the night because there were no blankets with which to cover himself. At one

point, he was so cold that he considered breaking open a bale and covering himself with hay. He would have, but he was too cold to stand up.

He did manage to fall asleep at some point during the night. When he woke up in the morning, he was surprised to find a heavy blanket over him.

Had he given in to the cold last night and gone into the family cabin for a blanket? He couldn't remember. It was a missing memory like how many drinks he had downed at The Queen's Crown.

David climbed out of the hay house and stretched while he stood on the race plank. He was tempted to walk into Cumberland, but he knew that he would have to face Alice at some point. Best to get it over with now than to let the situation simmer.

He walked into the family cabin and smelled ham cooking for breakfast. Alice stood at the stove preparing the meal. She looked slightly flushed from standing over the stove and working. An image of her dressed in Sarah's red dress flashed through David's mind, and he blushed at the picture.

"Good morning. Breakfast will be ready soon. Sit down," Alice said.

David did as she directed. "Did you put the blanket on me?" he asked.

"Yes," Alice said without turning to face him.

"I guess I acted like a child again."

"I didn't say that."

Why wasn't she yelling at him or at least scolding him?

"But you treated me like one," David said a bit defensively.

"I treated you like someone who was cold."

Alice set the plate in front of David without saying anything else to him.

"Children! Breakfast!" Alice called loudly.

While Alice and David were waiting in silence for the rest of the family to join them, he said quietly, "Thank you."

"You're welcome," Alice answered.

10

FOR THE CAUSE

FEBRUARY 1863

Elizabeth answered the knock at the door to the Armentrouts' home and was surprised to see a soldier standing in front of her.

The man was young with dirty blond hair. He smiled at her and took off his hat.

"Is Dr. Armentrout home?" the soldier asked.

"Yes, who is calling on him?" Elizabeth asked.

"He doesn't know me, ma'am, but I have a message from Dr. Oliver that I am supposed to deliver to the doctor."

Elizabeth held out her hand. "I can take the message to Dr. Armentrout."

The soldier shook his head. "No, ma'am, I need to wait for a reply and return to Dr. Oliver."

Elizabeth nodded and wondered what could be so important that the soldier needed an immediate reply to the message. This was the first time she had seen a soldier come to the house. She wondered if Dr. Oliver needed Dr. Armentrout's help with a case. But why would a soldier be sent?

"Follow me, please," she said.

Elizabeth walked down the hallway to the library. Harlan Armentrout was seated in an armchair reading the newspaper and smoking a pipe.

"Dr. Armentrout, there's a soldier here to see you. He said he has a message and needs a reply," Elizabeth said quietly.

Harlan closed his newspaper and stood up. He dropped the paper into the chair and walked over to stand next to his desk.

"Show him in, Elizabeth."

Elizabeth stepped back and allowed the soldier to walk into the room. The young man stopped in front of the doctor and saluted him.

"Put your hand down, Private. I am a doctor, not a soldier," Harlan said.

"Yes, sir. Dr. Oliver sent me to you with this."

The soldier pulled a folded piece of paper from his belt. Harlan unfolded it and read the message. Then he closed his eyes and sighed.

When Harlan opened his eyes, he straightened his back and wadded up the note and tossed it into the burning fire.

"How many men are there this time?"

"At least two regiments, sir. Clarysville is overflowing, and since some of them have the fever, Dr. Oliver is sending them to the Old Mill on South Mechanic Street...the ones with the fever that is. The others he is sending to the Academy," the soldier answered.

"The note asked me to go to the Academy, but the more pressing problem will be the soldiers with typho-malaria. Is there a doctor at the Old Mill to care for the ones being sent there?"

The soldier nodded. "Dr. Healy should be on his way. I was sent to fetch him first. As you said, that is the most-important place that needs staffing."

"Then go tell Dr. Oliver that I'll collect my things and head to the Academy."

The soldier saluted Harlan, but he quickly pulled his hand down before Harlan could correct him. The young man turned on his heels and walked quickly from the room.

Elizabeth watched Harlan take a black medical bag from a shelf behind his desk. He set it on his large oak desk and opened it. Then he went to a wooden cabinet and took bottled medicines from the shelves and set them in the bag.

"Is something the matter, Dr. Armentrout?" Elizabeth asked.

Harlan looked up as if seeing her for the first time. He managed a small smile.

"It's the war. Even when the enemy isn't killing those young men, nature seems to be. In fact, nature seems to be killing more soldiers than both sides combined," Harlan said.

"I'm sure you can help them, sir."

Harlan raised his eyebrows. "I only wish I could be so sure." He snapped his bag shut. "If my wife asks after me, tell her I am at the Allegany Academy and that it may be a day or so before I can return home."

70

A day or two? What did he have to do?

"Is there anything I can do to help?" Elizabeth asked as the doctor walked past her toward the hall.

Harlan waved a hand at her. "No, thank you, dear girl." Then he stopped in the doorway and turned back to Elizabeth. "Isn't there fresh bread in the kitchen? I thought I smelled it baking earlier."

Elizabeth nodded. "Yes, sir."

"What about vegetables and fruits?"

"Not fresh, but there are canned fruits and vegetables in the pantry. My mother and I have made sure that the pantry is filled."

"Fresh meat?"

"Only what we needed for the meals today, a chicken and a few steaks."

Harlan rubbed his chin. "Bring the bread and what vegetables you can spare to the Allegany Academy as soon as you can. It's the two-story building with the large white columns that sits on Washington Street and Prospect Square. You probably pass it on the way here from the canal."

Elizabeth nodded. "I know the place."

"Good. Then will you do that for me and do it quickly?"

"Yes, sir."

Harlan nodded sharply and left the house. Elizabeth watched him leave for only a moment before rushing to the kitchen to gather the items Harlan had asked her to bring. She filled the shopping basket with the cans first and then set the two loaves of bread on top of them so they wouldn't be squashed. It was a heavy load to carry because of the cans, but the Allegany Academy was only three blocks away. She would manage.

She put on her coat and headed out with the items. She wondered what good food would do for helping soldiers, but she wasn't a doctor. Dr. Armentrout had asked her to bring the food items and she would do as he asked. He was the doctor.

When she entered the Academy through the front doors, she was surprised to see a group of boys standing near the stairs and talking. They kept looking up the stairs, but none of them made a move to go up.

One of the boys was Michael Armentrout. He stood out among the group because he appeared to be older than the others were.

Michael saw her walk in the door and smiled. "What are you doing here, Elizabeth?"

"Your father asked me to bring these things, but I thought there were sick soldiers here," she said.

Michael nodded. "There are, but they are upstairs. The army converted the upstairs classrooms to a hospital last year when some of the other places they were housing soldiers filled up. They haven't used it much since the Clarysville Inn became a hospital, though."

"Is your father in the army?"

Michael laughed. "No, he just works for them. The army doesn't have enough doctors, so they hire local doctors to help them. My father gets eighty dollars a month to serve as acting assistant surgeon."

Elizabeth raised the basket to eye level. "Well, he asked me for these things. I had better take them upstairs to him."

Michael took the basket from her. "Here, I'll carry this for you. Follow me, I'll show you upstairs."

They walked up the switchback stairs to the second floor. Elizabeth noticed a different smell. The air here was filled with chemical smells, vomit and something else she couldn't identify. It was an unpleasant smell that she didn't like having to breathe.

The first room was filled with cots that lined the walls all the way around the room. Each cot had a thin, straw tick on it and on top of that was a soldier huddled under a blanket. Two men moved about between the cots wiping down sweaty brows and feeling foreheads to gauge fevers.

Elizabeth frowned at the sight. She had never been in a hospital before, but she had always pictured them as places where people were being made healthy by lots of doctors. This room just looked like there were soldiers being left on their own to heal.

"It's not very pleasant to look at, is it?" Michael said.

"There's a lot of misery in there."

As if to emphasize her point, one of the men started to groan. Then the man rolled over and threw up into a basin. Elizabeth's stomach clenched at the sight.

Michael took her by the arm. "Let's find my father."

There were four other rooms that looked just like the first room. They were filled with soldiers who were sick and wounded. Elizabeth and Michael found Harlan Armentrout in the back room, checking an unconscious soldier's pulse.

Harlan saw Michael and Elizabeth and stood up. He walked over and took the basket from Michael and handed it to an orderly who was standing nearby.

"See that this gets distributed to those who can handle it. Give bread and broth to the weaker," Harlan ordered.

"I can do that, sir," Elizabeth volunteered.

Harlan's eyebrows shot up. "You? I would think you would want to be as far from here as you can. It's not a pleasant place to work."

Elizabeth was tempted to tell him that his home could be just as unpleasant with Minerva hovering around and criticizing. She wisely decided not to insult Dr. Armentrout's wife.

"These men need help and what you need is a cook and serving woman to help them. I can do that," Elizabeth said.

"Fine. We can certainly use the help. Let me tell you what I need. You've seen the wards?" Elizabeth nodded. "None of these men have been wounded in battle."

Elizabeth looked around incredulously. "Then what happened to all of them?"

"Their living conditions did them in. A soldier's camp is not a healthy place to live. Some of the camps are short on fresh foods. Others have poor sanitary conditions. Add this winter weather on top of those problems, and you have a lot of men who are ripe for sickness. One of our main jobs here is to try and nurse them back to health so that they can fight. To do that, they need good food, plenty of rest and a warm room. Getting good food into them is where you come in."

Elizabeth nodded. "I understand, but I didn't bring that much. Certainly not enough to feed all of these soldiers. There must be a hundred men here."

"I had you bring these things to add to what I've sent some of the orderlies out to get. They have orders to buy what they can. Michael, show Elizabeth downstairs to the kitchen and fetch her whatever she needs," Harlan explained.

Elizabeth followed Michael down the back stairs and into the dark basement. It smelled of moist soil.

"Are you sure you want to do this?" he asked as they walked.

"Yes, I am."

"This is not part of your job to us."

Elizabeth nodded. "I know. It's part of what I need to do for my country. My mother and I used to knit socks and mittens for the soldiers. This is the same thing. You do what you can."

The kitchen in the basement was empty, though a fire was burning in the fireplace. Elizabeth set the basket down on the table and then walked around to see what the kitchen contained. She counted the bowls and plates in one of the cupboards.

"There's not near enough to feed everyone at once. I'll have to feed them in shifts," Elizabeth said to no one in particular.

"I can help," Michael said.

"You?"

Michael put his hands on his hips and threw his shoulders back. "Yes, me. I'm not afraid to work. You help where you can. Remember?"

"I thought that you would have classes to attend."

Michael shrugged. "I think I'll learn more helping out here. Besides, my father is always telling me I need to understand what he does if I'm to become a doctor like him."

"Do you want to be a doctor?"

"I'm not sure I have much say in the matter."

Elizabeth pulled the cloth off the basket. She set the loaves of bread aside and pushed the basket toward Michael.

"Empty the cans of vegetables into a cook pot. We'll get a vegetable stew started. Depending on what the orderlies bring back, we can add to it."

Michael did as he was asked while Elizabeth began slicing the bread. The kitchen did have butter, so she slathered the slices with plenty of butter. If the soldiers were undernourished, some extra fat in their meals would do them some good.

By the time Michael finished emptying the cans into the cook pot, the orderlies had begun to return with food. She added to the stew from their supplies and started cooking it.

"If nutrition is the problem with these soldiers, why doesn't the army just buy more food for them?" Elizabeth asked Michael as he stirred the warming stew.

"They don't have enough money."

"But there's enough money to buy rations now."

Michael shook his head. "Not really. My father is using the money the army pays him each month to buy the food for the soldiers. Sometimes he buys medicine for them, too, but that's harder to come by. Last December, there was absolutely no medicine to be had for any of the soldiers that were in Allegany County. Dr. Oliver...he's the army doctor in charge of the hospitals out here...he sent to Baltimore for supplies, but when the supplies came through Washington County, the doctors there took them and used them on their patients because they were out of medicine, too."

"That's horrible."

"They needed the medicine, too. At least it went to help a sick soldier somewhere."

"How many hospitals are there in Allegany County?"

Michael thought for a moment. "Not too many now. The main hospital is in Clarysville outside of town. That one opened up last March. It's out of the way, but there's a lot of space there to hold a lot of soldiers. After Dr. Oliver did that, he closed a lot of the hospitals in town. There used to be more than a dozen. All of the hotels and some churches were used as hospitals. Any place that had a lot of room was used. Now there's only a couple of places that the army uses in town for when the soldiers first come in off the railroad or when Clarysville gets filled up."

"Like now," Elizabeth said.

Michael nodded. "Like now."

Elizabeth carried the dishes up to the first wardroom and set them on a table in the middle of the room. Some of the soldiers began to perk up when they saw the dishes. They knew that it meant their meals would soon be arriving. Elizabeth was more worried about the men who didn't perk up, though. If they weren't interested in food, how could they be made to eat?

What would happen to them? How sick were they?

"What's for dinner, ma'am?" one of the soldiers called.

"Beef stew and fresh bread if you can hold it down."

The man smiled. "For homemade beef stew, I'll find a way to hold it down even if I have to pinch my lips shut. It certainly beats the salt pork and hardtack we've been eating since November."

Elizabeth went downstairs to get the bread. In the kitchen, she saw that Michael had put some of the other orderlies to work slicing bread, chopping up fresh meat and drawing water. He was making himself helpful just as he had promised.

Elizabeth piled the bread on a tray and took it back up to the ward. She worked her way around the room, giving each soldier two slices of bread. Most of them devoured the bread quickly. Others took their time to savor each mouthful.

The last soldier she came to didn't rise to take the bread. He just lay on his back staring at the ceiling. His skin was pale, and he rarely blinked. It was as if he was asleep with his eyes open.

"Don't you want dinner?" Elizabeth asked.

The soldier didn't say anything. Elizabeth wondered what she should do. This man was probably one of the men who needed to eat the most.

"That's Calhoun, ma'am. He probably won't say anything, and if he does, it won't make no sense," the soldier in the next bed said.

"What's wrong with him?"

The soldier said, "The same thing that's wrong with all of us, dysentery. But I think Calhoun might have gotten hit harder than the rest of us. He never did seem too healthy even when the rest of us were doing all right."

Elizabeth looked closer at Calhoun. This corner of the room was farthest away from the fireplace. It was cool, but there was a thin sheen of sweat on his pale face.

Elizabeth went into the hallway and saw Harlan Armentrout walking from one ward to another. She wondered how often he rested.

"Dr. Armentrout, what's wrong with Mr. Calhoun?" Elizabeth asked.

"Which one is he?"

"He's in the last bed in this ward. He doesn't move. He just stares at the ceiling."

"Oh, him." Harlan paused and considered his words. "The truth is I think he's dying. Most of these soldiers will recover unless their weak state leads to them contracting something worse. Private Calhoun was already sick when this latest wave of dysentery ran through his camp. Now he's so far gone, I don't think he will recover."

"You can't do anything for him?"

Harlan shook his head. "I don't think so. I'll try to get him to take some broth, but that's not much nourishment and certainly much less than he needs."

"That's not right!"

Harlan laid a hand on her shoulder. "It's life, dear girl. I can't save every person who comes under my care. My goal is to make sure that I help many more people than I lose. Since the war began, I've treated saber wounds, shrapnel wounds, and bullet wounds. I've stitched boys closed and amputated numerous limbs. Those are the types of things you would expect from a war. However, I've also had to treat diarrhea, dysentery, typho-malaria, pneumonia, bronchitis, consumption, pleurisy, asthma, rheumatism, scrofula, chronic gastritis, partial paralysis, hepatitis, jaundice, abscesses, and ulcers."

Elizabeth didn't recognize many of those diseases, but none of them sounded pleasant. There were too many ways for a person to take sick and die.

"I've only read about some of the things I've been forced to treat here, Elizabeth. I may be a doctor, but I don't know everything. In fact, this only shows me how little I do know. There is so much about the human body that even doctors don't understand," Harlan told her.

He shook his head slowly. Then his gaze focused on Elizabeth once more.

"Don't you know that you, with your delicious filling food, will do more for many of these men than I can with my medicines?"

"I'm just doing what I do at your house," Elizabeth said.

"But it's something these men don't get when they aren't living in a house. You are an angel with manna from Heaven for these men. If they don't thank you, I will."

Elizabeth felt herself blushing. "Thank you, sir. I'll get back to work."

She turned around and headed back down to the kitchen. The stew would be ready, and there were a lot of soldiers who wanted to eat.

11

YOUNG LOVE

FEBRUARY 1863

The Armentrouts sat around their large dining room table as Elizabeth served dinner. Harlan used his fork to make sure that each food occupied a separate area of the plate so that nothing touched its neighbors. Minerva seemed to be inspecting each and every item of food.

Elizabeth was sure the woman was looking for something to complain about. Minerva Armentrout was never short of criticisms, whether it was how food was prepared, how the house was cleaned or how clothes were washed. Minerva had probably never done any of those things for herself, but she knew how they should all be done to perfection.

Elizabeth set the steaming plate of roast beef, green beans and mashed potatoes in front of Michael Armentrout. He inhaled the savory scents deeply and smiled up at her.

"This smells great," Michael said.

Elizabeth smiled broadly. "Thank you."

"Did you prepare it?"

"I did the vegetables. My mother cooked the roast beef."

He cut into the beef and ate a bite. Then he nodded.

"I love it. Tell your mother she's a great cook," Michael said.

Elizabeth's hands hung down at her sides so that they were below the edge of the table. Michael reached out and took her hand in his and gave it a light squeeze. Elizabeth nearly jumped to feel his touch. When she looked at Michael, he was smiling. She smiled back.

Minerva coughed. Elizabeth looked up with a start. The woman glared across the table at her. Although she couldn't see Michael holding Elizabeth's hand, Elizabeth released his hand. Minerva did not approve of Michael's attention.

"You can back into the kitchen now," Mrs. Armentrout said. "We will call you if we need you."

Elizabeth curtsied and left the room.

Minerva Armentrout watched Elizabeth leave. Then she turned her glare on her son. Michael ignored her and concentrated on his dinner.

"You shouldn't tease the help," his mother said.

Michael swallowed his beans and looked over at his mother. He tried to muster his most-innocent expression, but he kept thinking about Elizabeth, and his thoughts were anything but innocent.

"Excuse me," he said.

"I said that you shouldn't tease the help," his mother repeated.

"You'll have to explain that to me, Mother. I don't understand what you mean."

"Yes, you do," she snapped, "but you are deliberately playing dumb. I am talking about that girl. You've made her become infatuated with you." Minerva waved her fork in the direction of the kitchen, sending drops of gravy flying. "She's probably having visions of marriage and living in a home like this. That's teasing her."

"Why is that teasing her?" Michael asked.

"Because she has no chance of seeing those visions come true!"

His mother seemed to be choosing who was good enough for him to fall in love with and who wasn't. Michael didn't like that. He had no control over his heart so why should his mother?

"I'm not teasing her, Mother."

His mother's eyes narrowed. "What's that mean?"

"Just what I said." He tried to keep from grinning. She could chew on that comment and all its interpretations for a while.

His mother waved a finger in his direction. "Your father and I didn't keep you out of the army just so you can go and waste your life on a girl who works on the canal."

Michael had suspected that his parents had paid for a replacement for him to go into the army. They hadn't discussed it with him, but he had been wondering why he hadn't been drafted into the army. It wasn't that he wanted to go fight. He could have joined up himself if that had been the case. He just wondered why he had remained behind when so many of Cumberland's young men had marched off to war.

He had watched his classes at the Allegany Academy dwindle as the older boys joined the army. Now, with the school being used as a hospital, he wondered how long it would be before he started seeing some of his friends on the second floor of the school.

"What do you both expect of me so that I might know what is a waste of my life and what is not? I need to be able to plan for the future, you know," he asked.

"Don't be impertinent, young man," Minerva said, "We expect you to succeed as we have."

"How have *you* succeeded?"

"Your father is a wealthy doctor. We can afford this life that you take for granted."

"I don't take it for granted. I'm helping him at the hospital, aren't I?" He hoped his father would jump to his support, but Harlan continued to concentrate on his food.

"It's not a hospital. It's a school. You should be studying while you're there," Minerva snapped.

She glared for a moment at Harlan. She probably blamed him for turning the school into an army hospital as if he could have done anything about it.

"Why? What right do I have to act as if the war isn't going on and soldiers aren't suffering and dying above my head! If you want me to be a doctor, then I'll have to actually work with patients like Father does," Michael defended himself.

"You aren't acting as a doctor. You are acting as an orderly."

"I have to start somewhere."

"You can start by doing well at school so you can go to medical school. Then you will become a successful doctor like your father."

Michael closed his eyes and sighed. "So that brings us back to me doing what I need to to be successful like both of you."

Minerva nodded. "Yes. Exactly."

"Father is a doctor. How have you succeeded?"

His mother slapped the table. "Don't play games with me, young man. I am your mother, and I will be respected. I helped your father to be successful. I have helped him at each step along the way. His success is as much mine as it is his."

Michael glanced at his father. What did he think about all of this? He wasn't saying anything. He was studying the roast beef as if he was operating on it. Michael was tempted to ask his father's opinion, but his father never contradicted his wife openly.

"I'm helping him at the hospital. Doesn't that mean, by your measure, that I'm already successful because I'm helping him be successful?"

"That is a temporary thing."

"Don't worry, Mother. I am studying hard, and I'm sure I will be accepted into whichever college you feel is fitting. Hopefully, I will be lucky enough to find a woman who will be the support to me that you have to Father," Michael told her.

His mother seemed to want to find fault with what he said, but she couldn't. She began to eat her dinner, and they finished the meal in silence.

After the meal, Michael said he was going to study in the library. He left the table, but instead of stopping in the library, he walked through the room to the swinging door that led into the kitchen. He cracked it open slightly and looked through. Elizabeth was washing the dinner dishes in the wash basin. She smiled brightly and chatted with her mother about the soldiers at the hospital and how they were recovering.

Michael smiled. She made it look like fun to wash dishes. He wouldn't even mind washing them himself if Elizabeth was there smiling and talking to him.

What would his mother think of that?

Maybe he wasn't the one doing the teasing. He was the one being unknowingly teased. He was having visions of a life with Elizabeth Fitzgerald that he wasn't going to be allowed to have.

Michael stepped back and let the door close quietly.

12

A MULE-HEADED BOY MEETS A MULE-HEADED MULE

FEBRUARY 1863

Alice walked to the doorway into the mule shed and looked inside. Thomas had filled the feed bin in front of Ocean, Seamus, and Jigger. The mules munched happily on oats and corn. While the mules ate, Thomas brushed them down with a hand brush.

"Thomas," Alice said.

Thomas looked up, but he kept brushing. "Hi, Mama."

"The mules look good."

Thomas smiled. "Papa always said if you treat your mules right, they'll pull hard for you."

Alice nodded. She had heard Hugh say that same thing about mules many times, but she was surprised that Thomas had listened, much less remembered. It just reinforced for her that she was making the right choice.

"Besides, they like to be brushed. It makes them feel good. If you hit the right spot, it makes the muscles twitch funny," Thomas added.

Alice chuckled. "We have a problem, though."

"What's that?"

"Mules were meant to work in teams. We only have three mules," Alice said.

"I know."

"When the canal opens again, I want to have four mules so we can work them in pairs again. The two-shift-on, one-shift-off method we were using slowed us down, and it wasn't treating the mules right."

Thomas finished brushing Seamus. He wiggled in between Seamus and Jigger and began grooming Jigger.

Alice had come here with an idea, but now she wasn't so sure. Thomas was so young. He was just nine years old. How could he make the decision she wanted him to make? Hugh had always said that Thomas had a natural way with animals. He was the one who spent extra time with the mules since the canal had been drained. He was the one who exercised them daily.

Alice said, "Thomas, you know a lot about mules. Do you think you could find a good mule that would work well with our mules?"

Thomas stopped working and looked around the end of Jigger.

"Me?" he said.

Alice nodded. "I don't have the time to hunt all over town for a mule that we can afford. Both Elizabeth and I are working most of the day for the Armentrouts, and Tony and David don't have the skill set to pick out a mule. That leaves you, and you are probably the best one to pick out the mule anyway. It will be like finding another one of your pets."

"I'll find you one today," Thomas said quickly.

Alice held up her hands. "There's no rush to get one today. Make sure that you find the right one. It needs to be healthy and strong."

"Oh, I will. I'll get started right after I'm finished here."

His brush strokes became faster as he worked on Jigger.

"No, you won't. You'll go to school when you're finished here. You can search for a mule after school," Alice told him.

Thomas stopped working. "Aw, Mama. Finding a mule is important."

"Learning how to get along in the world beyond the canal is more important."

Alice shook her head and walked back toward the family cabin. She had to get ready to join Elizabeth at the Armentrouts. She had a feeling that Thomas would be on the trail of a good canal mule like a beagle after a rabbit.

Tony and Thomas walked along Oldtown Road on their way to school. Tony had his books bound together with an old belt, and they hung over his shoulder. Thomas kept looking around and rushing up to buildings unexpectedly and then wandering away.

He kept thinking about where he was going to find a canal mule. There were stables near the canal that sold horses and mules, but he had already seen most of the animals there during his explorations of the basin area. Any of the mules that would be good on the canal were very expensive. They might be able to do what his mother wanted, but they would cost too much.

There were other stables in town, and there were farms outside of town. Those were the ones that Thomas needed to explore. He would find the new mule there among one of those stables.

Thomas stopped walking. Tony noticed and turned to him.

"What's wrong?" Tony asked.

"I can't go to school," Thomas said.

"Why not?"

"Mama wants me to find a mule to replace King Edward. Do you realize how many mules there are in Cumberland? I don't have time for school. I've got to find the new mule and train it. Who knows how long all of that will take?"

"If your mother finds out you didn't go to school, she'll be mad," Tony warned him.

"If you don't say anything to anyone, how is she going to know I wasn't there? Are you going to tell her?" Thomas countered.

Tony considered it for a few moments. "I won't say anything, but you had better make time to help me with my school work. I don't want to fall behind."

Thomas smiled. "Thanks, Tony. It's a deal. I'll find Mama a mule today and be ready to help you with your work tonight."

Thomas took off running up Oldtown Road without glancing behind him.

"Do you even know where you're going?" Tony called.

"I'm going to find the first stable I can and work from there," Thomas called over his shoulder.

Thomas ran four blocks up Oldtown Road before he noticed the first sign advertising a stable. He stopped running, bent over and caught his breath. Then he walked into the large barn.

There were ten stalls in the barn, five on each side of the main aisle. An old man shoveled fresh straw into one of the stalls. He stopped when he saw Thomas and leaned his pitchfork up against the wall.

"What can I do for you, young man?" he asked.

"Do you have any mules for sale?" Thomas asked.

The man nodded and pointed to a stall near Thomas. "Got that one there."

Thomas walked over and looked in the stall. He could tell immediately that the mule was too old for canal work. It had been well cared for, but its age would mean that it might not be able to generate the power needed to pull a loaded canal boat or last more than a few seasons.

Thomas stepped back and shook his head.

"What's wrong with it? I take good care of my animals!" the man said defensively.

Thomas was startled at the man's tone of voice, but he wasn't going to change his mind.

"Yes sir, you do take good care of them. It's a fine-looking mule, but it's too old for what I need. I'm trying to find a canal mule."

"Oh!" The man scratched his whisker-stubbled chin. "You've got a good eye for animals if you can recognize that mule's not suited for canal work."

"Yes sir, he's too old."

"You're right. You're a good judge of animals."

"Just don't ask me for an age. You've kept him in such good shape I might under guess by about five years," Thomas said.

The man chuckled. "That's right. People around here know that my animals are quality."

"Well, I need to know where I can find a quality, young mule that won't cost a lot."

The man walked up and clapped a hand on Thomas's shoulder. "You want what everyone wants, but I think you would recognize hidden quality if you saw it."

"I think I would. My Papa taught me a lot."

The man nodded. "Good. Good. A father should always teach what he knows to his children." He paused. "I suppose you looked at the places around the canal."

"Yes, sir. They were either too expensive, or their mules weren't near as nice as the one you've got here," Thomas explained.

The man's head bobbed up and down. "You're right about that. I'm surprised to see such sharpness in a young boy."

Now it was Thomas's turn to smile. "I like animals a lot."

"I can tell. Well, let me give you some advice then. There's another stable at the intersection of First Street and Grand Avenue. It's actually a livery stable, but you can buy there, too. The owner's name is Phillip Caul. He raises good horses and gets good prices for them. He doesn't value the mules as much. He uses them for work animals, but he'll sell them, too. He has a good eye for animals just like you do so I'm sure he'll have quality mules, they just might not look so nice. You seem to be able to see through stuff like that."

Thomas shook the man's hand. "Thank you for the advice, sir. I'll go see Mr. Caul now."

Thomas left the stable and followed the directions he had been given until he came to Caul Livery Stables. The horses were all in an outdoor pen walking around when Thomas arrived. There were also two mules huddled together close to the stable.

Thomas walked around the pen so that he could get a closer look at the animals. Both were excellent quality animals. Their legs were straight, and there were no cracks in their hooves. They were young, but they were thin. Thomas didn't think that would be a significant detriment. Many canal mules weren't taken good care of when the canal was closed and spent the first month of the season picking up lost weight. These two didn't look too different from those mules.

"You like mules, boy?"

Thomas looked toward the stables. A middle-aged man was walking toward him. The man had a full brown beard and mustache that nearly covered his face.

"Are you Mr. Caul?" Thomas asked.

Thomas straightened his shoulders and tried to look older.

"I am, but I don't believe that I know who you are."

Thomas held out his hand to shake Caul's. Caul didn't offer his hand.

"My name is Thomas Fitzgerald. I'm looking for a canal mule. Would you be willing to sell one of your mules?"

The man laughed. "Are you buying?"

"Not me, but my mother is. If you want to sell, I think she would be willing to buy one of your mules," Thomas explained.

"How much are you paying?"

"How much are you selling?"

"Fifteen dollars, Union."

Thomas nodded. It was a fair price, but he thought he could get it even lower later. He would have to take some time to think about it.

"I'll let my mother know, and I'll bring her out here either tonight or tomorrow," Thomas said.

Caul nodded and grinned. "You do that, Thomas Fitzgerald. I'll be around."

Thomas waved to the man and headed back to the *Freeman*. The family cabin was empty when he got there, so he cut himself a piece of the bread that was sitting on the table and ate it in his bunk. Then he took a nap. Finding a good mule had been hard work, but at least he hadn't had to go to school.

Thomas was sitting on the mule shed roof when his mother came home from working at the Armentrouts. It was just beginning to get dark. He jumped down on the race plank when his mother walked up the fall board.

"I found a mule, Mama," Thomas said excitedly.

"Did you?"

"Yes, we can go see it now if you want."

"I'm tired, Thomas," Alice told him.

"But you don't want someone else to buy her, do you?" He grabbed her hand and began to pull her back down the fall board.

"Where is this mule you want me to see?"

"She's at Caul's Livery Stable at the corner of First Street and Grand Avenue. Come on, we don't want to be too late."

Alice rolled her eyes, but she turned around and followed Thomas. He was nearly dragging her along with him.

"This must really be some great mule," Alice commented.

"It can be. I know it can be."

When they neared the livery stable, Thomas broke away from his mother and ran up to the barn.

"Mr. Caul. Mr. Caul!" Thomas called.

The man swung open the wide door.

"Why hello, Thomas Fitzgerald!" the man said

"I brought my mother back just like I said that I would," Thomas said.

Phillip Caul nodded. "I can see that. I'm pleased to meet you, ma'am. Well, the mule's inside if you want to see it."

Caul stepped aside and ushered them inside the stables. He walked them down the center aisle and pointed to one of the smaller stalls.

Thomas hurried forward. He looked over the half wall and then

87

stepped back.

"Where's the other one?" Thomas asked.

"This is the better mule if you're looking for a canal mule, Thomas. It's the bigger one," Caul said.

"I like the other one."

Caul nodded toward another stall. Thomas walked over and looked inside. This was the mule he wanted. The mule was small right now, but it had large hooves, and that told Thomas that the mule had a lot of potential to grow larger. He guessed it was younger than the larger mule, too.

His mother came up and stood next to him. She frowned when she saw the mule.

"This is the mule you want to pull our boat?" she asked.

"Yes, Mama."

"Thomas, this is a nice farm mule, but I would guess our mules are a hundred pounds heavier, if not more," Alice said.

Thomas was hoping his mother would react that way. "But he only wants fifteen dollars, Mama."

"That would be fine if this was a mule that we could put right to work, but this one won't ever be a worker," she said.

"I think it will. What if Mr. Caul sold it to us for ten dollars?"

"Now wait a minute, Thomas," Caul said. "I never said anything about selling that mule for ten dollars. It's worth fifteen dollars."

"Not to us. I'm sorry, Mr. Caul," Alice said.

His mother started to walk away, but Thomas jumped in front of her. "What about twelve dollars, Mama? Would you buy the mule for twelve dollars?"

"Mr. Caul said it was fifteen dollars," she said.

"What about it, Mr. Caul? You said you don't need two mules. Would you sell the smaller one for twelve dollars?" Thomas asked.

Mr. Caul ran his fingers through his beard as he thought. He looked from Thomas to Alice.

"Are you willing to buy it at twelve dollars?" Caul asked.

Alice looked at her son. "Thomas, are you sure?"

Thomas nodded.

Alice sighed and said to Caul, "Yes. I'm willing to buy it for twelve dollars."

Mr. Caul held out his hand. "Then you have yourself a mule and a bargain at that."

Alice and Caul shook hands. Thomas clapped his hands and jumped in the air.

As Alice passed the money over to Caul, Thomas slipped into the stall and put a halter on the mule. He talked softly to the animal and stroked her neck.

"You're going to like the *Freeman*. We've got three other mules there. They'll work you hard, but you'll get treated well," Thomas said.

He led the mule out of the stall.

Caul said, "You bought yourself a good mule, Thomas, but I'm still not sure why you wanted this one and not the bigger mule."

"You wouldn't have sold that one for twelve dollars and this one can grow a lot bigger. She just needs plenty of food and hard work."

"You're probably right." He held out his hand and shook Thomas's hand, too. "It was good to do business with someone who knows what he's talking about."

Thomas smiled as he led the mule from the stables. His mother walked beside him.

"I just spent a lot of our money on that mule, Thomas. Will she be able to pull?"

"I'll start her pulling logs tomorrow, and I'll feed her more to help her gain some weight. She'll be ready," Thomas explained.

"I'm trusting you on this, Thomas. This mule is not another one of your pets. We need her to work," his mother said.

Thomas nodded. "I know, Mama. She will work hard."

He turned and patted the mule's neck.

"So what should we name this mule?"

Thomas grinned. "That's easy. We'll call her Bargain."

Alice laughed.

13

WINTER WORK

FEBRUARY 1863

David stared at his reflection on the small mirror that hung on the wall in the family cabin. His brown beard and mustache had come in fully. He tugged at his beard and scratched underneath his chin where the beard still itched. He turned to the side and looked at himself by looking to the side.

He still looked like David Windover. Just hairier.

How could he expect to fool anyone?

Too many people had seen him working on the *Freeman* last year. Sooner or later someone would identify him to Union soldiers as a spy, just as they had last year.

What would happen then?

He was no longer moving around on the canal between Georgetown and Cumberland. During the season, it was fairly easy to stay out of sight along its 184-mile length if you wanted to, but David was stuck in Cumberland now. How could he hide if he needed to? What could he do to protect himself?

"What if I get caught?" he mumbled to himself.

"Then we would help you again," Tony said from his bunk.

David turned and saw Tony watching him test his beard. Tony rubbed his hand along his own smooth chin.

"How long do you think it will be before I can grow a beard?" Tony asked.

"Why would you want to do that? It itches like crazy," David said.

"It looks dignified. It would make me look older."

"That's right. No one expects an eleven-year-old to have a beard.

90

They would assume that you were at least thirteen." David paused. "You know, if I get arrested, I won't be traveling overnight to get someplace. I'll be in the city jail under guard, not in a tent in the middle of the woods."

When Union soldiers had arrested David a few months ago, they had started to march him to Frederick. Tony had followed and had helped David escape by slicing open the back of the canvas tent where David had been held when the patrol camped at night.

Tony lay back in his bunk. "You forget that I spent most of my life in Cumberland and a lot of that time was spent in the jail. I am very familiar with that building."

"And why did you spend so much time in the city jail?" David asked.

"Because it's hard to be a good thief when you're starving."

"Really?" David said with a touch of sarcasm.

"Yes. I'd try to steal food to eat, and my rumbling stomach would give me away. At least when I was in jail, Sheriff Whittaker would feed me."

David turned away from the mirror and leaned against the side of the bunk. "And, my young convict, in all the time you spent in the Cumberland City Jail, did you ever manage to escape?"

David's question didn't phase Tony. "No, but that was because I was always on the inside of the jail trying to get out."

"What difference does that make?"

Tony rolled his eyes as if David had just asked a foolish question. "Jails are made to keep people in, not out. If I'm on the outside trying to get in, I can hold open the door on the way in to let someone inside get out. It doesn't work that way in the other direction."

David just shook his head. He was always amazed at some of the things Tony said. His mind worked differently than any child David had known, but Tony had lived a life very different than the life of any child David had known.

"You know, that beard will help you stay warm during the winter. You won't have to pull your blanket up to your chin," Tony said.

"But it doesn't make me look different."

"Of course it does."

"Would you recognize me if you saw me?"

"Yes, but I'm not most people."

David chuckled. "That's for sure."

Tony's eyes narrowed as he stared at David and tried to figure out what David meant by the comment. David tried to keep an innocent look on his face.

"I just mean the type of people who would want to turn you in as a spy are not going to be looking for
David Windover. They aren't paying that much attention to you specifically. On the other hand, if you say something about Virginia or the Rebels when you shouldn't, someone might turn you in no matter what you look like," Tony explained.

David had no reply to that because he agreed with Tony. David had to watch his tongue. What he said could cause him more trouble than what he looked like.

"How long do you think we'll be in Cumberland?" David asked.

Tony shrugged. "This is new to me, too."

"But you lived here. You saw how often the basin was closed."

"Sure I saw, but I didn't pay that much attention to it. I wasn't working on the canal. I was trying to survive in town." He paused for a moment. "Since Mrs. Fitzgerald and Elizabeth got their jobs with the Armentrouts, I would guess they think it might be a while before the canal opens again."

"We're halfway through the month. Surely, the canal could be kept open by March," David suggested.

"Every year is different. Look how late it was before they finally closed the canal. Even I know that was unusual."

"Maybe I should see if I can find some winter work to help out with the expenses. It would also give me something to do to keep both my mind and body occupied."

David wondered what kind of job his experience might have prepared him for. He'd been a soldier and a pampered plantation owner's son. What did those experiences prepare him for? He was educated. That had to be something he could use to his advantage.

David stepped out of the family cabin. The air was cold, and he pulled his coat tight around him and shaved his hands deep into the pockets. He stood for a few minutes on the quarterdeck just looking over the town.

Scanning the waterfront, he saw a building that offered some promise of a job for him. He walked across the fall board to the shore and headed for the Lewis Boatworks. It was a large warehouse set on the southern end of the canal basin and one of a handful of boatyards in Cumberland.

David walked inside and saw a half dozen men hammering molded planks to the frame of a canal boat. He watched them for a few moments and marveled that a city so far from the ocean and the Chesapeake Bay should be known for its shipbuilding.

He walked up to the nearest man and asked, "Where can I find the owner?"

The man pointed to an enclosed office at the other end of the warehouse. David walked to the office and knocked on the door.

"Enter."

David walked inside and closed the door behind him. A man sat bent over a set of account books in a cluttered office. He looked up when David came in.

The man had thinning hair, and because the hair he did have was blond, it almost appeared as if he was bald. When the man looked up, a lock of hair fell down into his eyes. He brushed it back onto his head. He had wide shoulders and a body frame that could hold a lot of weight without looking fat, but he still appeared very heavy. He pulled his cigar from his mouth and blew out a stream of smoke.

"I don't know you," the man said.

"I'm David Windover."

"I still don't know you."

"I was hoping to find work here."

The man rolled his blue eyes. "I've got all the carpenters I need."

"I was thinking of a different position."

The man stopped his work and stared at David, but he still looked impatient to be done with the conversation.

"What other position? We build canal boats."

"I can read plans. I can balance books. I can negotiate for prices."

The man waved at the papers on his desk. "I do those things now."

"But if I do them, you'll be free to do things that will expand your business, or you can relax without worrying about whether things are getting done," David said.

"How do I know they'll get done?"

"You can watch me for as long as you want to see how I work."

The man rubbed his chin and stared at David. David wondered if the man was trying to come up with another reason why he shouldn't hire him.

"Are you a canawler?"

"Yes."

"And you know how to keep books?"

David nodded. "Among other things."

"I suppose you'll be leaving when the Canal Company reopens the canal."

David hesitated momentarily, knowing that his answer would endanger his chance of being hired. "Yes."

"Then when you leave, things will be just like they are now."

"But until then, you can benefit."

"Aren't you going to give up?"

"Not until you're ready to hire me."

The man laughed. It was a great belly laugh that didn't match his stern expression. When he laughed, though, his entire face seemed to change.

"Okay, canawler, I surrender."

"You're hiring me?"

"If you can help me, you've got a job, but mind you, I'll keep you around only as long as you can make things easier for me. I've been straining to keep up with work now that so many of my men have gone off to war. You're right. If you can bring me even a month or so of relief, that will be more than I can get otherwise," the man explained.

"Can I ask one more question?"

The man nodded.

"What's your name?"

The man laughed again. "I'm Amos Lewis. I'm the proprietor of this business you just talked your way into." He held out his hand, and David shook it. "Now for your first duty, I'll give you a choice. That boat out there needs to be checked out to make sure it meets what the plan calls for, or you can run these numbers and make a list of the accounts that need to be paid up and collected this week."

"Which one would you like to do?"

Amos smiled. "You and I are going to get along just fine. I've been working on these books for an hour. I could use a break. You take over here, and I'll check on how the latest boat is progressing."

"I'll take care of it."

Amos stood up and stretched. It lifted his stomach up over the edge of the desk, and it plopped down on the desk. He stepped around from behind the desk and clapped David on the back. Then he went outside to look over the construction of the new canal boat.

94

David sat down and began looking over the figures. He took a few moments to familiarize himself with Amos Lewis's system of accounting. It wasn't much different from the books his father kept at Grand Vista. They just kept track of different items.

He listed all of the items that had payments due this month. What David thought was interesting is that Lewis collected money from canal boat captains who were paying on their boats, but he also paid canal boat captains who were working for him on his boats. Lewis was more than a boat builder. He owned fourteen boats that captains were still paying for and operated five more boats.

The bad year that the canal had had last year had hurt Lewis, too. It hurt Lewis's cash flow so that while he had plenty of work, most of the money earned from one project was needed to pay for other supplies and labor for new projects.

There had to be a way David could help make Amos Lewis's business more efficient. If he could do that, he would ensure his job. Well, this job would certainly help keep David's mind off being arrested for a Southern spy.

Tony closed his primer when Mrs. Fitzgerald walked into the family room. She looked tired, but she still smiled at him.

"How is your reading coming along?" she asked Tony.

"It's going slow, but I'm not going to give up."

"That's good. You won't regret being able to read."

Tony nodded. "I know I won't, and I sure would regret not being able to read."

"That's right. If you know how to read, it opens up a lot more opportunities for you."

"Well, there's that, but if I don't learn how to read, Thomas would never let me forget that he could read and I couldn't."

Mrs. Fitzgerald laughed. "If that's what it takes for you to learn to read, then I hope that it works."

She sat down in a chair and cracked the window open a bit to allow some cool air into the warm room. She looked tired to Tony. Minerva Armentrout worked her and Elizabeth hard. Because they were expected to begin working very early and stay until it was very late, they worked staggered hours. Mrs. Fitzgerald went to work early to get things going. Elizabeth went in later and stayed later into the night. In that way, they covered all of the hours of the day that Minerva Armentrout demanded.

Tony was distraught that Mrs. Fitzgerald and Elizabeth had to work so hard for the Armentrouts. He would be glad when the canal opened again, and they were moving.

He reached under his mattress and felt his money bag. The bag had replaced the can when Tony had moved to the bunk. This bag represented his future. It was his way to get to California when he earned enough money for a train ticket. Once he was in California, he planned on making his fortune by mining gold.

That had been his dream when he had been living with his mother. His dreams had changed a lot since then. He wasn't living with his mother now. He was a part of the Fitzgerald family now. That meant he had a responsibility to help them like he did when he worked on the boat. Even David realized he had a responsibility as part of the family. He had gone off to find his own job to help the family.

Tony hopped off his bunk and took out his cash bag. He held it out to Mrs. Fitzgerald.

Mrs. Fitzgerald looked at the bag and said, "What's this?"

"Look inside and see."

Alice opened the bag and looked inside. Her eyes widened at the sight. She upended the bag and dumped the contents on the table. There were a few paper dollars, but most of the money was coins.

"That's a lot of money," Alice said.

"It's all the money I've got in the world. Twenty-eight dollars and two cents."

"What are you going to do with it?"

"I'm giving it to the family."

"What?"

"I'm giving it to you to use, so you and Elizabeth don't have to work so hard. If we need money to get by, then I want to do my part."

He noticed tears forming in the corners of her eyes and wondered if he had said something wrong. Or maybe his money was insignificant compared to what they needed to live.

Mrs. Fitzgerald slid the money back into the bag. Then she handed it back to Tony.

"You keep this," Alice said.

"Isn't it enough?" Tony asked.

Alice suddenly hugged him tightly.

"What's wrong, Mrs. Fitzgerald?"

Alice pulled back and kissed him on the forehead. "Sometimes I wonder if you're not a little angel who came down from Heaven and is hiding out under a layer of dirt."

"I'm no angel. Ask the sheriff."

"Why do you want to give me the money you worked so hard for?" Alice asked him.

"I was saving to go to California."

"Why did you want to go there?"

"Because that's where the gold fields are. I wanted to go out there and stake me a claim and pan for gold until I was a rich man," Tony said.

"And you don't want to go there anymore?"

Tony shrugged. "I don't know. Maybe someday, but right now, I'm part of this family. I like being with you and Thomas and Elizabeth and David. I've never been a part of a family before. I like how it feels."

She suddenly hugged him again. He liked being hugged by her, but he didn't know why she kept doing it. It wasn't like he was sweet-talking her or anything.

14

HUGH

FEBRUARY 1863

Alice watched David finish his breakfast and then leave for his job at the Lewis Boatworks. He was wearing Hugh's clothes and sometimes when she glanced at him out of the corner of her eye, she almost believed she was staring at Hugh.

Elizabeth was already gone to work at the Armentrouts. She and Alice switched which one of them worked early and who worked late from time to time. Sometimes, Elizabeth worked twice as long. She would work at the Armentrouts until Alice came and then work at the hospital until she was exhausted. Alice was proud that her daughter was helping out the war effort but worried that she would wear herself down too much.

Today, Alice would be going to the Armentrouts' home later and staying later into the evening until after the supper dishes were cleaned.

When David was gone, Alice called, "Tony. Thomas. It's time for you two to leave."

They came in from outside where they had been picketing the mules and feeding them. They had been attending school for nearly two weeks. Thomas already seemed to be getting bored with going into school for most of the day. Tony was very interested in what he was learning, and he was making leaps and bounds in his progress.

She passed them their lunch pails. Tony and Thomas each took one of the metal buckets. They grabbed their books and headed toward the door of the family cabin. Alice kissed them each on the forehead as they left the room.

Then she was alone.

Alice sat down in a chair and took a deep breath. She couldn't get past the feeling that everything was right. Everything was as it should be. Then the guilty feeling returned. She shouldn't be feeling this good when George was fighting somewhere in the war, and Hugh was dead and buried in Cumberland.

She worked through the morning cleaning the family cabin, but the feeling of guilt still nagged at her. It got to the point where she had to get off the boat, or she would scream. It was still two hours before she needed to go to the Armentrouts.

She dressed for work and headed for the west side of town. She walked up Washington Street and past the Armentrouts' home. She turned left down Allegany Street and walked for a block. From there, she was within sight of the cemetery where Hugh was buried.

She walked through the cemetery until she found Hugh's grave. It had a simple headstone on top of it listing his name and birth and death dates. She sat down on the cold ground next to the grave and stared at the stone marker.

She sat there and remembered the details of his face — the lock of hair above his ear that always seemed to stick out, his quick smile, his brown eyes — how he spoke with an Irish brogue that he had learned from his parents, not because he had lived in Ireland, and how he laughed his deep belly laugh. She remembered all the years that they had spent together, the good and the bad.

How much had changed last year! Their Sharpsburg home was destroyed in the Battle of Antietam. George had run away to join the army. Hugh was dead, killed by railroaders. It might have even been worse if David hadn't helped them save the *Freeman* when it had been swept into the Potomac River.

So much had changed. She wasn't sure how well she was handling it all.

She missed Hugh! He wasn't supposed to have left her like this.

It wasn't fair! It wasn't right!

She bent over and sobbed in great heaves until she exhausted herself. Then she sat there taking deep, gasping breaths. She took a handkerchief from her purse and wiped her eyes and tried to gather herself together before she left.

Alice stood up. It was time for her to get to the Armentrouts. She walked out of the cemetery and headed back toward Washington

Street. Near the entrance to the cemetery she saw a man dressed in black walking in the same direction. He looked familiar.

When he turned to look at her, she recognized him.

"Henry?"

The man stopped walking and stared at her. Then he smiled. "Hello, Alice."

"What are you doing here?"

"A funeral. A railroader I know was shot by guerillas while he was taking a train through Virginia. It's very dangerous to be a railroader now," he said. Henry Danforth was the railroader who had been courting Alice before she had met Hugh. That had been nearly twenty years ago. He still looked the same. He had blond hair and blue eyes. He was average height, but he had wide shoulders, probably from shoveling so much coal on the trains.

"What brings you here?" he asked

"Hugh is buried here."

"Hugh?"

"My husband."

"I'm sorry for your loss. Was this the same man I used to fight with?" Alice nodded. "Ah, those were the days. I used to look forward to our fights almost as much as I looked forward to seeing you. It was one of the joys of being young."

Alice couldn't help it. She laughed.

"You're not old."

Henry shrugged. "It depends on how you look at it. From this end, I'm not old at all, but we're as old now as our parents were when we were courting."

"Stop it, Henry. You're depressing me more than I already am," Alice said.

"Sorry, I can't help it sometimes. What happened to Hugh?" Henry asked. "He was as young as you and I are."

"I'm not that young."

"Now who's being depressing? You just said a moment ago that we weren't that old."

"I said that you weren't old."

"Well, you're no old lady. Let's see if I can remember...I'm thirty-eight so that would make you thirty-six. So if I'm not old neither are you."

"You have a good memory."

"I'd like to think so." He paused. "May I walk with you? Where are you going?"

"I'm working for the winter at Dr. Armentrout's house as one of his servants. He lives on Washington Street down by where it intersects with Lee Street."

They began to walk side by side up the hill toward Washington Street. Henry shortened his long stride to match hers.

"So you still work for the railroad, I take it," Alice said.

Henry nodded. "I think I always will. I love the feel of the power that is in that engine, and to think that I can control it." He sighed. "I sometimes wonder what I would have done if there was no railroad? That's how perfectly the work suits me. Are you still on the canal?"

"Yes, I love the canal just as much as you love the railroad."

"Then I guess we're enemies," Henry said simply.

Alice stopped walking and turned to look at Henry. "Do you think so?"

He grinned. "No, but that's what we're told."

"You seem much more" she searched for the right word "relaxed than you used to be."

"I'm not eighteen years old anymore. I grew up and discovered what life is about." He grinned again. "That's not to say that I still don't like to get into a fight now and then. There always seems to be some youngster who needs to have some common sense pounded into his head."

"You sound a lot like Hugh."

"What happened to Hugh, if you don't mind me asking?"

"He was killed in Shanty Town."

"Fighting?"

Alice shook her head. "No, he had calmed down somewhat, too. He went to Shanty Town to fetch our oldest son who is one of those youngsters you just mentioned. There was trouble, and Hugh was stabbed. We got him back to our boat, but he died there."

Alice started to cry. Henry pulled his handkerchief from his pocket and handed it to her. She wiped away the tears, but they kept rolling down her cheeks.

"I'm sorry I upset you," Henry said.

"That's all right. It's just that it's still pretty new not having him around."

Alice stopped walking in front of the Armentrouts house. She

101

passed the handkerchief back to Henry, but he shook his head.

"You hold onto it. You still look like you could use it," Henry said.

"Thank you, but what if I don't see you to return it?"

Henry smiled. "It just gives me an excuse to find you again so I can get it back."

He unlatched the gate and held it open for Alice. She walked through and waved goodbye to Henry.

Elizabeth was waiting for her just inside the door to the house. She helped her mother out of her coat.

"Who was that I saw you with?" she asked her mother.

"Were you spying on me?"

Elizabeth blushed to the point that her cheeks matched her strawberry-blonde hair. She said, "I was dusting in the sitting room, and I saw you two coming up the street."

"His name is Henry Danforth. He's an old friend."

"How come I've never met him before?"

"He's not been around. I haven't seen him for years. Your father and Henry did not really get along all that well."

Elizabeth's eyes widened. "Is he that railroader you told me about?"

Alice nodded.

It had been a shock to see Henry again. He looked much the same as he had when he was a teenager, but he was much calmer now. He had grown into what seemed to be a successful man who was comfortable with himself. Alice wondered how he and Hugh would get along if they were to meet now.

"You're crying," Elizabeth said.

"I was visiting your father's grave. That's where I ran into Henry. It was quite a surprise to see him again."

She wiped her eyes once again with the handkerchief and then paused to stare at it. She wondered just how this handkerchief would find its way back to Henry. She was surprised to find that she was looking forward to seeing him again.

15

ANIMAL ATTRACTION

FEBRUARY 1863

Tony and Thomas walked quickly from the loading basin toward their schoolhouse on Virginia Avenue. It was still cold outside, and cold without snow to play in wasn't much fun. Neither boy was anxious to be in school, but the huge pot-belly stove that heated the one-room schoolhouse held a certain attraction to their cold fingers and toes.

Thomas held a long branch that he kept swinging in front of him like it was a sword. Tony figured it would be safer for him to stay behind Thomas. Tony didn't want to get swatted in the stomach or head by Thomas's imaginary sword or very real branch.

Suddenly Thomas stopped so quickly that Tony nearly ran into his back.

"Why'd you stop?" Tony asked.

Thomas didn't answer him. Tony walked around in front of him and looked at the younger boy. Thomas was staring in the backyard of one of the buildings on Virginia Avenue.

A bald man with a brown apron on was leading a steer into the back of the building. Tony thought that was odd until he looked at the front of the building. McKenney Meats. This was a butcher shop. The man in the apron was getting ready to slaughter some fresh meat. If this had been last year, Tony would have been trying to figure out how to steal one of those steaks that the steer would yield.

"That's not right," Thomas said.

"What's not right?"

"He's taking that steer inside to kill it!"

103

"Should he kill it outside in this cold weather?"

Thomas's head snapped around to glare at Tony. The young boy looked angry enough to get into a fight with Tony. Tony wasn't used to seeing Thomas angry.

"He shouldn't be killing the steer!"

Tony shrugged. "Why not? That's what he does. He's a butcher."

"It's not right."

Thomas shook his head and then flung the branch up the street.

Tony rolled his eyes. "How can you eat meat, Thomas, and not understand how it gets from a steer like that to your table?"

Thomas punched Tony in the arm. "I know where it comes from. I've just never seen it happening before."

Tony walked up to the fence to watch the butcher lead the cow into the butcher shop. The butcher waved to the boys.

"Good morning, lads. Tell your parents I'll have fresh steaks available this afternoon. I've got the best meat and best prices in South Cumberland," the butcher said.

Tony waved back. Thomas simply stared back at the man without waving.

"Look at the steer's eyes. He's scared," Thomas whispered.

"He doesn't know what's happening, Thomas. Cows are stupid," Tony told him.

Thomas turned to him. "People are stupid, too, but we don't kill them."

"This is the way of things."

The door to the rear of the butcher shop closed. Everything was quiet, and then Tony heard a heavy thud, which was probably the steer falling to the floor of the butcher shop. The butcher had killed it.

Tears started to roll down Thomas's cheeks.

"It's not right," he whispered.

"What are you going to do, Thomas? Capture a cow and turn it into a pet? I don't think you'd be able to keep it in a bucket or in a cage in the hay house."

Thomas was notorious for capturing animals to keep as pets. It didn't matter whether it was a fish or a dog. Last year, he had nearly been killed when he tried to capture a black bear cub. His older brother George had managed to get Thomas safely aboard the *Freeman* before the she-bear caught him.

Tony tugged Thomas's arm. "Let's go. It's getting cold."

They started walking again. Thomas was no longer dancing around. He shuffled along with his hands in his pockets. He stared at the frozen ground.

The schoolhouse was a one-room building on Virginia Avenue. It usually had about twenty students of all ages in it, but with the canal closed, enrollment had swelled to twice that number as canallers sent their children to receive some limited schooling during the off season.

Most of the canalling children filled the benches that ran along the outside of the room. They would write with their slates on their knees because there were not enough desks for everyone. The room was packed so tightly that it was difficult to move around. They almost didn't need to use the stove because everyone's body heat kept the cabin warm.

Miss Grabenstein sat at the desk at the front of the room watching the students file into the room. Their coats lay on the floor near the door because all of the coat hooks were filled. The idle chatter in the room was so loud that Tony could barely hear what Thomas was saying next to him.

Miss Grabenstein was a young teacher, and Tony thought that she looked barely older than Elizabeth did but Elizabeth was a lot prettier. Miss Grabenstein just looked tired.

Tony sat next to Thomas near the front of the room. They put their lunch pails under the bench and set their books on their laps.

Tony looked up and watched Laura Anderson sit down at the desk closest to him. She was the same age as him. She had brown hair tied back in a long ponytail and blue eyes. They had spoken occasionally since Tony had begun attending the school, but she wasn't a canaller like him. Her father was a bookkeeper for one of the banks in town.

"Hi, Tony," she said.

"Good morning. That's a pretty ribbon in your hair," Tony said.

Laura smiled and touched the back of her head.

Then Miss Grabenstein clapped until everyone quieted down. Tony had the impression that the size of the class overwhelmed her and she would be happy when the canal opened again. She would have her normal size class back.

"Good morning, class. Today we are going to start by talking about the president of the United States. February is his birthday month, and I thought it would be appropriate to talk about him. Can anyone tell me who the president is?"

Most of the hands in the class were raised. She called on Tim Canfield, an eight-year-old.

"Honest Abe," Tim said.

"That's more of a nickname, Tim. Can you tell me his Christian name?" Miss Grabenstein asked.

"Abe Lincoln."

Miss Grabenstein nodded. "That's right. His name is Abraham Lincoln. He is President of our country. He is the most-powerful man in the country, maybe the world."

She held up a picture of the president. Then she held up a picture of a large mansion.

"This is the White House in Washington City," Miss Grabenstein said. "This is where Mr. Lincoln lives. Does anyone know what the house looked like where President Lincoln lived when he was a young boy the age some of you in here are?"

No one raised his or her hand. She held up a picture of a log cabin. Tony noticed some surprised expressions on the faces of his classmates. One of them was his. How could a powerful man have been raised in a log cabin?

"Mr. Lincoln was born in Kentucky and raised in a log cabin in Indiana. He didn't begin life as the son of a wealthy, powerful family. He began as a poor child. I want all the boys to think about that. If this man could raise himself up from these beginnings (She jiggled the picture of the cabin) to this point, (She jiggled the picture of the White House.) then why can't you? Why can't one of you be President of the United States? Or if not that, why not president of the canal or railroad or at least a successful businessman? It can be done, and President Lincoln has shown you how."

Tony raised his hand.

"Yes, Tony?"

"How did he get from one place to the other, and how do we do it?"

"Well, that's what we're going to talk about today."

Tony was very interested in this lesson. He paid attention to Abraham Lincoln's hard work and determination to better himself. The President had struggled throughout his life, but in the end, his hard work had paid off. He'd been elected President of the United States.

Tony found himself nodding along with the points Miss Grabenstein made in the lesson. If a man like Abraham Lincoln could succeed, so could Tony. He didn't want to be President of the United States. He just wanted to feel like he was successful. He wanted people like the sheriff to be able to look at him without suspecting he was up to no good. He wanted to be respected.

He was going to find a way to do this.

16

SHIPBUILDING

FEBRUARY 1863

David was enjoying a day working in the shop while Amos went over the book work David had been doing for the past week. Amos had kept him working in the office the past few days to sort through the ledgers that Amos kept on his business ventures.

David measured out the cuts for the wooden planks that would form the mule shed of a new canal boat. Harris Mueller and John Conlon were working with him today as he measured the opening that would house the mule shed.

He called down the measurements to Conlon while Mueller brought in the planks from the lumber pile to be cut. When David had finished his measurements, he climbed down to mark the boards.

"Do you think you'll get drafted, Mueller?" Conlon asked.

Mueller was eighteen years old. He was in excellent physical shape, but he wore glasses. He was not a likely candidate for a soldier, but the draft didn't care who it marked for service.

Mueller shrugged. "I'm not anxious to go, but if they think they can use me, I'll go fight. I'm not going to rush off to get shot at, though."

With most of the fighting died down for the winter, war talk now around the boatyard centered on how the war should be run rather than where the armies were and when they were fighting. People didn't have to read the newspaper to see which local boys had died in the latest fighting.

David didn't say anything. He concentrated on marking the charcoal lines on the planks. He had found in his week of working at the

Lewis Boatworks that much of the spare conversation either focused on drinking or the war. David had no desire to talk about either one, so he didn't take part in too many casual conversations with the carpenters. He was friendly with his co-workers; he just didn't encourage conversations that might put him in an uncomfortable position.

"Just think what the women in town would think of me if they saw me wearing a uniform," Conlon said with a slightly dreamy sound to his voice.

Josh Conlon was twenty-two years old, though he looked younger than Mueller. Conlon was as thin as one of the wooden planks they were cutting. Conlon did have muscular forearms, which came from his working with the tools of his trade.

David thought the young man was too young to understand what war was genuinely like. It wasn't fancy uniforms, marching, and swooning women. It was the smell of gunpowder, going hungry every other day and death.

"They would think you stole that uniform," Mueller said with a laugh.

Though David usually helped Amos Lewis with clerical duties, when he got the chance, he liked to come into the shop and work on whatever boat was being built. David had originally thought he would simply check the cuts and decipher the plans for the canal boats. The first time he had put a saw in his hand, though, he had realized his knack for carpentry. He could cut fast and true. His portions of the projects always fit tighter than other sections.

David truly enjoyed the work. It amazed him that he had never discovered this in his life before now. Of course, carpentry was not something the son of a plantation owner usually did, even if he was the younger son. It was still considered beneath his station.

Now that David was no longer considered a plantation owner's son, he could find out what made him truly happy because he considered nothing below his station. He didn't even know what his station was.

"I think the women would want to share a going-away kiss with me since they wouldn't be seeing me for a long time," Conlon said.

"Only if you pay them, which I hear you do," Mueller quipped.

No one knew that David had been a soldier, let alone a Confederate soldier. He didn't want the military troops in town to put him in the town jail until they could cart him off to a prison camp. If he ever wound up there, he was sure he would die.

So David stayed quiet, and he stayed apart from his work companions. He was friendly, but not too friendly. He worked hard, but he didn't go out to share a drink with his companions because he was afraid the alcohol might loosen his tongue and make him careless.

Despite his isolation, David was discovering that his life even as a younger son of a plantation owner had been privileged. He had lived with the Fitzgeralds and seen what other people did to make a living. This was a world that he had lived in for most of his life but never been a part of it. Now that he was experiencing the life most people knew, he found that he enjoyed it.

"David, can you come in here when you've finished out there?" Amos called from the office.

David waved to him as a sign that he had heard. He finished marking the last of the cuts and then headed to the office.

"You think you'll be back, David?" Conlon called behind him.

"I have no idea. I'll make sure if I don't come back that Mr. Lewis gets someone else to help you, so you aren't left short-handed," David answered.

Conlon smiled. "Thanks."

In the office, Amos was sitting behind his desk. He brushed his thin hair out of his eyes and then struck a match and lit the cigar he held clenched in his teeth. Amos waved David to a chair.

"Sit down, David. There's no problem. I just need to talk to you," Amos said between puffing on the cigar.

David did as he was asked.

"You've been doing good work, David, both in here and out there. You've kept your side of the deal and made life easier for me. I can see that quite easily."

"I'm glad, sir."

"I heard while I was out today that the Canal Company is pushing to get the canal open at the beginning of March. They lost a lot of money last year and want to have a long season this year to try and make up for it. That means you'll have a decision to make."

"What's that, sir?"

Amos took the cigar from his mouth. "I'm willing to offer you full-time, year-round work here. That's how much of a benefit I think you can be to me. You're a good, solid worker and they are few and far between with the war going on."

110

David smiled. He liked Amos and was glad the man appreciated his efforts. "I'm glad you think so highly of me, sir."

Amos held up a hand. "If you take the job, it means you'll have to give up canalling."

"Oh" was all David could think to say.

How could he tell Amos that he couldn't stay to work full-time no matter how much he would like to? David had cast his fortunes with the Fitzgeralds. They had believed in him and trusted him when they had no cause. He wouldn't desert them now. The five of them were a team. They were committed to each other. They were…a family.

David shook his head. "As much as I appreciate the offer and enjoy working here when the canal opens I'll have to go."

"Why? If you're just a hired crewman, I'm offering you a better deal. You'll be my assistant," Amos said.

David shook his head. "I'm not a hired crewman, Mr. Lewis. I'm working with…well, I'm working with my family."

17

A BOY AND A GIRL

FEBRUARY 1863

Michael walked downstairs from his room. His mother had finally stopped talking to him about what was expected of the son of Dr. Harlan Armentrout. The lecture had taken an hour, and all he had done was earned a B on a geography exam.

How was he expected to concentrate on geography when soldiers no older than him were dying on the second floor of the Academy? It didn't make sense. He was at the Allegany Academy to learn about the world, but the world was happening on the second floor where he and none of the other students were allowed to go.

The one small pleasure Michael did get is that his mother had been furious when the Academy had been turned into a hospital. She didn't want being able to give sick and wounded Union soldiers a little comfort to interfere with her son's education.

Well, his test grade certainly seemed to confirm to his mother that she was right.

He doubted that his mother could have done as well if she had taken the exam, but no one was talking to her about what was expected of a wife of Dr. Harlan Armentrout. Maybe less was expected.

All Michael wanted now was some pleasant conversation with someone who wasn't always judging him to be lacking in one area or another.

The dinner dishes were cleared from the dining room. He walked into the kitchen. Mrs. Fitzgerald was arranging some items on the counter and reading a menu of what his mother wanted to eat tomorrow. She looked up when she heard Michael come in.

"Hello, Michael."

"Good afternoon, Mrs. Fitzgerald. What are you doing?"

"I'm getting things set up for supper, so I'll have an idea of how much cooking time will be needed to have everything ready on time. Sometimes your mother selects some fairly time-consuming menus and having a meal served late is unacceptable to her."

"I'm not very surprised."

He glanced around the kitchen, but Mrs. Fitzgerald seemed to be the only one there.

"Can I help you with something?" Mrs. Fitzgerald asked.

"Is...um...where...um..." Michael asked nervously.

Mrs. Fitzgerald grinned. "Elizabeth left a few minutes ago. She's heading back to the *Freeman*. She's finished for the day."

"How did you know I was looking for her?" Michael asked, slightly amazed.

Mrs. Fitzgerald's eyebrows arched. "You are a young man, Michael. I know you didn't come in here to talk to me."

Michael didn't worry about putting on his coat. He hurried out the kitchen door and ran around the house to Washington Street. He was sure that his mother would tell him that a son of Dr. Harlan Armentrout shouldn't run anywhere, but she wasn't around. Michael turned east on Washington Street and ran toward the canal basin.

He caught up with Elizabeth near Emmanuel Episcopal Church on the downhill walk towards Wills Creek. He stopped beside her, panting.

Elizabeth stopped walking and raised an eyebrow. "Is something wrong? Did more soldiers take ill?"

Michael shook his head. He wanted to say something to her, but he was out of breath. Now that he was standing with her, he wasn't even sure he could say it if he had his breath. Elizabeth waited patiently for him to speak.

He stared at Elizabeth's strawberry blonde hair and her green eyes. He watched as the corners of her mouth turned up into the smile that warmed his insides.

"I wanted to talk to you," Michael said finally.

"You're not doing too good a job of it so far," she replied.

"I didn't want to wait to see you tomorrow, so I ran from the house to catch up with you."

Elizabeth suddenly frowned. "Your mother certainly wouldn't like that."

113

He wasn't sure whether Elizabeth meant his mother wouldn't have approved of him running after Elizabeth or catching up with her. Michael would have guessed both.

"No, she wouldn't." He paused, not because he was out of breath but because he didn't know what to say. "I'm sorry for the way she treats you and your mother."

"We're just the help."

"No, you're not. It's not right, but it's not just you who she treats that way. She does it with everyone," he said quickly.

"Then why don't you stand up and defend my mother or me? My mother can't do it if we want to keep our jobs," Elizabeth told him.

"My mother treats me the same way. You're just the help. I'm just the son. If I don't do what she wants, not only does she lecture me, she withholds my allowance."

"A pity."

Michael couldn't detect any sympathy in her words. Then he realized why. Elizabeth and her mother were working at a miserable job to get through the winter while all he had to do was behave properly to get more cash each week than Elizabeth and her mother together made in two weeks.

"Why do you think my father stays in his office as much as he can? I think he tries to stay away from my mother, too. As you probably already know, we're not a happy household," Michael said.

"Then maybe if the two of you reacted instead of avoided her, she might calm down. Maybe you could make things happy in your house."

Michael shook his head. "Now you're defending her?"

"I'm not defending or attacking, Michael. I'm just trying to understand why she acts the way she does when she doesn't have to. It sounds like neither you or your father tries to do that," Elizabeth said.

Michael shrugged. He turned away to walk back up the hill. This conversation hadn't gone the way that he thought it would. She'd quickly torn his reason for coming apart. She wouldn't want to spend time with him when she seemed to despise his family.

"Where are you going?" Elizabeth asked.

"Home."

"Why? I thought you wanted to talk to me."

"I did, but if I wanted to be yelled at, I could have stayed home."

Elizabeth hurried after him and grabbed his arm. "I'm sorry, Mi-

114

say in front of my brothers?" Elizabeth asked.

Michael sighed and shook his head. "I just enjoy being around you. You're nice to talk to, especially after I've been lectured to by my mother," Michael said.

"Did she lecture you today?" Elizabeth asked.

Michael nodded slowly. "Yes, but that's not why I wanted to talk to you. It's why I was late catching up to you, though."

"Why did you want to talk to me?"

"Well, I thought that you might...I mean if no one is courting..." Michael sighed. "Why can't I seem to speak correctly around you?"

"Because you keep remembering that your mother told you that you shouldn't be talking to me," Elizabeth suggested.

"You're not making this any easier for me," Michael said.

"Just say what you want to. How can I react until you say what you mean?"

Michael took a deep breath and quickly said, "There's a show at the Strand on Friday night. Will you go with me?"

"Yes." Elizabeth paused. "Now was that so hard?"

Michael grinned. "No, it wasn't. This is great. I'll ask your mother for her permission when I go back to the house. They'll be plenty of people there so we'll be properly chaperoned."

"What about your mother?"

"What about her?" Michael said quickly.

"Are you going to tell her?"

"Not if I don't have to." He stood up and drained his cup of cider. "I'll go ask your mother about it right now so she can tell you when she comes home. This is great. We'll have such a good time."

He headed out the door and nearly ran all the way back to his house. It wasn't until he walked in the door that he realized that he had forgotten to tell Elizabeth goodbye.

18

HELPING WHERE NEEDED

FEBRUARY 1863

Alice rubbed her eyes and glanced one more time around the Armentrouts' kitchen. She went through her mental checklist item by item and finally nodded. Everything was in order. She had even cooked extra loaves of bread for Elizabeth to take with her when she went to help Harlan Armentrout with his patients at the Allegany Academy Hospital.

With the extra duties that Elizabeth had taken on helping Harlan, Alice wanted to make sure that things around the house would be as easy as they could be for her daughter. Elizabeth wouldn't have to do any cleaning before she started working tomorrow morning. Alice had even left her some instructions about what needed to be done.

She took the lantern and walked into the dining room. She was careful to tiptoe so as not to bring Minerva Armentrout downstairs from her bedroom. Everything in the dining room was fine and clean. If it hadn't been, Minerva would have made some viperous comments. There was just no pleasing that woman, although as far as Alice could see, the woman had plenty to be happy about. She had a good son, a successful husband and wasn't being shot at while she worked.

Alice walked back into the kitchen. She set the lantern on the counter. Then she took her coat off the hook by the door and put it on. She blew out the lantern and walked out the back door, locking it behind her.

She walked around the house to Washington Street and started walking back toward the canal basin and the *Freeman*. She hadn't gone too far when she heard someone walking behind her. She glanced over her shoulder and could just barely make out the outline of a man about thirty feet behind her. She wondered who else would be out this late on a cold Cumberland night.

Another servant leaving work?

She quickened her step, and the man accelerated his step.

Why would he be hurrying unless he wanted to catch up with Alice? He hadn't said anything to her. Why was that?

Alice was about to panic when she heard, "Mrs. Fitzgerald, wait!"

Alice stopped and turned again. The man came closer.

"It's James O'Shaunessey, ma'am. I'm sorry I startled you, Mrs. Fitzgerald. I've been watching the house for you to come out all night."

Alice did know the man. He was one of the contacts she and Hugh had used along the Underground Railroad. O'Shaunessey would help slaves move into Somerset County in Pennsylvania when they came through Cumberland. The Pennsylvania border was only a few miles north of here.

Alice put her hand to her chest. "I'm glad you said something, Mr. O'Shaunessey. I was about to run."

He dipped his head. "Again, I'm sorry. I should have said something earlier, but I didn't want to yell out to you out in the open like we were."

"Why didn't you just come to the house and ask for me?"

"I couldn't. Dr. Armentrout knows who I am," James said.

"Does he work with the Underground Railroad?" Alice asked.

James shook his head. "No. He's sympathetic, but his wealth has made him fearful of taking any direct actions."

"I don't understand," Alice said.

"He's afraid to do anything that might cost him his comfortable living. He doesn't want to be caught transporting escaped slaves to safety. If he had seen me come to meet you, he would have suspected you to be working with us. He isn't trustworthy enough for that." There was a lot of disdain in his voice that Alice didn't fully understand.

"He is helping heal Union soldiers. Isn't that enough?" Alice asked.

She hated to hear someone speak poorly of Dr. Armentrout. Alice had come to respect him and his abilities more after hearing Elizabeth talk about his work on sick and wounded soldiers. Alice only hoped that if George was ever hurt or taken sick during his fighting that he would be under the care of a doctor like Harlan Armentrout.

"He does a fine thing helping them, but if he can help hundreds of soldiers who are fighting against slavery, why can't he bring himself to help one slave? We have a more direct impact on the lives of slaves than what Dr. Armentrout is doing," O'Shaunessey explained.

"But I'm not doing anything."

"I came to try and persuade you differently, Mrs. Fitzgerald. With the war going on, many slaves have the opportunity to escape from their captivity. Some are trying. Even now they are making their way north. It's a dangerous journey that doesn't need to be made any tougher once they get above the river," James said.

Alice shook her head. "Mr. O'Shaunessey, I don't do that anymore. Things have changed. My husband is dead, and I've got a boat hand that..." Alice stopped herself before she revealed that David was an ex-Confederate soldier. She didn't want to endanger him. "Well, I don't know where his sympathies lie."

"We need you, Mrs. Fitzgerald. We need your help. We need your boat."

"If the war goes badly for the Union, many slaves will be left at the mercy of the plantation owners, living in conditions that even the poorest white men in Cumberland don't live in."

Alice shook her head. She knew what James was saying was true, but she didn't want to hear it. She didn't want to deal with the guilt.

"Isn't there anyone else?"

"There's always room for one more person to help. In your case, your canal boat is invaluable. It allows us to move the escaped slaves quickly out of an area where people may be searching for them," O'Shaunessey explained to Alice.

Alice was tempted to help, if for nothing more than to honor Hugh's memory. She knew if O'Shaunessey had been asking Hugh, Hugh would have said yes without hesitation. Alice wasn't the anti-slavery zealot that Hugh was, though. She had never been a slave nor lived as close to one as you could and not be called a slave. That had been Hugh's experience. His family had been tenant farmers in Ireland before they emigrated to America to help build the canal.

But things were different now! Hugh was dead, and David was staying with them. He had been a Confederate soldier. He had grown up on a plantation that owned slaves. If he should find out that Alice was transporting slaves along the Underground Railroad, what would he do?

"The canal is closed right now," Alice said.

"That's a temporary thing. It will be open soon enough. Please, Mrs. Fitzgerald, help us. Your experience helping us is useful, invaluable even. You've done this work before and won't panic at the sight of a sheriff or slave hunter."

Alice sighed. "What is it you want me to do?"

They began to talk as Alice walked down Washington Street. James O'Shaunessey explained how he wanted to incorporate the *Freeman* into a slave's escape route. It was much the same thing Alice was already familiar with doing. O'Shaunessey left her before she reached the canal basin and Alice wondered if she was going to regret agreeing to help.

How could she regret helping to free someone, though?

19

COURTING IN CUMBERLAND

FEBRUARY 1863

Alice was surprised the next night when she had a different man waiting for her as she finished her work for the day.

Henry Danforth.

He walked up to the door of he Armentrout home right before Alice was supposed to leave. Alice answered the door, expecting it to be a sick person who needed immediate attention.

"Good evening, Alice," Henry said.

He was wearing blue jeans and a heavy coat.

"Hello, Henry. Do you need to see Dr. Armentrout?" Alice asked.

Henry shook his head. "No, I probably couldn't afford to see him on my pay. I'm here to see you."

"Me?"

"I've been thinking about you since we met at the cemetery the other day. Before then, I hadn't really thought about you for a long time, but now you're in my mind again." He tapped his temple. "I thought the only way I might deal with that was to come and visit you and invite you for dinner."

"Alice, who is at the door?" Minerva Armentrout called from the parlor.

"Someone to speak with me, ma'am," Alice told her.

"You're still working. It's no time for gossiping. Send the person away."

Alice rolled her eyes. She waved Henry into the foyer and put her finger to her lips. She looked around the doorway into the parlor. Minerva was sitting in an armchair facing the fireplace and warming herself. Her back was toward Alice. Alice took Henry's hand and led him through the hallway and into the kitchen.

"Does this mean you'll go to dinner with me?" Henry whispered.

Alice remembered the question Henry asked just before Minerva had interrupted them. Henry wanted to spend time with her again. He wanted to court her.

"I was just trying to keep you from getting into trouble with Mrs. Armentrout," Alice said.

"Oh," Henry said, clearly disappointed.

"I've only been a widow for half a year, Henry. I'm not sure I'm ready to accept offers like yours," Alice said, but she felt flattered.

"But we're both in Cumberland now. I don't know when I will see you again once your season starts. We'll both be moving around a lot."

"Maybe that would be for the better."

Henry nodded and looked at the floor. "I understand."

He started to head for the door. Alice stopped him. She couldn't let him leave like this. She didn't want him to be angry with her.

"I'm a different person now, Henry. When you last saw me, I was newly married. That was twenty years ago. I'm not the same person. You're not the same person," Alice said.

Henry stopped walking, but he didn't turn around.

"I realize that, but I also realized that when I spoke with you the other day that the only things that have changed have just changed the outside of you, and me not who we really are." He patted his stomach. "It's like these extra pounds I've put on since I was a teenager. They've changed how I look, but only on the outside. I'm still pretty much Henry on the inside."

Alice knew he was right, but if she accepted his invitation, what would that lead to? Was she ready to begin life as a single woman who was courted by men?

"You're right, Henry, but everything is so confusing right now," Alice said.

"Meaning that you don't want to be a widow, but you are."

Alice nodded.

Now he turned to face her. "I know that, Alice. Heck, I saw you coming from your husband's grave. I'd be a fool not to realize that, but I'm not saying I'm going to propose to you tonight or even try to kiss you. When people are hungry, they eat. I was hoping that we might be hungry at the same time."

Alice chuckled. "You're right."

Henry smiled. "I try my best."

She held up her hands in surrender. "You win. I am feeling hungry."

Henry's smile broadened. "You know, I'm feeling hungry myself. I guess that could be because I haven't eaten since noon. I wanted to make sure I was hungry when you were."

"What should we do about that?"

"Well, I know a nice tavern on Mechanic Street. It's not too far from the basin, and it serves excellent chicken."

"That sounds fine. Just let me tidy up here."

Alice finished straightening the kitchen so things would be in place for Elizabeth in the morning. She put on her coat and then she and Henry left the house. They walked down Washington Street and crossed Wills Creek.

The tavern on Mechanic Street was called Wills Creek Inn. Alice was surprised at how it looked inside. She had expected it to be more of a saloon where railroaders gathered. Instead, she found a clean dining room with no bar. It was in an entirely separate room. The only other people in the dining room at this hour were another couple who looked like they were permanent residents of the town.

"This is a nice place," Alice said.

"I'm not married, so I eat in taverns a lot. I like to try out the different places in each of the towns that I visit. That's how I got these extra pounds," Henry said as he patted his stomach.

"You keep making fun of your stomach, but you don't really look that bad," Alice told him.

"Thank you, but it depends on who you are comparing me to."

"Who are you comparing you to?"

"Me about fifteen years ago."

Henry held out the chair for her and Alice sat down. Henry sat down across from her. When the waitress came by, he ordered two chicken dinners.

"Do you eat here often?"

Henry shrugged. "Maybe once a month. It's one of my favorites. That's why I wanted to bring you here. I was hoping that you might like it, too."

"Do you live in Cumberland when you're not working?"

"Yes. I inherited my parents' home. They died a year ago."

"I'm sorry."

Henry shook his head. "It's all right. I was the youngest child, so my parents had seemed old to me for a long time. Once my father died, my mother faded quickly and died a month later. All my brothers and sisters already had their homes and lives, so I was the one who inherited our home although I was the youngest."

The waitress brought their meals and set them down before them. Alice inhaled. The roasted chicken smelled great. Her stomach growled its agreement. They ate mostly in silence, but they began to speak more as they got through their meals.

"I'm surprised that you are still with the canal," Henry said.

"Why?"

Henry frowned as if he didn't want to say anything. He stroked his mustache.

"I don't know that we should have this conversation. I don't want to upset you."

"Well, you brought it up," Alice said.

"Yes, I did. See, I still haven't curbed my mouth. I still say the wrong things at the wrong time," Henry said as he nodded his head.

"And I'm still curious. What did you mean, Henry?"

Henry sighed and said, "The canal is dying, Alice. You have to realize that."

"I don't realize that." She did, but she just didn't want to admit it to a railroader since the railroad was what was replacing the canal.

"The railroad can move coal quicker and cheaper than the canal. It can also move people and other crops and items. It can run year-round, and it can go farther away from water than a canal and not just the C&O Canal, all canals."

All of those things were right. Alice knew they were right.

"The canal isn't dead yet. In fact, I think we probably ran more last year than the railroad and last year was a bad year."

The B&O Railroad had only carried coal during May, June, July, August, and September last year. The C&O Canal had been shut down in May and October and sporadically throughout the rest of the year.

"These are unique times. We're at war. The B&O runs through the Confederacy for a stretch. That's the problem we're having right now. Once this war is over, we'll be running smoothly again. The canal gets stopped by the weather every year, and that won't change."

125

"The war will last long enough for the Confederate soldiers to dismantle the B&O Railroad. Then where will you be?"

"Perhaps, but what can be torn up can be rebuilt. I'm not just talking about the B&O and the C&O. I'm talking about railroads and canals in general. Canals have seen their heyday. Railroads are the new thing, and sometime in the future, I think they'll probably be replaced with something newer and better. With what I don't know, but this country is full of thinkers. People are coming up with new ideas all of the time. One of them will eventually replace the railroad like the railroad is replacing the canals," Henry explained.

"And how much time do you give the canal before it dies?" Alice asked, trying to keep the sharpness from her voice.

Henry shrugged. "Some might last longer than others. The C&O will last no longer than the coal in the mountains. When the coal is gone, there will be nothing left for the canal boats to carry and the canal will die."

"The B&O won't?"

"No, because we can still transport people west and crops east. The railroad isn't nearly as limited as the canal," Henry said.

Alice nodded. She agreed with Henry, but the question was: When would all of the coal be out of the mountains? It seemed endless, and the mountains were so large. There had to be millions of tons of coal left beneath the jagged hills. That could mean decades of life for the canal.

They finished their meal and Henry walked Alice back to the canal basin.

"I'm sorry about what I said in the tavern about the canal. I would have preferred to talk about more pleasant things."

"Did you believe what you said?" Alice asked.

"Yes, but that doesn't mean I had to tell you, especially knowing that you work on the canal," Henry said. He sounded truly contrite. Alice was upset about being angry with him.

"If you believe it, then you shouldn't be ashamed to say what you believe. I can't say that I haven't thought about some of the same things."

"Thank you, Alice." He paused. "You're still the same Alice, always worried about everyone else more than you are about you."

As they reached the basin, Henry said, "I'll leave you here. Some of the captains know me. They may not like to see me here and may take advantage of the shadows."

"I understand." She would have felt the same in the rail yards.

126

"Do you think we might be able to have dinner again sometime?" Henry asked quietly.

Alice nodded and smiled. "I think I would like that."

They said goodbye and Alice walked to the edge of the basin, across the fall board and onto the *Freeman*. The lanterns didn't seem to be lit. She wondered if everyone had gone to bed already.

"You're coming back late."

Alice looked around and saw David sitting on the roof of the family cabin, hidden in the shadows formed by the canopy.

"I stopped to eat on my way home. What are you doing out in this cold?" she asked.

"Thinking."

She noticed that he was looking across the river and into Virginia. He was looking at his homeland. Would he always be drawn south?

"What are you thinking about?"

"I'm a traitor."

"A traitor?" Alice sat down beside David on the roof of the cabin. "How do you figure that you're a traitor?"

"I'm a traitor to my country and my family. They expected me to fight for their freedom, but I'm here making canal boats."

"Are we going to go through this again?" Alice said. "You're no traitor. You are an American. This is the United States of America. If anyone is a traitor, it is the people who are across the river and fighting against their country. You aren't. So how does that make you a traitor?"

"Mr. Lewis asked me to stay with him," David said, changing the subject.

"What did you tell him?"

"I told him that I couldn't stay. My place is with you and your family."

Alice laid a hand on his arm. "Thank you. We would have missed you if you had chosen to stay here without us."

"That was an easy decision for me to make." He paused. "I told Mr. Lewis you were my family."

"I'm honored."

"I don't know that you should be. Look how I've treated my real family. I've turned my back on them," David said.

"No, you haven't. If you had, you wouldn't be out here fretting. You still care for them. You just don't agree with them."

"But what if I do something like that to you?"

"You won't."

"How can you be sure?"

"How can you not be? You've proven multiple times in the short time we've known you that you are loyal. Those things add up and strengthen the bond between all of us, David."

They sat in silence for a while, side by side, looking at the lights of Ridgeley.

"I think I know how you feel," Alice said, finally.

"How do I feel?"

"It hadn't dawned on me until now. You've lived all your life on your family plantation. You haven't had to work at a job or support a family."

"Yes."

"Most children leave their parents in their early twenties. They experience the unknown of being independent. They suffer the separation pains from their parents. I know I was scared when I went to live with Hugh. It was so different from what I had known."

"What did you do?"

"I adapted. I made new connections to Hugh and my children. I still had my connections, my love of my family, but I was no longer a part of that direct group. They were experiencing things that I wasn't a part of, and I was experiencing things that they weren't a part of. But Hugh was a part of my experiences, and the more those shared experiences grew, the stronger my bond was to him."

"So you're saying at thirty-four that I'm finally growing up?" David said.

"Not like that. I'm saying you're finding out how much you've lived and believed up until now is truly because you lived and believed it and how much is because your family lived and believed it."

David nodded slowly.

"So does that mean if I stay with your family long enough that I'll feel more a part of your family than my own even though I'm not a part of your family?"

"That's not it at all, David. You are a part of my family, our family, now because of the experiences we shared. Does that make sense?"

David nodded. "It does. I think I'll go inside. It's pretty cold out here."

"That's a good idea."

20

A NEW FRIEND

FEBRUARY 1863

"**H**ello! Good morning!"

Tony heard the voice calling from outside of the *Freeman*. He stopped working on his school lesson and looked around. The person didn't sound drunk, but why would anyone be making so much noise this early in the day? A good many canallers would still be sleeping off their drunk evenings.

Mrs. Fitzgerald seemed to recognize the voice, and she smiled. She laid down the book she was reading to Tony and walked out of the family cabin door. She stood on the race plank so she could see over the top of the family cabin.

"What are you doing here, Henry?" she asked.

"I thought that I would walk you to the Armentrouts."

"I don't go to work for a couple hours yet. Elizabeth and I stagger our time there. Won't you come in?"

A few moments later, Mrs. Fitzgerald came into the family cabin with a stranger. The man wore clean overalls and a red shirt. He had red hair and green eyes and had a young look about him, though he was obviously about her age.

"Children, this is Mr. Henry Danforth. He's an old friend of mine," Mrs. Fitzgerald said.

Tony looked at Thomas, who seemed just as surprised to see the man. Henry Danforth must be a very old friend. Tony wondered if Elizabeth knew him, but she was already off to work.

"Henry, this is my youngest son, Thomas, and my...well, I guess I can call him my adopted son, Tony," Alice said.

Tony grinned at being called her adopted son. He didn't mind that at all.

Henry shook their hands and smiled. "Nice to meet you both. You two look enough alike that I don't think that anyone would not think that you weren't natural brothers."

"Would you like some coffee, Henry?" Alice asked.

"That would be wonderful, thank you," Henry said. "Are you boys getting some schooling while the canal is closed?" Henry asked Thomas and Tony.

"We go to the Virginia Avenue School. It's crowded. I'm sure Miss Grabenstein will be thankful when all the canal kids leave," Thomas answered.

Alice handed the coffee mug to Henry, and he sipped at it.

"I've never been on a canal boat before. Is this all the room you have?"

"Well, there's the hay house. Someone sleeps out there occasionally and when it really gets hot in the summer, we may sleep on the roof."

"And you have...what...five people living in here? I'm surprised you don't trip over each other," Henry said.

"We manage to get by," Alice said.

She motioned for Henry to sit down at the table. Then she sat down with him.

"We don't usually spend that much time in here anyway," Tony said. "There's work to be done, and it doesn't get done by staying in here."

"Isn't it time for you and Thomas to be getting to school?" Alice said.

It was, but Tony didn't feel comfortable leaving Mrs. Fitzgerald alone on the boat with this man. Though she knew him, he was a stranger to everyone else around. Tony didn't know Henry Danforth, but he knew the look in Danforth's eyes. It was the same kind of looks men used to have for his mother. Not as fierce, maybe, but the attraction was still there.

"I don't know that we should go," Tony said, looking at Danforth.

"Nonsense. You both will go to school. I thought you liked learning," Alice told him.

Henry seemed to understand what Tony was getting at. He finished the coffee and stood up.

"Your son is looking out for your virtue, Alice. He's not going to leave you alone with a strange man. Isn't that right, Tony?" Henry asked.

Tony nodded.

Alice laughed. "Oh, Tony, don't be silly. I've known Henry for years. He's not a strange man."

"I don't know him," Tony said.

Henry said, "It's all right, Alice. I'm sure you have things to do this morning, and so do I. I would like to walk you to work, though, if that's all right?"

"That would be fine, Henry."

"What time do you leave?"

"If you come by about eleven o'clock, I'll be ready to go. I need to be at the Armentrouts in time to help Elizabeth get dinner ready."

Henry took his watch out and glanced at it. "That should work out fine. I'll be here at eleven o'clock then."

He shook Tony's and Thomas's hands again and walked to the door of the cabin. He paused there and turned around.

"You did the right thing, Tony. It's good to know that Alice's sons are looking out for her," Henry told them.

Then he walked out the door. Tony could hear his heavy footsteps as he walked over the hatch covers and down the race plank to where the fall board was.

Alice handed Thomas and Tony their lunch pails and kissed them each.

"Now that I am safe, you two get off to school," Alice said.

"Are you mad at me?" Tony asked.

Alice ruffled his dark hair. "Of course not. I'm happy to know that I have a guardian angel."

She gave them both a hug and sent them out the door. Thomas and Tony walked toward Virginia Avenue and their school.

"I like him," Thomas said. "He's a nice man."

"Would you like him as a daddy?"

"I already have Papa."

"This man may want to marry your Mama at some point, Thomas. If he does, he becomes your daddy like I'm your brother. So he may be a nice man, but you have to think will he be a good daddy to you," Tony explained to the younger boy.

Thomas was quiet after that. Tony wondered if it was because he was thinking of Henry Danforth as a daddy or Thomas just didn't have anything to say.

Thomas slowed his steps near the butcher shop, but the backyard was empty. Tony kept walking Thomas stared at the vacant lot for a moment and then caught up to Tony.

Laura Anderson came out of one of the houses along Virginia Avenue as Thomas and Tony walked by.

"Hello, Tony. Hello, Thomas," she called.

"Hi, Laura," Tony called back.

Thomas said, "Is that where you live?"

It was a two-story brick home with a wide, front porch. The house was narrow in the front, but it seemed to stretch quite a ways back.

"Yes. My bedroom is in the back. I have a porch that looks over the yard."

"That's nice. Would you like to walk to school with us?" Tony offered.

Laura smiled. "That would be great. Let me get my things."

She disappeared back into the house. Tony and Thomas sat down on the front porch to wait for her. Laura didn't take long. She was back outside in a couple of minutes with her books and lunch pail.

She was wearing a long pink dress and a red coat. Tony thought she looked pretty in it and he told her so. That brought a large smile to her face, and he thought she looked even prettier.

As they walked, they talked about the school work that Miss Grabenstein had assigned them to do last night. They were being asked to make a presentation about a famous American. Laura had chosen George Washington. Tony had chosen Abraham Lincoln. Thomas had chosen Daniel Boone.

They had only walked a few blocks when two older boys stepped out from an alleyway as they headed toward school. They stopped and faced Tony, Thomas, and Laura. Tony recognized them. They were two thirteen-year-old boys. One was Josh Tuckett, and the other was Andy Cardeson. Tony didn't like either one of them. They talked politely in front of adults, but when the adults were gone, the boys were bullies to younger and smaller children.

"Josh, why don't you take Laura and head along to school?" Andy suggested.

"I'm walking with Tony and Thomas," Laura said.

"You'll go with Josh," Andy threatened.

"But I don't want to."

"You'll go, or I'll tell your Papa that you're hanging out with canal trash."

Being younger, Laura backed down from Andy's threat. She cast a sad look at Tony and then walked away with Josh. Tony suspected he knew what was coming next. He wondered if Thomas did.

Andy walked up to Tony. Because he was big for his age and Tony was small for his, he was able to look down on Tony.

"You stay away from Laura," Andy said. To emphasize his point, he shoved Tony. Tony took a few quick steps back to keep from falling.

"Don't let me catch you with her again," Andy said as he walked away.

"Are you going to let him get away with that?" Thomas asked.

"It's not time to fight yet," Tony replied.

"What do you mean 'not time to fight'? He called us trash and pushed you."

"But Laura was willing to go with Josh. Why should I fight when she isn't willing to stay with us?" Tony asked.

"Oh. Are there rules for fighting then?"

Tony grinned. "Not written down. You just have to learn when the time to fight is. Now's not the time."

"When will it be time?"

Tony shrugged. "I don't know, but you can be sure I'm going to find out."

He clapped Thomas on the shoulder. "Let's get to school before we're too late. Won't it make Andy mad when he sees me sitting next to Laura?"

21

THE DEFENDER

FEBRUARY 1863

Andy Cardeson's threat didn't discourage Tony from wanting to be around Laura Appleton. In fact, it made him more interested in her. Laura liked him, and he thought that she was pretty with her long ponytails and bright smile. She was funny and smart. In short, she was worth the risk of getting into a fight with Andy Cardeson and Josh Tuckett.

Tony and Thomas stopped by Laura's house the next morning to walk with her to school. Thomas shook his head as Tony stepped onto the porch.

"What's wrong?" Tony asked.

"You're crazy. Andy and Josh are probably lurking around waiting for us just because they know you'll do this."

Tony shrugged. "We can't let them tell us what to do."

"Who says we can't? I'm fine with it. Laura's nice, but I don't want to see her bad enough to get punched in the nose."

"Then leave."

"I can't."

"Why not?" Tony asked.

"I don't want to see you get punched in the nose either," Thomas told him.

Tony smiled. It was nice to know that he could depend on his brother.

Tony knocked on the door. Laura answered the door, and her eyes widened when she saw them. She leaned out the door and looked down the street.

"Tony, Thomas, what are you doing here?" she asked.

"We didn't get to walk with you to school yesterday, and I was looking forward to that. So I thought that we could walk together today," Tony told her.

"What about Andy and Josh?"

Tony shrugged. "I'd rather not walk to school with them."

Laura laughed and then said, "Andy will hurt you if he sees you with me. He seems to think that I'm his girlfriend."

"Are you?" Tony asked.

Laura drew back and had a disgusted expression on her face. "No. I don't even like him."

Tony was glad to hear that.

"Laura, would you like walk to school with us?" he asked.

"Sure, but..."

"Do you think either Thomas or I are canal trash?"

"No, but..."

Tony held up his hands. "Then don't worry about Andy. As long as I know where things stand between us, I'll know what to do if something happens. Now why don't you hurry up and get your books so that we're not late getting to school," Tony said.

Laura hesitated a moment and then disappeared into the house.

"Do you know what you're doing?" Thomas asked.

"Probably not, but I'm not going to let someone bully me around. That just means I'll get a reputation of being someone who can be picked on."

"What do you care? We don't live here all the time," Thomas countered.

"It's a matter of pride."

"Pride could be painful."

Laura came back outside, and the three of them began walking up Virginia Avenue toward the school. Laura and Tony walked in front, and Thomas walked behind them.

Andy appeared at the same place and stopped in front of them. Thomas had been right. Andy must have expected Tony to return as he did. That was fine. Tony expected that he would have to confront Andy again. If not today, then tomorrow. The two of them understood each other.

"Go on to school, Laura," Andy said.

"I don't want to. I want to walk with Tony and Thomas," Laura said.

135

Andy grinned. "I don't think Tony will be making it to school to-day. He and I have to talk about his listening problem."

"No, Andy. This is wrong," Laura said.

Tony was surprised at her defense of Thomas and him. She did like them.

"Get out of the way, Laura," Andy said.

Andy grabbed her by the arm and pulled her away. Laura cried out in pain and dug her heels into the ground.

"That hurts," Laura said.

Tony knew what Andy meant to do to him, and he wasn't going to stand by and just let it happen. Tony stepped forward and acted.

He kicked Andy between the legs as hard as he could. Andy let go of Laura and doubled over grunting in pain. Tears ran down the side of his face.

Tony pulled back his arm and punched Andy as hard as he could squarely in the nose. Blood spurted from his nose, and Andy fell backward onto the street.

Tony backed away a step and prepared for Andy's attack. Andy didn't get up, though. He rolled around on the ground, moaning. So much for Andy the bully. Shanty Town brats younger than Tony were tougher than Andy Cardeson was.

"You won," Laura said.

She stared wide-eyed at Tony.

"You sound surprised," Tony said.

"I am. I thought he would be tougher."

"I am, too."

"Will he be all right?"

"He'll be sore for a while, but…" Tony started to say.

"What's going on here?"

Tony spun around and saw Sheriff Whittaker approaching at a hurried walk. Tony sighed and wondered if he should run. It wouldn't do any good. Laura would just tell the sheriff who he was.

When the sheriff saw it was Tony, he frowned. "What are you do-ing here?"

"I go to the school on this road."

"It looks like you're causing trouble as usual," Sheriff Whittaker said.

Between his moans, Andy pointed at Tony and said, "He…he at-tacked me. I…I didn't…do anything to him."

136

Sheriff Whittaker grabbed Tony by the arm and shook him. "You always have to cause trouble, don't you? Well, this time I've got you, and you're going to spend time in my jail, and that canal woman can't do a thing about it."

"But I didn't do anything wrong," Tony said.

"You're a liar. Just look at that boy lying there. You might have killed him."

Laura stepped forward. "Tony was helping me, Sheriff."

"Who are you?"

"My name is Laura Anderson. I live over there." She pointed down the street to her house.

"What happened then?" the sheriff asked.

"We were walking to school. Andy doesn't like Tony. He tried to make me go to school by myself, so he could beat up Tony. When I wouldn't go, Andy grabbed my arm and was hurting me. That's when Tony hit him to help me."

The sheriff looked back and forth between Tony and Laura. Then his eyes narrowed as he glared at Tony. Tony didn't flinch.

"One day your luck is going to run out, Tony. When that day happens, you will be mine, and I will make your life miserable," the sheriff said.

Why did the sheriff want to see him fail so badly? What satisfaction would the man get from seeing Tony suffer?

Sheriff Whittaker looked at Andy and said, "Where's he live?"

"On Arch Street," Laura answered.

The sheriff bent down and scooped the boy up in his arms. Then he walked off, grumbling about brats who made his life harder. Tony assumed Sheriff Whittaker was going to carry the boy home. Tony wondered what story the sheriff would tell Andy's parents when they saw their son.

"Thank you for helping me," Tony said to Laura.

"Thank you for helping me," Laura replied.

Tony grinned at her as he picked his books up off the street.

"The sheriff really hates you."

"He and I go back quite a way," Tony said.

"You had better not get into any trouble with him around," Laura warned him.

Tony nodded. "I think you're right."

Tony looked around. Thomas was nowhere around.

"Where'd Thomas go?" he asked.

"He was with us when we started walking. Do you think he ran off when Andy came out of the alley?" Laura suggested.

"Thomas is not a coward. He probably wandered away before Andy showed up. Wherever he is, though, he's probably creating mischief," Tony said.

What kind of mischief would Thomas be creating?

22

THOMAS THE FREEDOM FIGHTER

FEBRUARY 1863

Thomas squatted down next to the fence and peered between the slats. A pig and a cow stood inside the yard behind the butcher shop. Both of them were nervous because they could smell blood from inside the building. Both of them would be dead before the morning was done.

Mr. Stouffer, the butcher, was inside the back of the butcher shop disposing of another steer. Every once in a while Thomas could hear the smack of the butcher's blade as it chopped the steer into pieces. Thomas had watched the steer go inside to his death.

It wasn't right.

Thomas couldn't explain why he felt this way. He ate meat just like everyone else in his family, and he realized meat came from animals. It just hadn't affected him until he saw the animals that would eventually become steaks, chops and roasts.

It seemed wrong.

It *was* wrong.

Thomas crept around to the yard's back gate. Animals entered through here, but none of them ever left. Thomas was about to change that.

He looked through the fence slats again to make sure that the butcher was still inside the shop. Thomas reached up and lifted the latch on the gate. He pushed open the gate and waited. He hoped that the animals would come out on their own.

They didn't. They were too nervous. They weren't sure what to do.

Thomas crept into the yard and began quietly shooing the animals out of the yard and into the alley. They swerved back and forth and eventually noticed the open gate. They slipped through and began to hurry down the alley.

Thomas stood up to proudly watch them run free. He grinned at the sight.

"What are you doing?"

Thomas looked over his shoulder and saw that the butcher had come outside, probably to take another one of the animals to its death. Thomas had rescued the animals just in time.

He ran down the alley, but the butcher was quicker than Thomas thought that he would be. Mr. Stouffer started running after Thomas and jumped the three-foot-tall fence to shorten the distance between them. His stride was longer than Thomas's was, so no matter how hard Thomas ran, the butcher gradually closed the gap between them.

Thomas panicked and tried to swerve between two houses. Mr. Stouffer stayed right behind him and drew even closer.

Then Thomas saw a large hand reach over his shoulder and clamp down. Thomas skidded to a stop as the butcher stopped running.

"Gotcha!" Mr. Stouffer yelled.

"Let me go!"

"I think not. You just cost me a lot of money, boy. I'll be lucky if I can catch those animals now. Someone will catch them for themselves and feed themselves for a month."

"I didn't want to see them killed," Thomas said.

The butcher grabbed him by the arm and started walking back up the alley. When Thomas tried to dawdle, the butcher just lifted him up and carried the boy under his arm.

"They're animals that were born to become food," the butcher said. "They're not wild game that can live free on their own. It may not be me that does it now, but those animals will still wind up on someone's plate. You didn't do them no favors."

"They're free," Thomas said defiantly.

"Maybe you would like to take their places?"

"No!"

Mr. Stouffer pulled Thomas into the yard. He leaned inside the house.

"Mrs.!" he called.

"Yes," came a feminine voice in reply.

"I've got to go downtown for a little bit. You'll have to watch the shop."

"Why? What's wrong?" the woman called.

"I caught a thief. He cost me a steer and a hog. I want to take him to Sheriff Whittaker. The sheriff can keep the thief in jail until I get my animals."

"Be quick about it. Don't be stopping in any of those Shanty Town taverns on the way home," the woman called.

Mr. Stouffer shook his head and closed the door behind him.

"Let's go," he said.

Stouffer grabbed Thomas by the arm, and they walked down Virginia Avenue and Maryland Avenue until they were near town. They passed Queen City Station and walked down Baltimore Street until they got to the center of town where the sheriff's office was located.

Thomas hesitated when he saw the jail. He knew what it was from having been there with his mother to get Tony and he had no desire to be placed under Sheriff Whittaker's care. He dug in his heels, but the butcher just gave him a hard shove, and Thomas staggered toward the door.

The sheriff wasn't inside, but a deputy was.

"What can I do for you, Charlie?" the deputy asked.

"This boy set some livestock free from my yard. He cost me a lot of money. The last I saw of my hog and steer, they were running down the alley behind my shop," the butcher explained.

The deputy looked at Thomas. "Is that true, son?" Thomas nodded. "Now why would you do something like that?"

"I didn't want them to be killed."

The deputy nodded slowly. "Oh. What's your name?"

"Thomas Fitzgerald."

"And where do you live?"

"On the *Freeman*."

"Is that one of the boats down in the basin?" Thomas nodded. "Well, I'll send someone for your mother. She and I have a few things we'll need to talk through."

"She won't be there, sir. She'll be up at Dr. Armentrout's house working."

"Then I'll send for her there. Until then, I'll have to lock you up."

Thomas gulped. The deputy opened one of the cells and Thomas walked inside. The deputy locked the door behind him. Thomas sat down on the cot.

"What are you going to do, Deputy?" Stouffer asked.

"I'll get the boy's mother down here to get him, and she'll have to agree to make restitution either by replacing the livestock or paying you their worth."

"Well, you tell her that I lost a hundred dollars worth of meat because of her boy."

The deputy cocked his head to the side. "No, Charlie, it might have been worth a hundred dollars when you dressed it and sold it, but dressed meat doesn't walk off. A steer and a hog might be worth about fifty dollars, I would say."

Charlie Stouffer grumbled something under his breath that Thomas couldn't hear.

"Don't worry, Charlie, I'll also charge her a penalty for all of the disruption that she's caused you, but it still won't be one-hundred dollars," the deputy said.

Charlie smiled at that. Then he looked around the deputy and told Thomas, "When you get out of here, don't let me catch you around my shop, boy."

Thomas sat up when the door to the jail building opened. The deputy had left a short time ago to get his mother, and Thomas was alone in the jail. Thomas hoped it was his mother coming to get him. He remembered how bold she had been getting Tony from the prison. Thomas hoped that she was just as bold now.

Instead of the deputy, Sheriff Whittaker walked inside. Thomas noticed that he swaggered when he walked. The sheriff stopped when he saw Thomas in the cell.

"Who are you?" he asked.

"Thomas Fitzgerald."

"Where's the deputy?"

"He went to get my mother."

The sheriff's eyes narrowed to small slits as he stared at Thomas. "So what did you do? Kill somebody?"

"Oh no, sir. I let a steer and hog go out of Butcher Stouffer's yard."

The sheriff put his hands on his hips. "So you're the one responsible for that. I caught the steer easy enough, but I was not going to run down Virginia Avenue chasing that pig with it squealing. It probably would have thrashed around and knocked me down even if I had caught it."

The sheriff moved up closer to the bars of the cell. "Don't I know you?" He leaned in and stared hard at Thomas. "You came with that woman to get that brat Tony out of here the other day."

"That was my mother I was with."

The sheriff nodded. "Well, she and I will have a few words when Ross brings her back for you."

The sheriff sat down. He took his pistol from its holster and laid it on the desk. It was a sign of his authority. Thomas wondered if the sheriff had ever shot anyone with it.

When the deputy returned with Thomas's mother, the sheriff sat up straight and squared his shoulders. Alice glanced into the cell to see Thomas, then she looked at the sheriff.

"I came to get my son," she said.

"It seems like you are making it a habit of coming here to get troublemakers out of my jail," the sheriff said smugly.

"Thomas is not a troublemaker."

"Then why else would he be here?"

"Because he made a mistake for which he will be punished," Alice said calmly.

"That's right. He'll stay in there until the butcher is paid fifty-five dollars. Fifty for the livestock he lost and five for the trouble you've caused him," Sheriff Whittaker said.

"Since when did you become the judge?"

"Don't get smart with me, ma'am. I'm trying to help you get your son out of my jail as quickly as possible. If you ask me, I think Tony is a bad influence on your son."

Alice cocked her head to the side and said, "Then who would you say is the bad influence on you?"

The sheriff stood up so that he could look down on Alice. Alice didn't back away.

"Mrs. Fitzgerald, if you don't have the money, why don't you leave until you get it? Until then, we don't have anything to talk about."

"But everything has been paid for."

The sheriff looked at his deputy. "What is she talking about?"

The deputy squirmed a bit and said, "Her son Tony caught up with us on the way here. He said that he and another little girl caught the hog and took it back to the butcher. When we went to the butcher, he told us that you had brought in the steer. I had Mrs. Fitzgerald pay him five dollars for his trouble, so she has paid for everything."

The sheriff glared at Alice and pressed his lips together in a tight line.

"And Sheriff, I find it odd that you were going to charge me for a steer that you had returned to the butcher yourself. Why is that? Were you seeking payment for your trouble?" Alice asked.

"I was doing nothing of the sort!" Sheriff Whittaker snapped.

Alice remained unflustered.

"I would like my son released now," she said.

The sheriff nodded his head in the direction of the cell. "Let the boy out, Ross."

The deputy walked back to the cell and unlocked the door. Thomas ran out and hugged his mother. She patted him on the head.

"We'll be going now," Alice said. "Thank you for your kindness, Deputy. It's nice to meet a lawman who upholds the law."

"Get out!" the sheriff shouted.

Alice and Thomas calmly walked out of the jail. Thomas clung to his mother's waist until they neared the canal basin. His time in prison had frightened him, especially with the sheriff sitting at the desk with his gun lying in front of him.

"You handled the sheriff great, Mama," Thomas said.

"I don't like people who abuse their authority," she paused. "Nor do I like my children being dishonest in their dealings with others."

Thomas gulped. "How are you going to punish me?"

He knew it wasn't a question of if but when.

"That remains to be seen," Alice said.

23

A Youth Protected

February 1863

Michael waited on Washington Street for Elizabeth when she finished her work at his house. He hadn't left by the front door, or his mother might have seen him. She would have peppered him with questions about what he was doing and where he was going. They were questions he didn't want to answer. Even now he wasn't standing in front of his own house. That would be inviting his mother to look out the window and see him. He walked two houses farther down the street in front of the Martins' home. The lights were off inside the three-story brick home. Michael sat on a low stone wall watching her walk toward him.

As she drew nearer, Michael stood up. He folded down the collar of his coat so that Elizabeth could see his face in the moonlight. Elizabeth smiled.

"Have you been waiting long?" she asked.

Michael shrugged. "I couldn't leave too close to when you left, or my mother would have suspected. She isn't dumb."

Michael held out his arm and Elizabeth looped her arm through his. Then they started walking along Washington Street toward the canal basin. The bells of Emmanuel Episcopal Church chimed nine o'clock as they walked by.

"I enjoyed going to the theater last Friday. Thank you again," Elizabeth said.

Michael smiled. He had enjoyed the time with her, too. He could barely remember the play they had watched because he had been staring at Elizabeth more than the stage. She had worn her Sunday outfit and had looked lovely, although she hadn't been dressed as elegantly as some of the other women at the theater. The dress had been gingham, but it wasn't the fabric or the style that had attracted his attention. It had been the young woman wearing it.

"Would you like to go to supper tomorrow?" Michael asked.

"I think that would be wonderful."

Michael felt a flash of warmth surge through him.

"Would you like to stay in Cumberland?" Michael asked.

"I don't see how I could. I'm a canawler."

"You don't have to be. You could stay here."

"And do what? Stay as your family's servant?" Elizabeth asked.

A cold wind blew off Wills Creek and chilled Michael's exposed skin.

"Would that be so bad?" Michael asked.

Elizabeth nodded emphatically. "With your mother watching me? Yes."

"But I would be there."

"Michael, I like you, and I don't know where things between us will wind up, but I do know that if your mother has anything to do with it, things will end."

Michael's back stiffened. "It's my life."

"It may be your life, but you're not ready to live it yet. You're eighteen years old, and you're still going to school. Other boys your age are off fighting in the war. You're no different than my brothers...my younger brothers," Elizabeth told him.

Michael stopped walking. Elizabeth had never spoken to him like that before. He wasn't sure whether she was angry with him or ashamed of him.

"Are you saying I should join the army?" Michael asked.

Elizabeth shook her head. "No. War is terrible. We've seen that in the hospital. I'm just pointing out the difference between the life you're living and how most other people live."

"But you said I'm not living my life," Michael said quickly.

Elizabeth sighed and said, "Things change too quickly, especially now with the war going on."

"What's the war got to do with life? You keep comparing the two."

He didn't like the way this conversation was going, but he wanted to find out what Elizabeth really thought about him.

"The war has a lot to do with life right now. More people are dying now than usual. War is death, and to fight war the best way you can, you need to make the most of your life."

"And you don't think I am." It wasn't a question because he already knew the answer.

"I can't really say to you how to get the most out of your life. That's for you to decide. I just know what I have to do because war keeps intruding on my life. Last year, Confederate soldiers tried to burn our boat and Union soldiers arrested a friend of my family. Plus, we were shot at a couple times. Then there was Abel Sampson," Elizabeth said.

Michael's throat tightened a bit as he said, "Abel Sampson? Who was he?"

Elizabeth took a deep breath and said, "He was a boy who I liked a lot, but he became a soldier. He didn't have to join the army. He wasn't drafted or anything, but he felt that it was his duty to serve his country. So he served, and he was shot and killed by a Confederate soldier." She paused to wipe away her tears. "Life's too precious to live in dreams. Life itself is what needs to be lived. That's why I won't dream about your mother accepting me."

Michael didn't say anything. He just kept thinking about Abel Sampson. Abel had probably been as old as Michael. Abel had gone to fight when he had the opportunity not to go. Michael's father had paid a replacement to serve for Michael. Michael never knew the other man's name. He didn't even know if the man was still alive or dead. What if the replacement had been one of the soldiers Michael's father was treating in the hospital? What if it had been Abel Sampson who had gone to war in Michael's place?

And now Abel Sampson was dead.

Michael shook his head. He didn't want to think about that.

He escorted Elizabeth to the *Freeman.*

"After you get off work tomorrow, plan on going to supper at a nice restaurant. You won't need to dress up like you did for the theater," Michael said.

Elizabeth smiled. "I'll be ready. I'll think about it all night."

When Elizabeth had gone, Michael turned to walk back home. Then he noticed the lights over in Shanty Town. They glowed brightly. Music from different pianos conflicted with off-tune songs. He had heard the stories about the place and his parents had warned him never to go there. It was beneath his station to be seen in such a place.

Why shouldn't Michael go? He was a man, wasn't he?

Life was meant to be lived.

Like Elizabeth had said.

Tonight, Shanty Town was precisely where Michael wanted to be.

He walked over to Wineow Street and looked at the different saloons with their painted signs, dark windows, and boardwalks. It was different from Cumberland. The atmosphere here was charged with tension. Life was being lived here.

He chose the first saloon he came to—McKenney's Tavern—and went inside. It was dark inside, despite the lanterns. The room was filled with tobacco smoke, loud voices and lots of bodies. The light was dim, but not so dim that men couldn't see their poker hands as they played cards at the half-dozen tables.

Michael pushed his way through the crowd of men and women until he reached the wooden bar that was damp from spilled drinks. He pulled a dollar from his wallet and laid it on the bar in front of him.

The bartender noticed the money first and then Michael. He walked down from one end of the bar and stopped in front of Michael. The man had on a dirty red-striped shirt and a clean white apron. Michael thought it odd. He would have expected it would be the other way around.

"I want a bottle," Michael said.

"We don't have any baby bottles in here, boy," the bartender said, grinning. He was missing one of his teeth.

Michael felt his face heat up as the men around him laughed. "I'm not a boy, and I don't mean a baby bottle," he said.

The bartender leaned closer to Michael. "A man asks for his drink by name."

"Whiskey."

"Oh, whiskey. You must be a big man then." The crowd laughed again.

The bartender took Michael's money, and it disappeared into the pocket of his pants. The big man turned around, took a bottle off the wall and set it in front of Michael.

"Do you want a nipple or a glass?" the bartender asked.

"I'm eighteen," Michael said to defend himself.

"That makes you young enough to be the son of most of the men in here if they chose to acknowledge the bastards they fathered."

148

Michael looked around nervously. Most of the men were significantly older than him. They were in their thirties or older. He was just a boy in here. Didn't any young men work on the railroad or the canal? Didn't they have homes or families they should be with?

"I'll take a glass," he said quietly.

Michael poured himself a glass and drank it in one gulp. He almost fell down. The whiskey felt like he had swallowed fire. The wine he drank at home never tasted like this. It was awful! He wanted to scream from the pain, but he wasn't sure he hadn't harmed his voice.

He looked around and noticed the men nearby watching him. Michael set the glass down and grabbed onto the edge of the bar to help keep him from falling.

He took a deep breath and let go of the bar with one hand. He poured himself another glass of whiskey. He held it up. Something was floating in the liquid, but Michael didn't want to think about what it might be. It would just give the men around him another reason to laugh. He closed his eyes and quickly drank it down. He just hoped that he wouldn't swallow whatever he had seen floating in the bottle.

Fire! Pure fire! He didn't think drinking kerosene would have been any worse.

He could feel sweat on his forehead, and his face was flushed.

So why was this bar filled with only older men? The younger men had gone off to fight in the war. Michael hadn't because his father had bought a replacement for him. None of the men who came to this bar could afford to do that.

That's why they stared at him. That's why they called him a baby. He wasn't fighting. They thought that he was coward.

He looked to the side and saw the men grinning at him as they swallowed their drinks without flinching.

It wasn't Michael's fault that he wasn't fighting in the war right now. He hadn't told his father to pay for a replacement for him. Michael hadn't even found out about it until after the fact.

"So I'm a baby, huh? Well, if I'm a baby then all of you must be old men who even the army doesn't want," Michael said, his words slurring slightly as the alcohol took effect. He should have eaten something first, but he hadn't planned on getting drunk tonight.

"You had better shut up, boy," the bartender said.

Michael turned around and poured himself another drink.

"Why?" Michael said. "You can say things about me, but I can't say things about you and these others? You think I'm a coward like the rest of you? Too old to fight? Hah! Have any of you seen Grant or Jackson or Lee? They're older than you and not afraid to fight."

The bartender shrugged. "It's your life to lose, boy."

Michael downed the drink and slammed the glass down on the bar.

"That's right. It is my life! I should be able to live it the way I want to!"

The man next to Michael said, "Why don't you quiet down, boy? I didn't come here to coddle you. I want to drink without your whining."

"I wouldn't want to be coddled by someone whose face looks like my rear when it has a rash," Michael said, surprised that the image had jumped into his head.

As he began to contemplate where the thought had come from, the man punched him in the jaw and sent Michael sprawling against the man at the bar who was standing behind Michael. That man and the men beside him fell like a row of dominoes. They yelled as their drinks spilled and they stumbled around. Someone pushed Michael back toward the man who had punched him in the face. The man hit him again, and this time Michael fell to the floor.

He saw a man try to kick him and managed to roll out of the way. Michael reached up to pull himself up on a chair. A fist hit him in the side, and he fell again.

Michael felt his pockets being rifled and then he was being lifted up and carried. Tears filled his eyes so he couldn't see clearly. His sides and chin hurt.

He heard the shouts of the men around him and then Michael was airborne. He hit the boardwalk hard and rolled off the low walk to lay in the dirt street on his side.

Michael tried to push himself up to a sitting position but decided he felt better lying on the ground. He collapsed and passed out.

Michael opened his eyes and immediately shut them. The sun shone brightly through a window right into his face. His head throbbed painfully with every breath he took.

Window?

He was lying in the street in Shanty Town. The last thing he remembered was the men in the bar had thrown him out onto the street. Where was he now that he had a window near him? Not that he cared

150

much. He was still alive, though judging by the way he felt, that might be debatable.

He forced his eyes open again and groaned in pain. He managed to see the window again before he had to close his eyes.

Where was he?

"About time you woke up, boy."

Michael slowly turned his head to the side and opened his eyes. It was easier to do without the sun shining directly in his eyes.

He was staring at iron bars and beyond them was a big man in uniform. Michael tried to say something to the man, but his tongue felt swollen so that he couldn't speak.

The big man rolled his eyes. He walked to the water bucket, which sat on a bench, and dipped a tin cup into the water. Then he unlocked the door in the bars and stepped up next to Michael.

"Here, drink this," the big man said.

The man held the water to Michael's lips. Michael sipped at it, surprised at how dry his mouth felt. The water didn't seem to help much, either. It was cool, though, and seemed to soak right into his tongue. He could at least move his tongue around in his mouth.

"Where am I?" Michael whispered.

"City jail, boy. One of my deputies drug you in here last night. Said he found you lying on Wineow Street," the big man said.

"Jail?"

"That's what I said. Are your ears swelled up along with the rest of your face? You took quite a beating last night."

"Who are you?"

The big man straightened up and drew back his shoulders. He tapped on the tin star pinned on his chest. "Sheriff Whittaker. Who are you?"

"Michael...Michael Armentrout."

"Are you the doctor's son?"

Michael nodded slowly. His movement felt stiff, but it might be because his head felt swollen. How badly had he been beaten?

"I'll send someone to fetch your father then," the sheriff said.

The sheriff turned and left Michael alone in the cell. Michael put his arm over his eyes and went back to sleep. He wasn't sure how long he slept before he was jolted awake by the sound of keys banging against the bars of the cell. Michael's hands grabbed for his head and moaned.

"Is that your son?" Sheriff Whittaker asked.

Michael forced open his eyes and was greeted by his father staring at him through the bars. His father frowned as sunlight glinted off his bald head. Michael closed his eyes and rolled away.

"That's him. What happened to him? He looks horrible," his father said.

"A deputy found him lying unconscious on Wineow Street."

"In Shanty Town?"

Sheriff Whittaker said, "He was right outside McKenney's Tavern. It looked like he had been beaten up and robbed by some of the wharf rats who had run out of money for the night."

"What was he doing there?" his father asked.

"He hasn't said anything. He's been sleeping off a drunk."

"He's drunk?" Michael heard his father sigh. "What do I need to do to get him out?"

"Just take him, Doc."

Michael heard the keys rattle in the door to the cell. He rolled over so that he could see his father step inside the cell.

"Hello, Father," Michael said.

His father frowned. It was an expression that Michael used to fear before he learned to fear his mother's expressions more.

"Get up, Michael."

"I'm not sure I can," Michael replied.

"How could you do this?"

Michael tried to laugh, but it came out a cough. "I didn't beat myself up and throw my wallet away. Two or three others helped me out."

"You put yourself into the situation where it could happen!" his father snapped.

Michael waved his hands at his father. "Please speak softer. You don't need to yell."

"Your mother will not like this."

"I'll tell you something, Father. I don't much like it myself."

Michael struggled to his feet. He started to sway as he stood, but he put his hand out to steady himself. The room wavered in front of him.

He threw his shoulders back and tried to straighten up. He told himself that he would never be a man unless he could stand on his own. That meant literally now and figuratively later.

He was ready to face both his mother and father. He expected the walls would be shaking with his mother's screams shortly. That would be painful. He wondered if his mother would wait until later today to scream at him. Probably not.

She would try to plan his life for him, but Michael was ready to begin making his own plans.

BIRTHDAY PRESENTS

FEBRUARY 1863

David began thinking about Alice's birthday while he worked on Amos Lewis's books. He had found out about it because Elizabeth had mentioned that it was a shame that her mother had to work on her birthday. When David had asked her why, she told him not only was Minerva sure to be her normal insulting self, but her father had used to pamper her mother on her birthday every year. He would serve her breakfast in bed and make sure that she didn't have to do any work. It had been his gift to her each year.

Now Alice's birthday was just a day away, and David wanted her to have a truly happy birthday given that the past year hadn't been a particularly happy one for her.

The question was: what could he do to make it so?

He didn't have much money, and what money he did earn, he put toward the family's expenses. What kind of present could he buy without money?

"Amos, what kind of presents do you buy women?" David asked his boss.

Amos wasn't a married man, but he never seemed to be without a pretty lady on his arm whenever he wanted one.

He dropped into a chair. "That's easy enough to answer. Perfume, clothes, candy, jewelry. You can't go wrong with any of those things as long as it's quality merchandise. A woman believes that the higher the quality of the merchandise, the more you think of her."

David had considered all of those, but good quality perfume, clothes, candy, and jewelry all cost money, particularly if they were quality merchandise. And Alice deserved the highest-quality merchandise by Amos's standards.

"What about when the man doesn't have much money?" David asked.

Amos bit off the end of a cigar and lit it. The office quickly filled with blue smoke. David knew that the cigar cost about the same amount that he made working half a day. He wondered if Amos's standard for buying gifts for women applied to things a man bought himself.

"Ah, now that's harder to accomplish, of course, because women like to have money spent on them. It also makes them feel good and gives them a sense of how you feel," Amos Lewis said as he folded his arms across his ample belly.

That didn't seem to match with the present Elizabeth said that Hugh had given Alice each year. He hadn't spent much on the gift other than his time. Did women see a financial equivalent in time?

"If you don't have money, then you have to instead give what you do have a lot of. What do you have a lot of, David?"

"Nothing."

Amos chuckled. "You're wrong there. Everyone from the youngest child to the oldest crone has something to share."

"What?" David asked.

"I don't know."

David's shoulders sagged. "You're teasing me."

Amos grinned. "No, I'm not. Each person's thing they can share is just that. *Each* person's not *every* person's. I can spend money. That's my ability, as it were. What's yours?"

David pondered that question for the rest of the day, and by the time he headed back to the canal basin, he had an idea forming about what he wanted to do. What did he have a lot of? What could he share with Alice that she would appreciate? What could he do so that she would recognize how he felt about her? He had a few ideas, and he was willing to give all of them to Alice as freely as he did his pay.

When David reached the *Freeman*, he found all of the children in the family cabin. Alice was working the later shift at the Armentrouts today. Luckily, Elizabeth wasn't at the hospital helping out there.

"Good, you're all here. I want to talk to you about something. Your mother's birthday is tomorrow, and I would like it to be a good day for her," David said.

"What do you want to do?" Elizabeth asked anxiously.

"When will your mother be home?"

"Not for a couple hours. She took the late duty today."

David nodded. "Good. That gives us time to figure out what we can do. I've got some ideas, but I want to hear what you three can think of to do as well."

If Amos was right, each of them would be able to offer something different, but together, the four of them should be able to plan something wonderful.

The four of them sat down at the table to begin their planning.

When Alice walked into the family cabin that evening, David looked up from reading his newspaper. The children had gone to bed an hour ago. David sat alone in the room or as alone as you could be in the family cabin with everyone pressed into a room that was ten feet square.

Alice wasn't.

She opened the door to the family cabin and stopped suddenly when she saw David sitting in the rocking chair.

"I didn't know you would still be up, David," she said from the doorway.

David could see a man standing in the shadows behind her.

"I was catching up on some of my reading." He rattled his copy of *The Alleghenian* to show what he had been reading. "You're getting home very late."

Alice stepped further into the room, and the man followed her. He was a tall man with wide shoulders. He was dressed in clean clothes as if he worked at an office job, but his hands were callused. The man didn't work from behind a desk.

"This is a friend of mine, David. His name is Henry Danforth. Henry, this is our hand David Windover," Alice said uncomfortably.

The men shook hands, and then Henry turned to Alice.

"I'll be going now. I will see you later," Henry said.

"Thanks for walking me home and for supper."

Henry bowed his head. "My pleasure."

He left the family cabin, and Alice shut the door. She faced David, who had gone back to reading his paper. He was tempted to make a snide comment, but it wasn't his place. Besides, what he felt wasn't sarcasm. It was more like jealousy.

"Aren't you going to say anything?" Alice asked.

"Like what?" David replied.

"I don't know. I just thought you would have some sort of comment."

David waved his hands at her. "Whisper. The boys are asleep," he warned her.

What did she expect from him, David wondered. He had no claims on her. She was an independent woman. If she had decided that it was time to move on with her life beyond Hugh, that was no business of his. She wasn't one of the children. She was an adult woman who could make her own choices.

"What do you want me to say? I'll say it."

Alice shook her head. "You don't have to say anything."

She watched him for a few moments as if waiting for him to say something. David could sense her waiting, but he let the silence fill the room.

"Goodnight, David," she said as finally she went behind the curtain and into the stateroom.

"Goodnight, Alice."

Alice awoke in the morning to the smell of sausage frying. She stretched out as much as she could. She could see the morning light peeking under the shutters to the window in her room. A cold breeze slipped beneath the shutters and chilled her. When would it warm up?

"Are you awake, Mama?" Elizabeth asked softly.

"Yes," Alice replied.

Elizabeth parted the curtain to the room and carried in a tray filled with breakfast dishes.

Alice sat up in her bed. "What's this?"

"This is breakfast," Elizabeth said, smiling.

"But why are you bringing it to me?" Alice asked.

"Today is your birthday, and this is my present for you. I'm serving you breakfast in bed just like Papa used to do. Minerva Armentrout would have to pay for something like this, but you get it as a gift from me because I love you."

Alice clapped her hands in front of her. "This is wonderful, darling. Thank you so much."

Elizabeth set the tray on her mother's lap. Alice inhaled the scent of warm biscuits covered with melted butter and honey. There were also fried eggs, sausage, and potatoes on the tray.

"This all looks so wonderful. Thank you," Alice said.

"This is just my birthday present to you."

Alice's eyes widened. "You mean there's more?"

Elizabeth grinned and nodded. "Much more."

"So what happens now?"

"You sit here and enjoy your breakfast and catch up on the news."

"The news?"

Elizabeth stepped back, and Thomas walked into the room carrying a newspaper. He sat down on the foot of the bed and opened the copy of *The Alleghenian* David had been reading last night.

"I'll read you the headlines. You tell me when you hear one that you like, and I'll read you the story," Thomas explained to her.

Alice looked back and forth between Thomas and Elizabeth. "This is wonderful. I've never had anyone read me the newspaper before."

"You just eat breakfast and relax. This is your birthday. By the way, I wouldn't mind having a day like this when I turn ten," Thomas said.

Alice laughed. "I'll try and remember."

"Don't worry. If you forget, I'll remind you."

Alice leaned back against the wall and cut up the eggs on her plate. Thomas began reading the different headlines. Alice listened and told him when she wanted to hear the rest of an article. She didn't get to read the newspaper often, let alone have it read to her. This was a real treat for her. Alice took her time and savored every word.

Elizabeth came in a short time later and kissed her mother on the cheek.

"I have to go to the Armentrouts. You can stay here all day if you want. I'll handle things there for a day," Elizabeth told her.

Alice shook her head. "I appreciate that, dear, but it's going too far. I don't want you to have to work fourteen hours for me."

"It's your day, Mama. Enjoy it."

"What will you tell Minerva?"

"I'll tell her that you are sick and vomiting. She wouldn't want you to get sick all over her clean, expensive furniture so she won't want you around."

Alice hugged her and Elizabeth stood up.

"Happy birthday, Mama," Elizabeth said as she left the room.

When Alice finished her meal, she set aside the breakfast tray and began to climb out of bed. Thomas quickly stood up. He took the tray from her.

"I'll take care of those for you, Mama. Tony and I will wash them, too. You don't have to do anything today that you don't want to," Thomas said.

He carried the tray into the family cabin. Then he came back into the stateroom and sat down. He glanced over his shoulder and nodded.

"Are you ready for me to read to you some more, Mama?" Thomas asked when he turned to face her again.

Alice shook her head. "No, Thomas, you read me enough. I know what's going on in the world thanks to you."

"Phew," Thomas said.

"What was that for?"

"I was worried that I was going to have to read the whole newspaper to you. It would have taken all day, and my mouth would have been as dry as dirt." He realized what he said and quickly added. "I would have done it, though. This is your birthday."

Alice smiled. She reached out and patted his cheek. "I appreciate your willingness to make that great sacrifice, Thomas."

"So are you ready to get dressed?" he asked.

Alice stretched and said, "I think so. I'm not used to sitting around doing nothing all day."

"You like it, don't you?"

Alice nodded. "Yes, I do. It's been wonderful."

It reminded Alice of Hugh's birthday gifts to her. She wondered if the children were trying to recreate that for her.

"I'll get Tony then," Thomas said.

"What's Tony got to do with me getting dressed?"

Thomas grinned and looked as if he was about to laugh. "You'll see."

He stepped out of the room and held the curtain open. Alice saw a beautiful, long pink dress and white, button-up shoes. Tony peeked around the side of the dress.

"Happy birthday, Mrs. Fitzgerald," he said.

Alice put her hand to her mouth. "That's a beautiful dress."

"I'm glad you like it. Elizabeth helped me pick it out," Tony said.

Tony carried it into her and laid it on the bed. Alice ran her hand along the soft fabric. She reached out and hugged Tony and then kissed him on the cheek.

"This is a wonderful gift. Where did you get enough money, though?" she asked.

159

"You wouldn't let me spend my money on the family, so I spent it on the next-best thing, you," Tony told her.

Alice began to cry.

"Thomas, something's wrong," Tony said, panicked.

Thomas shook his head. "No, she just does that when she's really happy."

"She's happy?" Tony didn't sound convinced.

Thomas nodded. "That's why those older boys at school always talk about girls being so hard to figure out. When boys are happy, they laugh. When girls are happy, they cry." Thomas shook his head in disbelief.

Alice laughed. She reached out and hugged both of the boys at the same time.

"Now she's laughing," Thomas said.

"I wonder if that means she's sad," Tony said.

Alice squeezed them tighter. "You two are scamps. Now get out of here while I put on this beautiful outfit. You two can be the first ones who see me in it."

Thomas and Tony left, and Alice climbed out of bed. She stretched and then paused to look at the dress again. How long had it been since she had bought a new dress? It had probably been two Christmases ago. And she hadn't gotten new shoes with them!

What a wonderful morning!

She had the most-wonderful children in the world. They had indeed gone out of their way and made sacrifices to make this a very happy birthday for her. How could it get any better?

Alice dressed in the new dress. It fit well. Elizabeth must have also helped Tony pick out a dress that would fit her.

When she was finished, she stepped into the family cabin. Tony and Thomas stopped talking to stare at her. Tony's mouth fell open and formed an "O."

"You look great, Mrs. Fitzgerald," Tony said.

"Thank you again for the dress, Tony. You all have made this a wonderful birthday," she told him.

She felt hammering as the floorboards vibrated under her feet. That told her it was actually coming from her boat and not somewhere else nearby.

"What's that?" Alice asked, looking around.

"If I'm not mistaken, I think that is your next birthday present," Tony said, smiling.

"My next one?"

160

She walked out of the family cabin and up onto the race plank, where she could hear the hammering clearly. She didn't see anyone on the boat, so she looked over the side.

David stood in the dry basin with two strangers she didn't recognize. He was directing the men as they replaced a worn plank on the hull of the *Freeman*. The hull had taken a beating on the rocks in the Potomac River last year when the boat had nearly washed downriver after it had gone into open water.

David saw her standing over him. He smiled and waved. "Good morning, Alice, and happy birthday to you."

"It certainly has been. I've been getting surprised since I woke up this morning. I never expected anything like this," she told him.

David nodded. "That's how it should be. I think one's birthday should be full of surprises. It helps it maintain that sense of wonder."

"What are you doing?"

"These gentlemen who I work with are helping me with my present to you. The *Freeman* took a bit of a beating last year. We are repairing her, so she is ready to help the family earn a good living this season. She'll be as good as new when we're done with her," David explained.

That was a generous gift. The *Freeman* certainly needed the repairs, but she couldn't afford to pay for that work. "Thank you, David."

"You're welcome, and I must add that Tony's gift certainly looks wonderful on you. He and Elizabeth did an excellent job in selecting a dress that suited you well."

Alice could feel herself blushing. She put her hands to her cheeks.

"This is the most-wonderful birthday I've had in quite a few years. I suppose you are the one who organized all of this?" she asked.

"It was a family effort. Everyone played a part, and they all did it well."

Alice nodded. "Thank you. Thank you all."

25

REJECTION?

FEBRUARY 1863

Elizabeth set the plate of ham and potatoes in front of Michael. She paused for a moment to look at him, but he didn't return her stare. He focused all of his attention on cutting his ham into small pieces. Elizabeth straightened up and finished serving the rest of the family their dinner.

Michael never looked at her once during the meal. Minerva Armentrout did, though. Michael's mother wore a self-satisfied smile on her face. Elizabeth tried not to frown as she walked back into the kitchen to prepare the next course with her mother.

What was wrong with Michael? Had Minerva finally convinced him to leave Elizabeth alone? Her mother said that the entire family had gotten into a huge argument this morning. It seemed now that Michael might have been on the losing side.

Elizabeth came through the door and turned to lean against the wall as tears threatened to roll down her cheeks.

"Is something wrong, Elizabeth?" her mother asked.

Elizabeth looked at the door and shrugged. "I don't know."

Alice pulled a peach pie out of the oven. It smelled wonderfully sweet.

"Did Minerva say something to you?" Alice asked.

Elizabeth shook her head. "No. She didn't say a word, but neither did Michael."

"Oh."

There was something in her mother's tone of voice that worried her.

Each time Elizabeth returned to serve a different course of the meal, Michael never once looked at her. It became torturous to walk into the dining room to the emptiness she faced. The room was silent except for the scraping of silverware against the plates. Minerva's eyes drilled into her no matter where she moved about the place. Michael never once looked at her.

What was wrong? What had changed since the night before last when he had walked her back to the *Freeman* and made plans for supper tonight?

Elizabeth couldn't ask Minerva anything while his parents were nearby, but she wanted to talk to him alone. She wanted to hear from his own lips what was the matter.

She kept replaying the walk home and her conversation with Michael. Should she not have told him about Abel Sampson? Abel was dead, though. Michael certainly couldn't be jealous of him. It had to be something else, but what?

As she cleared the empty dishes away from the table, Michael was the first person to excuse himself from the table. He stood up and hurried off to his room. Elizabeth didn't know what to do. He didn't seem angry with her, but he certainly wasn't happy. She wanted to reach out and touch him, but she didn't dare. Not with Minerva watching.

Elizabeth gathered the dishes and hurried into the kitchen. She and her mother washed the dishes in silence until Alice spoke.

"Elizabeth, he may be trying to keep peace with his mother. It was a very loud argument that they had this morning," Alice said.

Elizabeth shook her head. "It's not that, or at least not completely. He's always been able to deal with her. Something else is wrong. Something has changed."

"How can you say that? He hasn't done anything to indicate this is anything but a temporary disruption," said Alice.

Elizabeth rolled her eyes at her mother. "Because I know him, Mama. I've spent a lot of time with him. He didn't care what his mother said. He wanted to be his own person."

Elizabeth stopped washing as tears rolled down her cheeks. Alice dried her hands and reached over and wiped the tears away.

"It will be all right, Elizabeth."

Elizabeth shook her head. "It won't be. He won't even look at me. It's like he doesn't want to admit I'm alive. He's treating me the same way his mother does."

Her mind raced with all of the things that could be wrong. Should she have told him about her feelings for him? Elizabeth had thought she was falling in love, but how did this affect those feelings? Could she be in love with a man who rejected her like Minerva was doing?

After Elizabeth and her mother had finished washing the dishes and putting them away, Alice hesitated about leaving for the *Freeman*.

"I'm not sure I should go," she said.

Elizabeth waved her away. "I'll be all right, Mama. I'll finish up things, and then I'll be on the *Freeman* before too long. I doubt I'll be late tonight. There's nothing to delay me," Elizabeth said with a sigh.

Alice kissed her on the cheek.

"In the morning, everything will look different," she said.

Elizabeth doubted that, but she didn't say anything. After all, her mother was only trying to be kind. At least somebody was treating her well.

Once she was alone, Elizabeth straightened up the kitchen and then moved into the dining room. She would go through all of the downstairs rooms once more before she served supper to the Armentrouts. She had to make sure the lamps were full, logs were next to the fireplace, curtains were closed, and everything was in order. If not, Minerva would complain, and that was the last thing Elizabeth wanted to hear.

As she finished wiping off the dining room table, she was surprised to see Minerva watching her from the archway between the dining room and the hall. What had she done wrong now?

"It would seem Michael is growing up," Minerva said.

Elizabeth didn't say anything. She kept working. Minerva wasn't finished with what she wanted to say, though.

"Michael had his little dalliance with you, and now he has moved onto those who are worthy of him," Minerva said.

Elizabeth's back stiffened. She worked a little faster.

"And now you are once again what you always were and always will be...a servant, a common girl. You thought you could catch my son, didn't you? You thought if you married Michael, you would have money and live like we do and rise above your station in life, didn't you? You were wrong. You are no Armentrout and Michael was the one who set you right."

Elizabeth wouldn't have been surprised if Minerva started laughing. Minerva smiled. It reminded Elizabeth of a rabid dog she had seen once.

Elizabeth finally stopped working and straightened up. Her face was red from barely concealed anger. Minerva's condescension was quickly wearing thin. The woman was no better than her no matter what Minerva Armentrout felt.

"Who do you think you are?" Elizabeth asked.

Minerva's eyes widened slightly at Elizabeth's tone of voice.

"Who do you think you are to try and rise above your station in life?" Minerva said in a cold voice.

"What is my station? Who are you to judge what I do or don't do? Where would you be without your husband or your family name?"

Minerva put her hands on her hips. "How dare you!"

"How dare you assume that you are better than me! If you and I were to both leave this house today and fend for ourselves, I could live on my own. Could you? You are pampered and spoiled and lack basic human kindness for those you consider lower than you."

Elizabeth knew she was going too far, but a torrent of emotions had suddenly been released in her. If Minerva wasn't the direct cause for the way Michael was treating her, she was a contributor.

"Get out!" Minerva shouted

Elizabeth smiled. She took off her apron and flung it into Minerva's face. Then she turned and stormed out of the house.

It felt like Elizabeth had been freed from prison.

26

GOODBYES

MARCH 1863

Elizabeth walked into Allegany Academy, wondering if it would be her last time in the hospital. The Canal Company was supposed to start reflooding the canal today. That would mean her family would be leaving for Georgetown tomorrow.

She would miss this place.

It was an odd thought given all of the suffering that had occurred here, but that is how she felt. Elizabeth made a difference here. She was useful. She was wanted, even if she wasn't necessarily needed.

She hurried up the stairs to the hospital level, partly because she wanted to see the healing soldiers and partly because she didn't want to see Michael.

Elizabeth walked into the first ward. The room was filled with sunlight coming through the four large windows on two different walls.

Twenty-five beds had been crowded into this room. They had all been filled at the beginning of the month. Now slightly more were empty than were filled. Most of the soldiers had returned to their camp east of Cumberland, but five of them had died.

Some of the soldiers waved to her as she walked in. Depending on the age of the soldiers and their upbringing, they treated her like a maid, a sister, a girlfriend or even a mother.

It was still early enough in the day that she didn't have to start getting dinner ready yet. She had been stocking the Academy pantry all month, but it still needed almost constant restocking because of the number of meals she and the other cooks had to prepare.

Elizabeth walked to the first bed. The soldier in it was Sergeant Eugene Mason. He was one of the soldiers who treated her like a younger sister. He was in his mid-twenties, though he seemed older. He had been stocky at the beginning of the month, but now he had lost some weight. There were still circles under his blue eyes, but he seemed healthy and happy.

He was sitting on his cot with his back against the wall when he saw Elizabeth.

"How are you, Eugene?" Elizabeth asked as she sat down on a stool next to the cot.

"I feel fine. Dr. Armentrout said he would put me on the list of men to be let out of here today," Eugene told her while smiling.

"Congratulations."

"I don't think there's anything to congratulate me about. Camp won't be better than this. In fact, it will be worse."

"It can't be that bad."

Eugene nodded. "It's what brought most of us here. We need a cook like you in camp to keep us all fat and healthy."

"This is my last day here, too."

Eugene's smile fell. "Everyone will be sorry to hear that. Why are you leaving?"

"I'm a canawler. The canal is being reopened today."

Eugene leaned forward and shook a finger in her face. "You be careful, Elizabeth. The Chesapeake and Ohio is not the safest place to be at a time like this."

"I'll be careful," she agreed. Elizabeth patted Eugene's hand. "You take care of yourself, Eugene and stay out of places like this."

She moved from bed to bed talking with all of the soldiers who remained. Where the soldiers were still very ill, she would mop their brows with a damp cloth or put an extra blanket over them to keep them warm.

She finished her rounds and walked into the hallway to go to the next ward. Dr. Armentrout was standing there leaning against the railing and smoking a hand-rolled cigarette. Elizabeth started to walk past him. She didn't want to talk to him no matter how much she respected what he did for the soldiers.

"Nothing to say to me, Elizabeth?" he asked.

She stopped and looked up at him. "What do you want me to say?"

"I heard you say that today is your last day."

Elizabeth nodded. "Yes, tomorrow my family and I will be leaving for Georgetown."

"Would you have told me goodbye?"

"I think so." She hesitated. "I don't know."

"And to Michael?"

"No," she said quickly.

"A shame, a true shame."

Elizabeth crossed her arms across her chest, thinking she might be about to replay her scene with Minerva. "It's not my fault, Doctor."

"I didn't say that it was, dear girl, but that doesn't make it any less of a shame." Harlan shook his head and blew out a stream of smoke. "You have a talent, Elizabeth."

"For what? Cooking?"

"No, dear girl, for caring and healing."

That gave Elizabeth paused. She hadn't expected Dr. Armentrout to compliment her.

"Thank you," she said.

He bowed his head toward her. "No, I thank you. Your presence here and your food has helped these men in more ways than I think you realize. It has been at least as effective as my medicines and ministrations. I will miss you."

He smiled at her and then moved into the ward that she had just left.

Elizabeth watched him go, unsure of what to think. Why hadn't he said these things before? Why hadn't he defended her to Minerva?

Elizabeth walked into the second ward and saw Private Calhoun. He was still lying on his back and staring at the ceiling of the room. He should have each crack memorized by now. His condition hadn't changed all month. Elizabeth had managed to get him to take some broth, but broth wasn't what he needed to recover. No one seemed to know what would help him do that.

She squatted down beside the cot and held his hand between her two. Occasionally, when she did this, she was rewarded with a return grasp. This was not one of those times.

"Good morning, Private," she said cheerily.

No response.

"The weather's warming up. The ice and snow are melting away. If should help warm you up some. Your hand feels so cold."

She let go of his hand and reached up to brush his hair from his face. Then she drew her hand back. Something was wrong.

What?

She stared at the young soldier. He looked as he always had during the time she had known him.

Elizabeth took his hand again, but this time she felt for the pulse. There was none. She let go of his hand and fell back onto the floor resting on her backside and hands.

She felt like she should be crying, but there were no tears. Was that wrong?

She hadn't known this boy. He had never said a word to her. But someone knew him. His fellow soldiers who were recovering and returning to duty knew him. His family who right now didn't realize their loss knew him. Elizabeth felt like she should cry, too, but the tears weren't there.

She knew Private Calhoun had died long ago. Maybe not before he had been brought to the hospital, but certainly soon after. He had had no will to live.

Elizabeth reached up and shut his eyes.

"I hope the place you're at now makes you happier. I'm certain it has a better view than what you've seen here."

Then she knelt beside him and prayed to God to treat the boy well.

When she was finished, she stood up and went to find the doctor.

27

CANALLING

MARCH 1863

David walked into the office of the Lewis Boatworks and stood in front of Amos Lewis. The large man looked up from his work on the company books and grinned at David.

"You don't have to tell me. You've come to quit," Amos said.

David's eyebrows arched. "How did you know?"

"You forget that I run boats of my own as well as build them. I listen for news of the canal, and the reopening of the canal is big news for canawlers. The opening of the guard dams is the same as opening a bank for canawlers."

The Potomac River water, while a long way from being warm, was still warm enough to not freeze every morning when it was in the canal or if it did, it would only freeze with a thin layer of ice on it. Icebreakers could be used if needed. That being the case, the Canal Company had ordered the canal channel reflooded so that it could once again begin making money to try and make up for its losses last year.

"I'm sorry I couldn't give you more notice. I just found out this morning," David said.

Amos waved the apology off. "I only heard about it last night myself. I'm sorry you decided not to stay. You were worth the money I paid you."

"I did my best."

"You did that and more, my boy."

Amos reached into his pocket and took out a ten-dollar bill. He passed it to David.

"That's more than you owe me for the work I've done, Amos."

"I know. Consider it a bonus and if you want a job next winter, come and see me. I'll probably need a bit of a holiday then. Lord knows I don't get any rest the remainder of the year."

David smiled. "I'll do that."

He shook Amos's hand and then turned and left the building.

With ten dollars, he might take the family out for dinner at one of the fancier restaurants in Washington City when they reached there. Of course, Alice would probably want to put the money away for times when traffic on the canal might get delayed, and their money would start to dwindle.

He walked to the edge of the canal basin and looked over to the guard dam. Two men stood on either side of a large iron wheel that was parallel to the ground. They began to turn the wheel with some effort. Below them, a butterfly valve opened, and water from the Potomac River rushed into the dry bed of the canal. It moved across the canal bed in small rivers. The rivers ran together forming growing pools. Soon the bottom would be covered. Then the water would work its way down until it joined the inflow from the next feeder lock. Then the water would begin to rise.

David watched the water flow, trying to estimate how long it would take for the canal to fill up so that the boats would float when fully loaded.

He looked over to where the railroad tracks crossed over the basin. Already there was a line of cars filled with coal waiting to be unloaded into the holds of the empty canal boats. The canal boats could be loaded as quickly as they could be positioned to take on coal.

Tomorrow, the *Freeman* would be moving again.

David walked across the fall board and onto the *Freeman*. Alice and Elizabeth were in the family cabin when David came inside.

"They opened the guard dam," David said.

"And none too early for my taste," Elizabeth said.

She still looked depressed having quit her job two days ago. She had talked about her reasons for doing so with her mother, but neither Alice nor Elizabeth said anything to David. He didn't press the issue either. If his advice were wanted or needed, they would ask him about it.

"The boys will certainly be happy that they don't have to go back to school for a while, though we must make sure that they continue

171

their studies," Alice said.

"Do we need anything from town? Mr. Lewis gave me ten dollars to even things up with us," David said, holding the ten-dollar bill up.

Alice shook her head. "No, I've been stocking up on the necessary items as money has come in. We are set until we need some fresh items in a day or two."

"How fast will we be able to get underway?" David asked.

"Tomorrow. We're already in the basin, so we are one of the first boats the basin master scheduled to be loaded. I would say we should be underway by early afternoon and should be able to get to Oldtown before we tie up for the night."

"I have to agree with Elizabeth. I'll be glad to get underway again," David said. Despite enjoying his time at the Lewis Boatworks, he would feel more comfortable once they were moving again.

"Why?"

"Because I don't like being in one place. I've been afraid someone will catch up with me since we stopped," he explained.

"Who are you expecting?"

"The Union Army. The Confederate Army. It doesn't matter. They would both probably like to get their hands on me."

"I thought you had gotten over that," Alice said.

David shrugged. Some things were harder to get over than others.

That night as David tried to sleep, he thought he could feel the boat moving slightly beneath him. He found it hard to fall asleep. He was excited about the prospect of the canal reopening. It went beyond just being on the move again. He would be spending his days with his adopted family now rather than everyone going their separate ways only to gather together in the evenings. It would even be fun having the boys around despite all the trouble they tend to cause.

When David walked out of the family cabin in the morning, the canal was full or at least full enough to float unloaded boats. David noticed that all of the canal boats were beginning to bunch up in the hopes of getting a better position to have their holds filled.

David looked at the canal boat floating under the loading chutes getting ready to take on a load of coal. He thought it was the *Mount Savage*. It was hard to tell because the boat's colors were dirty and the nameplate wasn't facing David.

He checked the time on his pocket watch. If it was the *Mount Savage*, then things were moving faster than scheduled. The *Freeman* would be filled in about two hours. The *Mount Savage* would have to be loaded first. Then the *Laurel* would have its turn. The *Freeman* would follow the *Laurel.*

If things kept moving at this rate, they might be able to start toward Washington City early enough to get through the Paw Paw Tunnel before they would need to tie up for the night.

Alice walked out of the family cabin and stood beside David. She passed him a cup of coffee. It warmed his hands to hold the cup.

He smiled at Alice. "Thanks. It feels as good to my hands as it does to my stomach."

Alice glanced across the basin. "Is that the *Mount Savage?*"

He nodded. "That's what I think."

"We'd better get the hatch covers off soon. I'll have Thomas and Tony do it. They have more energy than any six people I know."

She went back inside, and a few moments later Tony and Thomas rushed out, stuffing their mouths with fresh-baked bread. Tony and Thomas got on different sides of the cargo hatches. They lifted each of the hatch covers up and walked sideways down the race plank until they could stack the covers on the family cabin, hay house or the mule shed.

The boys finished their work about the same the time that the *Mount Savage* filled the last of its holds. David hitched up Seamus and Ocean and got them ready to work. When the *Laurel* finished taking on its load, David had the mules tow the *Freeman* over to the coal chutes. The basin foreman waved them over to position themselves under the chutes.

The chutes dumped the coal from one rail car at a time into the front of the canal boat first. As the forward holds filled, the boat tipped forward so that the family cabin at the rear end of the boat tipped up slightly. Alice had secured everything in the family cabin to keep it from breaking if it fell. The mules moved the boat forward, and another thirty tons of coal was dumped into the rear of the boat. The boat settled level but deeper in the water. The canal boat moved forward again, and another thirty tons of coal were dropped into the front holds, and then the rear holds to fill them completely.

Listening to the coal fall into the holds was like listening to a thunderstorm, and the black cloud of coal dust that rose into the air reminded David of storm clouds. The family had to stand yards off to the side to avoid being completely coated with the dust. Even though

Alice had shut the windows in the family cabin, there would still be a coating of dust over everything inside the cabin that she would have to spend a day cleaning.

The basin foreman checked the filled holds, judging the weight of the coal loaded against what was marked on his manifest. He signed the drayage certificate for 121 tons of coal, payable on arrival when the *Freeman* arrived in Georgetown.

The mules realized it was time for them to begin their work again and obediently started down the canal. David waved to many of the people he hadn't seen for a month since the canal had been drained at the end of January.

"See you in Georgetown!" David called.

Shortly outside of Cumberland, a train passed the *Freeman* on its way to Baltimore by way of enemy territory. Trains might move faster, but the canal was still the most-efficient way to get coal into Washington City, now more so than ever because the railroad passed through Northern Virginia. As long as control of Northern Virginia was in dispute, so was control of the railroad, which gave the canal an advantage.

"Most of those people don't even recognize you, David," Alice called from the tiller.

"Why not?"

"You don't look the same."

David's hand went to his beard and scratched his chin. It was still cold out, and the beard would help keep his face warm, but it might be irritating when the summer heat hit.

Alice was right, though. He had a full beard and mustache. His muscles were thicker as well from his work in the Lewis Boatworks even for the short time he was there.

He was entering a new life as a new person, but he wasn't sure he could forget whom he had been.

28

A DEAL

MARCH 1863

Lee Whittaker sat down at his desk in the city jail to eat his lunch. He had walked across the street to buy a ham sandwich and white rice. He wound up with a beef sandwich and canned corn. Lee dipped his tin cup into the water bucket and filled it halfway. Then he pulled a flask from his desk drawer and poured whiskey into his cup.

Behind him, three whores rested in the two cells, contemplating their sins against the community. He usually ignored them unless they wandered from Shanty Town into the more-respectable parts of Cumberland. If he kept rousting them from Shanty Town, he would not only damage the economy there, he would force the cheap whores to relocate, and that would only bring more attention to the more-expensive brothels in town. If that became the case and citizens began to insist he deal with the problem all over Cumberland, some of the City Fathers might be embarrassed if it was discovered where they held some of their meetings.

Lee's position was an elected office, and therefore, political. That meant he had to think politically. Being sheriff wasn't a matter of doing his job well. It was a matter of finding the balance needed to continue to be elected. That meant pleasing slightly more people by doing his job than making them angry by not doing his job.

Usually, he felt like he was going to fall on his backside trying to keep his balance and his job. He certainly didn't need anyone trying to push him over. Embarrassing the City Fathers would certainly do that.

Lee turned in his chair and looked at the three whores. Two were sleeping, and one was staring back at him. They all looked familiar to him. He didn't know their names, but he had probably arrested them before. He might even have visited them if he couldn't afford a better woman.

"When are you going to let us go, Sheriff?" the one whore who was awake asked.

"When are you going to stop causing trouble? I give you a lot of freedom in Shanty Town. Why do you have to take it outside of there? That's when you get in trouble," Lee replied.

"Because we are meant for grander things than just a few streets in Shanty Town," the whore said. Then she smiled broadly. It was an inviting smile, but the expression in her eyes was one of disinterest.

The reason the women were in the jail now was that the three of them had gotten in a fight over a piece of silk at a local store. They had all apparently gone shopping for fabrics to make themselves new dresses. They also all had decided they liked the same piece of green silk. To solve the problem, they had resorted to the standard Shanty Town decision maker…fighting.

Lee finished his sandwich and wiped his mouth on his shirtsleeve. He would let the women go this afternoon once they were all awake and he could yell at them for taking their rowdiness outside of Shanty Town. Breaking up the fight between the three of them hadn't been easy either. He could sling one woman under each arm and keep them apart, but there had been three of them. Lee had done more work breaking up that fight than he did breaking up most fights between men.

He stared at the one woman who was awake. She wasn't particularly attractive, though she might have been years ago. Now she looked tired. Her make-up looked overdone in the light of day. She had lustrous dark hair, though. It was her best feature.

"See something you like, Sheriff?" she asked.

"I don't like anything from Shanty Town. The place has brought me nothing but trouble and grief. Nothing good has ever come from there," he said.

She pursed her lips and blew him a kiss.

"You've just been looking in the wrong place," she said.

Lee nearly shuddered. The woman actually thought he was attracted to her!

Only out of desperation would he ever touch a Shanty Town whore. He had no desire to be robbed or catch the clap. When the need in him arose, he preferred the Grand Avenue Gentleman's Club. It was a quiet place that didn't attract attention to itself, and the four women who ran the business were ladies.

"What's your name?" Lee asked.

"Carol."

"Just Carol?"

"This month, it is."

Then Lee remembered where he had seen this woman before. It wasn't her he actually remembered but her son. There was no doubting who this woman's brat was.

"You've got a son," Lee said.

The woman looked surprised. She shook her head. "No. What would I do with a son? I bed men. I don't raise them."

Lee ignored her denial. "You do have a son. A young boy about ten years old who goes by the name of Tony."

"No, no I don't."

The woman turned away from Lee to end the conversation. He wasn't going to let that happen. He walked up to the bars of the cell.

"You can't deny it. He looks too much like you," Lee said.

The woman spun around and said, "So what?"

"Do you know where he is?"

Carol snorted. "Do you think I care? Having a kid doesn't exactly help my business."

"I know where he is. I've seen him."

The woman smiled crookedly. "Well, that's just wonderful for you, Sheriff. Maybe you should go become a Pinkerton detective instead of the sheriff."

"Don't get a smart mouth with me!" Whittaker said sharply. He wasn't about to let a cheap whore talk back to him. He was a respected man in Cumberland.

An idea was forming in Lee's mind. Tony had caused him a lot of trouble of late; certainly more trouble than the boy was worth. Then there was that canalling woman. She looked pretty enough, but she was all spit and fire. They had embarrassed him more in the past month than he had been in the last year. Now he had a hint of how to repay them. He could teach them both a lesson about going against Sheriff Lee James Whittaker and enrich himself at the same time.

"Tony's living with a canal family now. He's got himself a job as a hand and making himself some steady money," Lee said. He wasn't sure if Tony was getting paid wages by the Fitzgeralds, but Lee's scenario fit his needs the best.

Carol seemed uninterested, but she was quiet, and that meant she was listening.

"I suppose now Tony will be sharing that money with you to pay you back for all the years that you helped him get along."

There was a long silence. Lee's plan depended on how it was broken.

"He's giving me nothing," Carol said finally.

"Oh, that seems ungrateful to me. After all, when you were caring for him, I'm sure there are other things you would have rather spent your hard-earned money on."

"There was. I would have gotten myself a better room or nicer clothes."

Lee shook his head in sympathy. "Ah, children can be so trying at times."

Not that Lee knew from experience. He had no children. He did know that Tony tried his patience, though. The boy was too clever for his own good. Luckily, his mother wasn't quite as smart.

"Is he making a lot of money?" Carol asked.

Lee shrugged. "I don't know for sure, but what's he have to spend his money on? He lives and eats on the boat and just collects his pay. I figure he's probably saved up at least fifty dollars by now. He's been on that boat since late last year."

The amount caught her attention.

Carol stood up. "What! That ungrateful little wretch! I gave him everything he needed. I raised him. I fed him, and now he goes and does something like this to me."

That was just what Lee wanted to hear. Some people were so easy to manipulate.

"I agree," Lee said in a commiserating tone of voice. "It is amazing that the child could be so ungrateful. However, you are the boy's mother, and he is still a young lad. Does he have your permission to do the type of work he's doing?"

"No, no he doesn't. What does that mean?"

Lee smiled. "It means I think you can strike an agreement with your son's employers. Maybe you should even have them pay you Tony's wages. It would still be his money, of course, but you could watch it for him since he is only a child and has no money sense."

Carol's eyes glinted with anticipation.

"That's right! I'm the boy's mother. I should be the one saying whether or not he should be working. He's too young to be earning wages. They should be paying me. Where are they? Who is he with?"

"He's with a family of canallers, but they are not in Cumberland right now. They will come back, though. When they do, we'll find them."

"We?"

Lee nodded. "I am sheriff after all. You might need some help to get what is your due. I can ensure things run smoothly and legally and for a reasonable cost."

Carol's eyes narrowed. "I should have known that you would be getting something out of this."

Lee smiled. "More than you realize, woman."

"What if I do it without you?"

"You can't make it work without me backing you, even if you could find Tony on the canal, which I doubt that you could. Canallers will ignore a Shanty Town whore but not the Cumberland sheriff."

Carol folded her arms across her chest and pouted. "How much do you want?"

"Half."

"Half! That's ridiculous! I'm his mother."

Lee leaned forward. "I'm the law. Neither one of us can do this alone. We have an equal share or I will find a way to do it myself."

Carol was quiet. Finally, she stood up and moved to the front of the cell. "Fine. You can have half, but I want out of here now."

Lee smiled and jangled his keys. "Certainly. I can't have my partner locked up now, can I?"

He unlocked the cell and let Carol out. Lee was actually looking forward to having Tony and the Fitzgerald woman return to Cumberland.

29

THE RAILROAD RUNS

MARCH 1863

Alice called to Elizabeth to stop the mules. The young girl halted Ocean and Jigger, and Alice pushed the tiller to the side. The *Freeman* gradually drifted to the far side of the canal until it was close enough so that the fall board would reach the shore. Tony jumped ashore with a rope over his shoulder and tied his end around a sturdy tree. It wasn't as if the canal boat would drift away laden down so heavy with 121 tons of coal that less than a plank of the hull showed above the water.

"Stopping early, aren't you?" David called from the doorway of the family cabin.

Alice nodded but didn't explain. She didn't want David to know she was stopping here to pick up a slave this evening. Gladys Island, Lock Island, Bealls Island, Minnehaha Island and some other little patches of ground dotted the Potomac River here. They made fine temporary refuges for escaping slaves who were escorted across the river. Alice had received a note from the sympathetic lockkeeper as they locked through Lock 21 that her help would be needed tonight.

Elizabeth unhitched the mules from the tow line, and David began to coil it up.

Alice stopped close enough to the lock so that she could return for the escaped slave in the evening. She was far enough away, though, that if David or one of the children suspected what she was doing, they wouldn't realize that the lockhouse at Lock 32 was a station on the Underground Railroad.

"Should I bring the mules around at the lock, Mama?" Elizabeth called.

"Yes. Tony should have the feed bin set up by then."

Tony was already leading Seamus and Bargain out onto the ground so they would have some room to move around. The mule shed was the same size as the family cabin, but it filled up quickly when four mules were crammed inside it.

Bargain was working out well as a canal mule. She took her lead from Seamus and pulled hard when she needed to.

Once the mules were picketed, Tony brought out the portable feed bin, which was a bin mounted onto a spike that could be driven into the ground. He hammered the spike into the ground until the portable bin was steady enough that it wouldn't fall over when the mules bumped it. Then he filled the bin with oats and grain.

"Why are we stopping so early?" David asked.

"I felt it was time to stop," Alice said.

"But it's still early. We could have made it past Lock 15 easily before we would have usually stopped for the night."

David was too curious for his own good. Alice didn't want to get into an argument with him. She had work to do.

"Look, David. I'm the captain, so I decide when we stop and where we stop. Tonight, I want to stop here," she said sternly.

He looked like he was about to say something else, but instead he shrugged and walked to the hay house to get some feed for the mules.

Alice sighed and relaxed a bit. She was going to have to deal with David at some point. He wasn't one of the children, and even among the children, only Tony knew who was sometimes hidden in the pantry. David had been hidden there himself to escape from a Union patrol. He had to suspect it was used to hide others.

When everyone was together, Alice began to prepare supper. She went to bed early, saying that they would get an early start and get into Washington City early. It was a poor reason, but the children didn't question her. They were tired from walking all day and went to bed.

Alice lay in bed beside Elizabeth, waiting for her daughter to fall asleep. When Elizabeth's breaths became deep and steady, Alice rose up and slipped out of the stateroom. She stood in the middle of the family cabin and made sure that the boys were asleep. With the warmer temperatures, David had gone back to sleeping in the hay house.

Alice walked onto shore and hiked back to Lock 21. Paul Breedan,

181

the lockkeeper, leaned against the lock door swing arm and held a lantern.

"Mr. Breedan?" Alice called softly.

"Evening, Mrs. Fitzgerald." He straightened up and removed his hat. "I have to say I'm glad you're still helping things here. It makes me nervous with all this fighting going on to have slaves in my house. It's hard to know who to trust."

"I can't say that I'm comfortable with it either," Alice said.

Breedan was a tall man. His skin looked yellow under the lantern. The light made his wrinkled skin look like rock. He led Alice around the house to the small shed where Breedan kept his work and garden tools.

He knocked lightly on the door.

"It's me, son. Don't be alarmed," Breedan said.

He waited a moment and then opened the door. The light fell on a young black man sitting on the dirt floor of the shed. The former slave stared back at Breedan.

"This is Mrs. Fitzgerald. She'll take you on the next part of the journey," Breedan explained.

Alice would take the young man into Georgetown. From there, he would be taken out to one of the coastal schooners that would take him to safety in the north.

Breedan reached down and helped the young man to his feet.

"You go with Mrs. Fitzgerald. You can trust her," Breedan said.

Breedan passed the youth's hand to Alice. She could feel the hand trembling. Alice patted his hand to reassure the young man.

"He's been running from slave hunters for two weeks now. I fed him when I brought him across the river, but I'm sure he'll be hungry before too long. He's looking a bit scrawny, and I know how hungry my boys were when they were his age."

"Thank you, Massah," the youth said.

Breedan shook his head. "There's only one Master, son, and he's the master of us all, me and you and Mrs. Fitzgerald."

"You're talkin' about God's young boy," the ex-slave said.

Breedan nodded. "Jesus Christ is his name."

"My Massah, he talked a lot about Jesus too."

Alice led the youth away. As they made their way back to the *Freeman*, she explained to him where he would be hidden in the boat and the importance of being quiet so that he wasn't heard by anyone.

The young man said that he understood.

Alice crept onto the canal boat with the youth and into the family cabin. She blew out the lantern so the light wouldn't wake the children. She could see well enough in the dark that she didn't need it. With the boy's help, they unloaded the pantry shelves as quietly as they could and she hid him under the quarterdeck.

"I will knock three times when I need to see you. Otherwise stay hidden. Don't make any noise or let anyone see you," Alice whispered.

The boy nodded.

Alice let the curtain fall back into place. As she was loading the shelves up again, the door to the family cabin opened. She spun around holding a crock of flour in her hands. She wasn't sure if she intended to throw it or not.

David stood framed in the doorway. He looked around the room, barely glancing at her, and then he turned and left.

Had he seen or heard something?

Alice sat the crock on the table and followed David outside. He was sitting with his back against the side of the hay house, facing the mule shed. She walked up next to him.

"Are you all right, David?" she asked.

"I should be asking you that," he said.

"Why?"

"Why were you moving things around in the pantry in the dark?"

"I wanted to get things ready for breakfast in the morning and I didn't want to use the lantern because it would have awakened the boys."

"Not a bad lie."

"It's no lie," she said defensively, which was the truth. She had told the truth, just not all of it.

"Then where is the black boy who came onto the boat with you?" David asked.

Alice swallowed hard. She hadn't expected her confrontation with David to come so early in the season. She should have spoken with him long before now.

"He's hiding in the same place you hid when the Union patrol was after you," Alice said simply.

"He's an escaped slave, isn't he?"

Alice nodded.

David was quiet. Alice watched a swirl of emotions pass across his face in the moonlight. Anger. Confusion. Fear. Humor.

"What you're doing is illegal," he said finally.

"Some would consider it that."

"The law would consider it that. If you are caught, a judge would consider it that! How can it be anything else!"

"Sometimes what the law says is wrong is not really."

"How can you say that, Alice? This country lives by the rule of law. Without law, we would have anarchy," David said.

"And you are a law-abiding citizen?" Alice countered.

David nodded quickly. "I am."

"Yet what you did by deserting from the army is illegal."

David glared at her. "I know. I think about it all the time, as you well know."

Alice held up her hands in surrender. "Don't misunderstand me, David. I am not accusing you of doing something wrong. I am just pointing out that laws are not always right because the men who make them are not always right."

"What gives you the right to pick and choose the laws you will obey?"

"The same thing that gives the men who wrote the laws the right to dictate life for me. Free agency. I am not a slave to have my every minute planned out for me, and as you can see by who is in my pantry, even slaves have choices they sometimes make."

David sighed. "You're going to get us all arrested."

"That is possible. I had to consider that in my choice. When Pilate took Barabas and Jesus before the people, they had their own choice to make. They could free a murderer or the son of God. They chose the murderer and Pilate obeyed them because it was the law. But was it right?"

"No, but Jesus had to die. It was part of his plan."

"Only because he understood the people he was dealing with. He knew their strengths and faults. He knew they would choose to free a murderer over him. He knew Pilate would be too weak to resist and would hide behind the rule of law. He knew the people would use the law as their excuse to destroy Jesus. Sometimes what is wrong in the eyes of man is not wrong in the eyes of the Lord."

David shook his head in frustration. He stood up and began pacing back and forth across the hatch covers between the hay house and the mule shed.

"What are you going to do?" Alice asked after he had made three circuits.

David lifted his hands into the air. "I don't know."

"Are you going to turn me in? That's what the law says you should do," Alice said.

She held her breath waiting for his answer.

"Of course I wouldn't turn you in."

Alice let out her breath. She was glad that he hadn't hesitated. It somehow made him seem more sincere.

"Then there are laws that you choose to obey or not, aren't there?" she asked.

David stopped walking. He stood in front of Alice and grabbed her by the shoulders. "I couldn't turn you in. You...and your family mean too much to me."

"You mean a lot to us, David. You meant a lot more to us than a law." She paused. "I suppose you have a lot of thinking to do and I'm very tired. We'll talk more tomorrow. Goodnight."

She turned and walked back to the family cabin. David leaned over the roof of the hay house and shook his head.

The only reason that David knew morning had come was because of the movement from the family cabin. He hadn't slept at all after Alice had left him. He had been wrestling with the situation in which Alice had placed him and come to no resolution.

She helped slaves escape from their owners! Why? Why would she do something like that?

He had found himself recalling the two dozen slaves on Grand Vista. He remembered their songs as they picked tobacco and other crops. He remembered Sally, the house slave, and her friendly smile whenever he sneaked into the kitchen for a snack. Then there was Robert, whose driver's hat was always too big for him so that it had to rest on his ears to keep from sliding over his eyes.

Grand Vista's slaves had been clothed and well fed. His father wanted them to have plenty of energy to work and maintain their health. Their rooms were not fancy, but they all had beds and dry rooms. The overseer carried a pistol to maintain supremacy but no whip to maintain discipline.

David had heard stories about how some owners treated their slaves. It was wrong. It didn't make sense to wear someone down in order to make him work harder.

Those slaves obviously weren't happy. How could they have been when they lived and worked in a state of constant fear?

But what about the slaves of Grand Vista? Were they happy? David had never really given it a thought because it didn't matter if they were happy or not.

They were treated well and that was enough. He gave them as much consideration as he did his hunting hounds. Slaves weren't people.

Someone pounded on the shutters and David nearly jumped to his feet.

"David are you awake?" Tony asked.

"Yes," David replied.

Tony opened the shutters. It was still dark outside, but it was only March. A canaller's day started much earlier than the sunrise this early in the year.

Tony held the lantern high and peered in at David.

"You certainly look a mess," Tony said.

"Thank you. I didn't get any sleep last night."

"I know. Mrs. Fitzgerald told me about what you saw."

"She told you. Why?"

"Because I was in the same position you are in last year. I found out about the extra riders we have occasionally and I wasn't sure what to make of it."

Tony set the lantern down on the race plank and then sat down so that he could look into the hay house at David.

"It's not that bad, David," Tony said.

David shook his head. "It is. What she's doing is wrong."

"How is giving help to someone who needs it wrong? She helped me. She helped you. She's helping the slaves. It's who she is. Could you expect anything less from her?"

"But slaves are someone's property. Someone paid money for those slaves and to help them run away is no better than what Thomas did in running off that butcher's cow and pig."

Tony shook his head. "Oh, it's a lot different, David. Did you ever see a cow cry? Did a pig ever talk to you and tell you what its life on a plantation was like?"

"I know they are not animals."

"You are talking about them as if they are. Look them in the eyes when you talk to them, David. There's a soul inside the body. There's a person under that dark skin."

"They're not people."

Tony shook his head. "They are just like you and me."

David was surprised at the passion in Tony's voice.

"Why are you so worried about what I think?" David asked.

"I grew up being treated like a slave by my own mother. If my skin had been black, I most likely would have been a slave in name as well by the way I was treated. As it was, I was white, so no one used the word with me, but they sure treated me like a slave. If I had stayed like that, I probably would have grown up to be the person who Sheriff Whittaker already thinks I am. Mrs. Fitzgerald treats me differently, though. She treats me like a person. She treats me like one of her sons and I try to act like one," Tony told him.

"I know she does, Tony. I like you, too."

"Think about what I'm saying, David. If you had seen me on the street in the town near your father's plantation, you wouldn't have spared me a glance. I would have been non-existent to you; even less than a slave would be. If you treat people like people and not like property, then you will see them as people and not as property."

"I'll think about it, Tony," David said.

Tony stood up and left David to get ready for working on the *Freeman.*

When David walked into the family cabin for breakfast, he stared at the pantry. Then he looked around the room. Alice and Tony were acting as if nothing unusual was going on. Thomas and Elizabeth didn't even notice that there was an extra person in the room.

David sat down at the table and Alice put a plate of ham and potatoes in front of him.

"Good morning, David," she said pleasantly.

David managed a small smile. "Good morning."

Everyone seemed at ease except him. He continued to look at the pantry from time to time, wondering what the slave inside was doing and thinking.

If what Alice was doing for the slave was wrong, then it was wrong that she helped him as well. He knew that hadn't been wrong, though. Alice had saved his life. He would have died in a Northern prison camp if the soldiers had managed to get him to Frederick for a military trial.

So if it was the right thing to do for him, then it was the right thing to do for the slave.

Besides, Alice wouldn't change her mind just to please him. If she felt that she was right, she would dig her heels in and change for no one.

His fork scraped across the plate and he glanced down. He had eaten his breakfast and couldn't remember tasting any of the food.

Alice walked over. She put one hand on his shoulder as she leaned over to pick up his plate.

"Don't worry, David," she said quietly. "Everything will be fine."

And the amazing thing was that David believed her.

30

HONEST WORK

MARCH 1863

Michael Armentrout paused at the edge of the canal basin and watched the long boats take on tons of coal. The rail cars emptied their contents down the chutes where the canal disappeared in a cloud of black dust in the holds of the canal boats. Michael wondered if the *Freeman* was among the boats. He couldn't tell. Once they were covered in coal dust, one boat looked pretty much like another.

How could he have been so foolish as to ignore Elizabeth as if she didn't exist? She hadn't been the problem. The problem was him.

His father had warned him that he was making a mistake. He hadn't believed him because Michael had seen how his mother controlled his father. How could a man like that know anything about women?

Michael had been so confused after his night in jail and his mother yelling at him for most of the next morning that he hadn't been thinking clearly by dinner. Elizabeth hadn't been the reason he had gotten robbed and beaten up in Shanty Town. She had nothing to do with that. He had simply walked her home. The trouble had come later and had been his own doing.

His house seemed so bleak without Elizabeth around. He hadn't ever noticed that before she had come to work for his family. She had brought life and beauty and energy into the cold house. Now that she was gone, he could see what he was missing. Too late.

His mother saw Elizabeth's leaving as a triumph. She felt she had won a battle. She walked around the house gloating as if she had won a great victory against a powerful enemy, not realizing she had lost.

She had lost because her victory made Michael realize the truth.

Michael began walking again. He turned toward the basin and looked for the building that said Lewis Boatworks. He paused for a moment outside the door and considered if this was something he really wanted to do. Then he nodded to himself.

If he was going to be the type of man Elizabeth could respect and appreciate, then he was the one who had to change. Not Elizabeth.

No, not her.

She was close to perfect. Michael was the one who was flawed. First and foremost, he had to grow up.

He walked into the building and across the open floor to the office. The large man inside looked up when Michael walked in.

"Can I help you?" the man said.

Michael nodded. "I certainly hope so. My name is Michael Armentrout," he said, trying to imitate his father's professional tone.

"I'm Amos Lewis. Are you Dr. Armentrout's son?"

"Yes, sir." Michael paused for a moment and then rushed on with what he had come to ask. "I'd like a job, Mr. Lewis."

Amos leaned back in his chair and clasped his hands across his belly. "I wouldn't think a boy like you would need a job, let alone one in a boatyard."

Michael stepped forward and leaned across the desk. "But I do need one. Not because of the reason you're probably thinking about. I don't need the work because I'm poor. I need the work because I want to be my own person, or rather, I want to find out who I am. I don't just want to be Dr. Armentrout's son. I want to be Michael Armentrout." He paused. "I want when I introduce myself, for people to say, 'Oh, you're Michael Armentrout the canaller' or 'You're Michael Armentrout the merchant or doctor or architect.'"

Amos smiled. "And you think a job on the canal can do that for you? If that were true, maybe I should have my employees pay me for the service I provide them."

"I'm not trying to be funny, Mr. Lewis. I know a couple of people who work on the canal. I admire them. They are good people, and they have worked on the canal all their lives. If working on the C&O Canal can make me half as good as them, then I will be thankful for the job."

Amos chuckled and leaned forward.

"What's so funny?" Michael asked.

"You rich people always think of good, honest work as earthy and

190

character building."

"You're rich, and I heard that you built this place by saving your earnings from your first canal boat. I also hear people say good things about the man who you are. My father is one of them. The canal seems to have built your character."

Amos shook his head. "The canal has built my fortune. I am who I am. If you want to learn character, you should look to your own father. He's a fine man. What he does for the soldiers in the hospitals around here is amazing."

Michael was surprised to hear Amos refer to his father. He had never seen his father as having a particularly strong character, but Amos Lewis saw him differently.

Amos said, "Canal work is not the type of job that builds a particular character. It's the person doing the work. You have to have the character in you already. The job just works away all the fat." He grabbed his stomach. "I'm talking character fat not body fat now."

"Yes, sir."

"Anyway, the work takes away the fat, and you're left with your character. If it's not there to start with, I doubt the job will give it to you," Amos said.

"So you think all rich people lack character? That sounds just as bad as the way you consider rich people thinking about canallers."

Amos shook his head. "It's not quite the same. It's just much harder for the rich, especially those who have always been rich, to develop character. It's like the Good Book says: It's easier for a camel to go through the eye of a needle than a rich man to get into Heaven. Nothing is wrong with wealth, but it's like rich food. It makes you fat."

Michael frowned. He felt that Amos was right, but it wasn't helping him out of his present situation. He had character fat, as Amos called it.

"Does that mean you won't give me work?" Michael asked.

"Do you think you need it for what you want?"

Michael nodded. "Yes, sir. If I stay here, I'll never have a chance to find out what my character is like because I can't live my own life. My mother and father seem set to live it for me. How can I know my character if I don't have a chance to exercise it?"

Amos put his hands together in front of his face and closed his eyes.

"Are you of age or are your parents going to come looking for you and drag you away if I put you to work?" asked Amos.

"I'm eighteen."

Amos's eyebrows raised. "And not in the army?"

Michael shuffled his feet. "My father paid for a replacement without me knowing."

"Well, there is a shortage of working men around here. The war's brought that on. That's why a lot of wives are running canal boats. If I give you a job on one of my boats, you'll be treated like Michael Armentrout and not anyone's son."

Michael nodded.

"Just so you understand that things will be different than they are now. You'll have to earn your respect. You'll take orders, and you'll obey them. You will be responsible for what you do."

"I understand."

"I'm not sure you do, but you will. Go out to the basin and find Jackson Howell. He's the captain of the *Annabelle*, which is one of my boats. Tell him I said to put you to work. I'll pay you fifteen dollars a month at the end of every month."

Amos held out his right hand, and Michael shook it.

"Thank you, sir. You won't be sorry," Michael said.

"I only hope that you aren't. It will be a big change for you."

Michael walked back outside into the cool, sunny day. He walked along the canal basin searching out each boat's nameplate to find the *Annabelle*. It wasn't floating in the basin, so he began to walk down the canal until he saw the *Annabelle* lined up with the other boats waiting their turn to fill their holds.

Michael stood next to the boat and called, "Hello, I'm looking for Captain Howell."

An older man with a thick, brown beard stepped out of the mule shed. He wore a white shirt and pants held up by suspenders. He smoked a pipe and held a brush in one hand.

"I'm Jack Howell," the man said.

"My name is Michael Armentrout. Mr. Lewis hired me to work for you."

Jack stepped onto the race plank and looked Michael up and down. Even through the beard, Michael could tell the man was frowning.

"Can you do anything, boy?" Jack asked.

"I can do many things, and what I don't know I can learn. I'll work hard until I learn it as fast as I can," Michael said with as much pride as he could muster.

"Why would Amos hire a green boy like you?"

"Because he believes I'll earn my keep. I'll work hard and be an asset to him. Mostly, though, I think it's because it's so hard to find help right now."

Jack laughed. "Well, you've got a sense of humor. That's a good thing at least."

"Does that mean I can come aboard?"

"It's Amos's boat. If he hired you, I'll work you. Just remember that while Amos owns the *Annabelle*, I'm her captain. When Amos is not around, my word is law."

"Yes, sir."

"Good. Then we understand each other."

Jack waved him onto the boat and shook his hand.

"I'll show you where you can stow your bag," Jack said. "Then we'll figure out where we can put you to work."

They walked into the family cabin, and Michael was struck by the clutter and disorganized way the room was laid out. The family cabin on the *Freeman* hadn't looked this messy. A young boy lay on the lower bunk writing on a slate. The boy sat up when Jack and Michael entered the room.

"That's my son, Edward. Edward, this is Michael Armentrout. He's our new hand," Jack said.

Edward waved.

Jack pointed to the top bunk. "You can have that one. Toss your bag up there and then come back outside with me."

Michael put the bag on the top bunk and then hurried outside. Jack was sitting on the roof of the family cabin.

"Canawling is not that hard. Most children can drive the mules. That's where we'll start you. Can you groom a mule?"

"Yes, sir. I've done it with horses before."

Jack nodded. "Good. How about cooking?"

Michael shook his head.

"That's too bad. Edward and I can cook passably, but the meals aren't that enjoyable. I sure wish Amos had sent us a cook. We're not going to have a lot of time to teach you because there's lots of work for three men to do. You'll have to watch and learn, and we'll straighten out any mistakes at night."

193

"Yes, sir."

"That's another thing. Don't call me sir. My name is Jack. Just do what I tell you, and I'll be happy," Jack told him.

"I'm glad to be here, Jack."

31

BURNING BRIDGES

APRIL 1863

David jumped to the bank of the canal basin and helped Thomas lay down the fall board. Then he and the youngster led the mules off the boat and picketed them on the bank.

"I'll check with the basin master for when we can take a load of coal," said David.

"I can do that," Alice told him.

"I don't mind. I wanted to go see Amos anyway." David took the opportunity to see his friend and former boss whenever the *Freeman* was in Cumberland, but he was more anxious than usual to see Amos lately.

David walked around the edge of the basin until he found the basin master's office. He scheduled the *Freeman* a time to take on a load of coal at the first opening. It looked liked they would be the first boat to be filled in the morning.

When he finished with the basin master, David walked around the basin to the Lewis Boatworks building. The workshop area was empty. Amos must be between projects. That probably meant he had the men out repairing the boats while he tried to negotiate the construction costs of a new boat.

David walked into the office. Amos was looking over a set of plans for a new boat. The older man looked up when the door opened. He grinned when he saw David.

"David! When did you get in?" Amos asked.

"A few minutes ago. It doesn't look too busy around here right now."

"We're waiting for a shipment of wood so we can begin another boat."

"One of yours?"

Amos shook his head. "No, this one we'll be building to replace the *Oldtown*. It's got more patches than original wood. Oh, by the way, the mail you were expecting came in. I wasn't sure it would get through, but you were lucky."

David felt his chest tighten. "It's here!"

Amos opened the drawers to his desk and pulled out a letter. He held it out to David. "I have no idea how this got here, you know."

The letter had come from Virginia and since Virginia was at war with the Union, it meant that the letter had to come through illegal channels to cross the Potomac. Amos still had connections across the river, as did many people, but he couldn't acknowledge them openly.

"I appreciate it," David said.

"I hope it was worth the trouble."

David sighed. "That remains to be seen."

David put the letter into his pocket. It seemed to hang heavy there, pulling at his shirt pocket. He would read it in private later.

"How are things here otherwise?" David asked Amos.

"We're doing fine and if the canal can stay open most of the season, we may do very fine. That certainly would make me happy," Amos smiled broadly.

David sat down and talked with Amos for a while, but he was constantly aware of the letter in his pocket. He wanted to take it out and read it, but it was something best done in private, particularly since he had no idea what it said.

When he finished his visit with Amos, David quickly walked back to the *Freeman* and climbed into the hay house so he could be alone. He pulled the letter out of his pocket and unfolded it. It was from his father.

David,

While I am glad to know that you are alive, I am ashamed that my son is a coward and a traitor to his country. Everything you are, you owe to Virginia and you have turned your back on her in her time of need. You are a black mark on the Windover name.

I only pray that you will come to your senses and return to the cause. If you do not, do not seek to return here. I have made Peter sole heir of Grand Vista. It was a present to him and his new bride Florence McCaffrey. They will not allow our hallowed Virginia home to be tarnished by your craven act any more than I will.

196

I'm not sure why you wrote me. Certainly you did not think I would approve of your actions. Think about what you are doing, David! Don't throw away your future and your family over some foolish notion you've taken into your head. Show some gumption, boy!

Benjamin Windover

David stared at the letter for a few moments longer. Then he wadded it up and threw it across the small room.

He took a deep breath. He felt he should be angry that his father valued Virginia over him. David had written out his reasons for not fighting, but they hadn't been good enough for his father. He had expected his father to react like this, but he had hoped he was wrong.

His father was a true Virginian. Benjamin Windover would never bend, never compromise.

Virginia was the same way. She would not compromise her positions even if it would cost her her western counties, those that tended to be anti-slavery and pro-union.

Just as Virginia would willingly lose a part of herself because she could not bend, Benjamin Windover would willingly lose his son because he could not bend.

David's father had once again proven himself to be a true Virginian.

And David's path home was gone. He was alone with no family. He should have seen it coming. His father had cut the final ties between David and Virginia and David and his family.

The weight that the letter had caused at first now had the opposite effect. It loosened the burden he had felt on his shoulders. David had made his decision and he knew it was the right one for him. If his father had supported him and said he missed him, David would have continued to feel torn, but the letter had only shown David that he had made the right decision.

The Fitzgeralds cared about him despite the fact that he was a Confederate soldier. They had risked their own lives to save him when the Union patrol had arrested him last year.

He may have been born to the Windovers of Virginia, but his family was the Fitzgeralds of Maryland.

32

THE PRODIGAL SON

APRIL 1863

Alice ate dinner with Henry Danforth at the Baltimore Street Tavern. It was the first time they had seen each other since the canal opened. They spent about an hour and a half together over their meal. She and Henry sat and talked about the opening of the canal and the beginning of spring. When they had finished their meal, Henry offered to walk her back to the *Freeman*.

"No, thank you, Henry. I'm going to walk to the cemetery and visit Hugh," Alice told him.

Henry nodded. "I understand. I'll keep watching for the *Freeman* to be in the basin then. Hopefully, it won't be nearly two months before we meet again."

Alice patted his hand. "I certainly hope not. Drive safely and thank you for dinner."

She walked up Baltimore Street and then crossed over to Fayette Street. It took about twenty minutes to make the walk, but she was used to walking six-hour shifts with the mules, so a twenty-minute walk was nothing. She didn't even break a sweat in the warm air.

As Alice approached Hugh's grave, she saw a young man standing at the grave with his back to her. Alice paused and stared at the youth. The realization of who she was seeing dawned on her gradually because he wasn't supposed to be there. It was almost like she was seeing a ghost.

Alice found herself running toward the young man.

"George!" she called. It sounded like a scream in the silence of the cemetery.

The youth turned and she saw that it was George. He had returned!

Alice threw her arms around his neck and hugged him tightly. Tears streamed down her eyes and she sobbed into his chest. She realized that he was taller than her now.

"Oh, George, you came back," she said.

"Yes, Mama. I'm back. I'm sorry about everything," George said.

Alice took a deep breath and stepped back. She wiped her eyes.

"Let me look at you," she said.

George was dressed in blue jeans and a flannel shirt. He wore a thin, light-brown mustache now, which made him look slightly older, but all Alice could see was her baby boy. Then she noticed his arm or rather the lack of his arm. His left arm ended above the elbow and the sleeve was folded up and pinned to his shoulder so that it wouldn't flop around uselessly.

Alice gasped. George turned his left side away from his mother. His face colored slightly.

"What happened to you?" Alice asked.

"In February, I was in what they called a small engagement down in Northern Virginia. Cannon shrapnel tore it up pretty badly. The doctors said they couldn't save it and so they cut it off." He took a deep breath. "It was only my first battle. Now it turns out that it was my only battle. One-armed boys don't make good soldiers." When he spoke, his voice was tightly controlled. The lack of emotion in his voice was frightening.

Alice hugged him. "I am so sorry, George."

"It is justice."

"What do you mean?"

"It was my foolishness that got Papa killed. Then I went and ran away from the family." He waved his stump around. "This is God's punishment to me for all that."

That was a lot of guilt for George to carry and Alice felt it was more than he merited.

"It is not. He does not act like that," Alice said.

"Then it's the result of my bad decisions," George said a bit too sharply.

"You are coming back to the *Freeman* with me, aren't you?" Alice asked.

George smiled a crooked grin and nodded. "I've been hanging around Cumberland for a week waiting for the boat to come in. I haven't been down to the basin yet today. I was heading there after I left here. How is everyone?"

"They'll all be so excited to see you and we've had changes, too."

"What kind of changes?"

"Tony is living with us and a new friend named David Windover. Oh, George, it's so wonderful to have you back," Alice said.

Tears ran down her cheeks. She brushed them away. She was afraid that if her vision blurred, George would disappear.

George laid a hand on the back of her head. "Please don't cry, Mama."

"I can't help it. You're home and you're alive."

She grabbed onto George's good arm and walked with him down the hill to Fayette Street.

"We've missed you so much. Everyone will be so surprised to have you back. We didn't expect to see you until after the war was over."

"Most of me at least. The rest is buried somewhere in Northern Virginia," George said quietly.

Alice's pace was quick as she led George back to the *Freeman*. As they walked across the fall board, she called, "Thomas! Elizabeth! Come here."

Thomas and Tony poked their heads out of the mule shed. Elizabeth and David walked out of the family cabin.

"George!" Thomas and Elizabeth called out at the same time.

They ran across the boat to hug him. Thomas reached him first and grabbed him around the waist. Elizabeth hugged him a few moments later.

Thomas stepped back, his eyes wide.

"George, your arm," he said.

George looked at the deck, embarrassed or ashamed. Alice wasn't sure which. She stepped forward and put her arm around George's shoulders.

"Your brother was wounded in the war. I, for one, am grateful for that wound because it brought him back to us alive," she said.

Alice hoped that would set the tone for the rest of them to follow.

Tony stepped forward and waved to George. "Hello, George."

Then David walked around to face George. He held out his hand. "Hello, George. I've heard a lot about you. I'm David Windover."

George shook his hand.

200

"I guess I should thank you for helping my family while I was gone. I guess it's still early enough in the season for you to sign on with another boat," George said.

David's mouth parted to say something, but then he looked back and forth between Alice and George.

"No, I guess not," he said finally.

Alice suddenly realized what had happened. "Don't be foolish, David. You're not going to leave us. Remember what we've had to go through to keep you with us."

"But..." David started to say.

"But nothing. I don't expect you to leave any more than I do the children," she said.

"You won't need a hand with me home, Mama," George said.

Alice nodded. "That's right. I won't need a hand, but I don't have one. My idea of who is part of my family changed considerably since last year. I lost your father and you, but I gained Tony and David. They have been part of our lives long enough for me to know that I would miss them fiercely if they ever left. I experienced enough loss last year to last me for quite sometime, thank you. I don't want to go through that for a long while yet."

George's eyes narrowed as he stared at David. "But you're a widow and David is..."

"David is a gentleman who has saved all our lives as well as shared them. He could have left us last season or earlier this year. He didn't and we are much the better for that," Alice finished for him.

"You returned that kindness many times over," David said.

"It's what family does. What we don't do is keep track," Alice said.

"It's what my family does."

Alice smiled. "It is now. Let's get inside. I'll get supper started. Then we'll have to make some adjustments to where everyone will be sleeping." She hugged George again. "It's feels great to have the family together again."

33

HIDDEN WORK

APRIL 1863

Tony sat on his bunk and watched David put together roast beef sandwiches and cooked carrots. Tony noticed that David kept glancing nervously at the pantry. The doors were closed and Tony knew they weren't carrying any extra passengers.

"You still haven't accepted things, have you?" Tony asked.

"Accepted what?" David asked, not turning from his work.

"I see you watching the pantry. You've never done that before and if you keep doing it, not only will Thomas and Elizabeth figure things out, but you could get us in trouble, too. There's not even anyone in there right now. So why look?"

David sighed and leaned against the table.

"I know, but I can't stop thinking about it. I don't know if I can get past this, Tony. It goes against everything that I was taught."

"You have to."

"I'm trying. I really am."

Tony patted David on the back. "That's all you can do."

Tony picked up two of the sandwiches and set them on a plate.

"I'll take Mrs. Fitzgerald her sandwich," Tony said.

He walked out of the family cabin to the quarterdeck. He held the plate out to her. She took her sandwich in one hand while piloting the *Freeman* with her other hand.

"Thank you, Tony," she said.

"David made them."

He sat on the roof of the family cabin and began to eat his own sandwich. The day was warm so it was comfortable outside.

"Are you going to continue transporting slaves?" Tony asked.

Alice nodded. "I feel that I must."

"You aren't helping matters any."

"I'm not trying to help matters, Tony. I'm trying to help people. I thought that you were past your feelings about slaves."

Tony nodded. "I am. David's not."

"Well, he'll understand. He's a smart man."

"Mrs. Fitzgerald, what if he doesn't understand? What then? If everyone on the boat is not in agreement, then we'll get torn apart. Someone will wind up getting their feelings hurt. There is already tension between you and David."

"There isn't," she said quickly.

"There is," Tony insisted.

Alice hesitated and then said, "Well then, it isn't my doing."

"But it is your doing."

Alice shot a sharp look at Tony.

"I'm not saying you're wrong, but you are the one who brought the slave onto the boat last month."

"This is my boat. It's my choice."

Tony nodded. "Yes, ma'am, it is, but if David can't accept that you help slaves escape, you might have to choose between him and a slave. Are you ready to choose?"

"I'll keep that in mind, Tony."

"We're a family now, Mrs. Fitzgerald, and families need to stay together."

She nodded.

34

A MOTHER'S LOVE

APRIL 1863

A rapping on the door to the family cabin awakened Alice. She rubbed her eyes and sat up in her bed.

"Open up. Open up in there!"

Alice pulled on her robe and stepped into the family cabin from the stateroom. David and George were both awake as well and sitting up in their bunks. Tony and Thomas had been moved into the hay house because there was more room for them there.

"Who is it?" George asked.

"I don't know, but I'm about to find out. It's the middle of the night," Alice said.

She opened the door and was staring at a dark-haired woman in a tight black-and-red dress. She wore narrow, high-heeled shoes.

"I want my son!" the woman said.

Alice was taken back for a moment, but quickly recovered when the woman tried to push into the family cabin. Alice blocked the woman with her body.

"I don't know who you're looking for, but you're in the wrong place," Alice said.

"My son. You have my son and I want him back."

The woman seemed to be on the verge of tears, but Alice still didn't know what she was talking about.

"Who are you?"

"I'm Carol and I want my Tony back."

Alice's chest tightened. Tony? Surely this woman couldn't be Tony's mother.

"We've come to take Tony back. If you surrender him peacefully, we won't charge you with kidnapping," said Sheriff Whittaker. Alice looked up the stairs and saw the man standing on the race plank. He was grinning so broadly that Alice wanted to slap him in the face.

"What is going on, Sheriff?" Alice asked.

"Just like she says, Mrs. Fitzgerald. This grieving mother came to me all upset and crying because her son was missing," Whittaker said. "I asked her to describe the boy to me and she described young Tony to the last detail."

"And I want him back," Carol said.

"Why?" Alice asked because this woman before her certainly didn't look like a grieving mother.

"Because he's my son."

Whittaker said, "The why doesn't really matter. Tony's still a child and Carol is his mother. You wouldn't have someone else take one of your children without your knowledge, would you?"

Alice glared at him. She walked past Carol up the stairs to the race plank. She was tempted to push Whittaker into the water, but instead she shooed him back so she could walk forward.

"What are you doing?" Whittaker asked. He looked around nervously as if he could read Alice's mind.

"I'm trying to resolve this."

Sheriff Whittaker moved backwards to stand on the hatch covers. Alice walked to the hay house and rapped on the shutter. They opened without hesitation, which told her the boys had been awake and listening to what was going on.

"Come out here, Tony," Alice said.

Tony climbed out of the window, followed by Thomas. When Carol saw Tony, she ran over and hugged him tightly. He wiggled to be free from her grip, but she wouldn't let him go.

"Oh, Tony. Oh, Tony," Carol cried.

He didn't say anything. He looked at Alice, but she didn't know what to do. Alice wanted to reach out and help him, but did she have the right?

"Is this woman your mother?" Alice asked. She almost hoped that he would say "no," but it was obvious from their appearance that they were mother and son.

"She is," Tony said.

Sheriff Whittaker said, "You see? The boy ran away from home. At least, I hope he ran away and wasn't taken away."

205

Alice understood his implication but chose to ignore it.

"I wasn't taken," Tony said quickly. "I didn't run away either. Carol kicked me out because she thought I ruined the way she could take extra money…"

Carol said, "Now, Tony dear, don't talk that way. I know we argued, but you shouldn't be spreading lies about what happened."

"I'm not lying," Tony insisted.

"He's just a child," Carol said, looking at Alice.

"Why don't you gather your things together so your mother can take you home, son?" Whittaker said in a soothing voice.

"But I thought…" Carol started to say.

Whittaker laid his hand on Carol's shoulder and squeezed gently. "I'm glad that I'm able to help resolve this for everyone."

Carol glanced at him and then nodded.

"What do I do, Mrs. Fitzgerald?" Tony asked.

"I don't know, Tony."

Whittaker said, "You don't have a choice, Mrs. Fitzgerald. If you don't allow us to take the boy, you will be charged with kidnapping."

"Tony, do you really like working on this boat?" Carol asked.

Tony nodded vigorously. "Yes, more than anything."

"Well, I want you to be happy, — I always want what makes you happy — but a child your age is not ready for certain responsibilities."

Something in her tone sounded a warning to Alice. The truth of the visit was about to be revealed.

"I don't know what you mean. I do my share of the work," Tony said.

Carol ignored him. "Take your wages for instance. A child your age doesn't know how to save for your future."

Tony laughed. "Save for my future? That's all I ever did when I was with you when you stuck me under the bed. While you were taking the dollars, I was taking the change."

Whittaker cuffed Tony on the side of his head. Tony grabbed his ear, but he didn't cry out. He just glared at Whittaker.

"Don't you touch him!" Alice shouted.

Whittaker spun around and waved a finger in Alice's face. "You have no word in this. So be quiet, woman, before I do charge you with kidnapping. Let's go, Carol."

He started across the hatch covers to the other side of the boat.

"Wait, Sheriff. I do want Tony to be happy. Perhaps something could be worked out to allow Tony to stay where he is happy," Carol said.

Alice was immediately suspicious. It was obvious that Carol and Tony didn't care for each other, but the woman had to have some plan she wanted to put into motion to have come here in the middle of the night. More than likely, the sheriff was in it as well, but to what purpose Alice couldn't be sure.

"He's your son," Whittaker said nonchalantly, but his eyes narrowed as he concentrated on the conversation.

"Well, Mrs. Fitzgerald?" Carol asked.

"Well, what?"

"Can something be worked out?"

Alice cocked her head to the side. "Do you have something in mind?"

Carol thought for a moment. "If you give me Tony's wages, I can put them in the bank for him. That way I can be sure that you aren't taking advantage of him by taking his free labor and he'll still be happy to be working on the canal with you."

"Mrs. Fitzgerald…" Tony started to say but Sheriff Whittaker cuffed him on the head again.

"Otherwise, I'll just take Tony home with me," Carol finished.

Alice looked at Tony. She didn't want him to go with this woman, but would Carol believe that Alice didn't pay Tony wages? The woman was actually trying to sell her own son to Alice. She couldn't allow Tony to stay with this woman, but if she began to pay for Tony, the money would not be saved for Tony and the request for wages would only get larger as his future *needs* grew larger.

Alice looked over her shoulder at David. He was staring at Tony. Alice looked at Tony. The boy was shaking his head back and forth in small shakes.

But was he telling her not to agree or not to send him away?

"We don't pay Tony wages. He works for his room and board and I buy what he needs. None of us on the *Freeman* draw individual wages," Alice said.

Carol glanced nervously at the sheriff.

"I guess if you want the boy back, you'll have to find a way to pay his wages. He's not your son after all, so I think it's unfair that he not be paid," Whittaker said.

Alice was sure now that it was a scheme to extort money from her. What could she do though? She didn't have enough money to pay Tony wages, especially an amount that would satisfy Carol and the sheriff.

"I'll have to figure out what we can afford," Alice said.

"How long will that take?" Whittaker asked.

Alice was stalling for time, but the longer she stalled, the longer Tony would be forced to stay with Carol. Then Alice got an idea.

"It may take a few days. We are getting our next load of coal this morning. I should know for sure on our next trip back to Cumberland."

"That's more than a few days," Whittaker complained.

"Oh, I'll know what we can afford in a few days, but if I'm going to be paying Tony wages, we can't afford to sit idle. We'll just have to finish our business in a week or so when we come back for more coal. Hopefully, things won't be too backed up at Georgetown or it might be two weeks," Alice explained.

"Two weeks?" Carol said.

"We'll hold onto Tony until then," Whittaker said quickly. "We wouldn't want him to disappear before an agreement was made between you and Carol."

Alice nodded.

"I understand. I hope that Tony isn't too unhappy while he is with you. You know how difficult he can be when he's not happy."

"How?" Carol asked.

Alice winked at Tony. "Oh, you're his mother you should know. When Tony's unhappy, he can be a handful to deal with. He can test the patience of even the most-caring mother," Alice told Carol, but she looked directly at Tony while she said it.

She saw Tony grin. He understood what Alice was saying to him. He would make sure that he was unhappy and that his mother would know it as well.

It also gave Alice time to figure out a way to free Tony and perhaps make Carol more agreeable to whatever solution Alice devised.

Alice looked at Tony and said, "We will come back for you, Tony. You're my son as much as George or Thomas. I love you."

"I know," Tony said quietly.

She turned away quickly when she saw the tears form in his eyes.

35

LONGINGS

MAY 1863

Elizabeth hung out the wet laundry on a thin line strung between the hay house and family cabin. When she finished, she stood on the hatch covers and looked around.

She felt out of place being out on the canal. She wanted to be helping people. She wanted to be useful. She didn't belong out here any longer.

She sighed and sat down on the hatch cover next to the empty basket. Tears rolled down her cheeks, though she didn't sob.

Everything was changing so fast. George had returned from the war. Tony was stuck in Cumberland with his mother. Michael had rejected her because she wasn't good enough for him.

That is what hurt her. Michael's mother had convinced Michael that Elizabeth was beneath his station in life. What was wrong with her? Elizabeth didn't have the right name, the right bloodlines and enough money to please Minerva Armentrout and apparently, her son.

She had never considered such things about herself before. Abel Sampson had never considered himself better than her or anyone else. He had liked her for whom she was. Abel had even gone to fight alongside farmers and businessmen on the Aqueduct Defense. Certainly his parents had never treated her like she was a servant, and Mr. Sampson was a congressman!

Dr. Armentrout hadn't been the problem, though. The problem had been Minerva.

Why had Minerva treated her that way?

George walked over and sat down next to Elizabeth. It was still odd seeing him with a mustache and no left arm. She wondered if it hurt him. She wanted to know about the hospital where he recovered. Had the doctors used morphine to kill the pain while they had operated? Had they fed him well while he recovered? Had they cared? She was too afraid to ask.

George reached over and wiped her tears off her cheek.

"What's the matter, Elizabeth?" he asked.

She shook her head. "I was just thinking about something I should probably try to forget."

"Something or somebody?"

Elizabeth nodded.

George took a deep breath and said, "Let me tell you from personal experience not to let what someone else thinks about you drive you to do something foolish."

"Personal experience, huh?"

George nodded. "That's right. Becky Crabtree was one of the reasons I joined the army. I saw how she fawned over that soldier when we had dinner at their last year. It helped me make my decision to join the army, and it was a big mistake."

"So are you afraid I'm going to join the army?"

George laughed. "Well, at least you're joking about whatever's made you sad. That's a start."

George stood up. Elizabeth noticed that he moved slowly like a much older man. She wondered if George had other injuries besides his arm.

"George, am I too much of a tomboy?" Elizabeth asked.

George stopped and looked at her. "I've never known a tomboy to wear a dress."

"It's more than that. How many ladies drive mules or steer canal boats?"

George pointed to his mother standing at the tiller of the *Freeman*.

"Mama does both those things, and she's the truest lady I know. You could do a lot worse than to be like her," he said.

Elizabeth stared at her mother for a moment and nodded. George was right. Still, even her mother wanted her to be more lady-like. What could she do to become more lady-like?

"Thank you, George," said Elizabeth.

He walked away to the mule shed. She watched him go inside the small stable and then stared out over the canal.

How could she become a lady on the canal?

No one questioned her mother and whether she was a lady, but her mother considered Grace Sampson a lady. Grace lived a completely different life from her mother. How could they both be ladies?

Elizabeth watched the boat traffic back up at Georgetown because there weren't enough coastal schooners to take on all the coal that had come down from Cumberland.

The delay made her mother even more nervous about leaving Tony in Cumberland with his mother. She considered Tony her son now and didn't want him to be with the woman in Cumberland who had claimed him only because she thought she could earn money from his labors.

Elizabeth took advantage of the delay and walked into town to the Sampsons' Georgetown home. The Pennsylvania couple lived in a three-story brick home on Union Street when they were in Washington City. Elizabeth thought it was a lovely home with white shuttered windows, white curtains and window boxes that were filled with flowers during the season.

Elizabeth knocked on the door. Chesapeake, the Sampsons' butler, quickly answered it. He was an older, free black man who worked for the Sampsons. He wore his familiar gray suit that matched his gray hair. He smiled when he saw Elizabeth.

"Good morning, Miss Elizabeth," he said.

"Hello, Chess. Is Mrs. Sampson home?" Elizabeth asked.

He nodded. "She is indeed. Come inside, and I'll announce you."

Chess opened the door wider, and Elizabeth stepped into the foyer.

Chess walked up the wide staircase to the second floor. Elizabeth studied the paintings around her as she waited. Besides being a congressman from Pennsylvania, Eli Sampson was a painter as well. He typically painted scenes from his home state so that he could always be reminded of the people he represented while he was in Washington City.

"Elizabeth!"

Elizabeth looked up the stairs and saw Grace Sampson hurrying down. Grace was one of Alice Fitzgerald's oldest friends. She stood in front of Elizabeth and hugged her tightly.

"Oh, I'm so happy to see you!" Grace said.

Elizabeth hadn't visited since right after a Confederate sniper had killed Abel last October while he was guarding the Alexandria Aqueduct.

"Did your mother come with you?" Grace asked.

"No, ma'am. I'm alone. I kind of felt the need to come visit you. I've been thinking about Abel a lot lately," Elizabeth explained.

Grace nodded. "Well, come into the sitting room, and we'll talk."

She ushered Elizabeth into one of the rooms off the foyer. A large fireplace against the far wall had a family portrait of Grace, Eli, and Abel. Heavy drapes covered the tall front window. They were drawn back, however, so that the room was bright with sunlight.

"Chess, could you fix us some tea?" Grace said over her shoulder.

"Certainly, ma'am. I'll be back right shortly," the butler said.

Elizabeth took a seat on the sofa, trying not to stare in awe at the fabric. She wasn't used to such expensive furniture. It was even nicer than the furniture in the Armentrouts' home had been. Grace sat down in a wooden rocking chair that had a plump cushion on the seat.

"What is troubling you, Elizabeth? You don't seem your normal, cheery self," Grace said.

Elizabeth sighed. "I really liked Abel. He wasn't anything like I thought a rich boy would be like. I found that I wanted to be a lady around him."

Grace gave her a slight smile. "Abel was a wonderful son. I wish more people in the world could be like him. Maybe we wouldn't be fighting this war then."

"When he was killed, I was upset for a long time. Then earlier this year I met a boy who reminded me a lot of Abel. He even seemed a lot like Abel at first, then he suddenly stopped talking to me. His mother said I was beneath him. I wasn't good enough for him."

Grace put her hand to her mouth. "That's a horrible thing to tell someone, but unfortunately there are people out there like that. It doesn't mean anything."

"Doesn't it? I know I'm not sophisticated like you, but I was never ashamed of who I was before now," Elizabeth said.

Grace took hold of Elizabeth's hand. "You shouldn't be ashamed. You have a wonderful family."

"Did Abel ever think of me as being beneath him?"

"Oh, no, Elizabeth. He was in love with you. He wanted you to be proud of him. I'll tell you something else. He complained a lot about being part of the Aqueduct Defense rather than a regular unit, but he liked being there because you saw him on duty when the *Freeman* went by. He thought it helped impress you that he was a good man."

The Aqueduct Defense was an army unit that patrolled the Alexandria Aqueduct to make sure the Confederate Army didn't use it as a path to invade Washington City. The aqueduct used to take canal boats across the Potomac River to a seven-mile branch canal whose tidelock was in Alexandria. Near the beginning of the war, the aqueduct had been closed and drained.

"I knew he was a good man from the first night I met him. It wasn't because of the uniform he wore. It was because he treated me well. He listened to my opinions and didn't make fun of them, but he also didn't take himself too seriously."

Grace nodded. "He had a talent for doing things like that. He gets it from his father. He would have grown into a great man," she said with a mix of pride and sadness.

Elizabeth began crying. "Why did he have to die? He was so good. Things were so much clearer when he was around."

Grace came across the room and hugged Elizabeth. "Things will clear up again, dear. This confusion won't last forever, but you'll have to learn to grasp those moments in life when everything is clear and right and enjoy them."

"I feel so ashamed now that I am who I am."

Grace grabbed Elizabeth's chin and turned the girl's face toward her.

"Don't you do that! Don't you let that boy and his mother win. The only way you will be below them is if you let them push you down there. Don't do it!"

"Then what do I do?"

"You find a way to be happy with whom you are. If you look inside yourself and you find...*you* find...there is a change that you need to make, then you find a way to accomplish it. I think, though, that when you do look inside yourself, you will find yourself not lacking," Grace explained.

Elizabeth smiled weakly. "You sound like my mother."

"Maybe she sounds like me."

Elizabeth laughed. "You two should have been sisters."

"We are. Sometimes your closest relations don't share the same name."

Elizabeth nodded. "You're right. It's like Tony and David."

"Tony and David?"

"Oh, that's right. You haven't met them. They are living with us now."

Grace arched her eyebrows. "I detect a story waiting to be told. You will have to tell me all about them over lunch."

Grace led Elizabeth to the kitchen, and they spent an hour talking over sandwiches. When Elizabeth headed back to the basin about one-thirty, she felt happy for the first time in weeks.

Grace had a talent for putting people at ease. It was a talent that Elizabeth wished she had. Maybe that was the change she should work on developing in herself.

Elizabeth smiled at herself.

36

A New Life

May 1863

Michael slumped against Hanna, a seven-year-old canal mule, as she walked along the towpath near Hancock. He was working on four hours sleep, and the blisters on his feet made each step feel like he was walking on nails.

"Don't hold her back, Mikey," Captain Howell called. "She's already pulling half a loaded barge. She shouldn't have to pull you along, too."

Michael took a deep breath and stood straight up. He clenched his jaw shut and held it in place. He wasn't going to yell or cry. Edward had already teased him for being a crybaby.

The brass horn blew the opening notes of "Red Rover," which signaled they were approaching a lock. Michael squinted into the distance, but he couldn't see the lock. It would be there, though. Jack Howell knew the canal like he did his boat. He could talk you through the entire length of the canal, lock by lock, level by level, turn by turn.

"We'll switch teams at this lock, Mikey," Jack called.

"Yes, sir."

Michael spotted the lockhouse and lock as the canal turned. The gates were open and set for a loaded boat. Jack straightened out the canal boat and put it in line for the lock. As the mules reached the lock, Michael stopped them walking to allow the *Annabelle* to coast into the lock.

Edward Howell tossed a snubbing line to Collin McNabb, the lockkeeper. McNabb caught it and wrapped it around the snubbing

215

post, a wooden post about eighteen inches around set into the earth next to the lock. Edward took a second snubbing line and jumped onto the shore on the north side of the canal. He also wrapped his rope around a snubbing post.

When the *Annabelle* was about halfway into the lock, the two men began to tighten their lines. The boat slowed even more until it stopped just before it crashed into the downriver lock doors.

Michael jumped on board and laid out the fall board. He led the second pair of canal mules, Mutt and Joe, onto the towpath. Then he unhitched Hanna and Half Step and led them across the fall board and into the mule shed. He hurried back outside and hitched Mutt and Joe up to the tow line, making sure the harness pads sat as comfortably as they could in the mules' necks.

From this point on, they were Edward's responsibility. Michael ran back on board and pulled the fall board onto the boat. He went inside the mule shed to begin to brush, feed, and clean the mules.

He patted them each on the neck. "You both did well today. I was surprised at how quickly you were able to get the boat started. You two are feeling strong today."

The mules worked hard pulling the boat. He had watched them strain to start a loaded boat that sat dead in the water. They deserved to be treated well when they weren't working.

He filled the feed bin first because the mules would be hungry after pulling the boat for six hours. While they were eating he picked the dirt from their hoofs and made sure their shoes were tight and not wearing too thin. He scraped the sweat from the coats and then brushed them

He talked to Hanna and Half Step while he worked. Sometimes he spoke of his pains in adjusting to the way things worked on the canal. Other times he talked about his family or Elizabeth.

"My mother didn't think I could learn anything from someone below my station. I wonder what she would say if she could see what you two have taught me about patience and caring," Michael said with a laugh.

The time he spent in the mule shed taking care of the mules was the part of his job Michael liked the most. The mules weren't as judgmental as people were. They appreciated Michael's hard work on their behalf, and they worked just as hard for him when they were on the towpath.

Michael then carried the harnesses out into the warm air. He had quickly learned that one of the keys to having a canal boat run smoothly was the harness. Edward was careless in the way he fit the harness to the mules, and it showed at times. It was one reason why Michael harnessed the mules instead of leaving it for Edward. Michael saw the harness as a mule's set of clothes. A suit should be made to fit the man, and a harness should be made to fit the mule that wore it.

He wondered what his father would say if he saw that his son was using the fashion principles he had been taught to fit harnesses to mules.

The first thing Michael always checked was how the padding in the harness held up. Once a mule started on a six-hour trick, it was leaning against that padding nearly all of the time, particularly when it was moving a canal boat from a dead stop. If the padding wasn't thick enough or if it got too compacted from constant pressure, the mules would get sores on their shoulders and not pull as hard because it would hurt them.

Michael had noticed that even this early in the season Mutt had sores because Edward had been careless about caring for the harnesses. That was why Michael had started harnessing all of the mules. He made sure Mutt's harness fit properly, and Michael gave the mule's shoulder extra attention when Mutt finished his tricks.

Mutt didn't get all of Michael's attention. He made sure to loosen the harnesses a bit when the mules were stopped at a lock. He would wipe the leather and mules' shoulders free from sweat because the moisture helped the harnesses slip and cause sores.

He would let the harnesses dry from the mule sweat while he scraped and brushed the mules. Then he would oil the harness pads to keep the leather supple, which also helped the mules' shoulders.

He finished his work with the mules and walked to the family cabin for a cup of water and something to eat. Because no one on the *Annabelle* knew how to cook well, their fare was simple. It was far from the meals Michael had eaten at home, but he didn't mind. He had grown used to meats with no sauces, boiled vegetables, and fresh bread only when they bought it at the locks.

"You take good care of the mules," Jack said as Michael turned to go downstairs to the family cabin.

Michael stopped and looked up to the captain. "Thank you. The

Annabelle won't move if the mules can't pull, so I try to make sure they can."

Michael was just pleased that the captain had noticed the extra care he took with the mules. He might not know everything about the canal or do things fast, but what he did do; he did as well as he could without taking shortcuts.

If only his father and mother could recognize such small details. Michael was their son after all. They had known him all his life. Jack had only known him for two months, but he noticed more in Michael than Michael's own parents.

Jack said, "Well, you keep it up, Mikey. You're turning into a good canawler."

Michael decided that it was time to bring up another idea he had been thinking about lately. He walked up to the quarterdeck and stood next to Jack Howell.

"Jack, I have an idea that I wanted to tell you about," Michael said.

"Take the rudder for a moment, Mikey. I want to fill my pipe," Jack said.

Michael put his hand on the rudder. It was the first time he had been in control of the canal boat. True, they weren't going through a lock or doing any steering that required skill, but he was in control of the *Annabelle* if only for a few moments. It was a beginning.

Jack filled his pipe with tobacco and lit it. Then he leaned back against the railing and put his hand back on the rudder. Michael reluctantly released his control.

"So what is your grand idea?" Jack asked.

"The lockkeepers sell fish that they catch in nets across the waste weirs." Jack nodded. "And they make a nice bit of spare money from it."

"Not from canawlers. They sell most of the fish to townspeople or eat it themselves."

"But they do make some money," Michael said. "We could make some money ourselves if we drag a net behind or off to the side of the boat. It would catch some fish, and we could sell what we don't eat. We could even keep them fresh by filling another barrel with water and leaving the fish we don't eat in it until we can sell them in one of the towns we pass through."

Jack ran his hand over his beard and puffed on his pipe.

"Do you think it will really work?" Jack asked.

Michael shrugged. "I don't know, but it would only cost us a net. We can get one fairly inexpensively in Georgetown. If we can't make the money back from the fish we catch, then I'll pay for the net."

"That sounds sure to me. I'll tell you what, Michael. Since it's your idea, I'll buy the net. We'll split whatever we make in half," Jack said.

He held out his hand, and Michael shook it. He wanted to cheer, but he refrained. He didn't want to appear childish to Jack after having struck a business deal with his captain.

Michael turned to walk back into the family cabin. He smiled broadly. He might just be able to make a life for himself on the canal after all.

37

HOME AGAIN

JUNE 1863

Tony sat on a wooden bench behind the bar in McKenney's Tavern. It was so low that when he was seated, Tony couldn't see what was happening beyond the bar. His position kept him below most of the thick tobacco smoke that filled the bar. Carter McKenney split his attention between serving drinks to the crowd of canallers and railroaders and glaring at Tony.

Tony stuck his legs out and leaned back against the wall to relax. He knew Carter couldn't maintain a constant vigil over both him and his tavern. It was just a matter of time before something happened that would force Carter to make a choice between keeping order in his bar or earning the dollar Carol had given him to watch Tony.

Tony could wait.

The crowd was heavy tonight and loud. It was a dangerous mix of men, which is why Tony was content to wait for things to happen. His plan was to create problems for his mother not run away from her.

He'd been doing his best to make her life miserable this past week. He refused her requests. He wouldn't talk to her. He ate her food.

One refusal had brought him more pleasure than he wanted to admit. Five days ago, his mother had planned for a night of work. She had said it was because she wanted to collect extra money for all the trouble caring for Tony had caused her.

"Tony, get under the bed. I'll be back in a few minutes with a man friend," Carol had said.

Tony had glanced at the bed and the small space beneath it. He felt his skin crawl. Under the bed was the last place he wanted to be. He was not that boy thief anymore. He wasn't even sure he would fit under the bed since he had put on some size during his time with the Fitzgeralds.

"No," Tony had said.

His mother hadn't understood his answer. "What do you mean, no?"

She had continued to dress in her tight red dress and had painted her face with creams and powders to hide the Shanty Town wear in her face.

"I mean I'm not getting under that bed," Tony had said.

He had crossed his arms across his chest and had stood defiantly at the foot of the bed. His posture had dared his mother to force him under the bed, which she couldn't do. She needed a cooperative partner for the theft to work.

"You have to. I'm your mother," Carol had said.

Tony hadn't moved. "I don't have to. You might be able to make me get under that bed now, but I wouldn't be under it when you get back from downstairs with your man friend, and I certainly wouldn't steal the man's money for you," he had said.

Carol had been flustered. She was in a hurry to get downstairs to pick out her mark before the most-willing men were taken by her competition.

"If you don't get under there, you won't get any food this evening," Carol had said.

It had been an empty threat because Tony had learned to be independent in his months away from his mother. He wasn't scared that he might starve or be alone in Shanty Town. He knew that he could feed himself and he knew that his family was coming for him.

Tony had shrugged. "Maybe I won't get food from you, but I can find my own food. Besides, what you feed me isn't all that great anyway."

"If you don't get under there, I'll beat you."

Tony had shaken his head. "You wouldn't want me bruised. That would endanger your chances of getting any money from Mrs. Fitzgerald."

Carol had fumed, but she had given in because she couldn't think of anything to do with him. She could hold Tony against his will, but she had nothing to use to force Tony to cooperate with her.

So her money had dwindled during the week Tony had been staying with her because she couldn't work and she couldn't let Tony out of her sight for fear of him running away. This had led to her idea of having Carter McKenney watch him. It would cost her a sizable part of the money she made tonight, but at least she would make something.

Then again, if Tony had anything to do with it, maybe not.

Tony yawned and stretched his arms over his head. His motion caught Carter's attention. The big man turned and glared at him.

"You just sit there, boy, or I might have to take my club to you," Carter said.

"No, you won't. I'd tell the sheriff," Tony replied.

They might have him, but they had to be very careful what they did with him. Tony was so tickled with the position of power they had placed him in that he nearly laughed.

"Not if I knock all of the teeth out of your head," Carter growled.

Tony shook his head. "Oh, it won't be me who would complain to the sheriff. You see, he's got a bit of a financial interest in me right now. If I were to suddenly turn up all beat up, it would harm my value to him. So hit me. Sheriff Whittaker will toss you in his jail pretty quick."

Carter scowled, unsure of whether to believe Tony or not.

"You just sit there," he said finally. Then he turned back to his work. He poured whiskey into empty glasses and collected coins from his customers.

Tony leaned back and relaxed.

A shout amid the crowd caught Tony's attention. He started to raise himself up, but Carter put a hand on his shoulder and pushed him back down.

The liquor and animosity had kicked in as Tony heard more shouts and something or someone crash into a table. After that, all hell broke loose in the tavern. Carter grabbed his club and went around the bar to break up the fight.

It was just what Tony had been waiting for.

He peeked over the edge of the bar and watched the fight going on in the middle of the saloon. About eight men swung fists and kicked feet at each other. They were a thrashing mass of bodies. Carter was in the middle of the group, trying to pull them apart before they busted up the tables and chairs.

Bent over, Tony walked to the opposite end of the bar. He peeked over the edge again to make sure Carter was still occupied. At the moment, Carter was lying on his back on the floor, trying to keep from being swarmed over.

Tony hurried around the end of the bar and up the stairs to the rooms above the tavern. He walked down the hallway until he reached the door to Carol's room.

He knocked loudly on the door. He heard a grumble from inside the room, but no one said anything. He rapped again.

"Go away," a man's voice said.

"I'm looking for my mother, Carol," Tony said.

He heard a flurry of whispers from inside the room. The door cracked open, and Tony saw his mother through the gap with a sheet wrapped around her.

"How'd you get up here?" she asked.

"I walked up the stairs," Tony said innocently.

"What about Carter? I paid him to watch you."

"He's busy downstairs right now."

"What do you want?"

He tried to push his way into the room, but Carol blocked him.

"I want to come in," Tony said.

"Go away," she whispered harshly.

"If you really want me to. I'd be very glad to."

He turned away and headed back down the hallway toward the door that led outside. He could leave now and always argue that his mother had told him to go away.

As he reached the door, Carol realized her mistake and called, "No, wait, get back here."

Tony sighed and walked to his mother. She grabbed him by the arm and pulled him into the room. He didn't resist.

"You think you're going to get away from me that easy. Well, you've got some learning yet to do, little boy," Carol said.

Tony looked over at the bed and saw a burly looking man lying there. The man had more hair on his chest than a lot of people had on their heads.

"Who's the brat?" the man asked.

"He's my…" Carol started to say. She paused, and Tony could tell she was preparing to lie.

"I'm her son," Tony said quickly.

"Your son? I thought you said that you were twenty-one!" the man said.

Tony laughed loudly. "You must really be drunk, mister, if you think she's twenty-one years old! By the way, are you my daddy?"

The man jumped out of bed, not caring if he exposed himself or not. He quickly grabbed his pants and pulled them up to his waist.

"I don't know what kind of scam you're running here, woman, but I'm not having any of it. You're not going to peg me as this kid's father and try to get money from me," the man said.

Carol rushed over to him and tried to hug him. He pushed her away so that she fell on the bed.

"He's not my son! He's just some brat off the street. Don't leave! I'll send him back downstairs in just a couple minutes!" Carol said.

"I want my money back."

Carol shook her head. "No! We were in bed."

"But we hadn't gotten to the part that I paid for. Now give me my money, or I'll take it."

The man held out his hand. Carol stared at it and then at the man. She reluctantly dug the money out of her purse and handed it over.

The man put his shirt on and left without buttoning it. Tony looked over at his mother.

"You should have let me go when you had the chance," he said.

Carol glared at him. "When those canallers get back, I am going to throw you at them. If they want to deal with you, let them. Good riddance!"

Tony smiled.

38

GEORGE

JUNE 1863

George held the snubbing line in his remaining hand and tried to turn and lower it onto the cargo hatches. Instead of coiling into a neat pile, the rope tumbled every which way. The resulting pile looked no better than what he could have done when he was six-years old.

He sighed and threw the rope down in disgust. Thomas could coil it later.

"Here, let me help you," Alice said.

She quickly coiled the rope into a neat circular pile on top of the hatch cover.

"I suppose you expect me to thank you for helping me," George said when his mother finished.

Alice shook her head. "No, I was just trying to help out."

"Because I'm a cripple."

"No, because you needed help."

"I don't need help!"

George turned and stalked away to the mule shed. Ocean and Bargain were inside. Jigger and Seamus were pulling the empty boat back to Cumberland. He slipped inside the shed and patted the mules. He couldn't pick their hooves with only one hand, but he could still do something. He picked up a brush and began to groom Bargain.

George felt next to useless. If one of these mules had lost a limb, it would have been put down. People were different, though. They were expected to be useful even when they weren't. What was he supposed to do without two good arms?

"George," Alice said from the entrance to the mule shed.

He ignored her.

"George, you lost an arm, not an ear," Alice said after a few moments of silence.

"What do you want?" George asked.

"I want to know why you were so rude to me out there."

"I could have coiled that rope."

"Yes, but you were having trouble, so I helped you. What is wrong with that?"

George spun around and shouted, "What's wrong is that I didn't have a chance to do it because you didn't let me!"

Alice sighed. "What would you have me do? Should I watch you struggle and get frustrated over a simple thing that I could do?"

"I don't know! It's simple for you, but I don't know what I can do!"

Alice walked down into the mule shed. She walked over to George and hugged him. George tried to pull free from his mother, but she only hugged him tighter.

"I love you with or without your arm, George," Alice said.

"Well, I don't love me."

That surprised Alice enough that George was able to break free from her hug. He turned and hurried out of the mule shed onto the race plank. Where could he get away from his mother on the *Freeman*, though? The boat was large, but there were few places for people.

He walked around to the front of the mule shed and sat down on the quarterdeck, hoping that his mother wouldn't see him for at least another few minutes.

He felt so useless! The doctors had told him that he would adapt to not having one of his hands, but it wasn't happening. Whenever he tried to do something nowadays, he only proved to himself that he was of less use than a child was.

"You can pilot the *Freeman*. You can drive mules. You can operate a lock."

George's head jerked around, and he saw his mother standing behind him.

"What?" he asked.

"You said you didn't know what you could do so I'm telling you some of the things you can do," Alice explained.

George shook his head. "It's not enough."

"Why not? It's enough to make a living. That's more than some

226

people with two hands can do," his mother told him.

George scowled.

Alice said, "I guess that's not what you're truly worried about then."

The *Freeman* floated to a stop. George looked out onto the towpath where David was driving the mules. He was were stopped and talking to Peter Miller, the lockkeeper from Lock 44. That surprised George because they were nearly a mile from the lock.

"Alice, we've got a problem," David called back to the boat.

"What's wrong?" she asked.

"Peter says the Confederates came across the river yesterday. They are on their way north somewhere but not before they try and do some damage to the canal," David said.

"Filthy rebels," George muttered.

Alice put a hand on his shoulder to calm him.

"Are they letting boats through?" Alice asked.

Miller stepped forward. He was a round man with a bald head. He said, "Of course not, Alice. We're lucky they haven't burned the ones that are nearby. Some of the men want to try, but the captain in charge won't let them. He sees the canal as a military target, but not the boats."

"What should we do?"

"There's nothing you can do except not get too close to them in case they change their minds about burning boats. That's why I'm out here. I'm trying to warn off boats. I've already stopped the eastbound ones. The *Freeman* is the first westbound boat. I'm warning you so you can warn the boats that come behind you about what's happening."

Alice slapped her hand against the roof of the family cabin. She was hoping to be back in Cumberland in three days so she could retrieve Tony from his mother. Now they might be stuck here for a week or more.

"The Rebs will blow up the aqueduct, and we'll be sitting in an empty canal until the Canal Company can get the patches in place," George said.

That was one of Alice's fears. They had lost a lot of time last year because of damage to the canal. If the Confederates succeeded in destroying an aqueduct here, her family might be delayed a month until repairs could be made.

David stared at Alice. "You're worried about Tony, aren't you?"

227

Alice nodded. "We can't be stuck here. He's waiting for us."

David sighed and stared at his feet for a few moments. He shook his head and muttered to himself. Alice wondered what could have made him so upset.

"Peter, how many men are there?" David asked.

Peter shrugged. "It looks like the whole damn army to me."

"How many are on the canal trying to damage it?"

Peter threw up his hands. "I don't know, maybe a dozen along the aqueduct and a few more spread out along the way looking for other ways to disrupt things. I'm worried that they'll destroy my lock. That would be a lot easier than trying to blow up the aqueduct."

"I assume since there's still water in the canal that they're not having much luck," David said.

"That's right. They're more interested in raiding the stores for food and supplies. I tell you, some of those soldiers are looking mighty ragged. If they hadn't taken the food stores from my house, I would have been tempted to feed them."

George jumped to the railing and yelled, "You wouldn't have!"

"Of course, I would have, George," Miller said. "I've got a sister that lives in Shepherdstown. My nephews could be part of that army. It's not the men who are angry. It's the governments. They just use the men to do their fighting."

George could tell Peter Miller about angry men. He had seen the savagery they inflicted on each other. He had seen them rifle the pockets of men slain on the battlefield. They were more than pawns in the war. They were active participants.

"Is there anything we can do?" Alice asked.

David nodded. "I think there is, but first I want to take a look at how spread out the soldiers on the canal are."

"How can you do anything?" George asked.

Who did David think he was? Did he think he could scare away the Rebs just because he had two good arms?

Miller ignored George and said, "I can show you. The main army is north of Williamsport, though they come into town to confiscate any food they can find. The ones on the canal are patrolling between my lock and the aqueduct. They're not bothering canawlers much unless they suspect you're armed."

"I won't be…at least not now," David said.

Alice said, "David, don't do anything foolish."

228

David smiled at her. "I won't. I'm just going to walk up the canal a bit and take a look around."

He clapped Miller on the back, and the two of them began to walk away. George watched, tempted to go with them, but what good would a one-armed, ex-soldier be to them?

He wanted to cry.

39

IMPERSONATION

JUNE 1863

Peter Miller halted David by holding his hand out in front of him. Peter pointed to the side of the towpath, and both men hurried to the side.

"They're just up ahead," Miller whispered. "How close do you want to get?"

"As close as possible. Can we walk through to the eastbound boats? I want to see how many officers are mixed in with the men. Didn't you say they won't bother us as long as we aren't armed?"

Miller nodded. "So far."

David tugged at his beard. It changed his looks enough that at least at a casual glance no one should recognize him. He didn't have to worry about being seen by a soldier who knew him.

"Let's take a walk," David said.

"I can think of things I would rather do."

David couldn't argue with that. He also had no right to endanger Miller when David didn't know what he was going to do.

"So could I. You stay here. I'll be back in about an hour, and we'll need to talk about plans then," David said.

"Plans? What plans?"

Sweat broke out on Miller's forehead and the top of his head.

"We need to get to Cumberland. Tony's waiting for us in some unpleasant circumstances. We're going to clear out these boats to-night and get everyone on their way," David explained.

"The soldiers will come after you and the other boats," Miller said.

David shook his head. "No, they won't. The boats are only a small piece of what they want. They would rather destroy the aqueduct than sink a boat, and they would rather accomplish their reason for crossing the river than destroy the aqueduct."

"How do you know that?"

David stared at him. Miller gulped "Sorry, I don't think of you like that," he said, referring to David's history as a soldier for the Confederacy.

David smiled. "Thank you."

"That being said, I think you're crazy to walk into a hornet's nest."

David stood up and walked onto the towpath. "I've wondered about that a few times myself."

He started to walk and noticed Miller beside him. "I thought you could think of better things to do," David said.

Miller nodded. "That's right, but I'd rather think of them while I'm walking and not sitting around wondering if the Confederates have arrested you."

David smiled. "Appreciate the company."

They approached the first pair of soldiers camped across the towpath. One man lounged around resting on the ground. The second man fished in the canal with a piece of string tied to one end of a broken branch.

"Hey, Lockkeeper! I see you picked up someone on your walk," one of the soldiers said.

"Just one of the canawlers you've stranded," Miller said.

"He'll be sitting in an empty canal once the powder gets here to blow up the aqueduct," the soldier said.

"Just leave my house alone, please."

The soldier nodded. "Sure. There's nothing to be gained by blowing your house up."

"Thank you."

Miller and David walked on. They passed the lock and another group of four men. Then they crossed the aqueduct. A pair of men was stationed on each end. The men were scattered around, and they were resting until another group came from town with a wagonload of black powder. Beyond the aqueduct, three boats and crews waited to see what would happen, and there would probably be more by this evening.

The first boat was the *Larkspur*. David walked up to the boat and saw the captain. Three men ran this boat. It was one of Amos Lewis's boats.

"Captain O'Shea, I'm David Windover. I did some work for your boss, Amos Lewis."

Benjamin O'Shea nodded his head toward the aqueduct. "Is it true what they're saying? Are they going to blow the aqueduct into pieces?"

David nodded. "They are going to try, but these aqueducts can withstand a lot." David paused. "Would you like to be on your way?"

The red-haired man squinted at him. "What do you think?"

David grinned. "Be ready then. Tonight will be your opportunity."

"You're daft, man. The sentries will stop us if we try to go through now."

"I have a plan. If it works, we can all be on our way. You'll need to warn anyone coming up the canal, and I'll warn anyone I see coming down the canal. My plan may only be a temporary solution. The soldiers will still be able to control the aqueduct later, and they won't be too happy that we were able to get through."

"What plan would that be? Have you got a way to turn us invisible so we can float past the soldiers?" O'Shea asked.

David shook his head. "I don't want to say right now. Just tell the other crews on the boats behind you to be ready to move once the sun goes down and to be quiet about what they will be doing tonight."

O'Shea nodded. "I guess I'm in trouble no matter what I do. I'd rather attempt to fix things."

"Good. Then we're both of the same mind."

When David returned to the *Freeman,* Alice questioned him about what he had seen. He described the situation to her as he opened his canvas bag and pulled out his old Confederate Army uniform. He laid it out on the table in the family cabin and studied it. It was still in good shape because he hadn't worn it much while he was working on the canal as a guerilla.

"Why did you unpack that?" Alice asked.

"I'm going to make some good come from it."

Alice raised an eyebrow. "How?"

"We need to get to Tony. If the Confederate Army blows up the aqueduct or the lock, it will be a long time before we can get back to Tony. This uniform will help us get to Cumberland."

David picked up the outfit. He walked into the stateroom and pulled the curtain shut behind him.

"It will help you get arrested," Alice said from behind him.

"I'll take the risk."

"Tony's mother won't hurt him, David. She thinks Tony's her way

232

to money she doesn't have to work for," Alice said.

"Tony is counting on us to come back for him."

"We will, but you getting arrested won't help him."

"When I was arrested last year, Tony came for me. I can't do less for him now."

Late last year, a Union patrol had arrested David as a spy and taken him off the *Freeman*. The soldiers had been marching David to Frederick when Tony had helped him escape the camp one night. If Tony could risk his freedom to held David, then David could do no less for Tony now.

"Is this some sort of competition between the two of you to see which one of you can risk his life more for the other one?" Alice asked.

David said, "Why are you upset? I would do this for you or Elizabeth or Thomas."

"I know, but that doesn't make it any less foolish," Alice snapped.

Why did he have to risk himself? What was he trying to prove? No one doubted his loyalty.

"Would you rather just wait and have the aqueduct destroyed?" David asked.

Alice shook her head. "No, but that doesn't mean I have to like it."

David stepped out of the stateroom dressed in his uniform. He raised his hand and put it on her cheek. He wiped away her tears, but then left his hand there. He stared into her eyes, wondering what he should do.

After a moment, David sighed and dropped his hand away.

"I will be careful. Could you heat some water for me? I need to shave my beard and mustache. Otherwise some of the soldiers I saw earlier might recognize me as a canawler."

"Without the beard and mustache, it just means they'll be more likely to recognize you as David Windover, a deserter."

David said nothing because it would get them back into the same argument they had just finished. Alice must have sensed he wasn't going to argue anymore.

"I'll get the water for you," she said.

"Thank you."

David rode up to the aqueduct on a horse he had borrowed from Peter Miller. David was wearing his uniform and looked every bit a Confederate lieutenant. He halted in front of the sentry, a young boy about eighteen years old.

"Who's in charge here, Private?" David asked.

The private saluted and said, "Captain Baker, sir."

"Where can I find him?"

"His tent is next to the lockhouse."

David nodded and walked his horse forward. He held his breath, wondering if the private would challenge him. The man didn't.

David rode up to the lockhouse and dismounted in front of the tent. He looked over at the barrels next to the lock and knew that the black powder had arrived. The tent flaps were open to let a breeze blow through. The captain was sitting at his desk looking at a side drawing of the aqueduct.

"Captain Baker?" David said as he saluted.

The man looked up and rose to his feet. He saluted. "Yes, Lieutenant."

David stepped into the tent. "I'm Lieutenant Windover, I've got some new orders from command. How goes it here?"

"The black powder arrived a short time ago. It's too dark to get to work tonight on the aqueduct, but we'll be right on it tomorrow morning."

"How long will it take?"

"Most of the morning I would expect. It's a well-constructed aqueduct. It will be hard to destroy and a darn shame, too," Baker said.

"But not impossible. We've wasted a lot of effort trying to explode the dams."

Baker shook his head. "I don't think it's impossible. Hard, yes, but we can bring it down if we have some time."

David sighed and shook his head. "I was afraid that was the case."

"Why?"

"You don't have the time. The army is moving out of Williamsport at first light. You need to collect your men now and join with the main force so you can rest a bit before the army marches."

The captain shook his head. "But half a day won't slow us up that much. We can bring the aqueduct down!"

David held up his hands to calm the man. "I agree, but I'm just the messenger here. You have to remember that the aqueduct is not our target. We can't stay here too long, or the Union Army might catch us here and squash us against the river."

Baker was silent but fuming. He wadded up the drawing and threw it out of the tent. Then he took a deep breath and saluted.

"I'll get the men ready on time," Baker said.

"I have every confidence that you will. Just remember that sometimes our short-term goals need to give way to longer-term goals."

Baker nodded. "I understand. I don't like it, but I understand."

"Do you need me to stay around to help you here? I was authorized to do so," David asked.

Baker shook his head. "No, Lieutenant. These are my men. We'll be ready."

David smiled and saluted. He turned and walked away from the tent. He rode back the way he had come. When he was out of sight of the sentries and anyone else in the camp, he circled back and rode the borrowed horse back to the canal.

Peter Miller was waiting for him and took the horse by the reins.

"How did it go?" he asked.

"We'll know for sure in a short time. You should go back to your house and wait. How are the lock doors set?"

"Downstream."

"Fine. When the soldiers leave, come back to the *Freeman*. We'll be ready to move. Once we're out of the lock, we'll send the first upstream boat into the lock and just alternate back and forth until we've got all the boats through."

"What happens when the soldiers come back?" Miller asked.

"They'll be upset, but they'll be looking for me, not you. You should be fine. I'm also guessing that they won't stay in the area long. They didn't cross the river with an army to blow up an aqueduct. They are pushing north, and they won't stay in one place too long until they get where they want to be."

Miller nodded. David shook Miller's hand and walked down the towpath toward the *Freeman*. He came upon George waiting with Ocean and Jigger.

"What are you doing in a Rebel uniform?" George asked.

"I cleared the way for canal boats to get through," David told him.

"But where did you get the uniform?"

"It's mine."

David walked past George and hopped onto the canal boat. Alice was standing on the quarterdeck at the rudder.

"You're safe," Alice said quietly.

"For now."

An hour later Miller appeared carrying a lantern. He stopped to talk to George. George quietly started the mules moving, and Miller hopped onto the boat.

"Your impersonation worked, David. The men moved off a few

minutes ago. I'm guessing it will take them about an hour to reach the main army. Figure a few minutes to find out that they were misled and another hour to get back here," Miller said.

"Is that enough time to get all of the boats through?" David asked.

Miller nodded. "But what do I tell the soldiers when they want to know where all the canal boats have gone?"

"Tell them the truth. Once the soldiers had gone, you got back to work."

Miller nodded. "You know you took a big chance. That captain could have asked you for orders or your credentials. Then what would you have done?"

David shrugged. "I guess I would have run like a scared rabbit."

Miller chuckled. "I like you, David. You may be a bit crazy, but I like you."

The *Freeman* entered the lock, and both David and Miller jumped ashore with the snubbing lines. They worked in silence, and ten minutes later, the *Freeman* moved out of the lock.

The boat passed the *Larkspur* and David waved to Captain O'Shea.

"I'm going ashore," David said to Alice.

"Why?"

"If there's trouble, I can lead off the soldiers and distract them from the boats."

He saw Alice roll her eyes in the dark.

"David, don't."

"I have to. I started all of this. I'll not have someone else finish it. You keep moving, and I'll catch up with you before morning."

He walked down to the race plank. Alice steered the boat toward the bank and David jumped ashore. He waved to her and then started back toward the aqueduct.

He stopped at the lock and helped Miller lock through the boats. He kept his eyes opens for lanterns in the distance that would signal the army returning. After two hours, David stopped working. The army should be returning soon.

"Do you have a rifle?" David asked Miller.

"The soldiers took it."

David unholstered his Navy Colt and checked it. It would only be accurate at close distances, but he could still shoot it into the army if they returned and put a good scare into them.

He walked north until he could see across the road the led into

Williamsport. He waited. He could fire shots to scare the army and warn Miller at the lock.

An hour later, Miller walked up beside him.

"The boats are through," Miller said.

"Good. Where are they?"

"Maybe they didn't check in with a superior officer and just settled down to wait until they supposedly break camp in the morning," Miller suggested.

David nodded. "Could be. I've got to get back to the *Freeman.*"

"Let me ride you back. There won't be anymore boats coming through tonight. They will have been warned off by the boats that we got through the lock."

Miller and David rode double on Miller's horse. They caught up with the *Freeman* about twelve miles further west. David shook Miller's hand and dismounted.

"Thank you. You saved me a lot of time."

"It was the least I could do. You saved a lot of boats tonight."

He wheeled the horse around and started trotting back toward his lockhouse. David walked toward the *Freeman.*

Alice waved to David. She moved the boat close to the shore, and he jumped aboard.

"Are you finished playing hero for the evening?" Alice asked.

"Yes, and this hero's feeling very tired."

"Go get some sleep."

David nodded and started to walk toward the family cabin.

"David."

He stopped and turned around.

Alice said, "I know if Tony was here he would say thank you."

"And I would tell him that's what family does for each other."

40

PAYOFF

JUNE 1863

Tony lay on the floor on a thin blanket in the corner of his mother's room. His mother didn't have company this afternoon. She was drunk, though. She lay on her bed mumbling to herself. Tony stayed quiet in the corner because he didn't want to attract attention to himself. He wouldn't be able to reason with her while she was drunk. He knew this from years of living with her.

Tony heard a knock on the door. He looked up and waited for his mother to answer the knock.

She acted as if she didn't hear it.

Tony heard another knock. When his mother still continued to ignore it, Tony stood up and answered the door.

Sheriff Whittaker stood outside the door, waiting impatiently.

"What took you so long to answer? Do you think I want to be seen standing outside of a whore's door? Where's your mother, boy?" Whittaker said quickly.

Tony stepped back and opened the door wider. Whittaker looked past him and saw Tony's mother on the bed. He shook his head.

Whittaker shook his head. "She would have to be drunk *now*."

He walked into the room and grabbed Carol by the shoulders. He pulled her into a sitting position and gently slapped her cheeks.

Carol saw him. She flipped her hair from her shoulders and smiled at the sheriff. "Two dollars first, big man. Then you will get an evening of pleasure."

Whittaker frowned and slapped her across the face with no hint of gentleness this time. "Sober up!"

Carol began to cry, and Whittaker let her fall back onto the bed. She rolled back and forth holding her cheek.

"How much has she been drinking?" Whittaker asked Tony.

"I don't know how much. She started after dinner and just kept going," Tony answered. That had been three hours ago.

"I'm going to get some coffee for her. You get a bucket of cold water and bring it up here," Whittaker ordered.

"She'll be alright tonight."

"That's too bad because she needs to be sober now. That Fitzgerald woman is back, and she wants to meet this afternoon so she can get you back."

Tony smiled.

Whittaker shook a finger in Tony's face. "Don't smile too wide, boy. That woman is going to pay dearly for you."

Tony walked out of the room to find a bucket of water for Whittaker. He had to find a way to help Mrs. Fitzgerald. She shouldn't have to pay to have him live on board the *Freeman.* She was going to have to pay to help him. It wasn't right.

He walked downstairs and filled a pail of water from the pump behind McKenney's Tavern. He was once again tempted to run. He would be on the *Freeman* in minutes, but Whittaker knew that he would eventually head for the canal boat. It would be the first place he would search. There had to be a way to ensure he could stay with the Fitzgeralds without them having to pay his mother and Sheriff Whittaker.

Tony lugged the full bucket up the stairs to the room. Whittaker was already there. He was holding Carol up and trying to get her to drink a cup of black coffee.

"Set the bucket next to the bed," Whittaker said.

Tony did so and then backed away and leaned against the wall. Whittaker dropped a towel into the bucket until it was soaked through. When it was saturated, he picked the dripping towel out of the bucket and slapped it against Carol's face.

She screamed and thrashed around on wet sheets, but Whittaker held her in place.

"You...you..." Carol muttered.

"Watch your mouth, Carol. There are children present," Whittaker said.

He grinned with pleasure at Carol's discomfort.

239

Whittaker got her to drink some more coffee. When she resisted the coffee, he slapped her with the wet towel again.

The process continued for about fifteen minutes, and Tony stood against the wall watching the whole scene. He wasn't thinking about what he could do to help his mother. She had put herself in this situation by throwing in with Sheriff Whittaker. Tony wanted to help Mrs. Fitzgerald.

"What do you want, Whittaker?" Carol asked finally, pushing away the cup of coffee.

"You've got to make yourself presentable. Alice Fitzgerald is coming to the jail to work out the agreement for Tony in (He glanced at his watch.) two hours. You need to have a clear head to make sure she doesn't cheat you."

Tony had his own opinion of just who was cheating whom.

"Just give her the kid. He's more trouble than he's worth," Carol said.

Whittaker slapped her with his open hand, and she yelled.

"Don't you think to do that! I won't let you back out of this now. We've gone this far, and in a little more than two hours it will be over, and both of us will have more money in our pockets," Whittaker said.

"I just want him gone," Carol said between her sobs.

Whittaker glanced at Tony. "Fine. I'll take him to the jail with me. We'll wait for you there. If you don't show up in time, I'll arrange it so I can sign the papers instead of you. That means I'll get the money...all of the money."

"But I'm the one who's had to watch him for the past week and a half!"

"Then I guess I'll see you at the jail within two hours. I'm sure that you know where it's at. You've been there enough times."

Whittaker grabbed Tony by the arm and pulled him out of the room. Tony didn't say anything to the large man on their walk to the jail. Whittaker was set on taking his revenge against Tony and Mrs. Fitzgerald. He wouldn't be as easily deterred as Carol.

At the jail, Whittaker pushed Tony into one of the cells and locked the door.

"Now we wait and see how much you're worth," Whittaker said.

"It's not how much I'm worth. It's how much a canal boat hand is worth. That's about fifteen dollars a month," Tony told him.

240

Whittaker shrugged. "I can do a lot with seven dollars and fifty cents a month, and if your mother doesn't show up, I certainly won't turn away fifteen dollars."

Carol showed up an hour later. She looked tired, but she was awake and coherent. She was also dressed in her most-modest dress. It was white and had a high neckline, but it still clung tightly to her.

"Sit down and relax," Whittaker said. "I'll get you a cup of coffee."

If the four cups of coffee she had had in her room weren't helping her, Tony doubted one more cup would do much good.

As it neared five o'clock, Whittaker unlocked the door to the jail cell and left it open.

"Harder to sell a prisoner, isn't it?" Tony commented.

Whittaker ignored him and waited.

Alice and David walked into the jail. Alice almost immediately bristled at the sight of the sheriff and Tony's mother. She knew they were robbing her, but she couldn't see a way to stop them. Not if she wanted Tony to stay with her. Whittaker had the law and Carol had Tony.

Then Alice saw Tony sitting on the cot in the cell. She smiled at the boy. It was good to see him again. She had missed him as much as she had missed George when he had been away.

"Hello, Mrs. Fitzgerald. I hope that we'll be able to put this unfortunate situation behind us quickly," Whittaker said. He had a smile on his face that Alice was sure was real because he knew that he would walk away from this meeting a richer man.

"What needs to be done to get Tony back and not have this happen again the next time you want money?" Alice asked calmly.

Whittaker held up a small packet of papers.

"There are two agreements in here. One relinquishes Carol's claims to be Tony's mother and makes you his guardian. The second is an employment agreement that pays Carol Tony's wages. She will invest them for his benefit, of course."

"I doubt that part is in the agreement," David said.

Whittaker glanced at David and just smiled.

"How much are you asking for?" Alice asked.

She was hoping he would simply say Tony's wages. That would be the loophole she was looking for because she could then argue that she didn't pay Tony wages.

"It asks for the going wage for a canal hand to be paid to me, as the go-between for you and Carol. I will then pass on the wages to Carol. It also says that the wages need to be paid for the month ahead and not the month worked," Whittaker said.

"That's not how wages are paid," David said.

Whittaker shrugged. "Well, that's how you will pay them. After all, we wouldn't want you to work Tony hard and then cheat him out of his wages."

"I won't leave Tony again," she said quietly to David.

David started to argue, but Alice laid a hand on his arm to quiet him. She took a five-dollar bill and a ten-dollar bill from her purse and passed them to Sheriff Whittaker. David's bonus from Amos Lewis had come in handy. Whittaker smiled and slid the money into his pocket.

"Now that that is settled, we'll sign these papers and finish our business. Your hand and I can sign as witnesses," said Whittaker.

He passed the papers to Carol and pointed to the places where she needed to sign the different copies of the agreements. Carol's handwriting was poor, and Alice wondered if Carol had ever completed her schooling.

As Carol dipped the pen in the inkwell, Alice watched Tony move up behind the sheriff. He paused momentarily and then gently slid his hands into the sheriff's pockets. Alice held her breath because if Tony were caught now, he would be in deep trouble. Sheriff Whittaker was not a forgiving man.

"How many copies do you have there, Sheriff?" David asked.

What was David doing? The sheriff had been concentrating on Carol signing the papers. Now he was talking and moving around. Then she realized that David was creating a distraction to make it easier for Tony to pick the sheriff's pocket.

"Six. Three copies of each agreement. One for Mrs. Fitzgerald. One for Carol and one to be filed in the courthouse," Whittaker said.

Whittaker straightened up and looked at Alice. She bent over and dipped the pen into the inkwell and then signed the six different documents. She paused to stare at her signature. For all intents and purposes, she was now Tony's mother.

Whittaker looked at the signed papers and smiled. Then he turned to show them to Carol. She grinned and began to rub her fingers as if counting the money she would receive.

"I guess everything is legal now and the boy is yours. I sure hope he's worth what he's going to cost you," Whittaker said.

"We'll be leaving then," Alice said. She had to control her anger; otherwise, she might have wound up in jail if she did the things she was thinking about doing to Sheriff Whittaker and Tony's former mother.

She took Tony by the hand and she, David and Tony walked out of the city jail.

"Thank you, Mrs. Fitzgerald. I'll make it up to you. I promise. This is a start," Tony said when they were outside.

He held out the fifteen dollars to her. She took it and slid it into her purse. She wanted to scold him for picking the sheriff's pocket, but the sheriff had only stolen the money from her.

"That was a very dangerous thing to do, Tony," Alice said.

"I think we'd better hurry along. Once the sheriff realizes the money is gone, he's not going to have to think hard about where it is," David said.

They began walking quickly along Mechanic Street toward the Canal Basin. David and Tony kept glancing over their shoulders to see if they were being followed.

"Mrs. Fitzgerald, I have to get a few things before we leave. Can I meet you back at the *Freeman* in a little bit?" Tony asked.

"Are you going to be getting into trouble?" she asked.

Tony shrugged. "I hope not."

Alice sighed and nodded. Tony grinned and turned and disappeared down an alley.

"What do you think he's going to do?" Alice asked.

"I haven't a clue. He's lived a life as different from mine as I can imagine," David said.

"And yet, look at how devoted you are to each other."

They walked to the basin and climbed onto the boat. Alice took the papers she had signed and stored them with other family papers she kept in a metal box under her bunk.

"Sheriff's coming, Alice," David called from outside.

It hadn't taken long for him to search his pockets and find them empty.

She walked outside to stand on the quarterdeck by the rudder. The sheriff stomped his way toward the boat with Carol a short distance behind him. She had to jog to keep up with him because he was walking so fast. Sheriff Whittaker stopped before coming onto the boat.

"Where's my money?" he demanded.

"How should I know where your money is?" Alice said.

"I put it in my pocket when you were signing those papers, and now it's gone."

"Maybe you have a hole in your pocket," David suggested.

Sheriff Whittaker turned to glare at him, but David just glared back.

"I thought the money you put into your pocket was Carol's," Alice said.

The sheriff pointed at Alice. "Your boy took it. I want to see him now. If he's got my...Carol's money on him, he'll spend the night in the jail."

"Tony's not here right now," Alice said.

"What do you mean he's not here? He left the jail with you."

Alice nodded. "He did, but he said he had...a few errands to run before we left."

"He's spending that money no doubt." Sheriff Whittaker looked around, trying to decide what to do. "I'll be back later. You had better have the fifteen dollars to return to me. If not, you're violating our agreement, and those papers might not get filed at the courthouse."

He turned to leave and grabbed Carol by the arm to pull her along with him. She whined in pain from his grip on her arm.

"So what have we accomplished except angering a man who can make life difficult for us?" Alice asked. She sighed and leaned against the railing.

"We got Tony away from his mother. You've given him a new life. I'd say you've accomplished a lot," David replied.

She shook her head. "And the first thing Tony does with that new life is get himself in trouble with the town sheriff."

Tony returned to the *Freeman* about an hour later. He was grinning widely. He handed Alice a roll of papers.

"What's this?" she asked.

"Look at them," he said.

Alice opened the roll. It was the other copies of the adoption agreement and the financial agreement that they had signed at the jail.

"Tony, why did you take these? I can't keep you officially until these papers are filed in the courthouse," Alice asked.

Tony shook his head. "Unless I misunderstood, the only paper that

244

needs to be filed in the courthouse is the adoption agreement. You can do that because you've got all the copies."

"And the other agreement?"

"If it's not filed, you can't be forced to pay the sheriff and my mother any money for me. That was their agreement by the way. They are splitting the money."

"Tony…"

"This way you don't have to pay anything for me. It's not right. Things will be like they were before," Tony said.

"You know the sheriff will come looking for this and for you," Alice told him as she looked through the papers. She now had all of the sets to both the financial, and more importantly, the guardian agreements.

Tony nodded. "I thought I might stay in the pantry until we leave. By then, you can file the agreement at the courthouse, and the sheriff can't do anything about it. He's not going to make too much of a fuss about the payment agreement because it will make him look bad if it comes out that he was getting part of the money."

Thomas rushed into the room. "The sheriff's coming, Mama, and boy, does he look mad."

"Go back outside, Thomas, and see if you can stall him," Alice said.

Thomas turned on his heels and quickly ran back outside. He knew Tony's safety was at stake.

Alice quickly threw open the pantry doors. Tony sat down and kicked the false wall back. Then he slid under the bottom shelf. They didn't have time to remove things and replace them.

Outside, she could hear the sheriff yelling at Thomas and David as he tried to come on board.

Once Tony was inside the hidden area behind the pantry, Alice handed him the papers.

"Hold onto those," she said as Tony slid the wall back into place.

Sheriff Whittaker stormed onto the boat. He slammed open the door to the family cabin without pausing to knock.

"Where is he?" Whittaker demanded.

"A gentleman would have knocked first, but seeing who it is, I understand," Alice said.

Whittaker ignored her. He parted the curtain and looked in the stateroom. Then he opened the doors to the pantry and looked inside.

245

"Where is he?" he yelled.

"He who?" Alice asked coyly.

Sheriff Whittaker spun around and glared at her. "Don't you play innocent with me! Where's your newest brat!"

Then his hand quickly snaked out and slapped her. Alice gave a startled yelp. She started to pull away, but Whittaker grabbed onto her arm.

"Oh, you made a mistake this time. We're not playing games here. No one makes a fool of Lee James Whittaker. I'll throw you in my jail and treat you like the rest of the whores," Whittaker said in a cold voice.

Alice drew her free hand back to slap him, but he squeezed her arm, and she winced in pain. He gave her a hard shake and pulled her closer to him.

She was suddenly scared because she realized Whittaker wasn't playing the part of the sheriff any longer. He was an angry beast who meant to hurt her because he had been cheated from his prize.

Then she heard a loud click.

Whittaker heard it, too. He loosened his grip on her and looked up.

"You'd better put that away," he said.

Alice looked over her shoulder and saw David standing in the doorway of the family cabin aiming his army pistol at Sheriff Whittaker's head.

"You'd better let her go," David said.

Whittaker grinned. "You won't shoot."

"Why not? You are assaulting a woman of good reputation. Where I come from being shot would be the best you could hope for."

Alice was surprised at the sound of David's voice. He sounded just as cold as the sheriff had seemed a few moments earlier.

Whittaker said, "I'm the sheriff."

"Then you should know better. Now let her go."

Whittaker opened his hand. Alice quickly backed away. David stepped into the room, still aiming his pistol at Whittaker.

"I want Tony," Whittaker said.

"Tony hasn't come back," Alice said calmly.

"Well, he outsmarted himself this time. He stole our documents. If they aren't filed, the agreement is not legal. I'll haul him out of here and make sure he spends his time with his mother from now on. We'll see how he likes that."

"I still have my paper that says it is all right for Tony to be with me," Alice said.

"It's not in force yet."

"But it will be tomorrow."

"Then tonight Tony is mine."

Alice felt her anger rising. How dare he try to hold a child hostage! If she had been a man, she would have been tempted to punch the sheriff.

"Only if you find him," she said. "Now that you see he's not in here, I'll thank you to get off my boat. I'm sure you have plenty of other places to search."

Whittaker snorted. "I'll leave when I'm ready. I'm the sheriff."

"I'm a canawler and a woman. If I scream, a dozen canawlers will be here in a few moments with guns," she threatened. "And they may not show the restraint that David has shown."

Whittaker's face turned red. He wanted to say something, but he didn't dare. He turned around and stormed out of the cabin. Alice followed him to make sure he went ashore.

"I'll be watching this boat. When he comes back, I'll get him," Whittaker said.

Alice wasn't distraught, seeing as how Tony was already hidden on the boat. She would file the guardianship papers tomorrow and burn the financial agreements.

"Just stay off my boat," Alice said. She turned to David. "Thank you."

"You're welcome," he said, watching the sheriff walk away.

"What would you have done if he hadn't let me go?"

"I would have shot him, and he knew it."

"But he is the sheriff."

"He couldn't hide behind the law with what he was doing in there. The law is written to protect and defend people, not to allow them to be abused," David explained.

Alice nodded. Then she walked back into the family cabin. David followed her.

"He's gone, Tony," she said.

Tony kicked open the pantry doors with his foot. He had pulled back the false wall, but he still stayed in the small room.

"What happened? I couldn't see anything. All I could do was listen," Tony said as he poked his head out from under the lowest shelf.

"David convinced the sheriff to leave," Alice said simply.

Tony shook his head. "The sheriff won't forget. He never forgets anyone he feels has done him wrong. He probably still hates the doctor who slapped him on the back end when he was born."

"Tony!" Alice said, shocked.

He looked surprised. "Well, it's true!"

David just laughed.

"Everything's going to work out, isn't it?" Tony asked.

Alice nodded. "Yes, Tony, it will."

Tony smiled.

"You won't be disappointed in me, Mrs. Fitzgerald. I promise."

"I'm not disappointed now." She paused and sat down on the floor in front of him. "You know, those papers will make you my son."

"How can they do that?"

"It's a legal thing. Your real mother is officially giving you up, and I'm officially taking over in her place," Alice explained.

"I like that."

"It means that you can start calling yourself Tony Fitzgerald if you want to," Alice said.

Tony nodded.

"It also means you can call me Mama if you want to."

Tears started to roll down Tony's cheeks. He quickly crawled under the shelf and wrapped his arms around Alice's neck.

"I'd really like that, Mama," he said.

41

TEMPERS FLARE

JULY 1863

Alice looked up from her pancakes and saw George glaring at David, which George seemed to do more often than not these days. David ignored him and continued to eat his breakfast, but she could tell David knew he was being stared at. His body was tense, and he went out of his way not to look at George.

Alice decided to lighten the conversation.

"Elizabeth, would you like to go into Georgetown for some material for a new dress when we arrive?" Alice asked.

Elizabeth looked up and thought about the offer. "No. The dresses I have are fine. I think I would like to visit Mrs. Sampson, though."

That surprised Alice. She knew that Elizabeth liked Grace, but Elizabeth had only ever visited the Sampsons to see Abel. He had been killed in the war, though.

"Grace? Why?"

Elizabeth hesitated. She glanced nervously around the table. "I really don't want to talk about it right now."

"Why, is something the matter?"

Elizabeth shook her head.

Alice said, "Then talk to us, Elizabeth. We're all family here."

Elizabeth stood up suddenly. "I can't talk about it here."

She nearly ran out of the family cabin.

Alice had certainly broken the tension in the room. She had been so worried about George's problems adjusting to life without an arm that she had missed something with Elizabeth.

"Women," Thomas said in mock disgust.

David nudged him in the side with his elbow and shook his head.

"Should I go after her or does she want to be alone?" Alice asked. She was suddenly unsure of how she should deal with her daughter.

"I think she needs to talk to you," David said.

Alice sighed. David knew what was wrong. It shouldn't be this way. She was Elizabeth's mother. Elizabeth should have come to her mother with her problem.

"Do you know what's wrong?" Alice asked.

David shook his head. "No, but I can guess."

"What would you know? Elizabeth's not your daughter!" George snapped.

"It doesn't take a father to listen to what she's been saying this season. It doesn't take a father to see how she's been acting since the season started. It takes someone who cares, and your mother can probably guess what Elizabeth is worried about, too," David said calmly.

Alice was silently grateful at David's attempt to spare her feelings, but she knew the truth. She had been distracted.

Alice stood up and followed Elizabeth outside. The girl was sitting on the roof of the family cabin looking east toward the rising sun.

"Do you want to tell me what's the matter now or do I need to follow you all over the boat?" Alice asked, remembering how George had been when she had tried to talk to him.

Elizabeth turned her head to look at her. Her green eyes were red from Elizabeth wiping tears from them. "I just didn't want to talk about this in front of everyone because I think it's going to hurt you."

Alice's heart clenched. Hurt her? What could Elizabeth say that would hurt her? Alice sat down beside Elizabeth and hugged her.

"We're by ourselves now. Tell me what's wrong, and we'll talk about that first. We can deal with it hurting me later," Alice said.

Elizabeth stared at her mother for a few moments. Then she took a deep breath and said, "I want to stay with Mrs. Sampson. I want her to help me become a lady."

Alice closed her eyes and told herself not to cry. Elizabeth was right. It had hurt Alice to hear her daughter say that she wanted another woman to lead her into womanhood.

"What can Grace show you that you can't learn with your family?" Alice asked.

Elizabeth held Alice's clasped hands between hers. "Mama, you saw how the Armentrouts treated us. You are a lady, but Mrs. Armentrout treated you like dirt. I want Mrs. Sampson to show me how to deal with that. I want to be able to fit in with society. I want to feel like I'm good enough for anyone."

"You do fit in with society, Elizabeth. You fit in with your society. We are not a part of the Armentrouts' society, so that is why they treated us the way they did. If they tried to be canawlers, many people would treat them the way they treated us."

"It wasn't right, and I don't want it to happen again!"

"Does Grace know about this?" Alice asked.

Elizabeth shook her head. "I was going to ask her if she would help me when I saw her. I was hoping you could help me ask her."

Alice hesitated, then nodded. If this is what her daughter wanted, how could she deny her? Elizabeth was a woman and had to find her own place in the world.

"We'll go see Grace when we get to Georgetown and see what she thinks."

Elizabeth hugged her. "Thank you, Mama."

"How long do you think you'll be with her?"

"I don't know, but I don't know if I want to come back to the canal even when I am finished. I'm just not sure I belong here anymore."

Alice chuckled and shook her head.

"What's wrong?" Elizabeth asked.

"I don't know how many times I argued with your father that you shouldn't be growing up on the canal. I wanted you to be a lady, and I didn't think that would happen on the canal. Now here I am, listening to you make my same arguments, and I'm sounding like your father."

"I'm sorry I've hurt you, Mama."

Alice shook her head and wiped away the tears on her cheeks.

"I'm not hurt. How can I be hurt when you're only repeating what you've heard me say time and again? It's the right thing for you to do. I just always thought that I would be the one who helped you become a lady," Alice explained.

She stood up and kissed Elizabeth on her cheek. "We'll visit Grace. I'm sure she'll realize how lucky she'll be to have you want her help."

Elizabeth suddenly grabbed Alice around the neck and hugged her tightly.

"You're wonderful, Mama."

Alice turned and walked back into the family cabin not feeling wonderful at all. Her daughter wanted to leave her. She knew that it would happen someday, but she had always thought that it would be when Elizabeth married.

Everyone was eating their breakfast in silence, and Alice wondered if they had heard her conversation with Elizabeth. The children studied their food without looking up. David smiled at her. They had heard. She wished things could be more private on a canal boat.

"I'll take the first trick with the mules," Alice said. She wanted the time to walk with the mules and sort through her feelings to herself.

"I'll pilot the boat then," David said.

"No, I'll do it," George said quickly.

David rolled his eyes and shrugged. Alice was going to have to talk to George again, but she didn't want to have another major conversation with one of her children right now. The last thing she wanted was for George to leave again.

She quickly turned and went back outside to get the mules ready.

George stood with his hand on the rudder and guided the *Freeman* along the canal. He felt almost normal. His concentration was on his good hand and not his missing hand. He felt as if he belonged here as a captain of a canal boat.

But this wasn't his boat. It was his mother's. She had made that all too clear last year. He could imagine, though.

His mother was driving the mules. David was brushing Ocean and Bargain in the mule shed, and Elizabeth was cleaning up the breakfast dishes and preparing for dinner.

Tony and Thomas were lying on their backs and talking to each other. The two boys rolled over and stared at George.

George tried to ignore them, but their stares disturbed his peace. Then he noticed they weren't staring at him so much as they were staring at his stump. He wondered what they had been saying about him.

Suddenly, their stares got to be too much for George to bear. He stepped forward and waved his stump toward them.

"Do you want me to take off my shirt so that you can see the scars?" George yelled.

Tony and Thomas drew back. They rolled off the family cabin roof onto the cargo hatches and hurried toward their bunks in the hay house.

David stepped out from the mule shed, glanced around and walked to the quarterdeck where George was standing.

252

"What are you yelling about?" David asked.

"Leave me alone, David."

"Do you need a break for a while?"

"No, I do not. I'm able to steer this boat! I've still got one good arm!" George shouted.

"It has nothing to do with your arm. It has everything to do with the fact that you're very upset right now. I just wanted to give you some time to calm down," David said.

George kicked his foot against the wall of the family cabin.

"I'll never need help from a Rebel," George said.

"It's not a Rebel who's offering you help."

George snorted. "It was your uniform you said. Do you think I'm an idiot?"

When George had seen David in his Confederate uniform, he had wanted to shoot the rebel. He couldn't believe that his mother knew about David and still let him stay on the *Freeman.*

"George!" Elizabeth said as she came out of the family cabin. "David is our friend."

"He's no friend of mine!" George said.

"He's should be. Without him, we might all be dead," Elizabeth told him.

"Well, his friends nearly did that job," George said as he waved his stump around.

"David didn't do that, and he didn't force you to run off and join the army."

George held up his arm. "No, but his people did this because I was defending my country."

David said, "My people?"

"Rebels," George nearly spat the word out.

"I can understand how you feel, George, but…"

"Understand how I feel! I see two arms on you, David. You look healthy," George said.

David was beginning to anger now. His words took on a sharp tone. "But I've lost friends in this war. I've seen men next to me die. The images haunted me any time I fell asleep to the point that I knew I could no longer fight."

"So you're a coward, too."

Elizabeth said, "He is not."

"George, if you want to think I'm a coward, then that's your opin-

253

ion. You should be glad I am a coward," David said.

"Why?" George snapped.

"Because if I wasn't, I would have killed your family."

David turned and walked back to the other end of the boat to work on the mules again.

Elizabeth shook her head. "I thought that you had grown up in the war, George, but I see that you're still as young as Thomas."

She went back inside the family cabin. George kicked the wall again, but he didn't say anything more.

Alice was not happy to hear the argument on the *Freeman*. She had wondered how George would react when he found out that David was a former Confederate soldier. Now she knew. She was going to have to deal with him some way, or he would rip the family apart. That was sometime in the future, though.

She kept one hand on Ocean's neck and absent-mindedly walked alongside him.

She began to notice the ground was torn up from horse's hooves. She stopped walking and looked further up the towpath.

"Not again," she muttered.

She looked around and didn't see anyone nearby but a lot of men had passed over the canal, and they had been headed north.

"David," she called.

He stuck his head up above the roof of the mule shed and looked at her.

"Can you come over here?" Alice asked.

She kept the mules moving so they wouldn't have to start the *Freeman* moving from a dead stop.

David climbed onto the race plank. Then he took a few running steps and jumped to the shore. He landed on the towpath and dropped to his knees.

As he walked toward Alice, he hesitated, and she knew he had seen the tracks. How could anyone miss them?

"Soldiers moving north," David said.

"Do you think they were Confederate or Union?"

"Confederate."

"Why?"

"We saw that large crossing of soldiers at Williamsport. This group is probably trying to join up with them at some designated point."

"Do you think they'll bother us?"

David looked around. "It doesn't look that way. They're not around here. If an army as large as this one looks were anywhere nearby, we would see more signs than we're seeing now. Just the same, I think it might be wise to go armed for a while."

Alice considered the option. She didn't want to have to worry about being shot at by soldiers. She also didn't want to have to feel like she needed to defend herself on the canal.

"What good would it do?" she asked.

"It would give us some protection against guerillas," David said.

"Would it? If guerrillas want to attack us, they are going to have more guns than we will. That's what happened last year." The only way the *Freeman* had escaped being burned then was the timely arrival of a Union patrol.

"Maybe not, but then none of the guerrillas are going to want to be shot either. Seeing a gun will make them cautious."

"That's your choice then. I don't want to carry a gun," she said.

David nodded. "We'll let everyone know at the next lock, and they can choose for themselves what they want to do."

Rather than jump back onto the *Freeman*, David walked along with Alice. They didn't speak, though Alice sensed David wanted to talk about something.

"I heard the argument, David," Alice said finally.

"Most of Maryland and Virginia did, I suspect. Is it going to affect my ability to stay with you?" David asked.

Alice stumbled. "Why would it?"

"George is your son. I'm just an ex-Confederate spy that you picked up like one of Thomas's pets," David explained.

"George is my son, but that doesn't mean George is right. You're a part of this family now, David, for as long as you want to be," Alice told him.

David smiled. "Thank you. George and I will make our peace somehow."

42

BECOMING A LADY

JULY 1863

Alice dreaded seeing Grace Sampson. It seemed like she was admitting her failure as a mother. She hated feeling that way, but Alice knew that she would be losing her daughter to her friend.

For her part, Elizabeth was excited about staying with the Sampsons but nervous about asking them if she could remain and learn to be a lady.

Chess answered their knock at the door and smiled when he saw them.

"Hello, Miss Alice and Miss Elizabeth," he said.

"Is Grace home?" Alice asked.

Silently, she hoped the answer was no, even though that would only delay, not end, the meeting.

Chess nodded. "She is. Come right in, and I'll fetch her for you."

He led them to the sitting room. Alice sat in one of the armchairs, but Elizabeth paced back and forth. She walked from the fireplace to the doorway, occasionally detouring to look out the floor-to-ceiling windows.

Grace came in a few moments later. She was dressed in a casual dress made of gingham.

"Alice! Elizabeth! It's good to see you," Grace said.

Alice stood up and hugged her. Grace sat down on a chair near Alice. They caught each other up on what had been happening since they last saw each other, George's return, the army trouble in Williamsport, Eli working long hours in Congress and how lonely Grace was. That conversation naturally brought Alice to the topic she had been dreading.

"Elizabeth has decided she would like to become a lady," Alice said.

Grace smiled. "She already is such a lovely young lady. You must be proud."

256

"I am proud, but Elizabeth wants to become the type of young lady who moves in higher social circles than canawlers usually move."

Elizabeth suddenly took over. She knelt down in front of Grace and held her hand.

"Mrs. Sampson, could you please help me?" Elizabeth said.

Grace freed a hand and stroked Elizabeth's hair. "Of course, dear. You should know I'll help you however I can."

"Can I stay here with you and learn about being a lady?" Elizabeth asked.

Grace looked at Alice then back to Elizabeth.

"Your mother…" Grace started to say.

Elizabeth nodded. "I know my mother is a lady, but she can't teach me about the social graces you know about. I want to learn how ladies in society behave."

"Is this because of that boy Michael?" Grace asked.

Alice was surprised that Grace knew about Michael. Apparently, Elizabeth had had some communication with Grace this season.

Elizabeth shrugged. "Partly, but I just don't feel like I belong on the canal anymore. I want to see if I belong here."

"What do you think about this, Alice?" Grace asked.

Alice sighed, knowing the question was bound to come up at some point. "I can't say that I'm thrilled, but if this is what Elizabeth feels like she needs, I can't think of anyone I'd trust to help her and love her more than you," she said.

Tears ran down Grace's cheeks. "Then, of course, you can stay, Elizabeth. And thank you, Alice, for trusting me with this great treasure."

Now tears started to roll down Alice's cheeks because she wasn't sure if she had just lost her daughter forever.

Michael Armentrout walked back to the *Annabelle* with money in his pocket. He had been paid at the end of this trip and had gone off into Georgetown and Washington City to spend it. Many of the other canallers were spending their money in the taverns, but Michael didn't drink. He had gone looking for a new shirt and pair of jeans, but he had been dismayed by the prices.

He had quickly learned that he needed to be thrifty with his wages. He had managed to save over eighty dollars so far this season. The fish sales had gone well. He and Captain Howell didn't get much money for the fish, but for the amount of extra work it required, the money was quite good. The captain was happy, too.

Michael wasn't sure why he was saving his money. Except for work clothes and a few books, he just hadn't found anything he wanted to spend it on so far.

He walked along the wharf toward the *Annabelle*. He was beginning to learn the names of both the boats and crews that worked the canal. He waved to those people he knew as he walked. Bill Hale with the *Potomac Dream*. Carl McElfish with the *Union*. Paul Donovan with the *Hancock*.

When he saw the *Freeman*, he stopped.

Elizabeth's boat.

He hesitated, but then he walked up to the boat and called, "Hello, the *Freeman*!"

A young man about Michael's age walked out of the family cabin. The first thing Michael noticed about the youth was that his left arm was missing.

"What can I do for you?" the youth asked.

"I'm Michael Armentrout. Who are you?" Michael asked.

"Oh, so you're Michael. I'm George Fitzgerald. What are you doing here? It's a long way from Cumberland," George asked.

"I work on the *Annabelle*."

"I thought you were a doctor's son."

Michael nodded. "I am."

Who was this boy who seemed to know him?

George walked over to stand across from Michael. Michael tried not to stare at George's stump, but his eyes kept getting drawn to it. Elizabeth had said George was fighting in the war. Obviously, he had been wounded and sent home from the fighting.

"What are you doing working on a canal boat?" George asked.

"I'm a hand on the *Annabelle*. I signed on in February."

"Yes, but why would you take that job when you don't need to work?"

"Oh, I needed to. I needed a job like this. I've learned a lot," Michael said.

George sat down on the hatch covers. "Nothing much that would be of use to a doctor's son, I'd wager," he said.

Michael shook his head. "You're wrong there. I've learned things that would be of use to anyone's son or daughter, for that matter."

Michael had learned that while he might blame his mother for trying to take control of his life, he hadn't been living it himself. Then he had met Elizabeth and wanted to live his own life, but he hadn't known how to do it. His work on the canal was his own to claim. He was living his life now. His actions were his. His decisions were his. He was Michael Armentrout, not Dr. Armentrout's son.

"I'm looking for Elizabeth," Michael said.

George frowned. "Well, you're too late. She's gone."

"When will she be back? I'd like to talk to her."

"She won't be back. She's going to be staying in Georgetown so she can learn to be a lady." The way the youth said it made Michael think that George didn't agree with his sister's decision.

Michael stared at his feet. "Oh."

"Don't sound so disappointed. She's only doing what you wanted," George said.

Michael's head jerked up sharply. "What I wanted?"

"You drove her away, didn't you? Turned your back on her because she wasn't good enough for you? Well, she agreed with you. She doesn't think she's good enough, so she wants to be a lady. She's no longer happy being a canawler."

Agitated, Michael began to pace in small circles.

"She doesn't need to do that. It wasn't that she was not good enough for me. I wasn't good enough for her," Michael said.

"I could have guessed that without even meeting you," George said. "The problem is that Elizabeth didn't believe it."

"Can you tell me where she is? I want to talk to her."

George shook his head. "I think you've done enough to confuse her."

"But I want to set things right, so maybe she'll come back."

"So you can confuse her on something else? No. I won't do it." He shook his head.

Michael turned and slowly walked away. He wasn't going to push George because he could understand how George felt. He would feel that way if he were in the same position.

Now, though, Michael was beginning to conceive an idea. He began to realize why he had been saving his money.

43

PATIENCE RUNS OUT

JULY 1863

The sun had just gone down in the west. David sat on the hatch covers with his back against the wall of the mule shed. He wasn't looking west at the last glimmers of sunlight. He looked south across the Potomac. He stared at West Virginia.

David still couldn't believe that Virginia had lost her western counties over the war. Virginia was broken. Had the war been worth it? Virginia was split and would never be reunited again...like his family.

George walked from the mule shed toward the family cabin. He scowled at David as he passed. David didn't give George the pleasure of reacting, but inside he wondered the same thing he had been wondering for the past couple of months.

Did he belong here? Would he now be the cause of the split in the Fitzgeralds?

He might no longer be a Confederate soldier, but that didn't mean he wasn't a Southerner. Did West Virginians still consider themselves Virginians or Southerners?

It didn't mean that David was a part of the Fitzgerald family because he lived on their canal boat. Tony had been adopted, but David was still a guest.

David probably would make a good Marylander since the state itself couldn't make up its mind as to whether it was Union or Confederate.

Tony climbed out of the hay house. He saw David and walked over to sit next to him. He didn't say anything to David. Tony just stared across the river also.

"Bored?" David finally asked.

Tony shrugged. "I'm just trying to figure out what you find so fascinating about the land across the river. It's the same as over here."

"It's my homeland."

"Not anymore it's not. Now it's West Virginia." Tony had accepted the split that was less than a month old with much more ease than David had.

"I still think of it as my homeland because it was when I was born," David told him.

"Cumberland is my homeland, but you don't always see me mooning over it like a drunk railroader staring at a fifty-cent whore."

"Tony!" David wasn't used to hearing such coarse language from the young boy.

"Well, it's true. You do look like that. I should know. I've seen how drunk railroaders look," Tony told him in all seriousness.

"I believe you, Tony. If I'd lived what you've lived through in Cumberland, I don't think I'd be looking toward it either."

"So you think you have a good life in Virginia?"

David pressed his lips together and nodded. "Yes."

Tony snorted. "I'm not so sure about that. I think if I had lived your life I would feel betrayed."

"Why?"

"I expected my mother to act like she did in trying to profit from getting rid of me. That's who she is and so what she did was no surprise. Your father is supposed to be a gentleman, and he turned his back on you for no good reason. That doesn't seem like something a gentleman would do. You wouldn't."

David regretted having told Tony about the disappointing letter David had received from his father. He had felt the need to share his sorrow with someone, but he hadn't wanted Alice to know that he had sent the letter.

"He had his reasons," David said lamely.

While David and Tony were speaking, George came out of the family cabin. He saw Tony and David talking.

"You had better consider who you associate with," George told Tony.

Tony looked from David to George and back. "I do. I'm very careful. That's why I don't talk to you much."

George scowled at him. "You may look like Thomas, but you have

261

a mouth on you worse than many adults."

Tony shrugged and stood up.

George continued, "As for you, Rebel, just know that I'm keeping my eye on you. My mother says you're a good man, but she's just a woman."

"If you think she's just a woman, you've got a lot to learn," David said.

"You fought for the South. You spied for them. You could very well be spying for them now. I wouldn't be surprised. You've shown your true color. It's gray," George said.

David sighed. He stood up to walk away. Unfortunately, if George wanted a confrontation, David wouldn't be able to get away from him on a canal boat.

Tony didn't take the insult so lightly. He stiff-armed George. The one-armed youth stumbled off the race plank and fell into the water of the canal.

"Tony, what did you do?" David asked.

Alice screamed and left her position on the quarterdeck. "George!"

David prepared to dive overboard, but then he saw George bob to the surface and begin treading water with only one arm.

David pointed. "He's all right."

Tony looked over the edge of the boat, not panicked by what he had done. He said, "I guess you're not so helpless after all, George."

Tony and David reached out and helped pull George onto the boat. George rolled dripping wet onto the race plank and lay there catching his breath. Alice knelt next to him and held his face in her arms.

"Are you all right, George?" she asked.

He pulled his face away and nodded.

"I'm fine. I'm fine. I guess it's a good thing you and Papa taught me to swim when I was little," George said.

"Why did you push him in?" Alice asked Tony.

"Because I was tired of him taunting David. David wouldn't do anything because everyone feels sorry about George because he lost his arm," Tony said.

"How did you know that he wouldn't drown?"

"I knew a boy named Isaac when I was younger. He fell under a train once and lost more of his arm than George has. The doctors saved Isaac, and he learned to get along without his arm. He could tread water just like George was doing," Tony explained.

262

George started laughing.

"Like I said, you may look like Thomas, but you sure don't act like him," George said.

Alice relaxed. David sat down and stared at Tony.

44

NORTH VERSUS SOUTH

AUGUST 1863

George drove Jigger and Bargain along the towpath as he passed Paul Twigg driving the mules for the *Flintstone*. He nodded to the young boy who didn't even notice George's greeting because he was staring at George's stump. George held his arm close to his body as if that would shield it from view.

He wasn't sure if he would ever get used to people staring at him. He could almost feel their stares moving around the end of his stump, crawling over the thick scar tissue at the end of his arm. It made his arm itch.

As George passed the *Flintstone*, Charlie Twigg, the boat owner, waved to him.

"You had better be careful ahead, George. We heard some gunfire a ways back. There might be some sort of skirmish going on," Twigg warned.

"Thank you, sir. We'll be careful," George said.

A few moments later, George heard Twigg deliver the same message to David, who was piloting the *Freeman*. George waited for David's command to stop the mules, but it didn't come. George looked over his shoulder. David was standing on the quarterdeck looking unconcerned.

Wasn't he going to stop until the battle was done?

Did David want them to be shot at? Did he want to see the family hurt? Did he want to see the *Freeman* destroyed? George would expect nothing less from a Rebel.

George grabbed hold of Jigger's harness and pulled. "Whoa."

The mules stopped walking, and the tow rope went slack and slipped under the water.

"What's wrong?" David called.

"You know what's wrong! There's a battle going on up ahead!" George yelled.

"We don't know that."

"Charlie just told you that. He told me the same thing."

"He said he had heard shooting and there was possibly a skirmish. That's no reason to stop. We should be careful," David said.

"What is a reason to stop...a bullet in Thomas or me?"

David shook his head. "Get the mules moving, George. We'll be all right."

"I will not."

"We're not going to get anything done sitting here. Are you planning on waiting out the rest of the war because there might be skirmishes nearby?" David asked.

George put his hand on his hip and faced David. "I will not take my family into danger. I don't want them to be hurt."

"Is it them you are worried about or yourself?"

"It's them! You wouldn't know about loyalty seeing as how you are here and not in Virginia," George shouted.

David tried to keep from shouting. "Get moving, George. We've got work to do."

"You're not the captain of the *Freeman*. You don't command me, and I wouldn't listen to a filthy Rebel anyway," George said.

Alice stepped out of the family cabin, frowning. "Now that you both are sharing family business with all of Maryland and Virginia, can we settle it?"

"Fine," David said. "Let's get moving. We've got coal to deliver."

"Mama, he wants to take us into a battle," George complained.

Alice cocked her head to the side. "I don't hear any shots."

"There's a battle ahead. Charlie Twigg warned us about it," George said.

"He didn't say anything about a battle. He said that he had heard shots and that we should be on our guard because there *might* be a skirmish," David said.

"I am on my guard. I want to wait them out," George said.

"Alice, the Twiggs just passed us. If there had been any real danger, they would have told us about it," David told her.

Alice rubbed her temples with her fingers. "I am not happy that the two of you have put me in this position of having to choose. You

265

---

should have been able to work it out between yourselves," Alice said.

"I tried," David said.

"I did, too," George said defensively.

Alice sighed. She looked around. The day was clear and sound would carry a great distance, but there was nothing to be heard other than the normal sounds of the canal; water flowing, birds chirping, mules walking.

Alice shook her head and said, "We're going to go forward. If we hear more-definite signs of a battle, we'll stop. Until then, we'll take Charlie's advice and stay alert."

George started to say something. He wanted to yell out that his mother was being foolish. She didn't know what it was like to be in a battle. She had never been shot. She had never been operated on. What did she know about what they were walking into?

His mother was the captain of the *Freeman*, though. She had made that clear last year when he had challenged her authority. This was her boat, and she would run it as she saw fit. If he questioned her, she would only be more determined to show him that she was captain even if it meant walking into the middle of a battle.

George bit back his snide comments and started the mules walking. He let the mules follow the towpath. They were familiar enough to know their job. George watched the trees and brush, looking for hidden soldiers waiting to ambush them. He listened for gunfire, Rebel yells and soldiers marching. He sniffed the air for the scent of gunpowder.

His nerves were taut. He expected to be attacked at any moment.

That was one lesson he had learned well during his short time in the army. Death did not do what was expected, nor did it take only those people who were fighting.

His family didn't realize that, but George did. He would have to protect them from their own innocence.

The *Freeman* stopped near Oldtown for the night, having heard no battle or even any shots fired during the day. After supper, Alice sat up reading her Bible by lantern light until she was sure everyone was asleep. She finished the chapter she was reading about Moses leading his people, the Egyptian slaves, out of bondage to freedom. God had approved of Moses's actions then. Why shouldn't He approve of her actions now?

She closed the book and picked up the lantern. Once she was off the boat, she and walked down the towpath to where the B&O Railroad crossed over the river from West Virginia into Maryland. She climbed up the embankment and onto the tracks.

Alice stood there looking south into West Virginia. She couldn't see anything, and she wondered if she had misunderstood the message. She covered and exposed the lantern three times. Across the river, another light returned her triple blink.

The light began to bob up and down and grow larger. A few minutes later, she saw Jacob Olander and a black woman.

"Good evening, Mrs. Fitzgerald. It's good to see you doing well," Jacob said.

He was an older man with white hair and a beard. His hands were gnarled with arthritis, but he never complained about the pain.

"How are you, Mr. Olander? I haven't seen you in a while. I guess I should congratulate you and your fellow West Virginians for taking a stand for your country."

Olander shook his head. "It's a sad thing. Nothing I am proud of. Virginia may be in the wrong now, but she'll find her way back. She always has, but now because of our impatience, we have lost that proud heritage. We are like orphans," the old man said.

Alice was surprised to hear that this man who was so in opposition with Virginia right now could still long to be a part of the state. It gave Alice a glimpse of what David was going through as he tried to figure out who he was without being identified as David Windover of Virginia. Virginia's sons and daughters loved her with a dedication Alice rarely saw in other states.

"Now you'll have to create a new heritage that you can be just as proud of. You've given West Virginia a good start."

Olander nodded. He pointed to the black woman. "This is Rose. She's on her way to Canada and needs a ride to Cumberland."

Alice reached out and took the young woman's hand. Rose was terrified. Her hand was shaking. Alice patted her hand. He skin was rough. She must have been a field hand.

"It's all right, Rose. I'll take good care of you while you're with me," Alice said.

"Thank you, ma'am."

"Take care, Mrs. Fitzgerald," Olander said. He waved to her and then walked back across the trestle.

Alice and Rose started to walk back to the boat. They had barely started walking when the night sky opened, and rain poured down. It was a heavy, drenching rain, and Alice and Rose were soaked in moments. Alice hurried her pace, but she couldn't move too fast, or she would get lost in the darkness and rain.

When they finally walked back onto the *Freeman*, Alice saw David sitting on the roof of the family cabin under the canopy. He didn't say anything as Alice and Rose walked by him. He just watched them cross the hatch covers and walk down the stairs into the family cabin.

Alice carefully helped Rose into the hidden area behind the pantry, making sure not to wake George. She also passed Rose some bread and salt pork to feed her until Alice had a chance to give her more food.

"Only open this if you hear me ask you, too," Alice told Rose as Alice began to slide the false wall into place.

"Yes, ma'am."

Alice closed up the pantry and went back outside where David was still sitting. She climbed up onto the roof to sit beside him.

"You'd better dry off before you catch a cold," David said.

"Have you made your decision yet?" Alice asked. She didn't mention what the decision was about, but they both knew. Had David come to terms with Alice transporting escaped slaves to freedom?

David shook his head and leaned back on his hands. "I am not sure yet, but I trust you."

Alice sighed, glad to hear the confirmation. She patted his arm. "I won't abuse that trust."

"I know, and that's why I trust you." He paused and then said, "I used to hate the rain when I was in the army. It made life miserable with water leaking into my tent and marching through miles of mud. I've learned to like it since I've been with you, though."

"Why?"

"Because the rain washes the coal dust and other grime off everything and you can see how things look clean and unblemished. You see things how they really are before the world comes in and dirties them up again," David explained.

"That's a nice way to look at things."

"Tonight I watched you, and that woman come aboard walking through the rain. I watched you and waited for the rain to show me how you really are."

"What did it show you?"

David shook his head. "Nothing. You've always presented yourself just as you really are. You don't let the world change who you are."

David slid off the roof and walked back into the family cabin. Alice sat on the roof and wondered what David had meant.

The *Freeman* passed under the railroad trestle at Lock 33 across the river from Harpers Ferry. David opened up a bag at his feet and began to line up throwing stones along the railing of the quarterdeck. He piloted the boat and Thomas drove the mules. From this point on until Nolands Island around mile 45, the B&O Railroad ran close enough to the canal to cause trouble.

The *Freeman* was coming out of Lock 32 when David saw a train approaching them. He picked up one of the round stones and got ready to throw it at the train.

Alice walked out of the family cabin with a load of laundry and saw David. She hurried up the stairs to the quarterdeck and stood in front of him. She dropped the basket and grabbed David's arm.

"David, don't!" she said sharply.

"He'll try to spook the mules," David said.

"Maybe not."

David stared at her for a moment and set the stone down. If the train blew its whistle, he could always grab another rock and get in at least one more throw. As if reading his mind, Alice swept all of the stones from the railing into the water.

David frowned and waited.

The train approached and passed the mules without blowing its whistle. The engineer leaned out of the window of the engine and waved. Alice waved back.

"It's Henry!" she said.

"Did you know he was on that train?" David asked suspiciously.

"How could I?"

"Then why didn't he blow his whistle?"

Alice sniffled. "Because for peace to begin, one side has to first trust the other. Trust must outweigh fear and hate. If this war is going to end, one side is going to have to do the same thing."

She turned and walked back around to the front of the family cabin to wash clothes in a half barrel sitting on the hatch covers. Alice sniffled a few more times while she was dunking clothes and David wondered if she was on the verge of crying or just catching a cold.

He stared at her and wondered if peace had begun between the railroad and the canal, which side had trusted the other first?

45

GEORGETOWN

AUGUST 1863

Elizabeth paused on her way back to the house and stopped in the middle of the road to stare at it. She thought that it was a beautiful home and she still found it hard to believe that she lived there. Grace had converted guest bedroom to Elizabeth's room, and it was twice as large as Elizabeth's old bedroom in Sharpsburg had been.

She walked to the door and entered quietly. She wasn't sure why, but loud noises seemed out of place in this house.

Chess looked up from his cleaning in the living room. He smiled at her.

"Good morning, Miss Elizabeth," he said.

"Good morning, Chess. It's a beautiful morning out."

"It is. It is. Have you been visiting the canal again?"

Not much escaped Chess's notice in this house. He moved in and out of rooms quietly so that no one even interrupted their conversations when he was around. He watched when people came in and out of the house. He knew what they ate or didn't eat.

"I didn't see the *Freeman* at the wharf, but I did see some friends of mine. They loved my dress," Elizabeth said.

Elizabeth watched for the canal boat every morning so that she could visit with her family. Her mother always asked about what she was doing and learning, but she never mentioned Elizabeth returning to the canal. Her mother respected Elizabeth's decision, but Elizabeth sometimes wished that her mother would ask her to come back to the canal. She wouldn't have the strength or desire to say "no."

"It's a beautiful dress," Chess said.

270

Elizabeth's worst dress now was better than her old Sunday dress had been. She had been surprised when Grace Sampson had bought her a new wardrobe. Elizabeth had argued with her that it was too expensive, but Grace had told her that most of being a lady was appearance. If you looked like what people thought a lady should look like, they treated you like a lady. If you looked like a maid, they treated you like a maid. That certainly described Minerva Armentrout.

"Do you like your work?" Elizabeth asked Chess when she suddenly wondered how he wanted to be treated.

Chess paused and straightened up from dusting a table. "That's an odd question, ma'am. I don't think anyone has ever asked me that question before." He rubbed his chin. "I've never given it much thought. I don't think it's a question of whether I like or don't like my work. It's something I have to do to survive, and I am good at this work, so I make a good wage. Mr. and Mrs. Sampson are very nice to me. So I guess I can't say whether I like it, but I don't mind it."

"Do you ever feel out of place?"

"Of course."

"What do you do?"

"Are you feeling out of place, Miss Elizabeth? Is that why you spend so much time at the canal?"

Elizabeth nodded. She had felt the need for change after being rejected by Michael and left everything she had known because she no longer felt comfortable on the canal. Now that she was with Grace Sampson, she still felt out of place. This was not her world, and it didn't feel like it ever would be.

Chess said, "The Sampsons love having you here."

"I know."

"And I'm sure your mama loves you. She let you stay here, didn't she?"

Elizabeth nodded. "I know, Chess. I agree. I know they care about me."

"Then the problem is not the canal or Washington. It's you, Miss Elizabeth. You're the one who's making you feel out of place. If you don't want to feel that way, you've got to make the change in you, because the canal and Washington aren't going to change so that you feel good."

"Me?"

Chess nodded. "I'm sorry I had to say that to you. It's not exactly kind, but I think you needed to hear it because you seem to think that some change outside of you is what you need. No outside change is going to help unless you fix what is bothering you inside."

Elizabeth didn't have any reply. She had loved working on the canal until Michael rejected her. The canal hadn't changed. She had.

What had she changed into?

What did she want?

Chess went back to his cleaning and Elizabeth walked through the house to the back porch. Grace was sitting in her favorite rocking chair reading the newspaper.

"Hello, dear," Grace said when Elizabeth came onto the porch.

Elizabeth sat down on the porch with her feet on the top step that led down to the backyard. She stared out on Grace's beautiful flower gardens. Flower beds filled the yard with color. They were Grace's pride, and she cared for them herself. A path led to a small gazebo, which is where Grace usually sat when she was outside.

"Has Eli gone into the city already?" Elizabeth said.

Grace laughed. "Already? It's nearly noon."

"But he worked so late last night I thought he would be going in late today."

Eli hadn't come home until midnight. The sound of him coming up the stairs to his bedroom had awakened Elizabeth.

Grace sighed and laid aside the newspaper.

"I hoped so, too. He works so much lately," she said.

"I guess the war takes up a lot of time."

Grace shook her head. "The generals run the war, not Congress. No, Eli started working longer hours after Abel was killed. I'm not sure what he hopes to accomplish by doing it. The most-successful war ever can't bring Abel back. I just don't know what I can do."

Grace's voice broke, and Elizabeth looked over her shoulder. Grace started to cry. Elizabeth hurried over to her and hugged her.

"Things will work out," Elizabeth said.

"How? I don't even know what's wrong," Grace said.

Elizabeth remembered what Chess had told her. It seemed timely, and she wondered if he had told her what he had because Elizabeth needed to hear it or Grace.

"Abel's death changed him, Mrs. Sampson," Elizabeth said.

"Changed him how?"

"I don't know. He doesn't know either, I would guess. He's trying

272

to find out who he is now that Abel's gone."

"Don't you think Abel's death changed me, too? I was his mother," Grace said.

"Of course, it changed you. Do you know how?"

Grace stared out over the backyard. "I asked Chess this morning if he could care for my gardens this year. They don't bring me joy anymore. I don't want to raise flowers just to watch them die. I want to see things live, not die."

Elizabeth just nodded. She wasn't sure what to say.

Grace continued to open up. "It hurts me inside to think of all those boys dying like Abel did. I cry when I think about all those mothers who are waiting for their boys to return home. Some of them will always wait and wonder. It's not right. There's got to be a way to help them by keeping more boys from dying."

There was, or at least Elizabeth thought that there was. She had caught a glimpse of it earlier in the year, and now it was giving her an idea. It would help Mrs. Sampson, and at the same time, she thought that it would help her, too.

Was this how she had been changed?

"I think I know what we can do, Mrs. Sampson," Elizabeth said.

Grace looked up expectantly. "What?"

"Let me ask around and see if it's even possible. If I think it will work, I'll talk to you more about it. We'll do this together. You won't be alone in this."

And neither will I, Elizabeth thought to herself.

46

AMBUSHED

SEPTEMBER 1863

The *Freeman* moved along slowly back and forth as the canal ran through Washington County near Sharpsburg. Thomas walked out of the mule shed where he had finished grooming Ocean and Jigger, who had ended their trick at Lock 37. He looked around for a moment and then ran along the race plank to the family.

Tony looked up from his school work when Thomas barged into the small room.

"Let's go play! I know some great caves to explore around here," Thomas said.

Tony shut his school book. He wasn't making much headway with his reading today anyway. He had improved a lot over the summer, but one look at his mother's Bible with all of its words and small print only showed him how far he had to go.

He wasn't going to accomplish it all in one day, though.

Tony followed Thomas outside. Thomas called up to his mother, who was piloting the boat.

"Mama, we want to go ashore and play. I finished taking care of the mules. Can we go, please?" Thomas asked.

Alice nodded. "I suppose, but don't wander too far from the boat. I want you to be able to hear me if I call for you."

"Yes, ma'am."

Alice steered the boat toward the berm side of the canal so that it was less than two yards from the bank. Tony and Thomas ran along the race plank and jumped ashore. They landed on the ground and rolled in the dirt. Then they were on their feet and running off into the woods that bordered the towpath.

"And try not to rip holes in your clothes," Alice called after them.

Thomas and Tony worked their way through the trees until they came out on the canal again.

"Why didn't we just follow the canal?" Tony asked.

"Because it winds around with the river. This is a shortcut so that we can have some time to explore the caves here," Thomas said.

"Won't we need a lantern?"

"Not for the one I want to show you."

They pushed their way through some brush and then began to climb a steep slope. Near the top of the hill, the shape changed so that it became a large overhang more than a cave.

"This is it," Thomas announced.

"This isn't a cave."

"It is, too. It's the Killiansburg Cave."

Tony stood in the cool shadows and looked around.

"What's so special about this? I saw real caves along this rise."

"Last year when the battle was fought near our old house, a lot of people from Sharpsburg hid out in this cave. This is like the Sharpsburg Town Hall."

"It's not a cave," Tony said.

"It is, too."

Tony walked further under the overhang. The sun was on the opposite side of the rise, so it got dark under the overhang quickly. The space kept going back. It was enormous space, and Tony understood how a lot of people could take shelter here.

"Can we climb up on top of the rise? I bet we can see a lot from there," Tony suggested.

"Don't you want to explore it?"

"You can't see anything. How can you explore it?"

Thomas pouted. "You're no fun, Tony."

"Do you want to go up on top or not?" Tony asked.

"I know a way. Follow me," Thomas said.

They walked back out into the light and Thomas began to pick his way along the side of the steep slope. Some of the rocks were loose, so he had to be careful where he put his feet.

Tony heard a shot, and then rock shards sprayed his face as a bullet barely missed his head. He yelled and jumped back, but there was no place to jump back to. He lost his footing on the slope and fell head over heels, crashing through brush and sliding across rocks. Loose rocks and brush cut at him.

"Thomas!" was all Tony managed to yell.

He thought he heard another shot, but he was making so much noise as he fell that it was hard to tell. He wondered if the second shot had also been aimed at him.

When Tony finally managed to stop himself, he lay on his back trying to catch his breath. He lifted his arms and legs to make sure that he hadn't broken any bones. He was covered with scrapes and cuts, but otherwise, he was unharmed. Boy, would he be sore tomorrow, though!

Who had shot at him and why?

"Thomas!" Tony called.

When there was no response, Tony called out again even louder. This time, he heard his brother respond, "I'm over here."

"Where?"

"I don't know. I fell, and I've been shot. Things look kind of fuzzy right now."

Ignoring his own pain, Tony suddenly stood up and scrambled in the direction from where he had heard Thomas's voice.

"Keep talking to me, Thomas, so I can find you," Tony said.

"What do you want me to say?"

"I don't care. If I hadn't asked you to say anything, you would have been talking my ears off," Tony told him.

Thomas started singing "Goober Peas." The song was a favorite of his since he had first heard it. The song was about peanuts and Thomas loved to eat fresh roasted peanuts with salt on them. He always made a point of buying himself a bag when they were tied up in Georgetown.

Tony hurried along the side of the hill, searching the brush for his brother. He wasn't moving too fast himself because his legs were throbbing with pain. When Tony found Thomas, the boy was laying on his back singing. His left hand was covering his right arm, but Tony could still see blood coming from between Thomas's fingers. It looked like a lot of blood.

"Did you break any bones?" Tony asked.

"I don't think so, but I'm so banged up that it's hard to tell." Thomas turned his head toward his arm. "Someone shot me."

"He nearly shot me, too."

"He? Did you see him?"

Tony shook his head. "I'm guessing."

"Who would do that? We weren't bothering anyone."

Tony snorted. "Who do you think? There must be some Rebels wandering around here."

"But we're not soldiers. We don't even look like soldiers. Why would they want to shoot at us?"

Tony pulled off his shirt and tied it tightly around Thomas's arm. He wasn't a doctor, but he knew he would have to stop the bleeding or Thomas might bleed to death.

"I don't know. Maybe they don't really care who they are shooting at. Can you walk?"

"My ankle is twisted, but I can limp."

"That will have to do. We need to get back to the canal and warn everyone and get that wound looked at," Tony said.

Thomas sat up, and then Tony looped Thomas's right arm around his shoulders and helped him struggle to his feet. Thomas was as large as Tony, so it was hard for Tony to lift his brother. Because they had fallen down the hill, they were fairly close to the canal. They walked north until they reached the canal and then headed west to meet up with the *Freeman.*

When Tony saw the canal boat, he called, "Mama! We need help! Thomas has been shot!"

George ran out of the family cabin when he heard Tony yell. Shot? Here?

Although his mother reacted quickly, the boat didn't. It gradually moved over to the berm side of the canal and George, and his mother laid out the fall board. Tony helped Thomas across the cleated board onto the boat.

Thomas sat down on the cargo hatch, and Alice ran to him. She pulled away the bandage and frowned.

"Get me some water and soap, Tony," Alice said.

Tony hurried off. He took a basin from the family cabin and filled it with water from a water barrel. He carried the basin and a bar of lye soap back to his mother.

"What happened?" Alice asked.

"We were trying to get to the top of the rise above Killiansburg Cave and someone shot at us," Thomas said. "They barely missed

Tony, and we both wound up falling down the hill."

"Did you see who did it?" George asked.

"No," Thomas said.

George clenched his fist at his side. "It had to be Rebels. It had to be."

It was impossible to see the bullet hole because there was so much blood on Thomas's arm. Alice dipped a towel into the water and wiped the blood and dirt from her son's arm.

George stared at his brother for a few moments and then turned away. He felt his throat tightening as if he was going to scream. He took a deep breath and closed his eyes.

Alice washed away most of the blood and then scrubbed her son's arm with the soap to clear the dirt away so that she could see what sort of damage the bullet had done.

"He was shot twice," Tony said, surprised.

Alice shook her head. "No, he wasn't. The bullet went all the way through his arm. That's a good thing. Otherwise, I would have to dig the bullet out."

She leaned in closer and prodded Thomas's arm around the wound. He winced.

"George, can you get my sewing kit?" she asked.

George nodded and hurried off. He was glad for an excuse to be away from the sight. He found his mother's sewing kit in her state-room and carried it back outside.

"What are you going to do, Mama?" Thomas asked.

"I'm going to sew the holes in your arm closed."

Thomas's eyes widened. "With a needle?"

"That's the only way I know how to do it."

"No! I don't want you stabbing me with a needle."

He rolled away to try and get away from his mother. Alice grabbed him and pulled him back. Thomas wasn't acting like he was wounded.

"Is he going to be all right?" George asked.

"I don't know."

"Bullet wounds can cause a lot of damage even if they only leave small holes."

"I know, George. Your sister and I worked in a Cumberland army hospital during the winter. I've seen what happens with wounds."

George knew, too. He had experienced it first hand and arm.

And the hospital! George shuddered. "How could you work in a place like that? It's a death sentence. So many soldiers...so many soldiers go in, and they aren't that sick, and they never come out. They just got sicker and died."

George backed away.

"Calm down, George," Alice said.

He shook his head. He could see the surgeons with the saws and blood-soaked aprons. He could hear the screams of the men who had to be operated on while they were awake. There had been too many wounded and not enough ether to put the wounded to sleep for their surgeries.

"George? Are you all right?" Tony asked.

"They're going to have to amputate. They'll take his arm," George said.

George remembered lying in a line of soldiers who were all waiting to lose a limb. The orderlies lifted him onto the operating table. Next, to him, he saw another soldier being operated on. The doctor was using his knife to cut away the flesh of the soldier's thigh to expose the bone so it could be cut. George looked at his mangled arm and realized it would soon look like the other soldier's leg. He gagged.

"Who's they?" Tony asked.

"The doctors. They'll come for his arm. They'll kill him."

George closed his eyes. He saw the pile of limbs outside the surgery tent as he walked to an ambulance that would take him from the field hospital to a hospital in Washington City. Arms, legs, hands, feet. Which one was his? The smell of rotting flesh turned his stomach. He cried for the loss of his arm.

George suddenly turned away from Tony and ran to the other side and threw up over the edge of the boat.

"George!" Alice called.

He waved her away.

"Tony, help him."

"Help him what? I'm not sure what's wrong with him," Tony said.

George began to sob. His arm was gone! He would never be whole!

"Don't let them take his arm! Don't let them do it! He's too young!" George yelled.

"David! I need your help over here!" Alice called.

David had been standing on the towpath with the mules, waiting to

279

see what would happen. At Alice's call, he dove into the water and swam across the canal to the *Freeman*. He pulled himself aboard and shook the water from him.

"Help George. Something's got him upset. I've got to stitch up Thomas's arm," Alice said.

David hurried over to George who was sobbing against the corner of the family cabin. David put a hand on his shoulder.

"George, what's wrong?" David asked.

George spun around. His eyes were red from crying, but there was also fury behind them. He poked his stump into David's chest.

"You! You did this to me, and now you want to do it to Thomas. He never hurt you! Why are you trying to hurt him!" George shouted.

"I didn't do anything to him."

"You're a Rebel. You're all alike. It doesn't matter who you can hurt as long as you can hurt someone."

George swung at David, but David ducked and then pinned George's arm against his side. George thrashed around, but David kept him under control.

Then Thomas walked over and lifted his right hand and laid it on George's chest.

"George! George! It's all right. I'm all right. Look, my arm is working," Thomas said.

George slowly stopped thrashing. He stared at Thomas as if he were seeing a stranger. Thomas held up his hand and wiggled his fingers. Then he bent his elbow and winced.

George's brow furrowed.

Thomas quickly said, "Mama's stitches are a little tight."

Alice walked over and stood in front of George. David let go of him but readied himself in case George took another swing.

"George, what's wrong?" Alice asked.

George looked around in a slight daze. "Oh, Mama, I was so scared."

"I know George. I know," she said in a soothing voice.

She hugged him while George sobbed into her shoulder. David tapped Thomas and Tony on their shoulders and led them into the family cabin so that Alice could spend some time with George.

Inside the family cabin, Thomas laid down on one of the bunks and said, "George wasn't talking about me when he said he was scared, was he?"

David began to take off his wet clothes and change into dry ones.

"I don't think so, at least not entirely."

Thomas thought for a moment and then said, "It must have been really scary fighting in the war."

David nodded. "It is, Thomas. If I had to describe what Hell might look like, I would picture it like the Battle of Sharpsburg."

David had fought in and been wounded during the battle last September. It had been the worst battle he had seen, mainly because he had seen the battlefield afterward. It had been a sea of dead bodies. Blue and gray uniforms had all been connected with red blood.

"Do you think George will be all right?" Tony asked.

David shrugged. "I hope so. I think whatever happened today was a good start."

"Why do you say that? He was crying like a baby."

David tried to think of a way to explain it to the boys. "If the bullet had still been in Thomas's arm, would Alice have stitched him closed?"

Tony shook his head.

"Well, that's what happened with George. When they sewed up his arm, the doctors left something in George."

"What?"

"Fear. Maybe a bad memory. I've had some experience with those, and I know how badly they can affect you. Whatever it was, seeing Thomas shot brought it all out or at least most of it. I hope he can heal now."

"Does that mean he will stop acting like an idiot?" Tony asked.

Thomas shook his head. "No, he acted like an idiot long before he lost his arm. I guess he'll keep acting like that."

47

WORKING FOR THE CAUSE

SEPTEMBER 1863

After Chess served the roasted chicken and rice to everyone, Elizabeth looked around the dining room table at Eli and Grace. Elizabeth was giddy with excitement, but she tried to maintain her calm demeanor as she had seen the ladies Grace associated with doing. She wanted the Sampsons to take what she had to say seriously and not dismiss her as a child.

"Mrs. Sampson, I think I found what I was looking for, for us," Elizabeth said.

Grace looked up from her food. "Looking for? Oh, that. Are you ready to tell me what it is that you have planned?"

"I think we should work in a hospital as nurses."

Grace's eyebrows arched. "Nurses? I don't know anything about medicine."

"You don't need to know much. Before the war started, there weren't any trained nurses in the country. Now look at how many there are."

"How are they being trained?"

"By doing the work. You just need to want to learn. The doctors will tell you what needs to be done. Most of what you'll do is just be kind to the soldiers. They are hurting and scared, and they need a kind voice and a smiling face. I did this for a while in Cumberland," Elizabeth explained.

"What makes you think that will help me? I don't see the connection," Grace asked.

"You told me you wanted to stop watching things die. This is a way do to it, and the hospitals need help," Elizabeth said. "I walked around today and asked about hospitals. They are all over the city now, and more are being built all the time. I was told there is a wounded soldier for every two people in this city."

Eli, who had listened carefully to the conversation, chimed in, "I'm not sure what the two of you are talking about, but Elizabeth is right about the hospitals. We've got patients being cared for in the Capitol and there is a hospital behind the White House."

Eli had lost a lot of weight in the past year because he ate very little as he buried himself in his work. Eating dinner at home, as he was tonight, was a rare occurrence.

"Are you saying I should become a nurse, Eli?" Grace asked.

Eli pursed his lips as he considered what to say. "If you want to help our soldiers, I can think of no better way to do so. Many of our soldiers are Abel's age. When they are hurt and confined in a hospital, I'm sure they would appreciate the soothing touch of a mother."

Grace looked back and forth between Elizabeth and Eli.

Finally, she said, "But won't they also be dying?"

Elizabeth nodded. "Yes, but the more you help, the fewer will die. You can make a difference. Isn't that what you want?"

"Where would we go?" Grace asked.

"I found a Methodist church nearby. They've just opened up as a hospital with 200 beds. They've got no shortage of patients, just nurses, and doctors. They can use us."

Grace was silent and stared at her chicken. She moved it around on her plate with her knife. Then she nodded.

Elizabeth smiled. "We'll go tomorrow then. You can see what is done and if it will help you."

Eli stood up. He walked around the table and kissed his wife on the cheek. "I am very proud of you, my dear. While other ladies might talk about helping their country, you will be doing something. I can see where Abel came by his dedication to his country."

Tears began to roll down Grace's cheeks.

Elizabeth and Grace stopped in front of the First United Methodist Church. Grace looked up at the steeple with her mouth hanging slightly open. The front doors were open, and soldiers were being helped into the church by other soldiers, some of who were wounded themselves.

283

"This is only four blocks from our home," Grace said.

Elizabeth nodded. "Hospitals are being created all over the area. When the war started, Washington had only two hospitals. Now there are dozens."

"How did you know that?" Grace asked.

"I've been talking to a lot of doctors to find out how things work here. The wounded who survive at the field hospitals from battlefields relatively close to here are brought here to try and recover. Think of how much fighting is done between here and Richmond. That's why they need such help. If they can't find enough places to put all of the wounded, just imagine the trouble they are having finding people to care for them all."

Grace took a deep breath and started forward. Elizabeth joined her, and they walked through the vestibule. Inside the chapel, the pews had been removed and replaced with lines of beds. Men in various stages of recovery were packed into the room. Some could sit up. Others were lying down. One nurse moved back and forth among all of the wounded.

Elizabeth noticed a life-size painting of Jesus Christ on the wall behind the pulpit. He looked out over the wounded with a compassionate expression. She wondered what he would think of this war.

The nurse hurried by, and Elizabeth grabbed her by the arm. "Excuse me, could you tell us who's in charge here?"

The older woman pulled her arm free. "That would be Dr. Wellstone."

She started to walk away, and Elizabeth asked, "Where is he?"

"Stocking the pharmacy upstairs," the woman said over her shoulder. Then she was leaning over another soldier, changing the dressing on his shoulder wound.

Grace and Elizabeth climbed the stairs to the second-floor loft and began looking in the three rooms that had once been classrooms. Two of the rooms were packed with church items that had been removed from other places in the church. Then they found one room with a man inside who was lifting bottles and vials and setting them on shelves.

"Dr. Wellstone?" Elizabeth asked.

The man stopped and looked up. He was a young man in his late twenties. His blond hair was unkempt, and his face looked tired, but there was a certain energy in his eyes. He straightened up, and Elizabeth saw that he was medium height and average build.

"May I help you ladies?" he asked.

"We would like to help you. My name is Elizabeth Fitzgerald, and this is Grace Sampson. We would like to become nurses and help you here," Elizabeth said.

Dr. Wellstone stared at them and rubbed his chin. "Pardon me for asking, but are you nurses or have you had nursing experience?"

Elizabeth shook her head. "We aren't nurses, but I had some experience helping wounded soldiers in the hospitals in Cumberland."

"Then perhaps I should give you a tour of what we are dealing with here before you volunteer your services. I need help here, but I can't waste it either. If I have the nurse I do have help train you, she won't be able to do her job. I need to know that the lack of attention the soldiers will face while you're being trained will be both worthwhile and as short as possible. I don't want the two of you running off the first time you see an amputation."

He stepped out of the room and led them back down to the main floor. He led them down the aisles, pausing so that they could see the wounded soldiers in the bed. Men were missing limbs. They were pale and sick looking. Others who were covered with spots looked near death.

Elizabeth was surprised that no one seemed upset that men were on the verge of dying.

"Things are quiet now because we are not fully operational. We will be full soon, though. If additional casualties start coming in, we'll be busy trying to take care of the wounded," said Wellstone.

Elizabeth waved to a young soldier who waved at her.

"How are you doing?" she asked as she stopped by the soldier's bed.

The soldier smiled. "Much better now. I love the nurse here, but she is old enough to be my mother. She's caring for my body, but seeing you makes my eyes feel better," the soldier said.

Elizabeth blushed. "Thank you. What's your name?"

"Arthur Lund."

Elizabeth smiled. "Well, Arthur, if my friend and I can convince Dr. Wellstone to allow us to help, you'll be seeing a lot more of me."

Arthur looked at Dr. Wellstone. "Aw, Doc, you can't be so cruel as to let her get away. She's making me feel better already."

Wellstone chuckled. "We'll see, Arthur."

They started to walk again.

"I can see that you will be a distraction here," Wellstone said.

"I will not. I will work hard," Elizabeth defended herself.

"You saw how that soldier reacted to you. He won't be the only one to act that way either. You are an attractive young woman," Wellstone said.

"But you need us," Grace said. "Even I can see that there's more than enough work for a dozen women here, and you only have one nurse."

Wellstone nodded. "I am not arguing that point. I am short of doctors here, too. When the war broke out, the army had only 114 medical personnel. Of that amount, twenty-four men resigned to assist the Confederacy, and three men were dismissed because of disloyalty. Now there are hundreds of doctors. I was drafted into the army right out of medical school last year."

"This is what you were trained to do, isn't it?" Grace asked.

"I was trained to treat corns and the grippe. I can deliver babies. How many pregnant servicemen do you see?" Wellstone sighed and shook his head. "I am sorry I snapped at you, but you have to understand that much of what we are dealing with here is beyond current medical knowledge. We lose as many men as we save, and still the number of incoming wounded continues to grow."

"But you are learning, and with each person you save, your knowledge grows. With all of these young men still alive, you should be a fine doctor," Grace said.

Wellstone smiled. "Thank you, ma'am. That is kind of you to say. I am lucky. I do my best to control the conditions that I can control. I work hard to get food and clean water for my patients."

"Don't you feed them?" Grace asked.

"We do, but it's no better than they get in the field. They deserve...they need more than fried cornmeal," Wellstone explained. "Things like blood poisoning, tetanus and gangrene are common here. We get typhoid, dysentery and malarial fevers all the time."

"It sounds horrid," Grace said.

Wellstone nodded. "Now you understand the problem. This is not a ladies' club luncheon. This is war. The soldiers fight their battles on the field. We fight ours in places like this." He waved his arms around the church/hospital. "It is hard on everyone involved."

Grace looked over the hospital again. She licked her lips.

"Half of these boys will die?" Grace asked.

Wellstone shrugged. "I certainly hope not, but the averages say that it what will happen unless we can feed them, care for them and treat them."

"And you can't?"

"Not like I would like to."

"So even the nurses can make a difference?"

Wellstone nodded. "You saw how Arthur reacted to Miss Fitzgerald. If we can keep the boys happy, then they will want to live and fight to stay alive. That helps us immensely."

Dr. Wellstone stopped walking. They had made the circuit through the hospital and were back near the vestibule.

Wellstone held out his hand to shake their hands. "Thank you for coming ladies."

"When do we come back to work?" Grace asked.

Elizabeth smiled. She thought this was what Grace needed, but Elizabeth worried that the death and sickness might scare her away.

"You really want to do this? Both of you?" Wellstone asked.

Grace and Elizabeth both nodded.

Wellstone sighed and shook his head. Then he looked at the two women and smiled. "If you come back in the morning, I'll arrange for Nurse Carlyle to help show you what needs to be done."

When Elizabeth and Grace were walking back to the house, Elizabeth asked, "Why did you say yes to becoming a nurse?"

"I saw those boys and thought many of them will die alone and scared. If I can't keep them alive, and I hope that I can help do that, I can make sure they know someone cares about them and will miss them when they are gone. I can make a difference."

Elizabeth nodded. It was what she was thinking. This was her way to help and do something that she was proud of.

48

DEVOTION

SEPTEMBER 1863

David watched Alice standing over the stove cooking supper. She coughed repeatedly, which is what had caused him to look at her in the first place. She looked pale, which he thought was unusual since she was standing over the stove. He would have thought her skin would be flush. She was sweating, though.

"Are you all right?" David asked.

Alice looked over her shoulder. "I'm a little tired, that's all." Then she coughed.

"If that's all, why are you coughing?"

Alice shrugged.

David let the topic drop when George came into the family cabin. He was acting a little bit less worried about David since he and his mother had spoken yesterday, but George still wasn't comfortable around David. He eyed David suspiciously, but at least he wasn't outright hostile anymore.

Tony and Thomas came in a few moments later arguing about whether Tony liked a young girl back in Cumberland. The argument turned into a wrestling match when Tony picked up a pillow off one of the bunks and hit Thomas in the head.

Alice turned and said, "Boys, please stop."

David was surprised that she was so calm about stopping them. Usually, she would have yelled forcefully. Alice's shoulders sagged as she seemed resigned that she couldn't stop them.

David grabbed both of them and separated them. "You two can take this up outside after you eat supper, but for now stop it."

"But I don't like her," Tony said.

"Do, too," Thomas said in a cooing voice.

Tony lunged for his brother, but David kept them apart.

Alice served the meal and then went to bed without even eating it. Now David knew something was wrong. Alice never missed a meal.

"Alice, what's wrong?" David asked.

"I'm just tired, David. We've been pretty busy lately."

She looked around suddenly and grabbed for the ash bucket. She bent over and gagged. Then she vomited into it.

David rushed over to her to help her into the stateroom to lay down.

"Tony, get me some clean water and a rag," David said.

Alice shook her head. "I'll be all right."

"Yes, you will be, but not right now. You haven't been well since you got caught in the rain in Oldtown," David told her.

He realized that she had been coughing and getting sick since then. They should have found some way to treat her before then. Now it was too late to do any good.

Tony came back with the water and set it on the floor beside David. David dipped the rag into the water and wrung it out. He wiped down Alice's face.

"You're burning up with a fever. How long have you had it?" David asked.

Alice shook her head. "I don't know. A day or so."

"Or so?"

David helped Alice slide under her blanket. She lay back in her bed, and he put the damp cloth on her forehead.

"I just need a good night's sleep," Alice said.

"It hasn't helped you so far."

"There's nothing else you can do for now. It has to run its course."

David left the stateroom. He didn't feel much like eating because he was so worried about Alice. After supper, he looked in on her. She was asleep, but sweat was still beading up on her forehead.

"Is she all right?" George asked.

"I don't know. I think she has pneumonia," David told him.

"How did she catch it?"

"I think it was when she got caught in the rain last week. She's been coughing since then."

George eventually fell asleep, knowing their day would start early

289

tomorrow. David sat at the table and read his book by Edgar Allan Poe by lamplight.

About midnight, he heard sounds from the stateroom. He stood up and walked over to the curtain. He listened and heard Alice mumbling.

"Alice, are you all right?" he said softly.

He continued to hear more mumbling, but nothing he could understand. He parted the curtain and looked in at her. She was under her blanket tossing and turning. She was still feverish.

David stepped into the stateroom and knelt down on the floor. He wet the cloth again and mopped her brow, hoping that it might ease her agitation.

He put the rag back in the bucket and since he was on his knees, he decided to pray. "Dear God, help her. She's a good person who hasn't hurt anyone. She's the type of person you want on earth when everyone else seems to be going crazy. Help her, please. I love her. Amen."

David sat back on his haunches, feeling uncomfortable. He had never said that he loved Alice before. He had never even thought about it. It had crept up on him this past year and saying it in the prayer had seemed so natural.

He wondered what Alice would think? Did she think of him as just her boat hand?

"Where am I?"

David looked over and saw that Alice's eyes were open. He grabbed her hand, happy to see her awake. Maybe now she could get well.

"You're on the *Freeman* in your stateroom," David said.

"Hugh?" She looked at David, her eyes not focusing on him. "Hugh, I had the worst dream. I dreamed that you were killed."

David's spirits sagged. She wasn't recovering. She was delusional.

"We all have bad dreams sometimes," David said. He patted her hand.

"I'm glad it was just a dream. I don't want you to leave me, ever."

David had longed to hear Alice say that, but he had wanted to hear her say it about him, not about her dead husband.

"I won't leave you, Alice," he said and meant it.

"I love you, Hugh."

"I love you, Alice."

She closed her eyes and slipped back into sleep. He continued to hold her hand and rested with his back against the wall.

He fell asleep until the boys awakened with their stirring around in the family cabin. He came awake slowly and realized he was still holding Alice's hand.

He looked at Alice, and she was still sleeping fitfully. He mopped her brow with water.

David parted the curtain and saw the boys eating oatmeal at the table.

"How is Mama?" George asked.

"She's sleeping, but not easily. She's still feverish," David told him.

"Has she thrown up anymore?"

"There's nothing for her to lose, but no, she hasn't even gagged."

Tony asked, "What do we do?"

"Keep her cool and hope the fever breaks. George, you'll have to be in charge until your mother recovers," David said.

George looked slightly surprised at being given command of the boat, but he nodded and said nothing.

David stayed in the stateroom. He sat next to Alice's bed holding her hand while George got the boat underway. Occasionally, one of the boys would poke his head in the open window and ask about Alice, but there was very little change.

Alice mumbled at times, but what she said was never understandable. He wondered if she was dreaming of the happier days she had spent with Hugh.

At noon, her forehead was so hot that he thought he could almost hear the watering sizzling against her skin. He was worried that she was too hot and he began to continually mop her face and arms with a cold, damp cloth in an effort to cool her down. He continued this for two hours so that his hands were shriveled and sore.

He dunked the cloth in the bucket once again, wrung it out and lifted it to Alice's forehead.

Her eyes were open.

"David," she said.

David smiled. He put a hand on her head. It was considerably cooler. Her fever had broken.

"You had me scared," he said.

"Why?"

"You've been delirious and burning up with a fever all night and day."

"Will I be all right?"

"I sure hope so. I think you're over the roughest spot. Your fever's broken."

"Where are we?"

David shrugged. "I'm not sure. I've been in here with you since last night. George has been in charge of the boat."

Alice grinned. "I'm sure he likes that."

She tried to push herself up, but she was weak. Her arms shook, and she looked dangerously close to collapsing. David reached out and helped her into a sitting position.

"That's as far as you go. I don't want you up until you are healthy again," David said.

"Yes, doctor."

At least she hadn't lost her sense of humor.

"Are you hungry?" he asked.

Alice shook her head.

"Well, you need to eat something. You haven't eaten since this time yesterday, and you lost all of that last night. You need nourishment to rebuild your strength. I'll draw some broth off the stew that Tony made, and you can take in that."

David stood up and stretched. His legs were cramped from sitting so long with her. Then he started to leave the stateroom.

"David."

He stopped and turned around. Alice reached out and took his hand in hers.

"I can't remember much of what happened last night. I can remember this, though." She squeezed his hand. "I remember you were there. Thank you."

David lifted her hand and kissed it. Then he set it back in her lap.

"I will always be there for you," he said.

"I know."

He turned and went to draw her broth.

ABOUT THE AUTHOR

James Rada, Jr. is the author of historical fiction and non-fiction history. They include the popular books *Saving Shallmar: Christmas Spirit in a Coal Town, Canawlers* and *Battlefield Angels: The Daughters of Charity Work as Civil War Nurses.*

He lives in Gettysburg, Pa., where he works as a freelance writer. Jim has received numerous awards from the Maryland-Delaware-DC Press Association, Associated Press, Maryland State Teachers Association and Community Newspapers Holdings, Inc. for his newspaper writing.

If you would like to be kept up to date on new books being published by James or ask him questions, he can be reached by e-mail at *jimrada@yahoo.com.*

To see James' other books or to order copies online, go to *www.jamesrada.com.*

PLEASE LEAVE A REVIEW

If you enjoyed this book, please help other readers find it. Reviews help the author get more exposure for his books. Please take a few minutes to review this book at *Amazon.com* or *Goodreads.com*. Thank you, and if you sign up for my mailing list at *jamesrada.com*, you can get FREE ebooks.

If you liked
LOCK READY,
you can find more stories at these FREE sites from James Rada, Jr.

JAMES RADA, JR.'S WEB SITE
www.jamesrada.com
The official website for James Rada, Jr.'s books and news including a complete catalog of all his books (including eBooks) with ordering links. You'll also find free history articles, news, and special offers.

TIME WILL TELL
historyarchive.wordpress.com
Read history articles by James Rada, Jr. plus other history news, pictures and trivia.

WHISPERS IN THE WIND
jimrada.wordpress.com
Discover more about the writing life and keep up to date on news about James Rada, Jr.

Made in the USA
Middletown, DE
29 August 2020